CROWNOMA

Jeremy Winstanley

AUGUST 3, 2023

Chapter I
Down the Rabbit-Hole

It always starts the same…

Shadowy figures in suits, their faces obscured, burst into the room, hands filled with guns and a glint of sliver on their lapels. I try to focus on the pin they wear, knowing instinctively that it is important, but everything is blurred, like looking through a Vaseline-smeared lens.

*The woman opposite me reacts, throwing out her left hand and somehow pinning the figures in place. She speaks in tones of urgency – I can't make out the words but get the feeling that it is imperative that I leave, for I have something that **must** be done.*

She thrusts her right hand towards me, and, with a jolt, I am suddenly falling backwards, away from the light…

I awoke with a start, banging my head on the coach window. Someone sniggered nearby, the sound somewhat jarring in my disorientated state.

It always takes your mind a few seconds to recalibrate when you wake, as information is gathered from your environment and your memories to fill in the nebulous period when you were wandering in the Land of Nod.

Certain information is usually a given, unless you've been drugged or are suffering from concussion, so you should at least know *who* you are. *Where* you are being a slightly more complex matter, as whilst you *should* be in the same place you fell asleep, this is not always the case. If you wake in familiar surrounding – your own bed in your own home – you will not experience that momentary panic you get when waking in a hotel room on the first day of your holiday.

I had woken on a coach, which appeared to be travelling down a country road, as I could see cattle in the fields across from me, between the trees.

As my mind processed this, alarm bells stared going off in my head, as various questions jostled for attention; Why did I think there was something fundamentally wrong with those cows? Why was I viewing what was obviously an Autumnal scene, in shades of red and gold, when it was surely May? And, most importantly, how the **fuck** had I ended up on what seemed to be, from glancing at the uniformed teens around me, a school bus?

Furthermore, my body felt…swollen, as though all my insides had been scooped out and then stuffed back into a slightly smaller frame. I looked at my hands, noting that they were slimmer and smoother than I recalled, no rings or liver spots and, from the cuffs of the jumper sheathing my arms, I appeared to be wearing the same uniform as those about me.

I turned to the girl sitting across the aisle from me and spoke; 'Excuse me, you wouldn't happen to have a compact with a mirror, would you?'

My voice was higher pitched than I remembered and the fear that had been lurking at the back of my mind raged forward.

The girl frowned, reached into her bag, and pulled out a compact, wordlessly handing it to me. With trembling hands, I opened it, dreading what I was about to see.

There, staring back at me, was MY face – but a face I hadn't seen in a mirror for a good 35 years… the face of my 16-year-old self.

What. The. *Fuck…*

Sherlock Holmes is often quoted as stating that *"when you eliminate the impossible, whatever remains, however improbable, must be the truth."* So, by applying deductive reasoning to the scant evidence that had been presented so far, what possible explanations could there be for my current situation?

Option 1 – Like the plot of a cheesy family movie, I had been physically regressed to my previous age, but remained in the same chronological year – no doubt to teach me some kind of valuable moral lesson that had so far escaped me in the 50-odd years I had been on the planet.

However, I currently had no way of discerning the date and no memory of making a wish via battered brass lamp, automated fortune-telling booth or ancient Buddhist skull, so whilst the evidence partially supported this, there was no way of telling for sure.

Option 2 – My mind had been thrust back in time to occupy my own teenaged body (rather than someone else's – à la *Quantum Leap*) to rectify a mistake made in the past. As with option 1, I had yet to find out *when* I was, so this was another unproven possibility.

Option 3 – I was currently inside a highly advanced virtual reality simulator, the creators of which had decided I was better suited to experience their creation as a teenage boy, rather than a grey-haired Saganaut. If the technology was advanced enough and I was connected to it physically or by way of a direct neural interface, there would be no way of telling whether this was real or not – at least until Laurence Fishburne showed up to offer me drugs.

Now, the main problem with all three options was they required certain things – a supernatural artefact in respect of option 1, mental time travel in respect of option 2 and highly advanced &/or alien technology in respect of option 3 – all things that exist within the annals of Science Fiction (emphasis on the last word) rather than in the world in which I was born into.

All this led to probable Option No. 4 – that I'd been involved in some kind of serious accident, was lying in a coma in a hospital somewhere and all of this was the product of my subconscious mind.

In which case, DCI Gene Hunt would be along shortly to call me a soft, Southern, lager-drinking twat.

Of course, that didn't happen. Instead, I got *this*:

'You Crowe?'

I looked up from my reverie, still clutching the compact, to find a blonde, muscular lad, swaying slightly due to the motion of the coach, leaning over me.

Now, there were a number of responses I could have given to this query, from the factual "Yes, I am Alexander Crowe" to the challenging "Who wants to know?" Due to my mouth not always checking with my brain first and the belief (whether justified or not) that I was a witty person, I chose to respond *thus*:

'Yes, I AM currently a Crowe, but am hoping that someday soon I will become a *beautiful* swan...'

The girl I'd borrowed the compact from snorted with laughter and I glanced across, grinning as I did so. She was stifling her laughter with her hand, and I passed the compact back with a nod of thanks, then looked up at the boy, who was frowning. I decided to give him a break.

'Yes,' I said, 'I am Alexander Crowe.'

'So...' he seemed to be having some difficulty marshalling his thoughts, so I took the opportunity to examine him more closely.

Blonde, muscular, handsome. Jumper sleeves pushed up and shirt cuffs folded back. Tie loose at his throat, top button undone. Nicely cut grey trousers and expensive shoes, so not off the rack. Home counties accent. Probably good at sports.

I focused on the uniform next – Navy blue V-neck jumper with silver trim on the neckline, embroidered silver tree of some description on the left breast, surrounded by the legend "Oakdene College" also in silver – which probably meant it was supposed to be an oak tree. Striped tie in the corresponding matching colours.

Oakdene College? Now, why did that sound familiar?

'...you must be the scholarship boy, then.' The boy eventually finished.

'I...guess so.' I answered. *Scholarship?* Interesting...

'So, that means your parents are poor then.' He said disdainfully.

And there we had it. Not asking out of genuine interest, but due to ingrained snobbery from hereditary entitlement. Probably flogged his servants too.

'Sorry,' I said, 'I didn't catch your name?'

'Bond,' the boy said, with a touch of pride, 'Aubrey Bond.'

'Now, scholarships are not only granted to those in financial need, you know...' I began before my brain caught up with my ears. 'Hold on, did you really just say *Aubrey Bond*?'

'Yes, why?'

'*Seriously? Aubrey Bond?*' I started laughing. 'I suppose it could have been worse - your surname could have been Shortcake. Or Jambe. Or Fields.' I paused for a moment in thought. 'Actually, that last one wouldn't have been too bad, especially if you're a Beatles fan.'

I looked up at Aubrey, smiling brightly. He did not look happy.

'Are you making fun of me?' He growled, clenching his fists.

I was just considering the best response to this, ideally one which not involve one of Aubrey's fists ending up in my face, when we were fortunately interrupted.

'Oi, you at the back there!' shouted the coach driver, 'Get back in your seat!'

Aubrey shot me a venomous look, muttered 'This isn't over, Crowe...' and made his way back to his seat.

Whilst this encounter had provided additional information and introduced me to the school bully, I was no closer to fathoming out whatever "this" was. However, I *was* starting to doubt whether this was all in my head.

The coach slowed, which caused an excited murmuring amongst the other passengers, then swung to the right, passing between two brick pillars topped with large stone balls. I briefly noted a large sign, which read "Oakdene College – Established 1922 – *Omnia Qua*", before the coach entered a green tunnel of trees.

This soon gave way to bright Autumn sunlight, as the coach began to traverse a long avenue bordered with grass and what I would later discover to be Giant Redwoods, although to my uneducated eyes, they just looked like *really big* Christmas trees.

Leaning into the aisle, I could see in the distance another set of brick pillars, through which I could just about make out some kind of large multi-storey structure, as the rest of the view was screened by trees.

Given the length of the avenue, the size of the grounds surrounding the building we were rapidly approaching, and the vague hints of architecture glimpsed through the gateway, it would appear that Oakdene College was housed in a Victorian/Edwardian mansion. Which meant (based on the date on the sign) that the original owners had fallen upon hard times and sold the property on – mercifully not to a theme park chain, so the original fixtures should remain largely intact, there would be no crowds of screaming children and I was highly unlikely to be accosted by park employees dressed as "humorous" animal mascots.

Passing through the gateway, the coach turned left then swung in a circle to the right across the tarmacked courtyard, before coming to a stop adjacent to the main building.

As I was sitting on the right-hand side of the coach, I had not seen very much as we had come through the gates, so was curious to see *where* I had arrived, but the usual bunfight had started as soon as the coach stopped – everyone had leapt up and was rapidly pulling bags from both under and over their seats, in an effort to be the first one off.

You see this kind of herd behaviour on trips abroad, as holidaymakers scramble to be the first off the 'plane, because that additional five minutes head-start might mean you can get to the baggage carousel before everyone else in the vain hope that your suitcase will be the first through the flaps.

It never is – but hope springs eternal, as they say.

Being of a more realistic bent, I remained seated as everyone else did the slow shuffle down the aisle, before getting up.

I stepped off the coach, noting as I did that the majority of the courtyard was in the shadow cast by the main building.

I looked up. Then up a bit more. Then quite a bit more.

Oakdene College towered above me, literally, as the main frontage was dominated by an enormous square tower. It was constructed of red bricks (4,477,000 I later found out, fired in the estates own brick kilns) with dressings in Mansfield stone and had a large porte-cochere leading into the entrance hall – which is the architectural term for a covered porch to stop the landed gentry from getting their frockcoats wet.

Oakdene College is what you'd get if you exposed Downton Abbey to Gamma radiation and then made it angry. And as every card-carrying geek knows, that's not something you want to do.

The other students had collected their suitcases and trunks from the coach and were gathering in front of the main entrance, where a bespectacled woman with a clipboard was checking them off a list, then sending them in. Standing to the left of the entrance were three men, dressed in navy waistcoats and bowler hats, which my brain immediately identified as college porters – although there did not seem to be much porterage going on.

To the right was a low slung, expensive looking car, surrounded by men in suits and sunglasses, who were keeping a close eye on both a middle-aged bearded man in an expensive suit and a slim blonde girl, whose expression suggested that she didn't want to be here.

As my mind processed this, I could feel it nudging me, saying *"you're looking, but not seeing…"* I re-evaluated the view and then it struck me – the car had no wheels and was hovering a good foot or more above the ground. I turned and looked back at the coach – no wheels and *also* floating. I crouched down next to the coach and looked underneath. No visible means of support, just a slight heat haze beneath it. I tentatively waved my hand through this, noting that there was some resistance, as though the air was slightly thicker beneath the coach.

'If you've quite finished,' said a voice, 'do you think you could move your trunk?' The coach driver stood next to a large metal chest, examining a tag tied to one of the handles. 'I take it you're Alexander Crowe?'

'Yes, sorry...' I blurted, straightening up.

I walked over, grabbed one of the handles at the end of the chest and lifted it. Or that's what I intended to do – the bloody thing weighed a ton. God knows what was in it, but there was no chance in Hell that I was going to move it without some help.

But surely that's what porters were *for*?

I approached the three men standing by the porch.

'Excuse me, you wouldn't happen to have a sack truck or trolley or something?' I asked, 'as my trunk is a bit heavy and I won't be able to move it otherwise...'

One of the men stepped forward, smiling kindly.

'Do you know what?' he said, 'You're the first student to actually ask for help. The rest of 'em just struggled with their stuff.' He reached into his waistcoat pocket and pulled out a flat disc, about four inches across and one inch thick.

'I think we can do better than a trolley,' he said, handing me the disc.

I examined the disc – it was flat on one side, the other side being slightly domed and glittery, like a bike reflector. A ring of brass, incised with symbols, circled the disc and as I was turning it in my hands, came free.

I looked back at the porter.

'Thanks... I think.' I said, 'Um...what's this?'

'You've not seen a lifter before, I take it?' said the porter. 'It's a pretty simple piece of kit and works on the same principles as hover-cars.' He took the disc from my hands. 'The main disc is filled with pixoleum, which when magically charged, causes the disc and anything attached to it to float. However, as there's no motive force in the disc itself, you use this,' he brandished the ring, 'to get whatever the disc is attached to, to follow you about. Try it.' He then handed the disc and ring back to me.

Pixoleum? Magically charged? There was me expecting some kind of high-tech explanation to the floating cars but no, apparently it was all done via *magic*...

Dubiously, I placed the disc on top of my trunk.

'How do I charge it?' I asked.

'Just put you hand on top of it and imbue it with some of your *Vitae*. And put the ring around your wrist.'

I placed my hand on top of the disc, closed my eyes, and tried to imagine that I was somehow powering up the disc. I felt a subtle shift in my head, as though a switch had been flicked, then a warmth under my palm. As I opened my eyes, I could see a golden glow coming from the disc and watched amazed as my trunk rose off the ground.

I moved away from the trunk and as I did so, it gently floated after me. Stretching out the arm with the control ring on, I moved it back and forth, grinning as the trunk followed its movements.

'That is *SO* cool...' I said, then turned to the porter. 'Thank you so much for your help, Mr...?'

The porter smiled. 'My pleasure, Mr. Crowe, and it's Beamish. Should you need any further help, just come and see myself or one of my colleagues.' He indicated the two other porters standing by the porch.

The number of students was thinning by the porch, so I ambled over, my trunk gliding along behind me. As I did so, a strident voice called out,

'You there, boy!'

I looked about and saw the slim blonde girl bearing down on me. She stopped and gestured over her shoulder.

'Fetch my trunk, boy,' she said imperiously.

'I'm sorry...?'

'You heard me, boy,' she said, 'fetch my trunk.'

I looked over at the expensive car and saw that several of the suited men were lifting an obviously heavy wooden chest out of the back of the car. The bearded man was watching our exchange with interest, whilst chatting with a severe looking woman in a burgundy two-piece.

'It would appear that your...um...*servants*?' I hazarded, 'are sorting that out for you.'

'They'll be leaving soon, so YOU will need to see it gets to my room,' she said.

I looked at her coolly.

'Unlike your men over there, I am NOT your servant, so that won't be happening,' I said, and began to turn away.

The girl looked incensed, stepped forward and poked me hard in the chest.

'Don't you know who I AM?!' She exclaimed. I leaned in and quietly said,

'Of course I know who you are – you're a spoilt brat with no manners. So, I suggest, and I say this with the utmost respect, that you bugger off.' I smiled politely and turned my back on her.

'Father! *That* **boy** was rude to me!' She screamed.

Oh shit...

The bearded man walked over to me, frowning slightly.

'Is this true, young man?' He asked, 'Were you rude to my daughter?'

As mentioned before, I do have a tendency to speak before thinking, but luckily my survival instinct kicked in on this occasion. This man reeked of power and therefore was not to be trifled with, so I decided that honesty would be my best policy on this occasion.

'Your daughter demanded that I fetch her trunk for her,' I said.

'Oh, did she now?' He said, smiling slightly and looking at his daughter, who was looking suitably sheepish. 'And what was your response to this?'

'I informed her that I was not her servant and that she was a spoilt brat with no manners.' It was my turn to look sheepish, 'and I *may* have told her to bugger off...Sir.'

'Really?' The man's eyes crinkled with amusement, 'Is this true, Penny?'

The girl was staring intently at her shoes and muttered something under her breath.

'Speak up, Penny,' said the man, 'is what this young man said true?'

'Yes...' Penny muttered resentfully.

The man turned back to me.

'Thank you for your honesty, young man.' He turned to his daughter, 'I think we need to have a talk, young lady...' He took his daughter's hand and pulled her away. She glared at me.

I really did seem to be making friends wherever I went today. If the rest of the students were as insufferable as the two I had encountered so far, this was going to be an interesting experience. And by interesting, I am of course referring to the mythical Chinese curse *"may you live in interesting times."*

And it wasn't over yet...

'Alexander Crowe!'

The severe looking woman was staring at me, arms crossed and an expression of annoyance on her face.

'With me.' She said once she had gained my attention. 'Now! Mr. Beamish, take Mr. Crowe's trunk to room 13.'

The porter looked taken aback.

'Room 13, Headmistress?' he asked, 'But I thought we weren't using that room because of the…'

'It's the only room we have left. Crowe, with me…' She turned and walked away.

I handed the control ring to Mr Beamish and followed.

It looked like I was *definitely* in trouble now…

Chapter II
Warnings & Portents

We entered the cool interior of the main building, our footsteps echoing on the flagstone flooring, then turned left into what was obviously the main reception area for the college.

The circular counter was manned by a couple of no-nonsense clerks, who were calmly handing out room keys attached to wooden tags, along with maps of the main building with the relevant student's accommodation marked in fluorescent pen.

I noted that both Aubrey and Penny were still awaiting their keys and, unsurprisingly, they both scowled at me as I went past.

I caught a snippet of conversation as we passed through: 'Up the main stairs to the first floor, straight on, then turn left down the Nursery corridor. Carry on past the back stairs, then turn left at the next corridor and your room is third on the right...'

We passed into another hallway, which was illuminated by a series of narrow windows that marched diagonally up the wall, following the course of what I assumed was the main staircase.

I stood at the base of the enormous square tower I had noted outside, the interior of which was dominated by an equally enormous staircase. This rose three, possibly four storeys, with intricately carved wooden balustrades and newel posts and was wide enough to drive a small car up, should you be that way inclined – such as if you found yourself being chased by the Italian police who were keen on recovering the gold bullion in the boot of your Mini Cooper.

The Headmistress noted I had paused at the foot of stairs.

'Come along, Mr. Crowe,' she said, 'you'll have plenty of time to sight-see later.'

'Sorry, Miss.' I said and hurried up the stairs.

The Headmistress' office was on the first floor, overlooking the courtyard, just to the right of the main entrance.

I sat on a wooden chair in front of her desk, on top of a particularly large and slightly worn Persian rug, which covered the majority of the floor. Dr Vayne (as per the polished brass nameplate facing me) appraised me from the other side of her desk, then reached out her right hand towards a set of steel filing cabinets, painted British racing green.

'Crowe, Alexander,' she commanded.

The first drawer on the left-hand cabinet slid open, there was the sound of riffling, and a brown manila file rose from the cabinet, then floated across to Dr Vayne, who took it from the air, as the cabinet drawer slid closed.

She opened the file in front of her, briefly perusing the contents before closing it and placing her fingertips on top of it. She looked directly at me.

'Up until this year, the students who have attended Oakdene have come from private schools, either here or abroad. Whilst this has produced a number of alumni who have gone on to excel in their chosen fields of study, it has excluded students who have just as much talent and the right to a decent education as those of a more privileged upbringing. Hence the scholarship programme and your enrolment.'

Dr Vayne rose from her chair and circled the desk, stopping in front of me and leaning back on the edge of her desk.

'However,' she said, 'We expect ALL our students to maintain a certain level of decorum and behaviour, no matter what their background. Telling the heir to the throne to "bugger off" does not generally fall into this category. You are fortunate that the King found it amusing, otherwise this could have had serious repercussions for both you AND the school.'

She let this sink in.

'I shall be watching you, Mr. Crowe. Make sure that the next time you find yourself in my office, it is not for a reprimand. Do you understand?'

'Yes, Miss.' I answered.

There was knock at the door, to which the Headmistress called 'Enter.' The door opened and a pretty blonde female student walked in.

'You sent for me, Headmistress?' she asked.

'Ah, Miss Bond. This,' she pointed at me, 'is Alexander Crowe, one of our new First Years.' She then turned to me. 'This is Ashleigh Bond, one of the Prefects assigned to your House. Mr. Crowe was unable to collect his room key, due to attending this meeting. Could you take him to his room and see that he joins the rest of the students in the Picture Gallery at 11.00am?'

'Of course, Headmistress.' Ashleigh said, 'Which room is he in?'

Dr Vayne handed her a tagged key.

'Room 13.' She said.

Ashleigh started, almost dropping the key.

'Ah. Right...okay.' She muttered. 'Er...you'd better follow me, Alexander.'

We walked in silence, until we were out of earshot of Dr Vayne's office, then Ashleigh asked, 'So, who did you piss off to get assigned to room 13?'

'As far as I am aware, room 13 was the only one left.' I said, 'However, everyone seems to react badly every time it's mentioned. Is there something wrong with it?'

Ashleigh stopped and looked up and down the corridor, checking to see if anyone else was about.

'No student who has previously been assigned room 13 has lasted in there for longer than a week.' Ashleigh explained, 'They originally thought it *might* be haunted, but Dr Gaunt gave it a clean bill of health, so whilst there's no ghost, there's still something... *off* about the room.'

'Lovely.' I said, 'Who's Dr Gaunt?'

'School Necromancer. You'll meet him when you have his class.'

If Dr Gaunt ended up looking like Peter Cushing and our class project involved furtive field trips to the local graveyard, suturing, and a really big lightning rod, I would be looking to drop this subject pretty sharpish.

We had traversed what Ashleigh informed me was known as the Nursery corridor, which ended at a large sash window. To the right was an open archway, leading into a narrow room equipped with a Belfast sink and various cupboards. A door to the right led into a bathroom, which Ashleigh advised me was supposed to be communal, but as it was so close to Room 13, no-one used it. So, I effectively had my own private bathroom, which was a bonus.

A second door in the left-hand corner, with tarnished brass numerals affixed to it, led into the dreaded Room 13.

Ashleigh handed me the key and I apprehensively approached the door, slid the key into the lock, turned it and pushed the door open. I was slightly disappointed that it didn't creak in approved Horror film fashion.

A short diagonal corridor led into a high-ceilinged square chamber, with sash windows on the back and left-hand wall. I later found out that my room was within what was known as the Water Tower, a smaller tower at the rear of the college.

Given all the dire warnings that had been attributed to this room, it was surprisingly… ordinary.

Also quite cosy, with a wingback chair in dark green velvet sitting on top of a grey shag pile rug, facing an open fireplace. There was also dark wooden wardrobe, a desk and what I assumed to be large free-standing mirror (it was covered with a patterned bedspread) along the left-hand wall. A wooden bed already made up with crisp linen lay beneath the back window, alongside which was a small chest of drawers. My trunk had been deposited against the right-hand wall, under a set of shelves.

I turned to Ashleigh, who was hovering at the threshold.

'You coming in?' I asked, 'Seems safe to me…'

She hesitated, then tentatively ventured into the room. When nothing untoward happened, she visibly relaxed.

'It's actually quite nice,' she said, then frowned. 'And it's bigger than my room…'

'If you want to swap, I can ask for you…'

'Um…no, I don't think so.'

'Okay,' I said, throwing myself onto the bed. 'Mmm, comfy.' I looked over at her.

'So, Ashleigh *Bond*… any relation to Aubrey?'

Ashleigh looked surprised. [OBJ]

'Yeah, he's my little brother. Do you know him?'

'We've met.' I said, 'He seems…. nice.'

Ashleigh cocked her head to one side, a hint of a smile hovering about her lips.

'Really? Is that the impression you got of him?'

'Well, that depends if you want me to be truthful… or diplomatic.' I said. 'I mean, not only are you his sister, you're also a Prefect, so if I say the wrong thing here, you could make my life a living Hell.'

'True,' she said, smiling.

'So, let's just say that he needs to work on his people skills.'

'You being an expert on that, I suppose?'

'You've spent some time in my company, can't you tell? I'm great.' I grinned, then frowned. 'Although Princess Penny would disagree…'

'You've met the Princess?!' Said Ashleigh excitedly, 'What's she like?'

'She's… a bit of a cow, to be honest.' Ashleigh looked crestfallen, 'but she might have just been in a bad mood. First day of school, outside her comfort zone, that sort of thing. I'm sure once you get to know her, she's perfectly lovely.'

I stood up and looked at my watch – it was about quarter past ten.

'Looks like I have about 45 minutes before I need to be in the Picture Gallery,' I said, 'and I'm sure you've got other stuff you need to be doing, do you want to give me directions and I'll find my own way there later? You know, rather than you hanging around?'

'I was supposed to make sure you got there on time…' Ashleigh began.

'Well, yes,' I interrupted, 'but if you give me clear directions, you'll have done your job, right?'

'I guess so…' she said dubiously.

'Plus I need the loo, and I'm sure you don't want to listen to me doing *that*.'

At that, Ashleigh relented and explained how to get to the Picture Gallery, which was actually not that far from the bottom of the main staircase.

'Thank you for all you help, Ashleigh,' I said, 'and please… call me Alex. That's what my friends call me.'

'Oh, is that what we are?' she asked, a half-smile on her lips. [OBJ]

I paused thoughtfully.

'Well, maybe not *quite* yet' I said, 'but we're getting there.'

She laughed.

'I'll see you later… Alex.'

I looked about my room.

Yes, I may currently have my adult mind trapped in my teenaged body, attending a magical college in what appeared to be an alternate version of England in which history had not followed the path I was familiar with, but I had a nice, decent sized room (which may or may not have some kind of curse attached to it), my own private bathroom and a pretty girl had smiled at me.

Small victories…

I spent the next 45 minutes investigating the contents of my trunk, in the hope that this would shed some further light on my current circumstances.

As the clothing in my trunk matched my vague recollections of what I would have worn when I was 16 years old, this suggested that not only was I in an alternate reality, but I had also been thrust back in time as well. This was confirmed when I discovered a pocket diary with *"1ˢᵗ day at Oakdene"* entered on Monday 1ˢᵗ September – the year being 1986.

This came as a bit of a shock, understandably, but did explain why my hairstyle made me look like I belonged in a New Romantic band, complete with blonde highlights. That would need sorting out, as whilst I recall believing at the time it made me look cool, one of the benefits of hindsight was the realisation that it didn't. I wondered if there was a school barber on site or if I would have to venture out of the school grounds in search of a local hairdresser.

The rest of the contents of my trunk were standard school supplies, a deck of playing cards and a selection of textbooks for the various subjects that I assumed I would be studying.

Whilst I was relieved that some of the textbooks were titled *A Beginner's Guide to Offensive & Defensive Magic* or *An Introduction to Basic Lithometry*, which meant I wouldn't be expected to know anything about the subject, copies of *Advanced Alchemy* and *Enhanced Illusioneering* concerned me, as they suggested that I should have some knowledge of the basics, which, of course, I didn't.

This was not good, as I had a gut feeling that I was here for a specific reason – currently TBC – and getting thrown out of Oakdene because I didn't know how to mix up a Potion of Healing or whatever they called it here, would seriously hamper that.

So, on top of discovering why the Hell I was here in the first place, I now needed to cram approximately 5 years' worth of basic magical theory.

Once I got hold of whoever was responsible for my current predicament, we would be having words...

I made my way downstairs following Ashleigh's directions, and easily found the Picture Gallery, which was thronged with both students and what I assumed were members of the faculty.

The Picture Gallery itself was pretty impressive - 70 feet long, polished wooden floors, cream walls rising to decorative mouldings surrounding the entire perimeter. Above this the ceiling curved inwards, painted a delicate shade of duck egg blue, interspersed with white painted "ribs," terminating in a vast central skylight that ran almost the entire length of the room. This was supported by a substantial iron grid, also painted white, made up of 2-foot diamonds, the points of which aligned with the walls of the room.

I could see Dr Vayne at the far end of the room, chatting with a bearded man dressed in scruffy tweeds. As his outfit screamed "gamekeeper," I assumed this was what he was, as the majority of the other staff were wearing academic gowns.

I spotted Ashleigh standing over by a flipchart crammed with information and started to make my way over, until the crowd shifted, and I saw she was talking to her brother.

On one hand, Aubrey was unlikely to start anything in a room crowded with students and staff, but on the other, me talking familiarly to his sister could get his back up even further, if that were possible.

I was still contemplating my options, when the crowd parted, and I saw *Her*.

A slim, attractive girl, with pale skin and long black hair, which fell in soft curls over her shoulders. She was watching the other students with a wry smile on her face.

I was overcome with a feeling of extreme annoyance upon seeing her and my legs marched me over before my brain could raise any objections.

'You!' I spat, pointing at her, 'You're the reason I'm here!'

'As chat-up lines go,' she said drily, 'that's not bad.'

'No! It's not a chat-up line!' I said angrily, 'You're Helena Morgan, right?'

'Yes, I am.' She looked at me with puzzlement, 'How do you know that? Have you been scrying on me?'

'What?! No! I *know* you, but...' I faltered, 'I don't know *how*...'

The sudden realisation that I was causing a scene struck me, and I felt my cheeks flush crimson with embarrassment. I backed away, muttering 'I'm so sorry...' before fleeing the room.

My flight took me down a corridor running perpendicular to the Picture Gallery, through a set of glass-topped double doors and out onto a wide, paved terrace at the rear of the college. As the cooler air hit my face, I began to calm down and cast about for somewhere to sit and take stock.

A stone bench to my left, backing on to the main building, beckoned and I sat down heavily, putting my head into my hands and groaning.

'Well,' I muttered sarcastically, 'THAT went well...'

'Oh, I don't know,' said a lilting Welsh voice, 'As first impressions go, that *was* pretty memorable.'

I looked up to see that Helena had followed me out and was standing over me, arms crossed, a look of sardonic amusement on her face.

'Oh God…' I said, 'Look, I'm *really* sorry about that, I honestly don't know what came over me…'

'Well, you certainly piqued my curiosity,' Helena said, perching on the bench next to me. 'How exactly do you know all that stuff about me?'

'That's the weird thing,' I said, 'As soon as I saw you, it was though a box had been opened in my brain and it was suddenly flooded with information. For example, I know that you're Helena Morgan from Builth Wells in Powys, born on 1st May 1969. You have a younger sister called Bethany, a border collie named Patch and your dad is a farmer.'

Helena nodded in agreement, so I continued.

'Now, I'm assuming that the majority of this information would be in your school file, so I *could* have read it in there… I didn't, but I could have. But if that was the case, how would I know that your favourite place to be alone is the suspension bridge over the River Irfon, behind the Caer Beris hotel?'

Helena started back, looking shocked. She then leant forward, a look of intense concentration on her face. She raised her hand, made a complicated gesture, and muttered something under her breath.

I felt a slight tingling at my temples, followed by a warmth suffusing my head. Helena seemed satisfied with whatever she had done, but also puzzled.

'Well,' she said, 'I know you've not been scrying my mind – which IS generally considered bad manners – but I'm at a loss *how* you could possibly know all that…'

'Imagine how I feel…' I said, sighing. 'Oh God, where are my manners? Here's me knowing all that stuff about you and I haven't even introduced myself - I'm Alexander Crowe, Alex for short.' I offered my hand.

Helena looked at it for a moment, the tentatively took it. She looked me up and down, then focussed on my face.

'There is something decidedly odd about you, Alexander Crowe.' She said thoughtfully, as we rose and started to walk back inside.

You don't know the half of it, luv, I thought. 🔲

As we returned to the picture gallery, Dr Vayne was just finishing a series of announcements, which unfortunately we appeared to have missed the salient points of:

'…and Mr Ware,' Dr Vayne gestured to the man dressed in tweed, 'has advised that it's bandersnatch spawning season, so the Arboretum is out of bounds after nightfall to ALL students. Thank you.'

An excited chattering arose, as both the students and staff began to disperse. Both Helena and I stood to one side, unsure of what we should be doing next.

Aubrey spotted us standing there and ambled over, a smug expression on his face.

'What's the matter, Crowe?' he asked, 'Bit out of your depth? Is all this…' he gestured about the room, 'a bit too much for someone like *you*?'

I consider myself a relatively laidback person, but Aubrey's entitled bullshit was really starting to grate.

'I wonder if you could explain something to me, Aubrey,' I said, smiling, 'How come your sister Ashleigh is such a nice person, but you're such a massive dick?'

Helena snorted with laughter. Aubrey's face darkened and he stepped forward, clenching his fists. Apparently, this was his standard response to any kind of retort he was not happy with.

'Everything okay here, Alex?' Interrupted a voice I recognised. Ashleigh was walking towards us holding a clipboard, a questioning look upon her face.

'Hi Ashleigh,' I said brightly, 'I had a bit of a meltdown and Helena kindly came outside to check I was alright, so we missed most of what the Headmistress said. As Aubrey here isn't being particularly helpful, I was wondering if you could fill us in?'

Ashleigh glanced at her brother, who was glowering at me.

'Of course, Alex,' she said, 'happy to help.'

She started checking her clipboard, then noticed that Aubrey was still lurking nearby.

'Anything you need, little brother?' She asked sweetly.

Aubrey muttered something unintelligible, then turned on his heel and stalked out of the room.

'Sorry about him,' said Ashleigh, 'He can be a bit of a handful.'

'That's one way of putting it,' said Helena slyly, 'although Alex used a more colourful term...'

I shot her a look and mouthed "shut up." She smirked back at me, eyes crinkled with amusement. I turned back to Ashleigh, an innocent expression on my face. She was eyeing me speculatively over the top of the clipboard.

'You were saying...?' I said.

'Yes, sorry,' said Ashleigh, checking her clipboard, 'Looks like both of you are in Dee House, along with Aubrey...' I groaned, 'and myself, of course. I'm your House Prefect, so if you have any problems, you can come and see me. The Dee House common room is opposite the back stairs, next to the Dining Hall. Your head of house is Master Tweed, who you'll meet after lunch.' She looked up, 'I think that's everything. Any questions?'

I looked at Helena, who shrugged.

'I guess not,' I said. 'When's lunch?'

'Midday,' said Ashleigh, looking at her watch, 'So, in about 10 minutes.'

'Right. And the Dining Hall is where...?' I said. 'Sorry, I didn't get a map earlier, because I had to see the Headmistress...'

Ashleigh sighed and rolled her eyes. She then checked the papers on her clipboard, pulled a map from amongst them, then leaned in to show me where it was on the map.

I thanked her and we parted ways. Helena and I started climbing the main stairs, as we had decided to freshen up before lunch.

'She likes you,' said Helena quietly as we reached the first floor.

I stopped and looked at her in stunned disbelief. She was smiling, eyes twinkling with amusement.

'Uh...' I was at a loss for words, which is pretty unusual for me.

'Can't see it myself,' she said, breezing past me.

I stood bemused at the top of the stairs, her fading laughter echoing about me.

Chapter III
Curriculum Magia

Lunch was an interesting affair, as it appeared that certain breeds that were extinct in my world had not only survived but had been domesticated and become part of the food chain.

This gave me the options of sampling dodo curry, roast ochs or grice and onions.

Now, I'm not usually one to balk at trying new dishes, as you cannot claim you don't like something unless you've actually tried it, but the idea of eating a dish derived from dodo just didn't seem right.

Ochs was short for aurochs, which I seemed to recall from my well-thumbed copy of *Purnell's Find Out About Prehistoric Animals* was the precursor of the modern cow – except here aurochs were the dominant breed. This would explain my conviction that there was something wrong with the cows I'd seen earlier – they were *significantly* bigger than the cattle I was used to.

I finally decided on grice and onions, as it turned out that grice were a breed of highland pig, similar to a small wild boar. Having tried and liked boar in the past, I thought it was probably the safest option.

Having collected my dinner tray, I turned and surveyed the dining room, looking for somewhere to sit.

Unsurprisingly, Aubrey and Penny had gravitated towards one another and were holding court – literally in Penny's case – on one of the long trestle tables.

So, that was a table to definitely avoid.

'You could always go and sit with Ashleigh...' muttered a familiar voice, as Helena walked past.

'Oh, Ha Bloody Ha,' I said, as I followed her across the room to a free table, 'You're not *still* going on about that are you? She's our House Prefect – helping me...us...is her job. I've talked to her about as much as I've spoken to you. If that's the criteria you're using, then that would mean YOU fancy me too.'

I looked across at Helena, who had paused with her fork halfway to her mouth.

'Which, of course, you don't...' I finished lamely.

'Of course I don't,' said Helena quickly, 'but that's because you're a weirdo.'

I gave this some considered thought – she wasn't wrong. Aspects of my current situation did fall quite firmly into the pigeon-hole marked "weird shit." However, as I seemed to somehow *know* Helena, she appeared to be the key to unravelling the mystery of why I was here. I therefore needed her help, so decided to be as honest as I could – bearing in mind that some of the stuff I *could* tell her would revise her opinion of me from "weirdo" to "crazy as a box of frogs."

'Fair point,' I conceded, 'but there IS a reason for that...'

I paused, thinking how best to explain. Helena was watching me with guarded interest.

'I have suffered...' *I am suddenly falling backwards, away from the light...* 'a fall. The result of this is that some of the stuff I *should* know, such as basic magical theory, has gone from my head. This has been replaced by knowledge about YOU – I don't know how or why, but there must be a reason for this, and I've got a feeling that you may be able to help me... get back to normal. That's if you're willing to help?'

I don't like lying, but omission of certain facts doesn't really count – at least, that's what I told myself.

'I suppose that does explain a few things,' Helena said thoughtfully, 'and I must admit that you are a bit of an enigma...' She bit her lip, brow furrowed, then obviously reached a decision.

'Okay,' she said, 'I'll see what I can do to help. But if it gets *too* weird, you're on your own.'

'Fair enough,' I said, '... and thank you.'

I really didn't think it *could* get any weirder than it already was – which just goes to show how little I knew...

We were just finishing our lunch when Helena noticed that Ashleigh was walking over, followed by a sullen Aubrey and a gaggle of other students. I recognised the girl I had borrowed the compact from on the coach earlier that morning, along with a boy who looked so similar to her that he must be related.

'Here comes your *girlfriend*...' whispered Helena, grinning. I rolled my eyes – she might have agreed to help me, but this obviously wouldn't prevent her from winding me up over this whole Ashleigh thing.

'Hi Alex... Helena,' said Ashleigh, 'These are the rest of the Dee House students. Master Tweed has asked me to collect you all and take you to our common room, so he can introduce himself and hand out timetables.'

We rose from our table, briefly stopping on the way out of the Dining Hall to drop off our trays, then followed Ashleigh and the other students.

The Dee House common room was literally just around the corner. It was a wood panelled chamber, about 20-foot square. A set of three windows looked out onto the main courtyard and the room was furnished with a mismatched selection of chairs and sofas. An open fireplace stood against the right-hand wall, in front of which stood a particularly rotund bald gentleman, dressed in a grey herringbone suit and academic gown. This, I assumed, was Master Tweed.

'Gather round, Ladies and Gentlemen,' said the man, waiting until we had all filed in before continuing. 'I am Master Tweed, school librarian and Head of both the Bibliomancy and History departments for this esteemed establishment.' He smiled kindly, eyes twinkling. 'More importantly for you, I am your Head of House, so you will be seeing rather a lot of me and, as you can see, there is rather a lot of me to see.'

This was greeted by a few titters of polite, if somewhat nervous, laughter.

'This sumptuous chamber...' he opened his arms wide, encompassing the whole room, 'is your common room, where you may gather to study, relax, and socialise with your peers. Please treat it with respect. You have all been introduced to Miss Bond, who is your House Prefect and your first point of contact, should you have any particular problems during your time here at Oakdene.'

He clicked his fingers and a slim, red-bound book zipped across the room from a sideboard into his waiting hands. This was greeted by a few gasps of surprise.

'Bibliomancy,' Master Tweed stated, winking. 'When you've mastered it, every book will do your bidding. Even such boring tomes as this – the House register.'

He cleared his throat.

'Right, we'd best see that every student who is supposed to be here, IS actually here.' He peered at the book, 'Bond, Aubrey?'

'Here.' said Aubrey.

Master Tweed looked over the book at Aubrey.

'It is customary to suffix your acknowledgement of your presence with "Sir," Mr Bond. However, I will overlook it on this occasion, but let's not make a habit of it, shall we?'

I stifled a guffaw – Aubrey being taken down a peg or two sat well with me. I think I was going to like Master Tweed.

Gabrielle Cloche was a petite French girl, Elizabeth and Jack Hart were the twins, Mason Stone was a black American boy, Ian Strange a thin, bespectacled chap and Alice White was a stocky redhead, her face spattered with freckles. With Helena and I, that made nine students.

'That just leaves the final member of our little family, our very first Geist student, Yarrow.' Said Master Tweed, looking over into the far corner of the room. I turned and noticed a tall, slender figure with long, pale blonde hair, standing quietly there, their features curiously androgynous.

'Here, Sir.' Said Yarrow, stepping forward.

At the mention of the word "Geist," the other students had erupted into frenzied whispering. I edged over to Helena and nudged her.

'What's a Geist?' I whispered. She looked at me with exasperation. I tapped the side of my head and made a gesture as though dropping something. Her face cleared and she pulled me to one side.

'This is something that you've lost, right?' She asked. I nodded.

'We call them Geist, but they call themselves the Hidden Folk. They're a particularly magical race, attuned with nature, who don't tend to interact with humans very much – other than for trading purposes. They farm pixies, faeries, and sprites, so the majority of the pixie dust, hunny and sprites come from them.' She looked speculatively at Yarrow, 'But I've never heard of a Geist ever attending a human school...'

'This may be a stupid question,' I said, 'but is Yarrow a boy or a girl?'

'Neither...yet.' Said Helena. I must have looked puzzled, so she elaborated. 'Geist children don't choose their sex until puberty. From what I've read, their elders expose them to strong role models of both genders – whichever has the strongest influence on the child determines their eventual sex.' She paused thoughtfully. 'If Yarrow is at that stage, that means that we might actually see them take their final form – which would be pretty interesting.'

'So, I'm assuming that we use non-gender specific pronouns when referring to them?' I said.

Helena looked at me in surprise.

'Um...I *guess* so...' She said, hesitantly.

'You are indeed correct, Alexander,' said Master Tweed, who had caught the end of our conversation. He looked at me with interest. 'That is a remarkably mature insight for someone of your tender age - I can see that you will be a student to watch.'

Not *too* closely, I hoped, as drawing too much attention to myself would underscore my woeful lack of knowledge. I resolved to be more careful in what I said, or at least check who was listening first.

'Righty-ho, ladies and gentlemen,' announced Master Tweed, 'I have the dolorous task of handing out your timetables for the rest of term. Or at least Miss Bond does...'

Ashleigh was slowly going around the other students, handing out timetables to everyone.

'As you can see, you have the rest of today free, before your lessons start in earnest tomorrow.' Said Master Tweed, 'I would suggest you use this free time to familiarise yourself with the layout of the school. I would prefer that the first time I hear any of your names uttered by members of the faculty will not be because you have arrived late to your first lesson.'

As Ashleigh approached, she was scribbling something on the back of one of the timetables, which she handed to me, passing another to Helena.

'See you later, Alex.' She said, smiling.

Helena frowned and turned over her timetable, which, when she showed it to me, was blank. I turned mine over and saw written there:

If you need anything, I'm in Room 23.

Ashleigh x

Helena looked over my shoulder, then snorted with laughter.

'Told you so...' she said, nudging me in the ribs.

Like I didn't have enough stuff to worry about already...

I asked Helena if she wanted to spend the rest of the afternoon exploring the school and its grounds, but she said she'd agreed to call her parents when she got a spare moment, so she said she'd catch up with me later – then slyly suggested I ask Ashleigh to be my tour guide, laughing at my pained expression and then wisely retreating before I thumped her.

It wasn't until I got back to my room that I realised I'd taken what she'd said at face value. I had just assumed when she said she'd call her parents that this would involve a telephone – but I didn't even know if that sort of technology existed here and, if it did, what form it would take.

This then led to thinking about MY parents - or, at least, the parents of the Alex of this reality.

In the 1986 of my world, my father was working for a satellite communications company based in Farnborough, but what path he would have followed in this world I had no idea – perhaps he was involved in the national crystal ball network or something.

I resolved to keep my eyes peeled during my exploration of the school, for additional clues that would help me gain a better understanding of to what degree magic had replaced the technology I was used to.

However, as it was sunny day, I decided to start outside to familiarise myself with the school grounds.

Exiting the school via what was noted on the map as the Garden Exit, I found myself once again on the rear terrace, but in a frame of mind more conducive to fully appreciating the view.

The terrace was bordered by a low wall to the South, with a double staircase which swept down to a gravelled path that ran parallel to the wall, known as the Dog Walk. The South Lawn descended in a gentle slope to Oakdene Lake, with the Arboretum encroaching slightly onto this from the left.

From my vantage point on the terrace, I could just make out the largest of the several islands that dotted the lake, which was marked on the map as Temple Island. Hints of a stone structure could be seen amongst the trees on the island, but I was too far away to see any real detail.

Turning, I identified the Water Tower to the far right and the South-facing window of my room on the first floor.

I checked the map, then followed the terrace around the left-hand side of the building, heading for the main courtyard.

As I passed along the side of the college, I noted a set of stone steps leading down, terminating in a wooden door, the sign on which read "Staff Only." From what I'd read in *The Oakdene Students Handbook*, I hazarded a guess that this led to *"the extensive storage cellars, which students are forbidden from entering unless accompanied by a member of the faculty."*

I continued to the corner of the building, then turned into the main courtyard. As this was North facing, the majority of this was in shadow cast by the main building.

I continued along the front of the building, noting the college theatre to the left and, just beyond that a small building which seemed to be quite popular with the other students, given the number of them gathered outside. A fair few of them were clutching pink and white striped paper bags and quick glance at the map confirmed that this was the Tuck Shop.

Whilst I had left my wallet in my room, I *did* have a pocket full of loose change, all bearing the profile of the gentleman I'd met that morning – identified as *"Cole II, Dei Gratia Rex"* – but did I really *need* any sweets?

The decision was taken out of my hands, as a brief glance through the open doorway revealed that Penny was inside, and after our encounter earlier and the warning from the Headmistress, I was trying to avoid her wherever possible.

I therefore decided to head back inside, as I'd spotted a room on the map that I had a feeling I would be spending rather a lot of time in – namely the Library.

The Library was on the ground floor, accessed via a large room off the Picture Gallery, which was marked as the Study Hall.

The Study Hall looked to be housed in what would have originally been the mansion's drawing room, although rather than leather sofas and armchairs facing the large fireplace, there were a selection of wooden tables surrounded by chairs.

Given that lessons were not due to start in earnest until the following day, I was surprised to see another student already hard at work, surrounded by books and making copious notes. As I walked in, he scowled at me and covered his notes with his arms, as though I was spying on him. I didn't recognise him, so assumed he was from another House.

The library was behind this, looking out onto the back terrace and I stepped through the archway into the library proper, pausing to inhale that particular scent you only get where a lot of books are gathered together in one place. Floor to ceiling bookcases lined the walls, with two rows of freestanding bookcases running parallel down the centre of the room, allowing light from the rear window to illuminate the aisles.

I walked along one of these aisles, fingers gently gliding across the spines of the books upon the shelves, which all appeared to be bound in the same dark blue leather, their titles picked out in silver script.

As I exited the aisle, I came across a large desk, situated in front of the rear window, at which sat Master Tweed, perusing a slim volume bound in green leather with gold writing, a frown of concentration on his face.

Master Tweed notice me standing there, marked his place with a bookmark and put the book down.

'Well, if it isn't young Master Crowe,' he said, rising to his feet 'It's always gratifying to see a new member of my House gravitating towards the college's font of knowledge.'

He glanced over my shoulder.

'Although the fact that Master Levin from Watkins House already appears to be hard at work means that my sister will be crowing about that in the staff room later...' He noted my puzzled expression. 'Dr Deidre Tweed is not only the Unnaturalism Master and Head of Watkins House, but also my sibling.' He smiled brightly.

'Is there anything particular I can help you with, Alexander?'

Given that I needed some basic knowledge about the world I found myself in but didn't want to give this away to one of the faculty, I decided that getting a general feel of where each particular subject was shelved and what restrictions there were regarding access would be a good start, so this is what I asked.

'A valid question, Alexander.' Master Tweed circled the desk and started pointing to the shelves. 'Starting from the door, the subjects are shelved alphabetically in a clockwise direction, commencing with texts on Alchemy and concluding with those tomes concerned with study of Necromancy. The two central cases contain volumes dedicated to Scrying, Thaumaturgy, Unnaturalism and Warlockery. Generally speaking, all books relating to a specific subject can be found on the relevant shelves, as long as the students have put the book back where they got if from, which, unfortunately, is not always the case.'

He snapped his fingers and a heavy volume slid from a nearby shelf and floated over, rotating so he could read the spine.

'Case in point,' he said, indicating the floating book, 'Farrow's *Guide to the Fauna of Great Britain* should not be amongst the Chimestry texts.' He shooed the book away and it turned, then sedately floated to the relevant shelf, jostling for room, before sliding home.

'Students can access the library from 6am until 10pm every day, outside of these hours the doors are locked. Whilst books *may* be removed from the library by students, this is generally discouraged, although special dispensation may be granted by myself, should I feel that it would be beneficial to the student concerned.'

As we had been talking, I had noted a bookcase separate to those Master Tweed had indicated, all bound in green leather, like the volume he had been reading when I'd come in.

'What about the green-bound books, Sir?' I asked, 'What subject do they cover?'

Master Tweed looked at me speculatively.

'You have a good eye, Alexander.' He said. 'The green bound volumes cover subjects not on the curriculum, magic that is no longer practised in our more enlightened age - blood magic and the like. These books are not available to the average student and can only be referred to by advanced students with my express permission.'

I looked at the bookcase with interest, then noted that Master Tweed was watching me.

'You have a question regarding the books, do you not Alexander?' he asked.

'Yes, Sir, I do.' I paused, thinking how to frame the question. 'The contents of these books have no bearing on my studies and therefore I would have no reason to refer to one of these volumes. However, curiosity being what it is, what prevents me from just taking one of the books off the shelf? There doesn't *appear* to be anything stopping me from doing so, but I have a feeling that there probably *is*…'

'Very perceptive, Alexander.' Said Master Tweed. 'To prevent unauthorised perusal, a blood-lock enchantment has been placed on each volume. Should any man or woman other than myself touch one of the books, they will be paralysed in place - unharmed, but completely unable to move, until such time as the enchantment is lifted.' He paused, 'and before you ask, any form of Bibliomantic manipulation, the wearing of any thickness of gloves or the use of a trained monkey to retrieve the books, would **not** prevent this. Does that answer all your questions?'

'Yes, Sir.' I replied. 'I'm guessing from your response that every year someone still tries to beat the system?'

Master Tweed summoned the green-bound volume from his desk, then sent it back to its place on the shelf.

'You are correct, Alexander.' He sighed, 'There is always someone who thinks the rules either do not apply to them or sees it as a challenge.'

He looked over my shoulder and raised his eyebrows.

'I'm afraid I must cut short our discussion, as I believe Master Levin requires my assistance…?' He queried.

I turned and saw that the student who had been studying earlier next door was quietly waiting to speak to Master Tweed, his arms laden with books. From the expression on his face and the way he kept shooting glances at the restricted bookcase, it was clear he had been standing there for a while.

Whilst I was curious as to what was considered "forbidden lore," the idea of being fully aware of my surroundings, but completely unable to react or move was a terrifying thought, so I resolved not to go anywhere near those books.

Chapter IV
Night Visitors

I was sitting in my room after dinner, gazing thoughtfully into the flickering flames of the fire, when there was a knock at my door.

Rising, I carefully made my way to the door, as the fire did not shed a great deal of light and I'd already tripped over the edge of the rug at least twice, painfully banging my shin on my trunk.

Opening the door, I was surprised to see Yarrow standing there. I had been expecting either Helena or Ashleigh, as I didn't think anyone else knew which room I was in.

'Are you Alexander Crowe?' they asked, blinking owlishly.

'Yes, I am,' I said, 'please, come in…'

Yarrow walked in and gazed around my room.

'Why are you sitting in the dark?' They asked.

This was sore point with me and the reason my room was currently only illuminated by the fire, which I'd luckily been able to fumble around in the dark to get lit. There was a glass globe hanging from the ceiling, which I'd assumed was a light fitting, but could I find a switch to turn it on? Of course I bloody couldn't…

'Um… I can't get the light on…' I said lamely.

Yarrow looked up.

'*Solas*…' they murmured, smiling as the light flickered, then began to increase in luminescence. 'It is an older model of sprite globe, before they trained the sprites to understand English. Say *solas* to wake the sprite, and *dorcha* to render it dormant.' As Yarrow uttered the second word, the light began to dim again.

'*Solas*.' I said, trying the word out, and grinning as the light started to increase again.

'Thank you,' I said, 'I wouldn't have worked that out for myself and would have been sitting in the dark for ages. Now, what can I do for you, as I'm assuming you're here for a reason?'

Yarrow looked a little nervous, so I offered them the chair by the fire, closing the door and then carrying over the folding chair from my desk. If I was going to have regular guests in my room, I would need to find another chair from somewhere, as the folding chair wasn't particular comfortable.

'My parents advised me before coming here…' they started, 'that the best way to integrate myself into human society was to find the most popular student in the year and offer them my friendship.'

I had a feeling I knew where this was going, but let Yarrow continue.

'I noted at dinner that Aubrey Bond was surrounded by a large group of people, so I visited his room afterwards to… to…' Yarrow faltered, eyes tearing up. I leant forward and gently took their hand, looking them in the eye.

'Let me guess,' I said quietly, 'Aubrey not only rebuffed your offer, but also made some kind of hurtful comment.'

'He called me a freak!' Cried Yarrow, furiously wiping their eyes. I sighed – Aubrey never failed to disappoint.

'And then sent you to see me, right?' I asked wearily. Yarrow nodded.

'He said that "all you freaks should stick together" …'

During my early school years, my dad was in the Army, so we moved around a fair bit. This meant that I was always the new kid at school – the one who didn't know anyone and was wearing the wrong uniform for at least the first couple of weeks.

School bullies are like wolves – they can sense and single out the weakest member of the herd, so I naturally garnered a lot of attention. Usually, you only have to deal with this once or twice during your school years, but I experienced this at least half a dozen times, so learned from experience what was the best way to deal with and deflect this unwanted attention.

Which is why I wasn't overly bothered by Aubrey's attitude towards me, as I knew that I could shut him down if necessary.

Yarrow, coming from a completely different society, had probably never experienced this kind of behaviour and was therefore ill-equipped to deal with it. Having been in Yarrow's shoes, I knew exactly how they were feeling – isolated, weak, and powerless – and we couldn't be having *that*.

'Right,' I said, 'Up you get, Yarrow. We're going to go and see Aubrey and get you an apology.'

'Is that a good idea?' they asked nervously.

'It's an excellent idea,' I said grinning, 'but first we're going to take a little detour…'

Aubrey had been assigned Room 3, which was first on the left after you passed the back stairs and entered the Nursery Corridor. As I stood in front of his door, Yarrow hovering at my shoulder, I could hear the sound of music coming from within. I guessed there was nothing better after a strenuous evening of narrow-minded bullying than relaxing to the sound of your favourite band.

Raising my fist, I pounded on the door, only ceasing when the door was flung open by Aubrey himself, looking suitably annoyed. He started when he saw me, as obviously I was not who he was expecting to be visiting at this hour.

'Crowe,' he spat, 'What the Hell are you playing at?'

'I do have a first name, you know,' I said, 'but that's not why I'm here.' I indicated the silent form of Yarrow, who stood nervously behind me. 'I think you owe my friend here an apology.'

'What?! Are you bloody kidding me?' He asked.

'Did you or did you not refer to my good friend Yarrow as a "freak" and send them to me so, as I believe you stated, they could "stick together" with another freak, namely me?'

'So what if I did?' Aubrey growled.

'Well, that's not a particularly open-minded attitude to have towards your fellow students, especially Oakdene's very first Geist student now, is it?' I said, 'I believe that you certainly owe Yarrow an apology and, whilst you're at it, I'll have one too.' I smiled brightly.

Aubrey surged forward, shoving me hard against the opposite wall and pinning me there.

'You must be an idiot if you think I'm going to say sorry to either you…' he slammed me against the wall again, knocking the breath out of me, 'or that goddamn freak.' He released me, and I sank to one knee, coughing.

'That's where you're wrong, Aubrey.' I wheezed. 'An *idiot* would have come to your room without any official back-up.' I rose to my feet, smiling.

'Have you heard enough?' I asked, turning to the figure who was stepping forward from the shadows, into the halo of light spilling from Aubrey's door. [OBJ]

'Quite enough,' said Ashleigh coldly, 'you were right to come to me with this, Alex. I'll take it from here.'

She turned on her brother and grabbed his ear, twisting it. He squealed.

'We are going to see Master Tweed and see what he thinks of this.' She said furiously. 'I *honestly* can't believe you sometimes...' She then marched him off down the corridor.

With some people, all you have to do is give them enough rope...

Yarrow was concerned that I may have been injured in my encounter with Aubrey, but I assured them I was fine. We chatted about inconsequential matters as I walked them back to their room, then wished each other a good night. [OBJ]

Returning to my room, I activated the light, then looked about. The covered mirror drew my eye and I decided that it was about time I uncovered it, wondering as I did so why it had been covered in the first place.

Dropping the cover, I examined the mirror. It was an elongated oval of glass in a carved wooden frame, suspended midway in its frame by two wooden knobs, which allowed the mirror to be angled.

I couldn't immediately see anything wrong with it, but then noted movement on the bed behind me, reflected in the mirror. I turned and looked at the bed, but there was nothing there. I looked back at the mirror, stepping slightly to one side to get a better view.

In the mirror there was a tabby cat sitting on the bed, watching me, its ears twitching slightly. I looked back at the bed – nothing. In the mirror – cat.

'Now, that's a bit fucking weird...' I muttered.

In the mirror, the cat stood up and walked to the end of the bed, rising, and placing its paws on the end of the bedstead, looking at me intently.

'You can see me, can't you?' It asked. 'How curious...' It cocked its head and looked me up and down. 'Hmm, there appears to be some tachyon particulate clinging to you, which would explain your ability to discern my projected form. However, given the degree of particulate, it would appear that only a *portion* of your being is chronally anomalous, which is rather intriguing...'

'A-Ha!' I exclaimed. 'I bloody *knew* it!' I looked at the cat in the mirror.

'Would I be right in assuming that you are some kind of quantum entity that exists outside of the normal flow of time?' The Cat nodded. 'And due to the "tachyon particulate" you referred to, whilst others can *sense* your presence, I'm the only one who can actually *see* you?'

The Cat nodded again. This would explain why other occupants of the room had sensed something off about it, but not been able to work out what it was.

'And when you refer to your "projected form," what I can see is **not** your actual form, as this exists in four-dimensional space/time and viewing this would cause my brain to explode and dribble out of my ears?'

'Colourfully put, but in essence, yes.' Said the Cat. 'What you perceive is the closest approximation to my actual form that your mind can accept. And no, before you ask, no tentacles are involved.' It paused.

'That Lovecraft chap has a lot to answer for...' It muttered.

So, my theory that some kind of mental time travel was involved had been confirmed. However, given that the reality I existed in seemed to have followed a different history than the one I came from, this *would* suggest that I had skipped timelines and ended up in a parallel reality. Or did it? I decided to question the Cat further.

'So, my mind is from the future, currently occupying my teenaged body in what is, from my point of view, my past…' I started. 'However, as the past I remember is significantly different from the past I am experiencing now, this would suggest that I am in a different timeline than the one I came from… I think.'

'Actually, no.,' said the Cat. 'At some point in *your* near future, i.e. from your current temporal point of view, a cataclysmic event occurred which caused the reality in which you currently exist in to be over-written, changing the fundamental laws of physics, and resulting in the reality that you believe you had experienced from that point backwards.'

'So, prior to the event you're talking about, *this* **was** my past?' I asked incredulously.

'Correct.' Said the Cat.

I gave this some thought.

'Does this mean that all the authors from the future I come from, who've written about magical schools or universities, may have been subconsciously remembering fragments of their own pasts?' I asked.

'Hmm,' said the Cat, 'I would estimate a 93% probability that that is indeed the case.'

"Out of nowhere, it just fell from above…," eh Jo? I thought, *I reckon you were just remembering one of your old school mates…*

'And what exactly *was* this event?' I asked.

'That I cannot tell you,' said the Cat, 'but it will occur in approximately 108 of your days…'

December 17th, which, according to my diary, was when Saturnalia was apparently celebrated.

I has a horrible sinking feeling that *this* was the reason that I had been sent back, to try and prevent whatever this cataclysmic event was from happening.

So, no pressure then…

Chapter V
Practical Magic

The following morning, I was sitting talking with Yarrow at breakfast, when Helena came over carrying her tray.

'Shift up,' she said, nudging me in the back with her knee. I shuffled down the bench to give her enough room to sit down.

'Seems you two had an eventful evening, from the gossip going around...' she said, frowning at the contents of her tray, then examining mine.

'Are you going to eat that?' she asked pointing at a bacon sandwich sitting untouched on my plate. 'Only, they'd run out when I got there.'

'Help yourself,' I said, then paused. 'It's got brown sauce on it, though...'

Helena's eyes lit up.

'Even better,' she said, snatching it off my plate and taking a bite.

Now, usually a bacon sandwich wouldn't have lain untouched on my plate, but bacon in this world came from a breed of pig called a rath – which looked exactly like the pigs I was used to, except they were green. Which meant that their meat was green as well, even after it was cooked.

Generally speaking, if meat is green, this is Nature's way of telling you not to eat it. So, whilst I had intended to at least try it, when it came down to it, my mind refused. Green ham was also on offer - but no green eggs, so Dr Seuss would have been *very* disappointed.

Helena seemed to be enjoying it though, so at least it wouldn't be wasted.

'What were you talking about?' she said, mouth full.

I looked at her in mock disgust.

'You are an animal.' I stated, which caused Yarrow to burst out laughing. Helena looked mortified and quickly finished up the sandwich, colour suffusing her cheeks. She then smiled sweetly at me, leaned in, whispered 'Git' in my ear and punched me hard in the leg, numbing it.

Which was probably deserved...

'Anyway, before you so rudely interrupted...' I said, flinching as Helena growled at me, 'Yarrow was just explaining what will happen when they transition...'

Yarrow paused to gather their thoughts and continued where they'd left off.

'Once I have received enough stimulus for a decision to be made, the transition to my final gender will begin and I will start to manifest both the physical attributes and the traits of that gender. I will also start to gain the standard abilities of an adult Geist, such as the ability to see in the dark and being able to sense *mícheart...*'

When Yarrow noticed that we both looked blank regarding this, they elaborated.

'I think you would call it...wrongness,' they said, 'It's when something natural has become corrupted by dark magic.'

I almost asked whether they would also be able to detect secret or concealed doors on a roll of 1-2 on a d6, but wisely decided not to.

As we were due at our first lesson in less than twenty minutes, we finished up and returned to our rooms to collect our books.

I have to admit that I was in two minds about this – excited to see what a magical lesson actually looked like, but in equal measure, extremely worried that I was going to look like a complete and utter fool.

Lessons in the first year at Oakdene were taken with the other members of your House, and Dee House's first lesson of the day was double Lithometry, which was taught by Dr Noyce, a particularly energetic Scotsman. As the textbook for this was *An Introduction to Basic Lithometry,* I was fairly relieved, as this *should* mean that I'd be on an equal footing with the rest of the class.

Dr Noyce man-handled a carved block of what looked like Preseli Spotted Dolerite onto his desk at the front of the class.

Now, that might sound like I know my rocks, but I only recognised what it was due to the fact that it's the same as some of the stones that were used to construct Stonehenge. And the reason I knew *that* was because I had an Archaeology O level and we'd studied Stonehenge in exhaustive detail.

Although, because of the whole false history/time travel thing, whilst I had this knowledge in my head, this was due to reality being overwritten which hadn't actually happened yet from my current temporal position, so how AND when did I learn this?

Time travel really fucks with your head, so it's best not to think about it too much.

Dr Noyce looked around at the expectant faces of the class and grinned.

'Now,' he said, 'who knows what this is?'

This was followed by the standard response to any question raised by a teacher, or any public speaker for that matter – a shuffling of feet and people shooting glances at each other, to see if anyone else was going to answer.

I sighed, then put my hand up, as this kind of thing is painful to sit through and I DID actually know the answer. I would, of course, be hated by the rest of the class for being a know-it-all, but sometimes you have to take one for the team.

'Yes...' Dr Noyce glanced at his register, 'Alexander, isn't it?'

'I prefer Alex, Sir,' I said, 'I believe it's a piece of Preseli Spotted Dolerite, more commonly known as bluestone.'

'Very impressive, Alex.' Said Dr Noyce, 'You are indeed correct. Does anyone else know why it's called bluestone?'

Aubrey, who was sitting behind me, and didn't want to be upstaged, put up his hand.

'⌖ it's blue, Sir,' he said. Dr Noyce looked at the rock on his desk, which was more grey than blue, then looked back at Aubrey.

'Umm...not quite, Aubrey.' Said Dr Noyce, 'Anyone else? No?' He turned to me.

'Alex?'

'Bluestone is a generic term used to describe rock types not intrinsic to the area in which they are found. Generally, they've been quarried elsewhere and then transported to their current location.'

Yes, they would all *despise* me...

'Very good, Alex,' He grinned, 'You'll be after my job next...'

Aubrey kicked the back of my chair, which was not unexpected.

'Now, you may be wondering why I am showing you a lump of rock and wondering what this has to do with Lithometry.' Said Dr Royce. 'Lithometry concerns the study of and practical utilisation of specific forms of stone. Almost all of you will have an icebox at home, but how many of you know how these work?'

Over the next hour and a half, we learnt that a fully trained Lithometrist could attune certain naturally occurring forms of stone to achieve specific effects.

For example, hoarstone naturally generated cold and was generally found at the tops of mountains, which was why mountain tops were snow-capped. I always thought this was due to the altitude, but as the Cat had pointed out, the fundamental laws of physics differed here.

Once attuned by a Lithometrist, the degree of cold was enhanced and attuned hoarstone could then be used to line a cabinet and chill its contents, creating what was known here as an icebox, but which was essentially what I would call a fridge.

Historically, hoarstone had been mined from mountain tops, which was as dangerous as it sounds. Then some bright spark realised that it was a combination of the ambient temperature and the initial structure of the stone which caused hoarstone to spontaneously form, so if you exposed stone with right attributes to the correct temperature, such as in a large room lined with *attuned* hoarstone, you could create it without losing half your workforce when they took a slight misstep in a blizzard.

At the end of the lesson, Dr Noyce assigned each student a small cube of raw hoarstone, a grey granite-like stone, cool to the touch. The idea was that each student would *attempt* to attune the raw hoarstone before the next lesson, referring to their textbook for guidance on this. He did stress that only a small percentage of students would be able to attune their hoarstone on the first attempt.

I looked dubiously at the small cube of stone, sitting in the insulated container we had been supplied with. After the successful activation of the lifter the previous day, I knew that I was *capable* of channelling magic, but this seemed a bit more advanced.

However, it would have to wait until later, as after morning break, we were off into the Arboretum for double Unnaturalism with Dr Tweed.

Dr Tweed was a stocky, solid-looking woman, dressed in hard-wearing tweed and sensible boots. The resemblance to her brother was obvious, although luckily she wasn't bald, having chestnut curls streaked with grey, which were fastened into a rough ponytail.

We had assembled on the rear terrace, after changing into a variety of footwear more suited to tramping across the fields than the traversing the school corridors. Unsurprisingly, Aubrey had on a pair of Hunter wellingtons and a Barbour jacket, because if you've got it, you have to flaunt it in front of the peasants.

'Good morning, Class!' said Dr Tweed cheerfully. 'Today we will be venturing into the Arboretum, as whilst we *could* study this particular creature in the classroom, there is a degree of risk involved with mature specimens and the Headmistress doesn't want the gym burnt down again. Everyone got their Farrow's guide? Yes? Good – follow me.'

With that, Dr Tweed turned and marched down the steps and started across the lawn towards the treeline.

I fell into step with Helena and Yarrow, who were discussing possible options for the subject of our first lesson.

'It's got to be salamanders,' said Helena, 'They're the only creature that I'm aware of that can generate heat.'

'Do not most human dwellings have salamanders as part of their heating systems?' asked Yarrow. 'If they can be as dangerous as Dr Tweed suggested, surely they would not be used? Might we be studying something else instead?'

'I suppose it's possible,' said Helena reluctantly, 'But I still reckon it'll be salamanders...'

By this time, we had entered the Arboretum, following a well-worn path through the trees. The woodland was quite dense, with very little light filtering through the canopy. I could imagine that at night it would be pitch black, because unlike all those Hollywood movies featuring the protagonists being able to see where they were going, in reality, unless the tree canopy was quite sparse, there would be very little in the way of ambient light once the sun had set.

After a short walk, we entered a clearing, in the centre of which was a bonfire merrily blazing away. To the back of the clearing, just within the treeline, was a low stone structure, with steps leading down into it. Standing just in front of this was Mr Beamish, holding what looked like a fire extinguisher. He smiled when he saw me and nodded a greeting.

Dr Tweed stopped and turned to the class, who formed a semi-circle around her, with their backs to the fire. As I took my place with them, I noted movement within the fire, as though something was crawling amongst the logs.

'As some of you may have already surmised,' started Dr Tweed, 'today we will we studying the common salamander. Domesticated salamanders are used in heating systems, as this proved to be a more cost-effective way of generating heat than by the use of coal or wood burning boilers, because as long as the salamander is regularly fed, they will maintain a constant temperature without having to replace the consumed fuel. The older and larger the salamander, the more heat it generates. Does anyone know the name of units we use to measure the amount of heat generated by a salamander?'

Mason Stone tentatively put up his hand.

'Is it Efts, Miss?' He asked.

'Correct, Mr Stone,' answered Dr Tweed. 'A juvenile salamander will generate 1-2 efts worth of heat, and this will increase as it grows.'

She pointed at the fire behind us.

'Lurking amongst the logs is a mature *wild* salamander, approximately 15 years old, which is currently generating around 17-18 efts of heat. Whilst we will be taking a closer look at this specimen, please do not get *too* close, as it is not domesticated. Salamanders are quite territorial and their defence against intruders is to spray a viscous flammable liquid towards them, which can reach up to 3 feet with a specimen this size. Hence why Mr Beamish is standing by, with an extinguisher.'

After this announcement, those of us who had stepped forward for a closer look immediately took a couple of steps backwards.

I retreated back next to Mr Beamish, who grinned at me.

'Enjoying your first full day of lessons, Alex?' he asked.

'It's been...interesting' I said.

I then noticed a familiar scent, which seemed to be coming from the low building behind me. Was that...malt? Mr Beamish noticed my shift of attention, as I turned and cautiously approached the building.

'Er...you're not allowed in there, Alex.' He said.

Mr Beamish looked a little shifty, so I stepped closer to him and whispered.

'Unless I'm very much mistaken, I can detect the specific smells that would be associated with the brewing of beer. If I were to enter that building, I *wonder* what I would find...'

Mr Beamish drew me to one side, out of the earshot of the other members of the class, whose attention was fixed on the fire.

'Keep your voice down, lad,' he said, looking suitably uncomfortable. 'If you were to enter the Icehouse, which of course you're not allowed to do, it is possible that you may discover certain things that, upon the surface, may resemble the kind of equipment that you might find in a small-scale brewing operation. However, as this sort of thing would be frowned upon by the Headmistress and could result is the dismissal of those involved, it is, of course, merely a storage shed for...uh...*alchemical* supplies.' He then tipped me a slow wink.

'Well,' I said, slowly smiling, 'As I'm only sixteen and have *never* drunk beer in any shape or form, I'm sure that I must have been mistaken. If a couple of bottles of "alchemical elixir," preferable of the darker type, ended up in my bag by the end of the lesson...' I placed my bag on the ground, 'I'm sure this conversation and everything leading up to it would completely vanish from my memory.'

'And if that were to happen,' he asked, looking at me shrewdly, 'would further requests of a similar nature occur?'

'No,' I said simply. 'I may be a bit cheeky, but I know when not to take the piss. Do we have an agreement?' I stuck out my hand. Mr Beamish took it and gave it a quick and firm shake.

'Agreed.' He looked slightly puzzled. 'There's more to you than meets the eye, young Alex.'

If only you knew, Mr Beamish, I thought.

As the mature salamander was purely for show, Dr Tweed had arranged several long trestle tables around the perimeter of the clearing, with ten small glass tanks containing juvenile salamanders, enough for each member of the class.

I'd retrieved my exercise book and copy of Farrow's guide and was referring to it whilst making notes on my salamander.

It was a small lizard with a blunt head, about two inches long, glossy black in colouration with several blotches in bright orange running along its back. This, according to Farrow's, meant that it was a male, as females generally had yellow blotches. I had decided to call him Errol, as it seemed appropriate, a name that would go over the heads of everyone else, as Terry Pratchett wouldn't publish *Guards! Guards!* for another three years – if he actually existed in this reality, that is.

'Right, Class,' announced Dr Tweed, 'Time to pack up. The salamanders you have been studying are now your responsibility, so take these vivariums back to your rooms. Using Farrow's, I expect you to study and care for these creatures, with a full report on how your salamander has developed before our next lesson. As salamanders are relatively easy to look after, I will be disappointed if any of you fail to have a healthy, living creature by next week.' She looked pointedly as Aubrey, who had been poking at his with a pencil. 'That especially goes for you, Mr Bond.'

Aubrey started guiltily, dropping the pencil, which his salamander immediately pounced on, grasped it in its mouth and then, in a flash of incandescence, incinerated. Aubrey scowled at it.

I walked back over to my bag and nudged it with my toe. It clinked. Smiling, I opened it and carefully packed my schoolbooks around the two crown-capped brown bottles nestling in my bag. It wouldn't do for them to announce their presence on the way back to my room. I nodded an acknowledgement at Mr Beamish, who pretended to ignore me, then went back to collect Errol.

Helena was still packing her bag when I got there and glanced across at me.

'And what was that all about?' she asked.

'I don't know what you mean.' I said innocently.

'Alex,' said Helena, 'You're hiding something – I know it. If you don't tell me, I won't help you with your problem.'

Bugger.

'Okay,' I said quietly, 'come and see me this evening and I'll explain.'

Now all I needed was a bottle opener…

Chapter VI
The Order of Vulcan

There are those who state that to genuinely appreciate real or cask ale, it must be served at "cellar temperature," so between 12 to 14˚ Celsius, which is colder than room temperature, but not what I would call chilled. However, and I may be scorned for this opinion, I cannot drink and enjoy beer unless it is served at what I consider "fridge temperature" which ranges between 3 to 7˚ Celsius.

Not having a fridge (or icebox) in my room, how could I chill the beer I had acquired to bring it to an acceptable drinking temperature? Furthermore, as I was *physically* only 16 years old, whilst technically I could consume alcohol in the privacy of my own room, according to the *Oakdene Students Handbook*, "*students found in the possession of or consuming alcohol on school premises will be subject to disciplinary action.*"

Now, it may seem on the surface that the solution to both these issues were unrelated and would have to be resolved separately, but this failed to take into account the ingenuity of a friend of mine called Matt.

Matt and I attended many house parties in my early twenties (which from my current temporal point of view was my future, but from my mental point of view, was *actually* my past – due to time travel, see previous notes) and it was expected that you didn't turn up on someone's doorstep empty-handed. Generally speaking, any alcohol you showed up with would be put on the side in the kitchen, as the fridge was usually already full, and you'd break off a can and mingle with the other guests.

The disadvantage to this was twofold – firstly, even if you'd brought pre-chilled beer with you, after sitting on the side for a couple of hours, it would be room temperature. Secondly, if, like Matt, you'd bought high-end beer, rather than cheap lager, some other bugger would have decided to help themselves to it, so when you went back, all that would be left would be the cheap stuff that no-one wanted to drink.

Matt's solution to this was to conceal his beer in the toilet cistern, as water straight from the cold-water tank is, on average, about 7˚ Celsius, and who in their right mind would think to look in there for beer?

As the bathroom I had access to was generally not used by anyone else and the ceramic toilet cistern was not boxed in, that was where the two bottles I had acquired earlier were currently chilling, floating next to the ballcock.

Two birds, one stone.

Whilst that was one minor problem resolved, I still had the greater problem of the impending catastrophe that I believed I had been sent back to avert. Thanks to the Cat, I now had a definitive date of when this was supposed to happen, but other than that, I had *nothing*.

However, I had a feeling that the recurring dream of armed men bursting into a room and me falling away from the light was more than just a dream – it was an incomplete memory. If I could somehow recall greater detail, ideally what I had been told prior to the interruption, this might shed additional light on whatever it was I was here to prevent.

Helena was key to this, as not only was there some kind of connection between us, but she was also a talented scryer, as had been shown during our final lesson of the day.

As had been explained by Dr Bell during our lesson, Scrying was the ability to mentally discern certain information at a distance. A talented scryer could, for example, tell the contents of a sealed box by extending their senses beyond the normal five. It could also be used to skim the surface thoughts of another, but as Helena had pointed out on our first meeting, this was generally frowned upon in polite society.

Unsurprisingly, I had proved to be absolutely rubbish at this.

Helena, however, was really, really good. Given that she been able to tell that the personal information I knew about her had not been the result of me scrying on her, this came as no great surprise. Prior to our arranged meeting this evening, I'd gone through my copy of *The History and Practical Applications of Scrying in Great Britain,* as I'd had a hunch that her talent for scrying may be able to help me clarify this suppressed memory. According to the textbook, this was a process known as "*verum mormoria*" and required the willing cooperation and trust of the subject, as well as the agreement of the person attempting it.

I was hoping that Helena would at least be willing to give it a try.

'So, Alex,' said Helena, after I'd ushered her in to my room, checking the corridor and antechamber leading to my room for prying eyes, 'why are you acting so mysteriously?'

'Okay,' I began, 'let's say that, hypothetically, you discovered something about a certain member of staff that, if revealed to those in charge, would result in the person concerned possibly being dismissed from their position...'

I let Helena absorb this information.

'Would you feel obligated to report them?' I finished.

'That depends,' said Helena. 'If what you've found out...'

'Hypothetically, remember.' I interrupted.

'Right, what you've "hypothetically" found out... is it something could endanger the students?'

I gave this some considered thought.

' No,' I said, 'I'd say it falls more into the category of "naughty," rather than dangerous.' [OBJ] n I'd say No.'

'In that case, can I interest you in a beer?'

Helena paused, then leaned forward.

'You've got some beer?' she whispered, 'You do know if we get caught, we'll be in serious trouble?'

'You do realise that you just said "we," don't you?' I said laughing. I watched as the realisation of what she'd just said dawned on her. She opened her mouth to issue a retort, paused, then scowled at me. I noticed that there was hint of smile at the corner of her mouth.

'You are a bad influence, Alex,' she growled, 'If we get caught...'

I chuckled as I went to retrieve the beer from its hiding place, directing Helena to the glasses and bottle opener I'd liberated from the Dining Hall earlier.

When I returned, I made sure the door was locked, as we definitely didn't want to be interrupted.

'So, what sort of beer is it?' she asked, eyeing the bottle with interest.

'No idea,' I said, 'But we'll soon find out...'

I cracked open the bottle and poured a generous measure into each glass, happy to note that it appeared to be either a stout or a porter, my preferred tipple, judging from the colour.

I handed a glass to Helena, and we retired to the chairs in front of the fire. I had managed to "borrow" another armchair from our common room earlier, although manhandling it up the stairs had been a bit of a chore. This meant we could both relax in comfort, cold beer in hand and the fire warming our toes.

'I'm impressed,' said Helena, after she'd taken her first sip. 'Not only with the beer itself, but also that you've managed to get hold of some *and* make it cold. Does this mean you've managed to attune your hoarstone?'

'No,' I said frowning, 'No joy on that front. Any luck with yours?'

Helena tucked her legs under her in the chair, making herself more comfortable.

'Not yet,' she said, 'but I'm sure it's just a matter of time.'

We sat in companiable silence for a while before I decided to broach the subject of my memory.

'You know you said you were willing to help me with my memory?' I asked. Helena nodded. 'Do you think that you could attempt a *verum mormoria* on me?'

Helena looked startled, then gave it some thought.

'I guess I *could* try...' she said warily, 'I've not tried it before, but do know the theory. There's no guarantee it will work, though, and unless you trust me implicitly, your mind will fight against the intrusion.'

'Given that I've trusted you not to report the illicit beer we're currently drinking AND that I really do *need* to recover this particular memory, I think we'll be okay.'

'Alright, I'll give it a go, but I think you'll need to lay down, just in case...'

'Are you trying to get me into bed, Miss Morgan?' I asked in mock surprise.

'Do you want my help or not?'

'Sorry.'

Helena got me to lay down on my bed, with my head at the foot of the bed, as she needed to be able to place her fingers on my temples, and headboard was against the wall.

'Now, you need to focus on the memory you are trying to recover,' said Helena, placing the tips of her fingers on my temples, 'and close your eyes – you staring at me will put me off.' I stuck my tongue out at her, then closed my eyes. I felt a slight tingling, then warmth spread from Helena's fingertips, infusing my head.

And I was back *there...*

The woman opposite leans forward, looking me intently in the eye.

'I know you're finding it hard to believe, but everything I've told you is true,' she says, 'If you don't save her, then the world we knew will never have existed, replaced by this false shadow.'

'Why me?' I ask.

'You're the only one left. They've already got to everyone else.'

'Wonderful. Last choice, as usual.'

'You've always been a suspicious and stubborn bastard, Alex, I'm hoping that will help.'

Shadowy figures in suits, their faces obscured, burst into the room, hands filled with guns and a glint of sliver on their lapels. I focus on the pin they wear, knowing instinctively that it is important - it is an inverted triangle, with what looks like a capital T inside.

The woman opposite me reacts, throwing out her left hand and somehow pinning the figures in place.

'We're out of time!' She shouts, 'Time for you to go!'

She thrusts her right hand towards me, and, with a jolt, I am suddenly falling backwards, away from the light...

'Whoa...' I said, 'That was intense.'

Helena stumbled backwards, dazed. I quickly jumped up and guided her back to the chair by the fire.

'Are you alright?' I asked.

'Uh...yes, I think so.' she said, 'That took a lot out of me...' She sipped her drink, the looked up at me.

'Did it work?' She asked.

'Kind of...' I said, 'it didn't restore the entire memory, but it did give me more details I previously couldn't recall. There were people wearing a symbol I didn't recognise though, an inverted triangle with what looked like a capital T in the centre.'

Helena looked up sharply.

'Could it have been a hammer?' she asked.

'Possibly...' I answered, 'It wasn't very clear.'

'Where's your copy of *Magic Through the Ages*?'

I indicated the bookshelves. Helena started to get up, wobbled slightly and sat heavily back down.

'Think I need to rest for a bit more...'

I retrieved the book and handed it to her. She referred to the index and then turned to the relevant page, flicking back and forth until she found what she was looking for. She turned the book towards me.

'Is this the symbol?' She asked. I took the book from her and examined the illustration – it was the same as those worn by the men from my memory, a hammer enclosed within an inverted triangle.

'Yes, that's it,' I said, looking back at the book, 'it says here it's the symbol of "The Order of Vulcan." Who are they?'

Helena rolled her eyes and sighed.

'You really are quite exasperating,' she said, 'This is stuff you *should* know. The Order of Vulcan started off as a cult in Roman times, promoting technological advances in the place of magic. They believed that magic should not be practiced by mortals, as magic belonged to the Gods alone, and man should reject magic and embrace technology instead.'

She paused to take another drink, then continued.

'Whilst it apparently died out nearing the end of the Roman Empire, it actually just went underground and regularly resurfaced over the years. James I was a member of the Order of Vulcan, as was Oliver Cromwell, which was one of the main causes of the English Witch War. Fortunately, this was the last major conflict involving them. They still exist as a fanatical anti-magic organisation, but their last terrorist act was two years ago, when they tried to assassinate the Prime Magister in Brighton.' She looked at me speculatively, 'Why would they be interested in *you*?'

'I don't think it was me they were interested in,' I said, 'I think I was just in the wrong place at the wrong time...'

Helena had finished her beer and was looking a little sleepy, so I thought it best to call it a night.

'I think it's time for bed.' I said. Helena giggled. 'And I think you've had enough excitement for this evening. Let's get you back to your room.'

Now, some may think, given that I had an attractive and slightly tipsy girl in my room, that this would be an ideal opportunity for me to make a move on Helena. However, there were two reasons that I didn't.

Firstly, as I needed her help, should I have tried it on and been rebuffed, it was unlikely she would continue to help me. This would not be a good thing.

Secondly, and more importantly, this was morally questionable ground. Yes, I may *appear* to be a reasonably good-looking 16-year-old, but behind my eyes was the soul of someone old enough to be her dad. Yes, I'll admit that I was probably the only person to ever be in this kind of situation and therefore, there were no specific rules to govern my behaviour, but it just seemed...*wrong*.

Besides, whilst I may be a bit of a flirt, I do consider myself a Gentleman, old-fashioned as this may be, so I helped her up from her chair and walked her back to her room.

She was a bit unsteady on her feet, but that was understandable, given her expenditure of *Vitae* combined with the alcohol she'd had.

As she was fumbling with her key, I gently took it off her and unlocked her door, then handed her the key. Her hand lingered on mine, and she stepped in closer.

'You know what, Alex,' she murmured, 'I'm beginning to see what Ashleigh sees in you.'

She then leaned in and kissed me on the cheek, then stepped back quickly with a look of surprise on her face, which swiftly reddened.

'Um...good night, Alex,' she said and quickly retreated into her room, closing the door behind her.

I stood still in astonishment, tentatively raising my hand to my cheek.

This was getting complicated, as what I'd failed to tell her was that the woman from my memory, the one who'd sent me back in time, was actually a future version of Helena herself...

Chapter VII
Further Complications

Thanks to the revelations of the previous evening, I was a *little* more informed regarding the reason I was here.

It would appear that some kind of plot had been hatched by the Order of Vulcan to overwrite reality on 17th December 1986, causing technology to become the dominant axiom of the future I had come from.

Helena had somehow not been affected, retaining her memory and powers, and had attempted to rectify this, her final act being to send my future mind back to before the event occurred, to hopefully prevent it from ever happening.

Now, various theories of time travel had been put forward in my time, predominantly through a variety of science fiction films and books, and the "laws" governing time travel were as varied as the source material.

As far as I could tell from the limited information I had manged to gather so far, there was a single timeline, running from beginning of time to the eventual heat death of the Universe. Had nothing interfered with this, then my future (from my current temporal point of view) would have continued as it was now, with magic being the dominant axiom and technology being relegated to a crackpot idea, upheld only by a fanatical terrorist organisation.

Imagine a straight black line, running from the beginning to the end of time – this is the timeline. Along this line we'll add three dots; one on 1st September 1986, one on 17th December 1986 and one in May 2020 (as I can't recall the exact date). From the December date, we'll recolour the line red, representing the overwriting of reality from that point onwards. We'll then add a further black line, curving back from the May 2020 point to the September 1986 point, representing my mind being thrown back into the past. This, therefore, indicates the current situation.

Now, it would *appear* that the laws governing time travel do not follow the "Many Worlds" theory, which suggest that any disruption to the timeline would cause the timeline to bifurcate, splitting into two separate strands – one of which would be the technological world of my future and the other being the magical world I was currently in.

This meant, if I was correct, that if I failed to prevent the event from happening, I would be stuck in a recursive time loop. The event would happen, reality would be overwritten, I would live on in the technological world until Helena sent me back. From both our points of view, it would be the first time this happened, but it could have (or already had) occurred multiple times, ad infinitum, and we'd be none the wiser.

If I *did* prevent the event from happening, then Helena would have no cause to send me back, reality would not be overwritten, and everyone would live happily ever after.

However, there was a slight wrinkle with this second option - there was the *possibility* that should I succeed, I would cease to exist.

Not completely, as there would still be an Alexander Crowe in this reality, but he would have none of the knowledge, experience, and memories I currently had in my head, as his mind would revert to the pre-cataclysm version of me.

The question I therefore had to ask myself was this – was I selfless enough to risk my mind and existence to save a world that, up to this point, I hadn't even known existed?

I guess we'd find out...

The prevention of reality-altering cataclysms aside, I had more immediate concerns - I couldn't find my hoarstone anywhere and Errol's blotches had changed colour from a vivid orange to an electric blue.

I'd checked Farrow's and, whilst it described a deepening of the hues in mature specimens, I could find no mention of a complete change of colour. Other than the colour change, he seemed to be fine, having eaten all the worms I'd given him earlier.

However, I decided better safe than sorry, so collected the tank and went in search of Dr Tweed.

As this was prior to lessons starting for the day, I knocked on the door to the staff room, hoping that Dr Tweed would be there.

The door was answered by Dr Noyce, who grinned when he saw me.

'Well, if it isn't our rock expert,' he said, 'what can I do for you, Alex?'

'I'm looking for Dr Tweed, Sir.' I said.

Dr Noyce turned and shouted out across the staff room.

'Dee, young Mr Crowe wants a word,' He turned back to me, 'She'll be with you shortly.'

As I was waiting, I took the opportunity to sneak a look at the staff room through the open door. A long, low oblong table sat in the centre of the room, surrounded by chairs, which were partially occupied by several members of the faculty, some of whom I'd already met. Some were planning lessons, others just drinking coffee and chatting, whilst a particularly dishevelled individual was obviously asleep.

Dr Tweed had been chatting with a muscular-looking woman with short hair, dressed in Khaki combat trousers and matching pullover, but when she'd been called, had bustled over to me.

'Good morning, Alexander,' she said, then noted the tank in my arms, 'Problem with your salamander?'

'I'm not sure, Miss,' I said, 'When I checked on him this morning, he'd changed colour. I couldn't find anything in my textbook regarding this and although he doesn't seem any worse for wear, I thought I'd better come and check with you.'

'Best bring him in, then, so I can get a better look.' She noted my hesitancy on entering the staff room, 'Don't worry, we don't bite.'

I carried the tank over to the central table and put it down. Dr Tweed leaned forward and examined Errol.

'Now that's something you don't see every day...' she muttered, then turned to me, 'Have you fed him anything out of the ordinary?'

'Um...no. All he's had is some worms this morning,' I paused, 'Although...'

'Come on, Alexander,' said Dr Tweed, 'Out with it.'

'Well, my hoarstone was missing this morning...' I said, 'So, it's possible that Errol could have eaten it...'

'Errol?'

'My salamander.'

'You've named your salamander... Errol?'

'Er...yes.'

'Any particular reason?'

'It seemed an appropriate name.'

Dr Tweed considered this, then turned.

'Bob, can I borrow you for a moment?' she called.

Dr Noyce came over, carrying a mug of coffee.

'How can I help?' he asked.

'Alexander believes that his salamander may have eaten his hoarstone,' said Dr Tweed, 'As you're our resident rock-head, could you speculate on what effect this may have had on it?'

Dr Noyce crouched down and peered through the glass at Errol, gently tapping the glass with his fingernail.

'Hmm…,' he murmured, 'If the hoarstone had been attuned, which I'm assuming it wasn't?' I nodded in agreement. 'I would expect this wee beastie to have been frozen solid. Unattuned hoarstone, on the other hand, I wouldn't have thought would have had any effect, other than giving it a bellyache. Might be worth waking Burton up, as this is more his field of expertise.'

Dr Tweed approached the dishevelled sleeping man and kicked his foot. He awoke with a start, then sat up bleary eyed.

'Wakey-wakey, Burton,' said Dr Tweed briskly, 'Time to earn your keep.'

This, I later learned, was Dr Burton Moore, Oakdene's Chimestry Master.

'I don't have a lesson until after lunch,' groused Dr Moore, 'So I can't imagine why you'd need me…' He noticed the tank and its contents on the table and his whole demeanour changed. He shuffled forward in his seat and stared intently through the glass.

'And what do we have here?' He asked, pulling out his spectacles and perching them on his nose. 'General form indicates typical specimen of *Salamandra salamandra*, but atypical colouring would suggest some form of cosmetic change…' he made a pass over the top of the tank with his hand. 'Hmmm, no detectable Illusioneering involved, so change is non-cosmetic, which would suggest some form of chimerical alteration…' He took off his glasses and looked at our expectant faces.

'What did you say happened to this creature?' He asked.

'Alexander here believes it may have eaten some hoarstone,' said Dr Tweed.

Dr Moore started to chew on one the arms of his glasses, deep in thought, then appeared to come to a decision.

'It *IS* possible that change may merely be cosmetic, with the minerals contained within the hoarstone being absorbed by the salamander and altering the pigment of its skin.' He said, 'but there does also exist the possibility that a fundamental chimerical alteration may have occurred, for reasons currently unknown. If so, this creature may start manifesting the properties typically associated with attuned hoarstone.'

'Which means what, Sir?' I asked.

'Which means, young man,' answered Dr Moore, 'We may have a salamander that generates cold instead of heat. And a brand new, if accidental, chimera.'

He looked at me with interest.

'Whilst I'll leave this in your care for the time being…Alexander, wasn't it?' I nodded, 'Could you bring it along to the Chimestry lab after lessons today, as I'd like to perform a few tests?'

I looked across at Dr Tweed, who nodded in agreement.

'No problem, Sir,' I said.

Now all I needed was five more impossible things before breakfast and I'd be done for the day.

After I'd dropped Errol's tank back to my room, I headed down to the Dining Hall, hoping I'd have enough time before our first lesson of the day to get some breakfast.

As I was running a bit late, there was a limited choice of hot food, so I went for cereal, supplemented with fresh fruit and a big mug of coffee. Helena was still seated, idly toying with the remains of her own breakfast and when she saw me approaching, started to get up, avoiding looking at me directly, her face flushed.

'Sit down,' I said, 'You and I need to have a little chat.'

Helena wavered and I wasn't sure if she was going to bolt or not, but her shoulders slumped in resignation and she resumed her seat, eyes downcast. I glanced around the room, checking if anyone else was in earshot before speaking.

'Last night...' I began, before Helena interrupted me.

'Alex, I...' she said.

'Stop.' I said, 'Before you say anything else, let me finish.' Helena subsided, still refusing to look me in the eye.

'Last night, you and I spent a pleasant evening together, chatting by the fire in my room. Then I walked you back to your room, we said good night and went our separate ways. And that is *all* that happened, right?'

Helena looked up at me in surprise.

'Now,' I continued, pouring milk on my cereal, 'whilst you may have a *slightly* different recollection of the events of last night, I can assure you that, as far as I'm concerned, that's all that happened.' I looked across at her, watching as realisation dawned on her face.

'We good?' I asked. Helena smiled at me shyly.

'Yes, I believe we are,' she answered, then frowned, 'You know, you don't act like a typical teenage boy...'

'Ah, that's because I'm not,' I said truthfully, 'I'm a weirdo, remember?'

Helena laughed and I watched as the tension drained out of her.

'What are you doing after lessons?' I asked. Helena looked at me quizzically.

'Why?'

'I've got to take my salamander to Dr Moore, as apparently, I may have accidentally created a "chimera," whatever that is, and I thought you might like to tag along.'

Helena leaned forward, a look of interest on her face.

'*You've* created a chimera?! How d'you manage *that*?'

'I don't even know what a chimera IS, so how I could have created one, even accidentally, is beyond me.'

Chimestry, from what I could gather from Helena's explanation, was magical crossbreeding, where the aspects of two or more unrelated creatures were combined into a new entity, known as a chimera. Due to the magical process, these new creatures were generally barren, so existed as one-of-a kind beasts with no prospect of propagating a new species.

This practice started in Ancient Greece, with a variety of chimeras created, usually for the purpose of guarding treasure of some kind. The practice spread across the rest of Europe and, up until the 1400's, was completely unregulated, so anyone with a modicum of talent and a menagerie could unleash weird and wonderful creatures upon an unsuspecting populace.

Then came the Wherwell cockatrice debacle, which resulted in a significant number of deaths in that community, until Magister Green was able to subdue and slay the beast.

From that point onwards, it was illegal to craft chimeras in Great Britain without a Royal decree, until this was reviewed in 1928 and the criteria changed. Those who wished to practice Chimestry had to go through an extensive interview process to decide whether they were of the right temperament to experiment in this fashion, before being issued with a government sanctioned licence.

Apparently, without formal training and knowledge of the correct enchantments needed, it was *extremely* difficult to create a chimera and even more so to combine the properties of inorganic matter with a living subject. An Oxfordshire don *had* managed to do so in 1871, combining a lizard, a badger, and a corkscrew into what became known as Toves, because he had also managed to overcome the fertility issue, meaning that Toves were now a species in their own right and the bane of anyone owning a sundial.

So, just how *I* had possibly managed to do this was a mystery.

Helena was equally puzzled and was eager to see what Dr Moore could discover, so agreed to accompany me after the final lesson of the day.

Chapter VIII
Cupid's Arrow

As our first lesson of the day was Warlockery, we gathered our copies of *A Beginner's Guide to Offensive & Defensive Magic* and headed for the tennis courts, which were across the West Lawn amongst the trees.

As we made our way across the grass, I could hear Aubrey boasting about his previous experience to Ian and Mason.

'Of course, I was a member of the combined cadet force at Eton before coming here,' he bragged, 'So I doubt they'll be able to teach me anything I don't already know.'

'We had something similar back home,' said Mason, 'so I've at least got some experience of combat training, but I'm curious to see how it differs here in England.'

I looked back, noting that Yarrow was bringing up the rear and seemed to be flagging slightly. I waited until they had caught up and walked alongside them. Yarrow looked quite nervous and was twisting their hair between their fingers.

'You okay, Yarrow?' I asked.

'Oh, hello Alex,' they said distractedly, biting their lip, 'I have to admit that I am a little anxious regarding our next lesson. Our people have a separate warrior caste who specialise in martial prowess, but other than formal displays, I have not had any exposure to this type of magic. I fear I may not be any good at it.'

'I wouldn't be too worried,' I said, 'I've not had any formal training in this either, so we'll both be on an equal footing. You never know, we might turn out to be really good at this.'

'But I have heard rumours that they pair up students and make them fight one another. What if I get paired up with Aubrey? I have heard him say that he is really good at combat magic and after the other night, he may take the opportunity to try and hurt me as revenge for getting him into trouble.'

'Aubrey got himself in trouble, we just helped expose him. But I do see you point. If we *are* required to pair up, I'll make sure it's me that gets paired up with him, okay?'

'But you said you have no formal training, so would not the same thing happen to you?'

'I said I had no formal *magical combat* training,' I said, 'but that doesn't mean I don't know how to fight. Or how to take a punch. And as it was me who got him into trouble, it should be me that he's got it in for.' I considered this for a moment. 'Actually, it might be worth reminding him of that fact, as that should deflect his interest from you.'

'Alex, why are you so kind to me all the time? Other than Helena, no-one else really talks to me.'

'You're my friend, Yarrow,' I said grinning, 'besides, aren't we "freaks" supposed to stick together? Now, let's go wind Aubrey up...'

I increased my pace, until I was level with Aubrey and his audience.

'Alright, Aubs?' I called, 'Did you get a bollocking the other night from Master Tweed? I bet your parents won't be too pleased when they find out. Although, I have to admit when your big sister grabbed your ear and made you squeal like a little pig it did make me laugh.'

I glanced across at Aubrey, who had gone dangerously quiet, his face like thunder. He was simmering nicely, so wouldn't need too much further prodding to blow.

'Talking about your sister,' I started, 'She's pretty fit and, do you know what, I reckon she'd let me...'

We'd never find out what I was going to suggest she'd let me do, as Aubrey surged forward, fists swinging.

'You're dead, Crowe!' he shouted.

I danced back out of his reach.

'You've got to be quicker than that, Aubs,' I said, darting out of his way, 'perhaps if your knuckles weren't dragging on the ground, you'd be able to catch me. Or maybe you like chasing after boys... is that it?'

With an inarticulate roar, Aubrey charged forward head down, tackling me midsection and carrying me backwards. I would have gone over, but as we'd reached the tennis courts by then, our momentum was halted by the chain link fence surrounding them. We bounced and once again the breath was knocked out of me. I felt my stomach churning and wondered if I was going to add injury to insult by throwing up down his back.

'That is quite enough of *that*!' barked a firm female voice, and Aubrey was thrown backwards away from me. I fell forward on to my hands and knees, stomach roiling.

In hindsight, this probably wasn't one of my better ideas, but you couldn't argue that it hadn't been effective. It was *highly* unlikely that Aubrey would be picking on Yarrow now.

Me, on the other hand, well, that was a different matter...

The muscular, Khaki clad woman I'd seen in the staff room earlier was standing over Aubrey, an angry look on her face.

'On your feet, Bond,' she said furiously, waiting until Aubrey had sullenly returned to his feet. 'Now - explain yourself.'

'He started it...' he said, glowering at me.

'*He started it...*' parroted the woman, mockingly, 'And did he "start it" the first time you assaulted him?' Aubrey looked startled.

'Yes, Bond, I am aware of your previous run in with Crowe. It may surprise you to know that the staff do discuss potentially disruptive students, so we can plan for any issues that arise during class.'

She turned away from him and walked over to where Yarrow and Helena were helping me up.

'You alright, Crowe?' she asked.

'I'm fine, Sergeant Hades,' I said, 'Aubrey has a hasty temper, which can be provoked by insults.'

A look of surprise appeared on her face and her eyes narrowed.

'Quoting Sun Tzu...' she said speculatively, then came to a swift decision. 'If you two could join the others on the courts, I'd like to speak to Crowe alone, please.'

Helena and Yarrow looked at each other in puzzlement, then slowly followed the rest of the class, glancing back over their shoulders as they went.

Sergeant Hades folded her arms and looked intently at me.

'I'm intrigued, Crowe,' she said, 'I'm assuming you noted the stripes on my arm indicating my rank, but am surprised that you'd know what they meant.'

'My dad was in the Army, Sergeant,' I said. She nodded in understanding.

'Well, that explains that,' she said, 'However, the context of the Sun Tzu quote you used would suggest that you deliberately provoked Bond into attacking you. My question is - why?'

'Aubrey doesn't like Yarrow and they were worried that he would use this lesson as an opportunity to get back at them, due to his perceived notion that it was both Yarrow and my fault that he got into trouble with Master Tweed. I was merely presenting myself as a more viable target for his attention.'

'You put yourself in harm's way to protect your friend?' She asked.

'Um…I guess so.' I answered, smiling ruefully.

Sergeant Hades gave this some thought.

'Whilst your courage and loyalty are to be commended,' she said, 'you should have come to me with this at the start of the lesson, rather than trying to deal with this yourself. The faculty are already aware of Bond's… views regarding our Geist student, partly due to your exposure of this the other night, so we would not have let any harm come to your friend. However, we need to resolve this enmity between yourself and Bond in a more controlled and constructive fashion than brawling on the school grounds. So, I think the best way to do this would be for you and Bond to compete against one another during this lesson. I think it will be instructive for all concerned.'

'Sounds like reasonable idea, Sergeant,' I said a little nervously, 'although Aubrey claims to be well-versed in combat magic and I've never had any formal training…'

'Shouldn't be a problem for a student of Sun Tzu,' she said, smiling at me, 'But I will be refereeing, so should you come off worse in this encounter, all you'll be walking away with is a few bruises – which you were prepared to take anyway. I think we've kept the rest of the class waiting long enough.'

With that, she marched off, with me trailing unhurriedly in her wake.

It looked like I was about to take part in my first ever magical duel, against an (allegedly) more skilled opponent, armed with nothing more than a few pithy quotes from an ancient Chinese general.

I was about to get my arse well and truly kicked.

'Right, Class,' said Sergeant Hades briskly, 'apologies for the delay in starting your lesson. My name is Sergeant Hades and it's my task to teach you the basics of offensive and defensive magic, which is more commonly known as Warlockery. However, before we start, we need to resolve a difference of opinion between Bond and Crowe and the most constructive way to do this is a duel between the pair, in a controlled environment.'

There was an excited whispering amongst the other students, although both Helena and Yarrow looked as apprehensive as I currently felt.

'As you can see,' continued Sergeant Hades, 'the courts have been set up as simulated combat environment, in which our two combatants will attempt to defeat their opponent. Bond claims to have had extensive magical combat experience, whereas Crowe does not – which would suggest that this is an unequal duel. However, I have a feeling that Mr Crowe may surprise us all.'

I looked around the courts with interest and some trepidation, as I did not share Sergeant Hades' faith in my ability. Scattered about the interior of the courts were a series of fences, some made from corrugated iron, some from wood and a couple of high platforms, accessed by ladders. It resembled the sort of terrain you'd expect to find on a paintballing site, but instead of coloured patches from paintball impacts, there were singe marks on some of them. This did not bode well.

Behind the gathered students, against the fence, were two long trestle tables loaded with a variety of weaponry and armour, most of which I was unable to identify.

'Both combatants will select their choice of arms from the selection available, as this is a training exercise and the use of hex bolts or defensive shields should be beyond students of your level,' said Sergeant Hades, indicating the tables 'Whilst they will be charging their weapons with their own *Vitae*, these have been specifically enchanted to limit the effects of any blows to stunning only, rather than to cause any actual physical damage. If they get hit, they'll know about it. Once they have selected their arms, they will take position at either end of the arena and begin the contest when I blow my whistle.'

Aubrey gave me a smug and condescending grin, then sauntered over to the tables and began examining the weaponry on display.

Sergeant Hades walked over to me, trailed by Helena and Yarrow, who were looking even more concerned.

'Right, Crowe,' she said, 'you may feel like I've dropped you in at the deep end, but I am confident that you'll be able to hold your own against Bond. Other than the tactical advantage you have over Bond due to your study of Sun Tzu, do you have any particular talents you feel may help in this, as I can then suggest the most suitable way to arm yourself?'

I looked over at Aubrey, who was hefting what looked like an elongated mace.

'Um...I'm not bad with a bow,' I said hesitantly.

'Excellent,' said Sergeant Hades, 'In that case, I suggest you play to your strengths.'

She walked me over to the table and selected a recurve bow from those lying there. 'Standard recurve bow, used by armed forces across the world. And these are your arrows.' She handed me a quiver, with a dozen or so arrows within.

She then showed me the charging patch on the exterior of the quiver, explaining that a single charge would empower every arrow. Apparently, once a weapon had struck a blow, it expended its some or all of its charge, depending on the strength of the blow. With arrows, as they were effectively single use, this wasn't a major problem, but melee weapons needed constant replenishing, so these tended to be pre-charged when used in actual combat.

As the expenditure of personal *Vitae* had a tiring effect, as I had witnessed the other night when Helena had when performed the *verum mormoria* on me, I could possibly use this to my advantage in the upcoming contest. This would mean I'd have to get Aubrey to hit something other than myself, which meant potentially getting rather closer than him that I would prefer.

Sergeant Hades left me to it and as soon as she'd left, Helena and Yarrow rushed over.

'You know you don't have to do this if you don't want to, don't you Alex?' asked Helena, a look of concern on her face. 'Aubrey's been looking for an opportunity to get back at you, and if he's as good as he says he is, you won't stand a chance.'

'Your faith in me is duly noted,' I said drily.

'Don't be like that, Alex,' said Helena, 'I'm just worried you'll get hurt.'

'I know and it's appreciated, Helena.' I swallowed nervously, 'I'm a bit worried myself, to be perfectly honest...'

'Sergeant Hades will not let you get seriously hurt though?' asked Yarrow.

'I would hope not,' I said, 'Duty of care and all that, but I guess we'll find out.'

Aubrey strolled over, confidently twirling his mace by its wrist-strap.

'Scared, Crowe?' he asked, smirking, 'You should be – I'm going to destroy you. In fact...' He stepped forward, mace extended 'why don't I give you a little taste of what you're going to get now?'

Both Yarrow and Helena stepped in front of me, blocking Aubrey's advance.

'Leave him be, Aubrey!' hissed Helena. Aubrey looked slightly taken aback at this show of solidarity but rallied.

'Oooh, getting your *girlfriend* to fight your battles for you, Crowe,' he said sneeringly, 'Doesn't surprise me – always thought you were a coward…'

'At least I've GOT a girlfriend, dickhead,' I said calmly, 'Not getting very far with the princess now, are you?'

Aubrey scowled.

'You're dead, Crowe.' He spat, then turned on his heel and stalked off.

'And yet here I am, still walking and talking,' I murmured, strapping on my quiver, and testing my bowstring, 'What a twat.'

Helena whispered something to Yarrow, who nodded and walked over to join the rest of the class.

'Alex…' she began.

'Yeah, sorry about the girlfriend thing,' I said, 'I was just winding him up. I mean, you are my friend and you're a girl, so technically, you ARE my girl **friend**, but not my actual *girlfriend*, if you get what I mean…' I paused. 'I'm rambling, aren't I?'

I looked up at Helena, who was grinning at me.

'You talk too much, Alex,' she said, then leaned in and gave me a quick peck on the cheek. 'Be careful.'

I watched her walk away, smiling to myself. I may be about to get the shit kicked out of me, but at least I knew there would be someone to pick me up afterwards.

Sergeant Hades directed Aubrey and I to our starting positions, out of sight of one another at either end of the courts. Once we were in place, she blew her whistle.

Aubrey was armed with a melee weapon, so would therefore be attempting to get as close to me as possible, as quickly as he could. My strategy, as I was armed with a bow, was to take him out at a distance, for which I needed a clear shot.

As the centre parts of the courts blocked line of sight, I had two alternatives. Either go to one of the sides and hope he'd venture out, which he *might* do, as it would give him a clear run at me, or take the higher ground on one of the towers and hopefully be able to pick him off. I felt that he wasn't *quite* stupid enough for the former and if I was on one of the platforms, he'd have to climb up to get to me, which would give me the advantage, so off I scurried.

Reaching the nearest tower, I stowed my bow and quickly climbed up on to the platform. As the ladder wasn't actually attached, I gave it a quick kick, grinning as it toppled to the ground with a crash.

Let's see him get to me *now*.

I crouched down, unshipped my bow, and nocked an arrow, noting a slight glow surrounding the bulbous arrowhead, then scanned the rest of the courts, searching for Aubrey.

From my elevated vantage point, I could just make out the top of his head as he moved amongst the barriers, drawing ever closer. Whilst there wasn't enough of him on show to present a viable target, he wasn't to know that and I did need a quick practice run with the bow, to familiarise myself with it before I attempted to take him down.

Rising to my feet, I brought the bow up and sighted along the shaft, tracking the top of his bobbing head. I deliberately aimed just behind him, as I wanted him to think that I wasn't quite as good as I was, but still wanted to put the wind up him. I released the string, then threw myself flat on the platform, chuckling as I heard the impact of the arrow followed by a squeal of surprise from Aubrey.

'That the best you can do, Crowe?' I heard Aubrey shout, although he did sound a little rattled.

'That was a warning shot, Aubs,' I called back, 'The next one will be right between your little piggy eyes...'

What I needed to do now was draw Aubrey into the open, so I could get a clear shot, ideally without him realising it was coming. I crawled forward and peered over the edge of the platform, looking for the best ambush spot.

There was a longish alley running directly from the base of the tower to just shy of where Aubrey was currently lurking, which would be ideal for this – I just needed to get Aubrey far enough down it so that he had no chance of retreat.

To do this, I need to convince him I was somewhere where I wasn't. The standard tactic for this, as seen in too many films to mention, was to toss a stone into the area you wished to distract the guard to. As I was currently lying on a wooden platform, 10 feet above the ground, this wasn't really an option and everything else was in my schoolbag.

'Who throws a shoe?' I muttered, untying my laces, 'Me, apparently...'

I lobbed the shoe towards the mouth of the alley, which bounced off one of the corrugated iron barriers, making a pleasingly loud noise. I watched as the top of Aubrey's head start making its way towards the sound, then slowly got to my feet and drew back out of sight, nocking another arrow and waiting patiently for Aubrey to make his appearance.

It's a little-known fact that people don't tend to look up, unless there is something that draws their eye. As Aubrey was unaware that I was above him, I watched him cautiously poke his head around the corner at the top of the alley, then sidle down the side, keeping his back to the wall. He reached the end of the alley and took a quick look around each corner, frowning when he couldn't see me. He then noticed both my shoe and the ladder lying on the ground, realised what that meant and looked up.

'That's not fair...' he whined.

'All's fair in love and war, sunshine,' I said stepping forward into sight, bow raised. I then shot him in the balls. Unsurprisingly, he went down like a pole-axed steer.

There were gasps of surprise from the gathered students, then silence as they waited for Sergeant Hades' reaction. She stepped forward, slowly clapping.

'Well done, Mr Crowe,' she said, then turned to the rest of the class, 'As you have just witnessed, a sound strategy utilising your environment to your advantage can overcome claimed combat superiority. Bond failed to take into account how his opponent was armed and therefore what possible strategies they would use, assuming his previous experience would be enough to defeat them. Fortunately, as this was a training exercise, his mistake merely resulted in a bruised... ego,' I could see she was trying not to laugh, 'rather than anything more serious.' She looked up at me.

'Do you have anything to add, Mr Crowe?' she asked.

'Um...yes, Sergeant,' I said sheepishly, 'Could someone help me get down?'

Chapter IX
Draco Britannica

The rest of the lesson passed without incident, but it was not until lunch I discovered how my victory had altered the perception of my classmates.

Normally, it would just be Helena, Yarrow and myself sitting together at lunch, but we were joined by almost all of the rest of our class. Mason had sat down first, followed by Jack and Lizzie, with Gabrielle following soon after.

'That was pretty impressive, Alex,' said Mason, 'And you've not had any kind of formal combat training, right?' I nodded.

'And that last shot!' chortled Jack, 'Right in the balls! I'll bet he'll be feeling that for a while...'

'It is no more that 'e deserves,' muttered Gabrielle darkly, 'that boy, 'e is, how you say, a pig.'

'Looks like you've got yourself a fan club, Alex,' whispered Helena, leaning in and nudging me in the ribs, a grin on her face. She then looked past me and pulled back, 'But *someone* might not be entirely happy with you...'

I turned to see Ashleigh bearing down on me, a frown on her face. The conversation petered out as the others noticed her presence.

'Alex, can I have a word,' said Ashleigh, 'in private?'

'Of course, Ashleigh,' I said, standing up, 'Rear terrace?'

Helena started to get up as well, but I gestured for her to remain seated. She slipped her hand into mine, gave it a quick squeeze and then released it. I glanced back as I followed Ashleigh out of the Dining Hall – Helena looked worried and, I have to admit, I was feeling a little apprehensive as well.

We exited the building, stepping out into the crisp September air and Ashleigh led me to low wall overlooking the South Lawn. Ashleigh turned to face me.

'Alex, I've heard about what happened with Aubrey...' she started.

'Am I in trouble?' I interrupted nervously.

'Is that what you thought I wanted to talk to you about?' she asked, a look of surprise on her face, 'No, no, you're not in trouble. I wanted to apologise for my brother's behaviour. My parents are a bit old-fashioned, so Aubrey, as the only boy, has been a bit spoilt – which means he thinks he's better than everyone else. And that's why he acts like he does.'

She sighed, then turned and leant on the wall, looking out over the lawn, towards the lake. I joined her at the wall.

'And although you're the older sibling, Aubrey gets most of the attention from your parents, correct?' I asked. She nodded. 'And no matter how well you do, I bet they just say things like "That's nice, but Aubrey will do *so* much better..." That must be pretty hard on you.'

'Yeah, it's not the best...'

'From what you've said, it seems to me that no matter what you do, your parents will always compare you unfavourably to Aubrey, due to a misguided belief that he will amount to something someday. So, rather than trying to attain an impossible goal, i.e. the approval of your parents which will potentially never come, perhaps you should concentrate on what YOU want to achieve. I mean, you're already a school Prefect, which means that the powers that be consider you responsible enough to guide other students, which is a pretty big deal.

Who knows what you could achieve if you put your mind to it? Stop worrying about what others want you to be and be what YOU want to be. Sometimes, it's alright to be a little selfish, especially if by doing so, you feel better about yourself.'

Ashleigh turned to me, a thoughtful expression on her face.

'That's quite a speech, Alex,' she said, 'and you do talk a lot of sense.' She paused. 'You know, you don't talk like a typical teenaged boy – you talk more like one of the teachers.'

'I'm just trying to help,' I said, 'That's what friends do.'

'Oh, so we ARE friends now, are we?' asked Ashleigh, laughing.

'I'm afraid so. It was inevitable, really – you're only human, after all, and I'm just such an incredibly nice person. Your brother seems immune to my charms, but that's because he's a fucking idiot.'

At the mention of Aubrey, Ashleigh became more serious.

'You do realise that he's not going to take what you did to him lying down, don't you?' she asked, 'He will try and get back at you and because he knows the teachers will be keeping an eye on him, he will be sneaky about it.'

'Trust me, Ashleigh,' I answered truthfully, 'Aubrey is the *least* of my worries.'

The rest of the day thankfully passed uneventfully and once we'd finished our lessons for the day, I arranged to meet Helena at the Chimestry lab once I'd collected Errol from my room.

When I'd checked on him before breakfast, the blotches on his skin had faded to a pale blue, but appeared to have expanded, so he was more blue than black now. A further change had occurred since then and he was now a uniform shade of pale blue, his skin was somewhat rougher, and a couple of nodules had appeared on his back, just above his front legs. Other than that, he seemed to be fine, although his appetite *had* increased.

I was hopeful that Dr Moore would be able to shed some light on this.

'Come on in, Alexander.' Said Dr Moore when we stuck our heads around the open door to the Chimestry lab, 'And who is this?'

'This is Helena, Helena Morgan,' I answered, 'one of my classmates and friends. We were discussing chimeras over breakfast, and she was curious to find out if I had accidentally created one or not. I hope that's okay, Sir?'

'Of course it is, Alexander,' said Dr Moore, 'We teachers are always pleased when students take an interest in our subjects, so she is more than welcome. Now, let's have a look at your mysterious anomaly.'

I carried the tank over to one of the workbenches, where Dr Moore had set out several instruments to help with his tests. Dr Moore crouched down and gazed through the glass at Errol, who stared back at him challengingly.

'Now *that* is unexpected,' he murmured, then stood up and turned to me, 'This is the same creature you showed me earlier, correct?' I nodded. 'Because if I'm not mistaken, this is no longer a salamander, but something else entirely. I think we might need Dr Tweed for this. Miss Morgan, would you mind fetching her? I think you'll probably find her in the staff room...'

Helena nodded and went off in search of Dr Tweed.

'Helena tells me there have been further developments with Alexander's salamander, Burton,' said Dr Tweed without preamble, as she strode into the Chimestry lab, Helena trailing after her.

'See for yourself, Dee,' said Dr Moore, indicating the tank.

Dr Tweed leant forward and stared intently at Errol.

'It can't be...' she muttered, then turned to Dr Moore, 'Have you got a copy of Lambton's guide about, Burton?'

Dr Moore looked around the lab vaguely. Paperwork and books were piled haphazardly on several of the workbenches along the walls, some which had the tell-tale brown rings indicating that coffee cups had been left on them.

'I *think* so...' said Dr Moore uncertainly. Dr Tweed rolled her eyes.

'I'm surprised you can find anything in this mess, Burton,' said Dr Tweed. She frowned, reached out her right hand with her eyes closed, then pointed to a large pile of paperwork next to the sink, 'Alexander, nestled amongst Dr Moore's research notes you should find a copy of *Draco Britannica* by John Lambton. Would you mind digging it out and bringing it here?'

I retrieved the book and handed it to Dr Tweed, who quickly thumbed through it until she found the page she was looking for. She then re-examined Errol, referring back to the book on several occasions.

Helena sidled over to me.

'What's going on?' she whispered.

'No idea,' I answered, 'Hopefully we'll find out shortly...'

There was a whispered discussion going on between the two teachers, who appeared to be quite excited about something. I decided that I ought to remind them that we were still here and cleared my throat noisily. Dr Tweed looked up.

'Please accept our apologies, you two,' she said, 'When you come across something as unprecedented as this, you do tend to get caught up in it.'

'What's going on, Miss?' I asked, 'Is there something wrong with Errol?'

'No, not at all, Alexander,' answered Dr Tweed, 'Errol is a remarkably fine and healthy specimen – he's just not a salamander. At least, not anymore.'

'I don't understand, Miss.'

Dr Tweed closed the book she was holding.

'What do you know about dragons?' she asked.

I was tempted to say that that they don't exist outside of myths, legends, and role-playing games, but that was based on MY future reality. I had no idea if they *did* actually exist in this reality, so decided to play it safe.

'Not a great deal, to be honest,' I said.

'Helena?'

'I know quite a bit about wyverns,' said Helena, 'as we've had problems with them on the farm back home. My dad set up post coch around the fields, which stops them eating our sheep.' She noticed my blank expression. 'Post coch is Welsh for "red pillar." Wyverns attack anything coloured red for some reason, so we put them up to protect the flocks.'

'That's correct, Helena,' said Dr Tweed, 'It's also the reason that both post boxes and Royal Mail vans are painted green in Wales. The wyvern is one of the few remaining extant species of dragon in Britain, along with the wyrm. Wyverns are predominantly found in Wales, whilst the few remaining wyrms can be found in Sussex. The last of the *true* dragons found on British soil was allegedly slain by King Athelstan – I can't remember the exact date, you'd have to ask my brother about that, as history is his forte – but it supposedly happened in Uffington, if I remember correctly. Which leads us to the final species of dragon native to these shores, *Draco parvus*, the petty dragon, or drake as it is more commonly known.'

'That's all very interesting, Dr Tweed,' I said, 'but what has this got to do with Errol?'

'I was getting to that, Alexander,' said Dr Tweed, 'You will have to forgive me for going into lecture mode, but I wanted to provide some context. As I explained earlier, wyverns and wyrms are the *only* two species of dragon that still exist in the British Isles – drakes were hunted to extinction. There are no drakes left. Or to be more precise, up until this point, there *were* no drakes left.'

She leaned forward and tapped the side of Errol's tank.

'However, it would appear that Errol here, even though he started off as a salamander, is now *somehow* changing into a drake, specifically an ice drake. If you look closely, you can see that he is developing scales and those lumps on his back are wing buds, which will develop into wings within the next week or so.'

She paused thoughtfully.

'Whilst I know that you are a responsible young man, Alexander, as you were concerned enough to bring Errol's condition to my attention, unlike certain other members of your class who will remain nameless, I think it best if Errol remains in my care for the time being. We will also need to ascertain *how* this took place, as this is a remarkable, and potentially historic, turn of events.' She looked down at Errol, beaming in excitement.

'I can't quite believe it – a real *live* drake...'

'Never a dull moment hanging around with you, Alex,' said Helena, as we made our way down to dinner, 'I wonder if they'll give Errol back to you after – might be worth checking *Draco Britannica* for tips on caring for drakes, in case they do.'

When I failed to acknowledge this, Helena stopped and touched me on the shoulder, a look of concern on her face.

'Are you alright, Alex?' she asked, 'You're awfully quiet.'

I am a time-displaced consciousness occupying my 16-year-old body in an alternate history, tasked with preventing the overwriting of your reality by saving a currently unidentified female on or before 17th December, which may or may not erase my own consciousness from existence, I thought to myself, *I have a fourth-dimensional entity manifesting as a cat via the mirror in my room, whom only I can see and hear, my presence here appears to be generating a localised reality warping field, causing spontaneous transmogrification, resulting in the resurrection of a previously extinct species AND at least two teenaged girls appear to be attracted to me. I am far from 'alright.'*

However, being the sort of person who doesn't like to burden others with my problems, I just said 'Yes, I'm fine – just a bit preoccupied.'

Helena turned me towards her, searching my face.

'Alex, I know we've only been friends for a short while, but you do know that if something's bothering you, you can tell me, don't you?'

'Yeah, I do – and I appreciate your support. The past couple of days have been a bit...overwhelming, to be honest.' I replied, 'I think I just need a decent night's sleep, possibly supplemented with some beer.'

Helena glanced up and down the corridor, checking to see if anyone else was about.

'You've still got some left?' she whispered.

'I *might* have a bottle left...' I said, smiling, 'but given that you're such a lightweight, I don't think you should have any this time.'

Helena scowled at me, then grinned.

'But if you don't give me any, what's to stop me from reporting you to Master Tweed?'

'Are you attempting to blackmail me, Miss Morgan?' I asked in feigned disbelief, 'I am shocked, absolutely shocked, at this behaviour. There was me thinking you were such a nice, innocent young lady and now I find out that you're a wicked, *wicked* girl.'

'You wish,' said Helena, realised what she'd said and flushed crimson, 'Um...what I meant was...' She then realised I was laughing at her, grinned ruefully and punched me on the arm.

'I hate you sometimes...' she muttered.

'If you hate me so much, you really should stop kissing me all the time.' I said grinning, then bolted for the stairs.

'Alex!' Helena shouted after me, trying not to laugh, 'Just you wait 'til I get my hands on you...'

'You wish,' I called over my shoulder, grinning as I heard Helena finally burst into laughter.

Yes, I may have been tasked with saving the world without any clear instructions on how to achieve this, but that didn't mean I couldn't have a little bit of fun along the way.

Chapter X
Truth

It had been a couple of weeks and I had now settled into the daily routine at Oakdene. Whilst ten subjects were taught as part of the curriculum, the teachers spent the first few lessons assessing the students and anyone who did not meet the minimum criteria for the subject no longer had to study it.

I had been a little concerned that I would be dumped from *all* subjects, given that I had no knowledge of them, but so far, I had only been dropped from Alchemy and Necromancy.

Dr Gaunt, the Necromancy master had been quite kind with his assessment, stating that it takes a particular spiritual mindset to connect with the souls of the dead and not everyone possessed this.

Dr Stone the Alchemy master, on the other hand, had been rather blunter. Her exact words were 'The most dangerous thing in my lab is YOU. Get out and never return, Crowe.' To be fair, I had just filled the lab with thick, purple smoke, which was not only slightly toxic, but had also melted most of the glassware it had come into contact with, so I could understand her reticence in letting me continue my studies.

Bibliomancy, however, it seemed I had real talent for, much to the delight of Master Tweed. I was currently sitting in the Study Hall, being orbited by various books that I was referring to for the essay that Dr Noyce had set during our last Lithometry lesson.

'Showing off again, Alex?' said Helena wryly, as she dumped her school bag on the table, 'Why can't you just pile them up on the desk like Mark over there? It's quite disconcerting to see them circling you like a flock of crows…'

I glanced over at one of the other occupied tables. Mark Levin from Watkins House was hard at work, with various volumes piled next to him, furiously making notes with a frown on his face. He always seemed to be in here when I came in, so I guessed he was either really dedicated or was struggling and needed additional study time.

The Study Hall was relatively busy, with a good half dozen students either hunched over their work or with the look of concentration on their face that meant they were using Bibliomancy to locate the books they needed. One of the latter, Katie Smith from Scot House, turned her head towards us, then rose from her seat and walked over.

'Hi…Alex, isn't it?' she asked, then pointed to one of the circling books, 'Have you finished with that, as I need it for my essay?'

'Sorry, Katie,' I said, mentally closing the volume and directing it into her waiting hands, 'All done for the time being.'

'You're very good at Bibliomancy,' she said, her head cocked to one side, a shy smile on her lips 'Maybe some time…you could give me a few tips?'

'Um…I could try, I suppose,' I said hesitantly, 'But I'm not sure I'd be much help…'

'I'll catch you later, Alex,' she said and sashayed away, book in hand.

With a gesture, I gathered the remaining volumes into a column, then stacked them neatly on the table next to me.

Helena was staring at me with a sour expression on her face.

'What?' I asked.

'Oh Alex, you're *SO* good at that,' she simpered sarcastically, fluttering her eyelashes, 'You *MUST* show me how you do it.' She paused, 'I think I'm going to vomit.'

As my memory from the future had indicated that to prevent the upcoming reality-altering cataclysm, I needed to save a currently unidentified female, I really needed to work out *who* that was.

As future Helena had stated I need to "save her," I had ruled out Helena herself, as I assumed that she wouldn't have referred to herself in the third person. I had also decided that it was unlikely to be one of the staff and *probably* not one of the Second Years, which left me with thirteen possible damsels in distress.

My plan therefore was to get to know as much about each of these girls as possible, to see if I could work out which of them was the most likely target. I had been doing this by introducing myself to and chatting with each of the girls individually.

Except Penny.

Because A) she despised me, and B) I'd rather eat my own feet than speak to that stuck-up bitch.

Whilst I considered this a valid plan, Helena, not knowing the reason for this, had become a little jealous that I was showing an interest in other girls. It didn't help that *because* I was showing an interest in them, some of the girls had started showing an interest in *me*.

As future Helena knew about the plot, at some point *before* reality was overwritten she must have become aware of it and I had the sneaking suspicion that this was because I was going to tell her – which *possibly* meant that in order for her to know about it and her future self to send me back to try and prevent it, I *may* have already failed at least once.

Funny how time travel in movies and books always appears *relatively* simple, rather than the total mindfuck it actually is.

So, I needed to keep Helena on side until such time as I gathered the courage to try and explain the whole mental time travel, old mind in young body, reality overwriting prevention thing, which I wasn't looking forward to.

The problem was that Helena and I had become quite close, and I did *really* like her, so I was worried that if I told her the entire truth, I would lose her.

However, as demonstrated in too many soap operas to mention, the number one cause of conflict amongst those supposedly close-knit communities is concealing the truth from one another, usually for entirely transparent plot-driven reasons.

That, and sleeping with people you shouldn't.

I honestly couldn't see the latter being an issue for me, but I did *need* to tell Helena the truth, because it was the right thing to do.

And sometimes, you have to do the right thing, even if it means you risk losing something dear to you.

Doesn't mean you have to like it though.

I stood up and with an assertive gesture, sent all my reference books back to their correct shelves, then gathered my notes and packed them away. I then looked Helena directly in the eye.

'You and I need to talk,' I said, 'Now.'

'Jeez, someone can't take a joke...' said Helena huffily, then saw the serious expression on my face, 'Fine, whatever...'

I led her outside, across the rear terrace and down the left-hand staircase onto the Dog Walk. There was stone bench nestled in an alcove, which I pointed at.

'Sit.' I commanded. Helena scowled, then threw herself onto the bench, crossing her arms.

'Right,' I said, 'I've been putting this off for a while now, partially because I couldn't work out the best way to do this, but mainly because I was scared.'

Helena stopped scowling when she heard this, concern for me warring with the annoyance she still felt for the perceived slights.

'Whilst I have tried to be as honest with you as I can, there are things about me I haven't told you. Really serious things. Things that I felt would damage our friendship and change the way you think about me. But I can't keep it bottled up any longer. It's not fair on either you or me and I *have* to tell you and risk the consequences.'

Helena's face had drained of colour, and she looked a bit worried.

'Alex... you're not sick, are you?' she asked, 'Like seriously, terminally ill?'

'No, it's nothing like that. And I'm not gay either, before you ask.'

'So, what is it? And why did you feel you couldn't tell me?'

'I really don't know *how* to tell you,' I said, 'but I *may* be able to show you...'

'What do you mean?'

'*Visum memoria.*'

'You want me to go into your head and view your memories? You do realise that I'll be able to see *everything,* and **nothing** will be hidden from me?'

'Yes, I am aware of that, but I really think it's the only way you'll truly understand.'

Helena looked quite shocked.

'I'm not sure about this, Alex,' she said, 'I know I helped you recover part of your lost memory, but this is different. You're giving me free access to the contents of your head and that's not something you do lightly. I know you're prepared to do it, but I'm not sure that **I** am.' She looked up at me, 'I'll need to think about it...'

She stood up and shouldered her bag, then reached up and touched me gently on the cheek.

'I'll speak to you later, okay?' she said, searching my face, then turned and walked slowly away.

There was a knock on my door later that evening and when I opened it, Helena was standing there, a resolute expression on her face.

'Okay, I'll do it,' she said simply.

I lay on the bed as before and Helena placed her fingertips on my temples. I closed my eyes, feeling warmth spreading from my temples through my head and images started flickering through my head, like someone riffling through a picture book...

...I'm standing underneath an archway, sheltering from the rain, cigarette in hand. An attractive woman with long curly hair walks past holding an umbrella, notices me standing there and smiles back at me, then carries on walking...

...the same woman, standing in a night club, having just been told by me that I really like her. She walks away and I later see her in the arms of another man, kissing. A hollow feeling in my chest at seeing this, I turn and walk out into the night...

...the same woman, naked beneath me, our moans mingling as we both reach climax at the same point...

...I stand nervously in a church, dressed in a morning suit, starting slightly when the music begins. There she is again, dressed in white, being escorted down the aisle by her father. I grin – she is the most beautiful thing I have ever seen, and she has agreed to spend the rest of her life with me...

...I stand in front of a mirror, 'phone pressed against my ear, face drained of colour. The man on the 'phone asks me if I am alright – how can I be? She's gone, taken from me in a crash of glass and metal...

I felt tears on my cheeks, as I tried to stifle a sob.

...an overcast day, the weather reflecting the sombre gathering. A scattering of black-clad mourners and well-wishers, gathered about the open maw. The priest is saying something, but I am numb, tears dried upon my face...

...more images flash past, but I curl around the kernel of grief, ignoring them all, racked with pain that had been buried deep, but was now unearthed once more...

Helena staggered back with a cry, overcome with what she had witnessed. I reached up to my face, fingers coming away damp, wet with the tears I had shed.

What a fool I had been.

The intention was to show Helena where I'd come from, so she would understand, but I'd failed to consider that a complete dredge of my memories would bring up those I had buried deep, to protect myself from the pain.

Not only that, but I'd also just exposed someone I held dear to grief on a level that they would not have previously experienced or been prepared for.

I quickly stood up and turned to where Helena was shaking against the wall, tears in her eyes and a look of anguish on her face. I started to reach for her but stopped as she flinched.

'I'm sorry,' I said, as there was nothing else I could think to say.

I walked to the door, opened it, and stood back, giving her a clear avenue. She looked fearfully at me, then quickly made her way across the room and out the door.

I walked over and closed it, then sat back down on the bed, head in my hands.

I did what I thought was right, but as usual, didn't think through the consequences of my actions, which resulted in me hurting someone I cared about.

The only positive thing I had taken away from this evening was the determination that I would do all within my power to save Helena's reality and, if this resulted in me being erased from existence, then it was no more than I deserved.

Chapter XI
...And Consequences

As I had spent most of the night lying awake, brooding on the various possible outcomes of my misjudged attempt to explain myself to Helena, when I finally managed to prise my eyes open, I felt like shit – mentally AND physically. A long, hot shower helped somewhat, but I knew I'd have to venture down to the Dining Hall for some breakfast, otherwise the headache I could feel developing would settle in for most of the morning.

To be honest, I was dreading seeing Helena, as whilst I had run through various scenarios in my head the previous evening, I genuinely had no idea how she was going to react.

Given that my head was filled with memories in which the Order of Vulcan had succeeded, and reality had been overwritten wiping all magic from the world, the possibility existed that she may believe me to be some kind of sleeper agent for the Order and would report me to the relevant authorities. Which meant that I could be looking at spending a long period of time in darkened rooms with serious looking men in suits, trying to convince them that I was not the threat they thought I was.

And also trying to convince them that there WAS a threat, but not being able to explain what it was.

Of course, this *might* prevent the reality-altering cataclysm from occurring, but somehow I doubted it. More than likely, I'd end up in whatever this reality's version of a mental institution was until the end of this world, three short months away, knowing that it was coming but not being able to do anything about it.

Which was a really depressing thought.

I've always lived by the precept of doing the job that's in front of you to the best of your ability, no matter what. True, I'd never had to save the world before, but that didn't mean I wasn't going to try.

I headed down to the Dining Hall, hoping for the best, but prepared for the worst.

I collected my breakfast and scanned the room. Helena was sitting with Yarrow and some of our other classmates, picking desultorily at her food. She glanced up, saw me and her face drained of colour. She started to get up, obviously intending on fleeing my presence.

I felt my eyes tearing up and a hollow, empty feeling in my chest, so quickly turned and made my way across the room, to the furthest available table. I sat heavily down, my back to the rest of the room and furiously wiped my eyes.

I was obviously still emotionally overwrought due to reliving my past memories last night - that *had* to be the reason for this reaction.

Okay, yes, I admit that I liked Helena a lot. She was funny, clever, and attractive and, had I been considerably younger (from a mental standpoint), I possibly would have fancied her. But I didn't – it was merely a combination of stress, lack of sleep and the hormones coursing through my 16-year-old body. *Had* to be. I mean, what other rational explanation *could* there be?

'What a fucking mess...' I muttered to myself.

'Talking to yourself, Alex?' asked a voice I recognised.

I looked up to see Ashleigh standing across the table from me, a look of concern on her face.

'Mind if I join you?' she asked and when I nodded, she quickly sat down, then leaned forward, 'I could say it's none of my business, but that wouldn't be true, me being House Prefect. But I'm also your friend, and it's fairly obvious that something's gone on between you and Helena, as you two are pretty much inseparable – yet here you both are, sitting on opposites sides of the room, both looking miserable. Is there something I should know? I know boys can be a bit...forward at times?'

It took me a while to work out what Ashleigh was insinuating.

'Oh God, No!' I exclaimed, 'It's nothing like *that...*'

Ashleigh had the decency to look slightly embarrassed.

'I'm sorry, Alex,' she said, flushing, 'But I did have to ask. You understand, don't you?'

'Yes, I do,' I said, 'But you should know me well enough to know that I'd *never* do anything like that.'

'Right...sorry - again,' she said, looking slightly uncomfortable, 'Look, you may not be ready to discuss it quite yet, but if you do, you know where to find me. And I will be making the same offer to Helena, just so you're aware.'

'That's good to know, Ashleigh, thank you. I feel that Helena probably needs your support more than me, though. Just...just make sure she's okay, won't you?'

Ashleigh looked at me thoughtfully.

'You care for her a great deal, don't you?' she asked.

'Yes,' I said, finally admitting it to myself, 'Yes, I do, and I would never intentionally cause her harm or distress. Sometimes doing the right thing, even if it's for the right reason, ends up hurting the people you lo...er...care about.' I finished lamely.

'You're a bit odd, Alex,' said Ashleigh, 'But your heart's in the right place. Helena may not realise it yet, but she's lucky to have someone like you.'

Ashleigh made her way over to where Helena was still sitting and there was brief conversation before Helena got up and left the Dining Hall with her. She kept looking back over her shoulder at me, her expression one of uncertainty, as though she wasn't sure what to make of me anymore.

Lucky to have me? I didn't think so. After what I'd put her through, I'd be lucky if she ever spoke to me again.

Whilst I'd managed to shake my headache, I was in no real mood to speak to anyone during that day's lessons, so ended up just keeping my head down and concentrating on my studies.

Yarrow, being a sensitive soul, had picked up on the atmosphere between myself and Helena and after several abortive attempts to get us to speak to one another and at my urging, paired up with Helena during those lessons where this was required.

This meant that I ended up with Alice White, who had a tendency to open her mouth and just say whatever came into her head, which was actually a bit of a relief, as I could just let her inane chatter wash over me.

After spending some time in her company, during which I heard about every member of her family in excruciating detail, what her favourite lesson was, her favourite teachers and her aspirations for the future, I had crossed her off my list of possible targets.

The only reason I could think that anyone would want to dispose of her was to get her to stop talking.

Alice's chatter was actually detrimental during Unnaturalism, as we were studying wysps, which were feisty little buggers with a tendency to bite if you weren't paying attention. As their bites were venomous, and produced a numbing effect, I currently couldn't feel my hands, having sustained various nips as I was trying to get them back into their cage.

Aubrey had been watching me struggling with them, a big grin on his face and was currently flapping his hands at Ian, both of them laughing at my attempts to try and pick up anything with my floppy hands.

It didn't help that I'd been trying to surreptitiously watch Helena during the lesson, pretending to be looking elsewhere when she caught me looking at her, so I really only had myself to blame.

Dr Tweed had noted my difficulties and provided me with a wooden bowl of anti-venom, instructing me soak my hands in it until sensation returned.

By the end of the lesson most of the feeling had returned, but I was a bit behind, having not been able to take any notes during class. I would have to spend some time in the Study Hall later, writing up what I could remember from the lesson.

'Feeling better, Alexander?' asked Dr Tweed, as the rest of the class packed up around me, 'Usually you're one of the most attentive students in my class, so I was quite surprised to see you having issues.' She followed my gaze, 'But it seems you might have other things on your mind. I have noted that Helena and you appear to have had a falling out and whilst "the course of true love never did run smooth," I expect a better performance in your next lesson.'

She waited until the rest of class had left, walking back up to the main building.

'Actually, it is somewhat fortuitous that your departure has been delayed,' she continued, 'as there was something I needed to discuss with you.'

She strode over to one of trestle tables, which was covered with a cloth, pulling on a pair of thick, insulated gloves. She then reached below the table and brought out a metal cage, within which I could just make out a blue form thrashing about. Holding the cage at arm's length, she walked back over. I noted as she drew nearer, the creature's exertions lessened, so by the time the cage was placed on the table in front of me, I could make out what was within.

It was a tiny blue dragon, about a foot long, with iridescent blue scales and a membranous pair of ivory-coloured wings folded along its back. When it saw me, it rose up on its rear legs, cocked its head on one side and made a chirruping sound. I reached out tentatively, gently poking my fingers through the bars and the creature rubbed its head against them, eyes closed.

Dr Tweed has watched this exchange with interest.

'Exactly as I had surmised,' she said, 'As you may have gathered, Mr Crowe, this is Errol, who has now fully transformed into an ice drake. We are still unsure how this has happened, but as Errol was becoming a little...fractious in captivity, I did some extensive research on the historical behaviour of drakes. Prior to their extinction, if a drake was caught early enough, it would form a bond with the sorcerer who caught it, becoming a steadfast companion. As recent attempts by me to perform tests on him have resulted in defensive frosting – hence the gloves – and the calm way he reacted to your presence, it would appear that Errol had bonded with *you*.'

'Sorry if I'm being a little dense here...' I said, 'Are you saying that Errol effectively *belongs* to me now?'

'Yes, Alexander, that's exactly what I'm saying. Now, I've checked with Dr Vayne, and she is happy for you to keep Errol in your room for the time being, but you will need to let him stretch his wings on a regular basis, so I would suggest you leave your window open during the day. I would also ask you to not parade around the school with him on your shoulder – that sort of thing can lead to other students becoming somewhat resentful of you.'

'He'd sit on my shoulder?!' I said, 'That is *so* cool...'

Dr Tweed smiled kindly at me.

'We may not know how Errol became an ice drake, but I'm confident that he is in good hands with you. Don't disappoint me, Alexander. And one final piece of advice. I would suggest you try and patch things up with Helena. Not only for the sake of your studies, but also for both yours and her peace of mind.'

Dr Tweed looked about the clearing.

'Now off you go, Alexander, I've got some tidying up to do before my next class,' she looked puzzled, 'I'm sure there were six cages of wysps, but I can only see five...'

'Would you like me to stay and help you look, Miss?' I asked.

'No, that won't be necessary, Alexander,' she said, 'I'm sure it's around here somewhere and you need to get Errol back to your room. Take this cover for the cage, so you can transport him free of prying eyes.'

I covered the cage with the cloth cover and began walking back to the main building. Helena may not be ready to talk to me yet, but she hadn't reported me, so I was hopeful that she might come around. *And* now I had my own teeny-tiny dragon, which was pretty damn cool.

Things were starting to look up.

I spent the early part of the evening in the Study Hall, writing up the notes I'd failed to take during the Unnaturalism lesson, referring to my copy of Farrow's.

Wysps were part of the faerie family, so like their relatives, were winged humanoids approximately two to three inches tall. Unlike their brethren, wysps had no commercial use and were considered a pest. Whilst annoying individually, due to their venomous paralysing bite, they could become a serious threat if encountered as a swarm, as once their target was paralysed, the wysps removed all their teeth and used them to build their nests. Farrow's had several illustrations showing what these nests looked like, and they were as horrific and nightmare-inducing as they sounded.

Wysps were more common in warmer weather, as cold slowed their metabolism and rendered them dormant during the winter months. This was why we had been able to study them during the lesson, as had the temperature been any higher, the wysps would have been too fast to be able to be caught and handled. Farrow's advised wearing protective gloves when handling wysps, something I had failed to do during the lesson, due to being distracted, so I made sure that I included this in my notes, so that Dr Tweed would know that I had learnt from my mistakes.

Once I was happy with my notes, I packed up my bag and headed back to my room, as I wanted to check if Errol had settled in.

The first thing I noted when I unlocked my door was how warm it was in my room, which was a little odd, as I was sure I'd left the window open prior to heading down to the Study Hall.

The window was definitely closed, and I could see Errol perched on the windowsill, scratching at the glass, so I dumped my bag and let him in. Rather than let me pet him, Errol pushed past me, his head questing back and forth, as though he was hunting something.

It was then I noticed a high-pitched droning noise and several shadowy forms that had been circling the sprite globe plummeted towards me, wings beating furiously.

I now knew where the missing cage of wysps had ended up.

The wysps started circling me, darting in towards my exposed face and hands, seeking to latch on and bite. I quickly dragged the sleeves of my jumper down over my hands, limiting the exposed skin on show and ran to the other window, rationalising that if I could reduce the overall temperature in the room, it would make them easier to deal with.

As I was struggling to get the second window unlatched, I felt a weight on my back, then a sudden sharp pain, followed by a spreading numbness across the back of my neck.

'Fuck!' I exclaimed, reaching round to try and dislodge the little bastard, but it was too quick for me. I heard the sound of wings, followed by an extended hissing, then something impacted on the floor behind me with a tinkling sound.

Having finally gotten the window open, I turned, my arms guarding my face to behold a wondrous sight.

Errol was weaving about the room, hunting wysps.

Once he got within range, his jaws opened and out came a jet of freezing white mist which, when it struck, covered the targeted wysp in rime, immobilising it. The tinkling sound I had heard was a frozen wysp dropping to the floor, its wings shattering as it hit.

Within the space of a few minutes, the floor was littered with small, frozen bodies, as Errol made short work of my miniscule attackers. Errol flapped in place, scanning for any remaining wysps and when satisfied, flew across to me and landed heavily on my shoulder. He nuzzled at my cheek, chirruping.

'Good job, Errol,' I said, stroking him gently under the chin, 'Not sure what I would have done without you, mate.'

Errol butted my hand, then descended to the floor and began to crunch his way through his disabled prey.

I had a strong suspicion of who was responsible for releasing the wysps into my room and, if I was correct, that wasn't just getting back at me, but a malicious attempt to seriously maim or injure me.

A cold fury descended upon me, and I marched towards the door, fully intending on confronting Aubrey right that second. I furiously threw open the door, but faltered as I saw that Helena was standing on the other side, hand raised as though she had been about to knock.

She looked startled and slowly lowered her hand, then noticed the look on my face and started to back away.

'I shouldn't have come...' she said, turning to leave.

'No, please, stay,' I said, feeling the anger drain away, replaced by a sudden need for her company, 'It's not you, it's...um...' I pushed the door open wide, indicating Errol finishing off the remains of the frozen wysps, 'I've had a little bit of a pest control problem...'

Helena peered around me, taking in the carnage and then spotted Errol, who peered up at her inquisitively.

'Oh my God…' she breathed, 'Is that Errol? He's so *cute*.' She brushed past me and cautiously approached Errol, kneeling on the floor in front of him. She tentatively reached out a hand towards him, then paused and turned to me.

'Does he bite?' she asked nervously.

'I'm not sure,' I said, 'He hasn't bitten me yet, but I think that's because Dr Tweed says he's bonded with me. I think you should be safe, as he only attacks things he considers are a threat to me – like these little sods.'

Errol had finished off the last of the wysps and stalked forward, sniffing Helena's outstretched hand. He then butted it with his head and made a chirruping sound.

'Um…what's he doing?' asked Helena apprehensively.

'He wants you to pet him,' I said, 'I think he likes you.' I took her hand gently in mine and guided it, 'stroke him under his chin, like this.'

Helena did so and Errol closed his eyes in evident pleasure. She turned towards me, eyes shining and a look of joy and wonder on her face.

'This is amazing…' she said.

You only get a handful of these type of moments in your life, where no matter what has gone before, everything falls into place – just so.

The tricky part is to recognise them as such and let your instincts take the next step. If you make the mistake of over-thinking them, you either do the wrong thing or you do nothing at all. Either way, the moment is lost, and your life will be that tiny bit worse because of it.

I knew instinctively that if I had leaned in at that precise second, our lips would have met, and Helena would have melted into my arms. And, for that perfect, blissful moment, everything that had gone before would have been forgotten.

But, and some may judge me a fool because of it, I chose not to.

I drew back, rose to my feet, and went to the open window, resting my hands on the sill and taking a deep breath of the chill Autumnal air.

I was shaking. Overwrought emotions, the sudden change in temperature or a combination of the two? I couldn't tell.

'You were going to kiss me, weren't you?' said Helena quietly.

'I was thinking about it, yeah,' I answered.

'And you knew that I would have let you, don't you?'

'Yes,' I said, 'I knew.'

Helena went quiet then, so I turned to face her. She was still kneeling on the floor and looked so lost and vulnerable that it took all my will power not to walk over and scoop her up into my arms.

'I like you, Helena,' I said, 'I like you a lot. In fact, I've not felt this way about someone since…' I faltered then, voice thick with emotion.

Helena looked up at me.

'What was her name?' she asked, 'Your wife?'

'Rachel, her name was Rachel.'

'And what happened?'

I turned back to the open window and took a deep breath.

'It was our anniversary,' I started, 'and she wanted to cook me the same meal we had had on our very first date. The weather was shitty, pouring down, but she was insistent that she go out and get the stuff she needed...'

I paused, feeling emotions that had long been buried surfacing and I stifled a sob.

'I'd opened a bottle of wine, her favourite, to let it breathe and looked at the clock. She'd been gone a lot longer than I'd expected, so I'd got out my mobile to call her. Then the 'phone rang. It was the police.'

I paused, wiped my eyes, took another deep breath, then continued.

'They told me there had been an accident. Another driver had lost control in the wet weather and ploughed into the side of her car. They said they had tried all they could, but it was too late... she was gone.'

My head dropped and I let the tears fall, impacting on the windowsill below.

I heard movement behind me and felt Helena approaching. She tentatively touched me on the shoulder, then gently turned me to face her. Her eyes were filled with tears, a look of sorrow on her face. She then tenderly enfolded me sobbing in her arms and just held me, as I finally let out all the pent-up emotion and grief that had been bottled up for far too long.

And it was enough.

Chapter XII
Cunning Plans

'So, does this mean you are now friends again?' asked Yarrow, joining Helena and I at breakfast the following morning.

I glanced across at Helena, who was pretending to be engrossed in her breakfast.

'We're getting there, yeah…' I answered. I could see out the corner of my eye that Helena had a half-smile on her lips. Along with quite a lot of brown sauce. I handed her a napkin, which earned me a scowl and an elbow in the ribs, but once she'd wiped her mouth, I could see she was trying not to smile.

'I am so relieved,' sighed Yarrow, 'I was so worried about you both. You are my closest friends and it pained me to see you not talking…'

There had been tears from us both the previous evening and a lot of talking. We had admitted that our feelings for one another went beyond simple friendship, but due to the uniqueness of the situation, were unsure how we should proceed. So, we had decided to play it by ear and see what developed if anything.

Helena has also stated that saving the world was not a burden that anyone should have to shoulder alone, so had agreed that she would help me in any way she could.

By the time we had finished, it was quite late, so I suggested that we really ought to try and get some sleep.

As I walked Helena back to her room, her hand naturally slipped into mine, which was unexpected but not unwelcome. We paused at the threshold to her room, both as awkward as the teenagers we appeared to be, unsure as to what the most appropriate way to part was.

'Um…I guess this is good night, then…' I said, releasing her hand.

Helena raised her hand and placed in on my cheek.

'Why did this have to be so complicated?' she asked wistfully, then turned and walked into her room, closing the door behind her.

I had been asking myself the same question ever since I woke up on the coach and was really no closer to having an answer.

As Helena and I couldn't really discuss anything of note whilst Yarrow was sitting with us, we spent the time in idle conversation, waiting until they left.

I found my eyes drawn back to Yarrow on more than one occasion, as something was nagging me about them. Yarrow's hair had always been pale blonde, but there seemed to be more of a slivery sheen to it now. Furthermore, they appeared to be hunching forward slightly unnaturally, as though trying to hide something. A sudden realisation hit me, and I had a strong suspicion I knew what they were hiding.

As Yarrow got up and walked away, I narrowed my eyes, watching how they walked away.

'Alex,' said Helena, nudging me in the ribs, 'Are you listen…'

'Shhh,' I interrupted, 'Watch Yarrow.'

'What are you on about?' she said, craning around me to look.

'Look at the way *she's* walking.'

'What do you mea…' she stopped, as the realisation of what she was seeing and what I'd said hit her, 'Oh…oh my.'

'I think you'd better go after her and tell her that you know.'

'Right…yes…' said Helena, slightly flustered. She started to get up, then stopped. 'Hang on, how did you know?'

'Because I'm awesome, of course.' I said smugly. This earned me a well-deserved punch on the arm. 'And bring her to the common room at lunch.'

'What?! Why?'

'You'll see…'

Helena looked as she was about to thump me again.

'She's getting away…' I said.

Helena scowled, then scurried off.

I'd just had a genius idea, but would need some help, so went in search of Ashleigh.

Helena badgered me unmercifully during our morning lessons, but I refused to tell her what I was planning. Yarrow kept shooting glances across at me, colouring every time I returned her gaze, as Helena had told her that it was me who had worked it out.

When I entered the common room after our final morning lesson, I was gratified to see that Ashleigh had managed to gather every female member of Dee House, as I'd requested. They all looked up as I walked in, followed by Helena and a bashful Yarrow. I glanced about the room, noting that I was the only male present, exactly as I had planned.

'Good afternoon ladies,' I began, 'You may be wondering why I asked Ashleigh to assemble you all here.'

There was some muttering at this, which was to be expected, as they'd probably thought that Ashleigh had organised this gathering.

'I want to talk to you about your underwear…' I said, then waited for the anticipated reaction.

I was not disappointed.

Several of the First Years went red and there were gasps of outrage. One of the Second Years, a tall redhead, whose name I think was Sophie, looked furious and stalked forward.

'Are you some kind of pervert?' she asked, poking me in the chest.

I have to admit I was enjoying this, as I had been deliberately provocative with my first statement, knowing the kind of reaction it would engender.

Sometimes I just can't help myself.

But now it was time to turn the tables.

'Oh God, I'm *so* sorry…' I said, putting on my best innocent expression, 'I probably didn't phrase that as well as I could.' I turned and beckoned Yarrow over.

'As some of the more observant of you will have noticed,' I said, 'Yarrow here has almost completed her transition to her final gender. As she was not aware which gender this would be, she had not fully planned for this and, therefore, is lacking in certain garments that the rest of you ladies take for granted. In other words, she has no suitable underwear. Isn't that right, Yarrow?'

Yarrow nodded, bashfully looking at her feet.

'Now, as I'm not an expert in ladies' underwear, I'm not really sure what size Yarrow needs. Hence why I asked you all here, as I thought that at least one of you might be of a similar size and therefore be able to help her out.'

I looked Sophie directly in the eye, an innocent expression on my face. She looked mortified and it was all I could do not to laugh.

'Oh God, I'm so sorry,' she said to me, 'I got *completely* the wrong end of the stick. I thought...well, it doesn't matter what I thought. It's clear that you were just trying to help your friend.'

I watched as the assembled girls of Dee House gathered about Yarrow, offering their support and, I assumed, their underwear. Some of the First Years hugged her and Yarrow noticed me watching, her expression one of joyful astonishment. She mouthed a "thank you" and I smiled.

Sophie was watching me with interest.

'You're Alexander Crowe, aren't you?' she asked.

'Yeah, that's me.' I replied.

'That was remarkably thoughtful of you. Not many boys would even think of something like that.'

'Well, I'm not your average teenage boy,' I said grinning, 'I have hidden depths.'

'So Ashleigh keeps telling me...' said Sophie speculatively.

'I'd best leave you girls to it,' I said, 'my work here is done.'

I could feel Sophie's eyes boring into my back as I left, but it was Helena who collared me in the corridor outside.

'You could have warned me what you were up to,' she said sourly.

'What, and miss the expression on your face?' I said, 'Where's the fun in *that*?'

'And you thoroughly enjoyed shocking them, didn't you?'

I looked at her with my best innocent expression.

'I have no idea what you're talking about,' I said solemnly. Helena's eyes narrowed and I quickly skipped back as she swung for me.

'Now, now, Miss Morgan,' I said grinning, 'There's no need for that.' I paused, holding my hand up to my ear, 'Hold on, is that...Yarrow, calling for you?' I stared pointedly at her chest, 'Yours might be just the right size, after all...'

Helena flushed and crossed her arms over her chest, but I could see she was trying not laugh.

'I hate you sometimes...' she said, then turned on her heel and re-entered the common room.

I rubbed my hands together in glee. Now that Helena, Yarrow, and Ashleigh were otherwise occupied and could not interfere, I could now initiate my *second* cunning plan of the day.

The Cat had confirmed last night that it was indeed Aubrey who had released the wysps into my room, having watched him do it.

Aubrey was about to discover that if you stamp on a scorpion, you best bloody well make sure it is dead.

'Oi, Fuckwit!' I called out.

Aubrey looked up from where he was frowning over the notes he was attempting to take in the Study Hall. He looked surprised to see me intact, especially when I grinned showing that I still had all my own teeth.

'You talking to me, Crowe?' he snarled.

I made a show of looking around the Study Hall.

'Can't see anyone else that fits the description...'

Aubrey started to get up but sat heavily back down as a large book slammed into his back at my bidding.

'You sit your arse back down, sunshine,' I said, leaning forward over the table opposite him, 'I'll keep this short and sweet. I didn't appreciate your little "gift" last night and am fed up with all your shit. I think it's time we settled this, man to man. I'll meet you in the clearing by the Icehouse, 9 o'clock tonight. No teachers, no prefects, no-one else – just you… and me.' I let this sink in. 'Unless you're scared, of course.'

I watched Aubrey's face as he digested this and saw the narrowing of his eyes as he thought of his *own* cunning plan.

Got you, I thought.

'Deal,' he said through gritted teeth.

I released the book, which thumped onto the tabletop, narrowly missing his hand. I then turned and walked away.

The bait had been laid, so it was just a case of setting the trap.

I headed for the Dining Hall – all this plotting had given me an appetite.

Chapter XIII
Season of Mists

I had positioned myself on the windowsill overlooking the rear terrace, curtains closed behind me and no light on, as I didn't want anyone looking up to my room to realise I was lurking there.

I'd been there since about 8pm, as I wasn't sure *exactly* when Aubrey and his cronies would make an appearance. The thing about bullies is that, at heart, they're cowards, so whilst I was knew Aubrey wouldn't be able to resist the opportunity to potentially give me a kicking, I was also certain that he wouldn't come alone. I was anticipating that he would have talked another couple of like-minded individuals, one of which would probably be Ian, into accompanying him.

As it was unlikely they would *actually* enter the Arboretum, they would probably attempt to set up their ambush on the Dog Walk, hiding out of sight until I made an appearance on the way to the planned meeting.

Which, of course, wasn't going to happen.

I may have *accidentally* let slip earlier to one of the Prefects from Scot House (as I didn't want to involve Ashleigh this time around) that I'd heard a couple of the boys boasting that they were planning on venturing into the Arboretum after nightfall to drink beer. I'd stressed that I wasn't sure if I'd heard them correctly, but as we'd been warned not to go in there because it was dangerous, I thought I ought to mention it, just in case.

Just after eight, I'd watched as Sergeant Hades (Head of Scot House) had met with Mr Ware and the three porters on the rear terrace, each of them carrying shrouded sprite lanterns. Sergeant Hades was clearly giving instructions and, when she had finished talking, they all dispersed, taking up a variety of positions out of sight, dousing their lanterns.

'And so, it begins...' I whispered to myself, grinning.

It was about twenty to nine before I saw three shadowed forms, wearing black hooded cloaks, flit across the rear terrace and make their way down the left-hand set of steps towards the Dog Walk. I eased the window up as quietly as I could, as although I couldn't *see* what was about to happen, I should be able to *hear* something.

I heard someone call out challengingly, followed by cries of surprise, then the sound of several pairs of feet attempting to run on gravel.

I cocked my head...yep, someone had just gone over. Gravel paths can be a bit treacherous in the dark, especially at high speed.

Two shadowed forms bounded up the steps they had not long descended but were suddenly illuminated as the porters closed in from either side, unshrouding their lanterns. Pinned by the light and surrounded, I could see the two figures' shoulders slump in resignation.

Sergeant Hades marched up the steps, holding tightly on to the upper arm of the third cloaked figure, who she thrust next to the other two. I couldn't hear exactly what she was saying, but the three figures sheepishly lifted their hands and lowered their hoods.

Unsurprisingly, it was indeed Aubrey and Ian, accompanied by Roger Bishop from Watkins House.

I threw open the curtains, activated the sprite globe and stood in plain sight at my window, gazing down. Of my three potential assailants, only Aubrey was aware of which room was mine and I watched as his head snapped towards the sudden light. I gave him a jaunty wave, then closed my curtains, grinning.

And that, my friends, is why you don't fuck with Alexander Crowe.

However, as usual, things didn't go *quite* as smoothly as I'd planned…

About ten minutes later, that was a hammering on my door.

'Alex!' I heard Helena calling urgently from the other side, 'Are you in there?!'

I opened the door and saw Helena standing there panting, her face flushed. She'd obviously been running.

'If you're here to tell me that Aubrey and his chums have been caught trying to ambush me on the Dog Walk, I already know,' I said laconically, 'I watched the whole thing unfold from my window, just as I'd planned.'

'What…you knew what they were planning?' she said in astonishment, 'And you set them up?'

'I did indeed, for it is said "Do not meddle in the affairs of Alexander Crowe, for he is subtle and will screw you over."'

'I expect you think you're really clever, don't you?' she asked, scowling when I nodded, 'Well, Mr Smart-arse, Yarrow overheard what they were planning and has headed into the Arboretum to try and stop them.'

It took me a few seconds to realise what she was saying, and I quickly rushed to the window and threw open the curtains. I could just make out a figure with silvery hair disappearing into the treeline.

'Shit, Bollocks, Wank…' I muttered, 'Right, we need to go after her - now.'

I ran to the wardrobe, dumped a load of clothes on the floor and pulled out the sprite lantern I'd concealed in there earlier, then grabbed the poker from beside the fire.

'Alex,' said Helena, placing a hand on my chest to stop me haring out the door, 'firstly, shouldn't we tell someone? and secondly, we won't be able to get out, as they've locked all the doors.'

I grabbed Helena's hand.

'Look, if you want to tell someone, go ahead, I won't stop you,' I said, 'but Yarrow's my friend and it's my fault that she's gone looking for me where I'm not, so I'm going after her. As for the second, that won't be a problem.'

I pushed past her and walked into the vestibule, put the poker and lantern down by my feet and ran my hands over the wooden panel next to the door to the bathroom. Helena followed me out and was watching me in puzzlement.

'What on Earth are you doing?' she asked.

'Secret door,' I explained, 'Just trying to remember where the catch is…'

As noted before, I am quite an observant chap and I'd noticed that there was a narrow circular tower that adjoined the Water Tower. As I'm also quite curious, I explored both the ground and second floors to see if I could work out how you got into it. As there was no obvious egress, I did a bit of research in the Library and found the original floor plans, prior to the mansion being taken over by the college.

These showed that the tower contained a staircase, which was used by servants to move between floors unobserved. After much probing of the panel on my floor, I'd discovered that if you applied pressure at a specific point, this released a catch into a cobwebbed stone staircase, which led both up and down. At the very base of the staircase was a second door

69

that led out onto the rear terrace, shrouded from view by a curtain of ivy. This had been a bit stiff, but I'd managed to get it open and went back later to oil the hinges and latch just in case I needed to get outside for any reason.

I pushed on the panel and heard the click I'd been waiting for, stepping back as the concealed door swung slowly open. I picked up the poker and lantern, then turned to Helena.

'You coming or not?' I asked.

I could see Helena wavering, then make her decision.

'I suppose someone has to keep an eye on you and make sure you don't get into any more trouble,' she said, 'But this is under protest and if there's any spiders in there, I'm coming straight back...'

'You'll be fine,' I said, as we stepped onto the staircase and closed the door, 'There's no spiders in here...' I paused and activated the sprite lantern, 'the rats have eaten them all.'

'You'd best be *fucking* joking...' said Helena nervously.

'I thought you lived on a farm?' I said, starting to make my way down the stairs, 'Don't you have rats in the barn?'

'And that's where they can stay, as far as I'm concerned...'

The spiral staircase was quite narrow and had no exterior windows, so the only light was from the sprite lantern. This illuminated the roughness of the unfinished brickwork on interior of the tower, which were festooned with cobwebs. I'd cleared the ones that blocked the staircase, as there's nothing worse than a face full of cobwebs, especially if things start to creep about in your hair after you've blundered into them.

Helena dug her fingers painfully into my shoulder the whole way down and, as soon as I'd got the door open at the bottom, barged past me into the night air.

'Ugh, that was *horrible*...' she said, shivering and brushing off her arms, 'Are there any on me? I can feel them on me...'

'You're clear,' I said, checking her back, 'Now, come on, we need to go get Yarrow.'

We headed quickly down the steps leading to the Dog Walk, then stayed close to the wall, to ensure we wouldn't be seen from the college.

I paused at the treeline, trying to make out anything in the inky darkness beneath the canopy, then turned and scanned the skies.

'What are you doing now?' Hissed Helena.

'Waiting for reinforcements,' I said, 'Ah, here he comes now...'

I could just make out a dim form winging its way towards me, which swooped down, hovered for a moment, and landed on my shoulder with a thump, almost causing me to drop the lantern.

'You're getting a bit heavy to be doing that, mate,' I said to Errol, who butted me on the cheek, chirruping, 'Right, into the woods we go...'

As I'd previously guessed, it was pretty much pitch dark in the Arboretum, so even had the moon been full, rather than waning, we wouldn't have been able to see bugger all.

I activated the sprite lantern, which cast a flickering light as the constrained sprite flittered about within, illuminating the path at our feet, then handed it to Helena.

'You carry this, just in case.' I said.

'In case of what?' whispered Helena, following me as I set off done the path.

'Why are we not supposed to be in here?' I asked.

'Because it's bandersnatch spawning seas...ohhh.'

'Exactly. Hence the poker,' I glanced at the poker, which looked a little puny in the flickering light cast from the lantern, 'let's hope we don't need it.'

We hurried forward as quickly as we could, trying to avoid the gnarled tree roots that seemed intent on tripping us.

When we reached the clearing by the Icehouse, Yarrow was nowhere to be seen.

'Where is she?' whispered Helena, spinning about, trying to illuminate all the shadowy corners.

'Don't know,' I whispered back, then called out, 'Yarrow? You here?'

There was movement by the Icehouse and Yarrow slowly crept into sight from where she had been hiding on the steps. She saw who it was and rushed forward, flinging her arms around me.

'Alex! I was so worried about you!' she said hugging me tightly, 'Are you alright?'

'I'm fine, Yarrow,' I replied, 'and I'm sorry that you ended up coming in here. I'd planned for Aubrey to get caught before he'd even got into the Arboretum and didn't realise until Helena told me that you'd overheard him planning his ambush.'

I detached myself from her embrace, then glanced about, noting as I did so that the ground fog was rising.

'Where's your lantern?' I asked.

'Don't need one,' she said grinning, 'I can see in the dark now, can't I?'

'That's... pretty damn cool, actually,' I said, 'but let's get back to the college before we run into anything unpleasant.'

'Alex...' said Helena warningly, 'I think there's something moving out there in the trees...'

The fog was getting thicker and also appeared to be localised within the clearing itself. Dark forms, low to the ground, were moving about within it, causing the fog to eddy and swirl. A sudden realisation hit me – this wasn't natural fog...

'Bandersnatch!' I shouted, 'Get behind me! Yarrow, take this...' I handed her the poker. Errol hissed and launched himself into the air, circling the clearing.

I cleared my mind and extended my hands. Whilst Sergeant Hades had said that my hex bolts were "lacking the necessary force to do any significant damage," she was of the opinion that my defensive shield was one of the best she had seen. I was hoping that it would be enough to protect us from the bandersnatch.

A shimmering dome of silvery light popped into existence, surrounding the three of us.

'Right,' I said, extending my hands to either side, 'the idea is to move slowly out of the clearing, whilst I maintain the shield, until we are clear of the trees. We should be alright after that...'

I'd read up about bandersnatch in Farrow's and was desperately trying to remember the salient facts. Largest member of the weasel family, carnivorous, aggressive, pack hunter, generated vapour from their bodies which could be mistaken for ground fog, which they used to cover their attacks, big bitey teeth. There was something important that I was missing but couldn't recall what it was.

'Alex...' said Yarrow faintly, 'I don't feel so good...'

She then toppled to the ground.

Then I remembered – bandersnatch fumes didn't just cover their attacks, they also had a soporific effect on their prey, causing unconsciousness if you were exposed for too long.

'Helena! Hold your breath!' I shouted, but it was too late. Helena staggered against me, then dropped to her knees, the lantern tumbling to the ground.

'Alex...' she murmured, eyelids fluttering, then slowly went over.

Calling out to Helena had cost me and I could feel a fuzziness in my head, as the effects of the fumes started to get to me.

The shield flickered and I shook my head, teeth gritted, and forced it back to full strength. I heard a snarl off to my right and a long, lithe form leapt forward, impacting on the shield, and bouncing off, back into the fog.

Errol, who had been circling above us, suddenly darted off into the trees, wings beating furiously.

What's that, boy? I thought to myself as my head filled up with cotton wool, *Timmy's in the well?*

Whilst I assumed my last thought before I lost consciousness would be that I *wasn't* going to be able to save the world, due to having been eaten by giant weasels, it was actually - *Where's that burbling noise coming from?*

Chapter XIV
Repercussions

The first thing I saw when I regained consciousness was the White Horse at Uffington.

Or to be more accurate, a Victorian illustration of the White Horse at Uffington. However, as I appeared to be lying on a flagstone floor, I was viewing it at 90°, so it looked like it was balancing on its tail.

I'd never really thought it looked like a horse, what with the two fangs or whatever they were protruding from its head, and seeing it from this angle just reinforced this, although there was something naggingly familiar about seeing like this, as though I'd seen another similar picture elsewhere.

However, as it felt like someone had filled my head with kapok stuffing, pinning down the elusive memory was like trying to catch a shadow.

A strong pair of hands grasped my shoulders and sat me upright, then a wooden beaker containing a steaming liquid was placed in my hands.

'Drink this,' said a rough voice, 'It will counteract the vapour.'

I brought the vessel towards my face, the steam bathing my face and took a tentative sip. The liquid was hot and laced with herbs I couldn't identify, but immediately the fog affecting my mind began to clear.

'Thank you,' I croaked, looking up at the owner of the voice. It was Mr Ware, the gamekeeper. I felt a sudden panic in my chest. 'Are...are my friends okay?'

Mr Ware glanced across the room, where both Helena and Yarrow were sitting on shapeless armchairs in front of a large roaring fire, wrapped in blankets and cradling beakers of their own. Helena smiled wanly and gave me a little wave.

'They're fine...now,' said Mr Ware, 'However, if it hadn't been for your little dragon here finding me...' I then noticed that Errol was calmly sitting on Mr Ware's shoulder, 'things could have gone a lot differently.'

'The last thing I remember was hearing a weird noise...' I said.

Mr Ware held up what looked like a larger version of a duck call.

'Burbler,' he explained, 'Bandersnatch don't like the noise, so it causes them to bolt. Although I wouldn't have needed it if you lot hadn't been in there in the first place. I won't ask for an explanation, as Dr Vayne wants you all in her office once you've recovered enough to walk back up to the college and I can listen in then.'

'Thank you again, Mr Ware,' I said, then looked around, 'Where are we exactly?'

'Keeper's cottage,' he said, 'In other words, my home.'

I remembered the picture I'd seen as I woke up and looked around until I found it.

'Any particular reason you've got a picture of the White Horse at Uffington on your wall? Are you from that part of the country?'

'Inquisitive lad, aren't you?' replied Mr Ware, walking over the picture, 'I suppose it's what you'd call an heirloom, a reminder of where I came from.' He looked at it introspectively for a moment, then turned back to me.

'Before I take you back up to the college, a small piece of advice for you, Mr Crowe,' At my look of surprise, he smiled slightly, 'Yes, I know who you are. I may not spend much time in the staff room, but I do hear the gossip. Of course, your dragon was a bit of a giveaway as well.' He reached into his waistcoat pocket and offered Errol a piece of what looked like dried meat, who snatched it and gobbled it down with obvious relish. 'The Arboretum is out of bounds after nightfall due the danger the bandersnatch pose to students, so no more wandering in the woods after dark.'

'Understood,' I said, 'they were particularly frumious, so I shall shun them in future.'

Mr Ware looked at me sharply.

'What did you just say?'

'That I will shun the frumious bandersnatch in future.' I paused, 'I suppose I ought to beware the jub-jub birds as well, if any happen to be flapping about in there too…'

Mr Ware looked at me speculatively.

'I'm surprised that someone of your age would be familiar with *The Ballad of King Athelstan…*' he said slowly.

The Ballad of King Athelstan? I thought, *I was quoting from Lewi Carroll's "Jabberwocky."*

The Cat had confirmed that subconscious echoes of this "true" history had potentially influenced *future* authors. However, it seemed logical that anything that had been written *prior* to the reality-altering event on 17th December 1986 would therefore have been "adjusted" to fit the new reality. Therefore, what was currently known as *The Ballad of King Athelstan* could, in the future I came from, actually be the supposedly nonsense poem *Jabberwocky*.

As we'd been served rath in the Dining Hall, toves had cropped up in the conversation I'd had with Helena regarding chimeras and I'd just had an unpleasant encounter with bandersnatch, it stood to reason that borogoves and jub-jub birds also existed.

This would mean that the last true dragon defeated by King Athelstan WAS actually the Jabberwock.

Curiouser and curiouser…

'My parents read it to me when I was younger,' I lied, 'and it stuck in my head.'

The way Mr Ware was looking at me made me think he wasn't entirely convinced. However, he seemed to recall that we were supposed to be elsewhere. He looked across at Yarrow and Helena.

'Do you girls feel well enough to walk now?' he asked.

'I think so…,' said Yarrow. Helena nodded and got slowly to her feet, discarding the blanket.

'Best not keep the Headmistress waiting any longer, then.'

When we were marched into the Headmistresses office, I was surprised to see not only Dr Vayne, but also Master Tweed and Sergeant Hades were waiting for us, each with a different expression on their faces. Master Tweed looked both relieved and disappointed, Sergeant Hades speculative and Dr Vayne looked furious.

'Thank you, Mr Ware,' she said, then looked coldly at us, 'You three – sit down.'

'When Sergeant Hades caught three students attempting to make their way in the Arboretum earlier, I assumed that would be the only misconduct I would have to deal with this evening,' she started, 'But then I received word from Mr Ware here that three additional students were actually found *IN* the Arboretum – which you were ALL told was Out of Bounds. You were fortunate that Mr Ware found you, as any punishment I may mete out would pale in comparison to what would have happened to you if he hadn't arrived when he did.'

'Pardon me for interrupting, Headmistress,' said Mr Ware, 'But I'd just like to state that Mr Crowe, even though he was partially unconscious when I arrived, had still managed to maintain a defensive shield around himself and his friends, which the bandersnatch couldn't penetrate.'

'Really?' asked Sergeant Hades with interest, 'Even half conscious? How big was it?'

'Well, it covered both him and the two girls, so about 20 feet across, I'd say...'

'That's pretty impressive...'

'If we could concentrate on the matter at hand?' interrupted Dr Vayne, raising her eyebrows. Mr Ware and Sergeant Hades lapsed into silence, muttering apologies. 'Thank you.' She looked back at the three of us, 'What do you have to say for yourselves?'

Both Helena and Yarrow opened their mouths to speak, but I cut them off.

'Helena and Yarrow are completely blameless in this, Dr Vayne,' I said looking her directly in the eye, 'this is entirely my fault and, therefore, any punishment should be applied to me alone.'

'When I heard you were involved, Mr Crowe, I did wonder if you were the root cause, as your time here at Oakdene has not been without... incident,' she said, 'Explain.'

I marshalled my thoughts and began.

'As you and the faculty are aware, Aubrey Bond and I have not... warmed to one another. Whilst I thought this was just a childish feud, I came back to my room last night to find that someone had released a cage of wysps in there and if it hadn't been for Errol, I could have been seriously injured. As the cage went missing during our lesson with Dr Tweed, I suspected that it had been Aubrey who had done this. Unfortunately, I have no proof of this, as Errol ate all the wysps.'

'That's true, Miss,' interjected Helena, 'I saw Errol eating them.'

There had been a collective intake of breath at this, and some serious muttering.

'Humphrey,' said Dr Vayne, 'Could you fetch your sister, so we can confirm this?'

'Of course, Headmistress,' said Master Tweed and left the office.

'Continue, Mr Crowe,' said Dr Vayne.

'I therefore decided to set Aubrey up, so challenged him to meet me in the clearing by the Icehouse at 9pm this evening. However, I anticipated that as he's a bully and a coward, he wouldn't come alone and would draft some additional muscle, with the intention of waylaying me on the way there. I then let slip to one of the Prefects that I'd heard some boys boasting that they were going to venture into the Arboretum after nightfall and this led to Aubrey, Ian and Roger being caught by Sergeant Hades and the porters earlier on the Dog Walk, as I knew they'd be too scared to go into the Arboretum itself.'

'Sound tactics,' muttered Sergeant Hades.

'Victoria, please,' said Dr Vayne, 'No more interruptions.'

'Umm...' my voice was getting croaky, 'Could I possibly get a drink, as my mouth's drying up?'

Dr Vayne nodded, and I heard the clinking of glassware behind me, and Mr Ware handed me a glass of water. I took a large mouthful, then continued.

'However, Yarrow had overheard Aubrey plotting and decided to go into the Arboretum to stop them.'

'Is this true, Miss Yarrow?' Asked Dr Vayne.

'Yes, Miss,' said Yarrow nodding.

'Helena came and told me what Yarrow was planning and we saw her from my window, so I decided to go after her. Helena tried to stop me, as she thought that we should tell someone first, but I convinced her there wasn't time.'

'I see,' said Dr Vayne, 'And how did you get out of the building, as all the doors were secured?'

'There's a secret door next to my bathroom,' I said, 'behind which is an abandoned staircase that leads down to the rear terrace.'

'Really?' asked Dr Vayne with interest, 'How did you know about that?'

'Um, I'd noticed there was a narrow tower next to the Water Tower, but couldn't see any way to get into it, so I found the original plans for Oakdene House, prior to it being taken over by the college.' I paused as Master and Doctor Tweed came back into the room, 'the plans indicated that the tower contained a servants staircase and showed that there *was* a concealed door on my floor, so I investigated the place where it showed the door was until I found how to open it.'

'He's not wrong, Headmistress,' said Master Tweed, 'I've seen the plans myself and this building is riddled with hidden doors and passages. There's a priest hole behind the main fireplace in the Library, for example, although it would be a tight fit for someone of my stature.'

'So, let me get this straight,' said Dr Vayne, 'the only reason Miss Yarrow was in the Arboretum was because she thought you were going to be assaulted by your classmates and the only reason Miss Morgan was in there was because you convinced her to follow you, even though she tried to stop you in the first place. Is that correct?'

'Yes, Miss.' I said, 'Which is why they shouldn't be punished, as this was all my doing.'

Dr Vayne frowned, then came to a decision.

'I concur, Mr Crowe,' she said, 'You two can go. Victoria, would you mind seeing Miss Morgan and Miss Yarrow back to their rooms.'

'Of course, Headmistress,' said Sergeant Hades, 'Come along, you two.'

I turned to watch them both leave. Just as Sergeant Hades was shutting the door, I could have sworn I saw her winking at me, a grin on her face.

'Deidre,' said Dr Vayne, addressing Dr Tweed, 'Is it true that a cage of wysps went missing from your lesson with the Dee House students yesterday?'

'That's correct, Headmistress,' said Dr Tweed, 'I remember because that's when Alexander took ownership of his drake and he'd offered to stay behind and help me look for them.'

'Hmmm.' Said Dr Vayne, 'Mr Crowe, I remember distinctly telling you on your first day that I hoped that the next time I saw you in my office would not be for a reprimand, yet here you are. Your teachers have nothing but praise for your attitude and dedication to your studies. You also clearly care very much for your friends, as indicated by how you thoughtfully dealt with Miss Yarrow's transition and bravely tried to protect them from harm this evening. You also took full responsibility for tonight's events and were open and honest when questioned.' She paused, 'However, had you not engineered this little scheme of yours in the first place, there would have been no need to break the rules AND potentially endanger your friends. By rights, you should be expelled.'

My heart dropped and I hung my head.

'However, given the other factors I've mentioned,' she continued, 'I really don't think that would be the best option in this case. You clearly understand your transgression and seem suitably repentant. This then leads us to the question of what is the most suitable and appropriate punishment for you?'

'As long as it's only me being punished, Headmistress,' I said, 'I'll accept whatever you decide.'

'Headmistress?' said Mr Ware, 'I *might* have an idea...?'

Mr Ware walked over and spoke quietly to Dr Vayne, who listened carefully, then smiled and nodded.

'Well, if she's complaining that she hasn't got enough help, then I think that's an ideal solution,' she said. 'Mr Crowe, for *at least* the next two weeks, after your evening meal you will report to Mrs Milano in the college theatre for detention. She apparently requires an extra pair of hands and I think you fit the bill perfectly. As it will probably involve a degree of manual labour, I suggest you wear appropriate clothing.'

When I returned to my room, I found both Helena and Yarrow waiting for me in the vestibule.

'I thought Sergeant Hades had escorted you back to your rooms?' I asked, unlocking my door, and ushering them both in.

'She did...kind of,' said Yarrow, 'She said she knew that even if she took us back to our rooms, we'd both just come and wait for you anyway, so there wasn't much point going the whole way. She left us at the top of the Nursery Corridor.'

'And there was no way we were going to wait until morning to find out what happened to you,' said Helena, 'How much trouble are you in?'

'That's not important,' I said, 'Are *you* both alright? If it hadn't been for my misguided attempt to set Aubrey up, neither of you would have ended up in such a dangerous situation. I am so, *so* sorry. If anything had happened to either of you, I wouldn't have forgiven myself.'

'Well, it was a little scary at the end,' said Yarrow, 'but it was kind of exciting too. But I'm not sure I'd want to do it again though...'

Helena stalked forward, a scowl on her face. I took an involuntarily step backwards, certain that I was about to get a well-deserved slap.

'Idiot,' she said emotions warring on her face, then swiftly stepped in, threw her arms around me and hugged me tightly. 'If you *ever* do anything like that again,' she murmured in my ear, 'I will personally cut off your balls.'

'That seems a little...extreme,' I said. Helena growled at me warningly, her hands inching downwards, 'Okay, okay,' I said, trying not to laugh, 'I'll be more careful in future...'

Seemingly mollified, Helena released me, but not before pinching me on the arse as a warning.

'Anyway,' she said, 'you didn't answer my question earlier... how much trouble are you actually in?'

'Not as much as I thought I'd be, to be honest,' I said, 'I've got two weeks evening detention, starting tomorrow. Not sure how long I'll be in detention for or what I'll be doing, but it does mean that any other *projects*...' I looked meaningfully at Helena, 'will have to wait until the weekend.'

Helena initially looked puzzled, then realised what I was going on about.

'Ah yes...' she said, 'Well, *I* can work on that in the meantime, and we can review it on Saturday.'

Luckily, our exchange appeared to gone over Yarrow's head.

'So, what do you have to do for detention?' she asked.

'Not sure yet,' I answered, 'but I've got to report to Mrs Milano in the theatre tomorrow evening. I'll guess I'll find out then…'

Chapter XV
The Fabrician's Apprentice

The following day passed without incident, although Sergeant Hades did pull me to one side during our Warlockery lesson to question me about my defensive shield and kept me behind so she could test its efficacy. Having spent a good twenty minutes attempting to breach it with progressively stronger hex bolts, she finally gave up.

'I have to admit that I'm impressed, Alex,' she said, red-faced from her exertions, 'I hit your shield with my best shot, and it just bounced right off. I'm not sure *any* physical force could breach it other than a Vorpal blade, but as they're extremely rare, I doubt you'll ever encounter one. However, do bear in mind that it will only protect you from *physical* attacks, as you found out last night, so don't rely on it exclusively.'

After dinner, I returned to my room and spread out my casual clothes on the bed. Dr Vayne had said to wear clothing appropriate to physical labour, which I took to mean that there was the chance I'd get a bit grubby.

As my selection of casual wear was, to quote the song, "acceptable in the 80's" it represented a snapshot of what *I* had considered at the time to be "fashionable."

In other words, it was bloody awful.

I sighed and threw on a vivid blue mesh t-shirt, baggy maroon jumper, and some hideous stone washed jeans, finished off with some truly ugly high-top trainers. Hopefully, I'd get them so dirty that I'd have no choice but to throw them out.

I quickly made my way across the main courtyard towards the college theatre, hoping to God that no-one would see me and made my way inside.

Passing through the lobby, I pushed open the doors to the theatre proper and walked down the aisle towards the stage.

The theatre was where we had Illusioneering lessons with Master Thare. Illusioneering was the projection of three-dimensional images from your mind. It was used for theatrical performances, to enhance the experience for the audience, as a troupe of trained Illusioneers could provide any scenery they could imagine, as well as imaginary creatures and brilliant pyrotechnics. So, a bit like computer-generated visual effects, but with the advantage that the actors could actually *see* the images and interact with them accordingly.

As Illusioneering took both a great deal of imagination AND concentration, it required the Illusioneer to remain still whilst projecting, as any distractions would cause the image to fade.

I quite liked these lessons for two reasons.

Firstly, I wasn't too bad at it, although producing images that moved convincingly was still a little beyond me, as my creations did tend to judder somewhat, like badly realised stop-frame animation.

Secondly, Aubrey wasn't in these lessons.

Master Thare had looked in horror at Aubrey's attempt to create a simple sphere, our first exercise, and banished him from the theatre, stating that if he believed that the grey amorphous blob he had produced was truly what he thought a sphere looked like, there was no helping him.

Someone cleared their throat, and I looked up to see a slim, elderly woman with long raven tresses, dressed in black, looking down at me from the stage.

'Hello,' I said timidly, 'Dr Vayne sent me. I'm looking for Mrs Milano?'

The woman adjusted her glasses and looked me up and down.

'You must be Alessandro,' she said, with a pronounced Italian accent, 'I am indeed Signora Milano. But, more importantly child, *what* are you wearing?'

I looked ruefully down at my clothes.

'Dr Vayne suggested that there might be some manual labour involved, so I wore clothes that I didn't care would get dirty.'

'Youngsters these days...' she sighed, 'No sense of style. Your clothing offends me. If you are to work with me, we must find you something else to wear. If I have to look at *that* all evening, I will be...' she made a gagging noise, 'physically sick. It is fortunate for you that I have much clothing at my disposal.'

She turned and started to walk away, then looked back over her shoulder.

'What are you waiting for, Alessandro?' she said, 'Come, come...'

And that's how I came to meet Mama Lucia.

I followed Signora Milano backstage and down a set of narrow stairs, to vast cavernous space beneath the theatre. Most of the space was taken up with rows upon rows of metal rails, densely packed with a dazzling variety of clothing, which I assumed were costumes for the various performances the theatre put on. In front of these rails was a relatively open area, with dressing tables and a small raised circular platform.

Off to one side, I could see a doorway leading into what I assumed was a storeroom, as I could see shelving with rolls of fabric in every shade imaginable.

Signora Milano turned to me and looked me up and down once more.

'Let us see...' she said, 'shoulders are quite broad, waist is slim... so a 34-inch chest and a 30-inch waist, am I right?' I nodded. She turned and gestured down one of the aisles between the clothing. 'You will find clothing in your size down there. You may choose what you like, as it is clear to me that what you are wearing is not what you would choose to wear, given the choice.'

'You're not wrong, Signora,' I said, 'Given a choice, I'd burn all my current clothes and buy a whole new wardrobe.'

'Pfft, we do not burn clothes here,' she said, 'With the correct fabricantation, the cloth, she can be repurposed.' She looked at my current outfit, 'Although, with these, there may be no hope. And as you will be spending much time in my company, you will call me Mama Lucia. Now, go, go. My eyes, they will bleed if I have to look at you much longer...'

I scurried off down the aisle and started to browse the clothing on offer. I wasn't sure what Mama Lucia was going to have me doing, but at least it looked like I'd get a decent outfit out of it.

I returned shortly with a pair of black chinos and a white linen shirt. Mama Lucia looked over my selection, nodded once and gestured to the platform.

I must have looked a little nervous, as she then rolled her eyes and sighed.

'You are not the first man I have seen in their underwear, Alessandro,' she said, 'many men have disrobed in front of me, for I am a Fabrician, and in order to create the perfect outfit, I need to see the frame I am working with.'

It was a fair point and as I'm not overly shy when it comes to my body, I hopped onto the platform and started undressing. Within a short while, I'd removed my ghastly clothing, which Mama Lucia took away, holding it at arm's length with a look of disdain on her face. I then dressed in my selection and checked myself out in the large mirror, adjacent to the platform.

'Much better,' said Mama Lucia walking back into the room, 'now you look like a man, not a *vagabondo...*'

'Thank you, Mama Lucia,' I said, smiling at my reflection, 'I do feel a lot better now.'

'That is because you are now *wearing* the clothes, rather than letting the clothes wear *you*. It is an important difference. Tomorrow, you will bring me the rest of your clothes and we will decide if they are also suitable.'

I turned this way and that, looking at my reflection.

'Right,' I said, 'I need some black patent leather shoes to finish this outfit off and the sleeves need rolling up a touch.'

I looked around at Mama Lucia, who was smiling at me.

'What?' I asked.

'I could see it in your eyes, Alessandro,' she said, 'Now that you are dressed correctly, it is time for you to *learn*...'

I had been expecting my detention to involve some hard manual labour, which it did, as bolts of cloth are not the lightest of things to be carting around. But I hadn't also expected that it would be so interesting AND so much fun.

Mama Lucia was responsible for the creation of ALL the costumes used in the theatre's many productions. I'd assumed she was a seamstress, but she was in fact, as she had said, a Fabrician.

Ars Fabrica, or Fabricantation as it was more commonly known, was the magical art of creating clothing from the whole cloth, if you'll pardon the pun. A competent and fully trained Fabrician, such as Mama Lucia, would mentally visualise the outfit they wanted to create and then, with the person for whom the outfit was being made in front of them (usually in their underwear), would craft the outfit around them, using whatever fabric was best suited to the particular garment being created.

As the Fabrician needed a clear visualisation of the finished article in their mind before they could create it, trainee Fabricians started their design process with hand-drawn illustrations, before moving on to the use of Illusioneering. The advantage with the latter was that designs could be tweaked in situ, rather than having to redraw the illustration each time a change was made.

Mama Lucia had set up a dressmakers dummy on the platform, and I was projecting a simple white shift dress on to it.

'We always start with white, as it is easier to see,' said Mama Lucia, 'Once the design is *perfetto*, then comes the colour. Now, take the hem up to just above the knee...good. Cinch in the waist... and add capped sleeves. Hmm...' She turned to me, 'Now, is your turn – the dress, she is good, but she is not great. Show me what you have learned.'

I cupped my chin in my hand, narrowed my eyes, and examined the dress. It was okay, but it wasn't *right*.

So, let's give it a full, pleated skirt, like so...a defined waistband and... yes, a sweetheart neckline.

'There...' I said, then turned to Mama Lucia, 'Better?'

Mama Lucia shrewdly looked over my design.

'Yes, *much* better, Alessandro,' she said, 'Now, what colour should it be?'

'Ah, well that depends on who's wearing it,' I said, 'Without knowing who it was for, I would probably leave it white or change it to black, as those colours everyone can wear.'

'*Molto bene,* Alessandro – you are a good student, for you *listen*. Now, do you want to try the fabricantation? I think you are ready.'

'Um…'

'You are worried that you will waste fabric, yes?' Mama Lucia reached behind her and held up an old bedsheet, 'I have this for practice, so not to worry.'

I took a deep breath, extended my hands and began.

The sheet was plucked from Mama Lucia's hands and swirled through the air towards the dummy, wrapping itself around it and slowly taking the shape of my projection. This was a bit more difficult that I had anticipated, as keeping the projection up AND casting the fabricantation was like trying to juggle with water balloons.

But did I *need* both? I could see the finished dress in my mind, so did I need the projection as well?

I paused, then closed my eyes, feeling the projection dissipate. Taking another deep breath, I rolled my shoulders, opened my eyes and continued. The dress continued to take shape before my eyes, the fabric rippling, flexing, and parting, as I exerted my will. A reel of cotton rose from the workbench, unspooling, the needle at its head swiftly darting in and out, as the pieces came together. A final push… and it was done.

I relaxed, then looked critically at the finished dress.

Mama Lucia stepped forward and spun the dummy, checking the dress over.

'Is not bad for a first attempt,' she said, 'a little rough around the edges, but that will improve with practice. However, there is one *piccolo* problem…' She tugged at the dress, which remained firmly attached to the dummy. 'You have sewn the dress *TO* the dummy – she does not mind for she does not feel, so will not scream and call you bad names. But you will need to practice much more before I let you loose on a real person, yes?'

Due to my detentions lasting well into the evening, by the time I was finished I was knackered, so had not really had a chance to catch up with Helena regarding the whole saving the world thing. When we were together during the day, either at meals or in lessons, there was always someone else about, so it was not really a good time to discuss it.

I'd arranged to meet her on Saturday morning in the Study Hall, so we could get down what we already knew and try and formulate some kind of plan to work out the information we were missing.

Helena was already hard at work when I arrived, with several books lying open on the table around her.

'I'm not late, am I?' I said, looking at my watch as I dumped my bag on the table, 'I was sure we agreed to meet at ten?'

'We did,' said Helena looking up, 'I just had an idea and came down early, as I wanted to check something.' She paused and looked at her notes, 'I think you might have been going about this the wrong way.'

'Really?' I said, 'In what way?'

'Well, you've been concentrating on trying to work out *who* you need to save, but without taking into account the other stuff you already *know*.'

'Uh…not sure I'm following you?'

Helena sighed, rolled her eyes, and pushed her notes towards me.

'Look,' she said, 'we know that we need to save a currently unidentified female, which you've narrowed down to one of the First Years, based on the fact that future ME wouldn't have sent YOU back unless it was someone that you would have access to. So, it's likely that it would be someone in the same year as you, correct?' I nodded. 'Right, now as future me said "save her," you reasoned that it wouldn't be me and you've already ruled out Alice, because you don't think she's important enough, so that leaves twelve possible targets, according to your list.'

'Thirteen.'

'What? There's only twelve on your list…'

'Ah, but I wrote that list before Yarrow transitioned, so I didn't include her, as she wasn't a *SHE* at the time.'

'Okay, so it's thirteen, then.' Helena paused frowning, 'Where was I? Ah, yes. So, the only other thing we know for *definite* is the date – 17th December – and I think that if we can work out *why* that date is important, it will help us work out the *who*.'

Helena looked at me triumphantly, grinning, then deflated slightly.

'Unless you think that's a stupid idea…' she said.

'Actually,' I said, 'I think that's *brilliant*… that's not something I'd even considered.'

'Well, you have had other things on your mind…' she said, flushing at the compliment.

'Okay, so is there anything special about the date?' I said, 'I seem to recall that my diary said it's the first day of Saturnalia.'

'Exactly,' said Helena, pulling one of the books towards her, 'But it's also a full moon on that date.'

'And that's significant…why, exactly?'

'The full moon is traditionally when sorcerers perform great feats of magic, as the light of the full moon is supposed to enhance any sorcery performed.' She said, 'In other words, it's more likely to succeed.'

'Right, so we're thinking that some kind of major sorcerous ritual will be performed on the night of 17th December, correct?'

'That's what I'm guessing,' said Helena, then showed me the book she'd pulled towards her, 'especially if you take into account that it's also the first day of Saturnalia. If you look here, you can see that one of the traditions of Saturnalia is an offering made to Saturn on that date. As Saturn is an agricultural deity, this used to be the best part of the harvest, but these days it's usually tins of beans and the like. However, in Ancient Rome, they offered the souls of dead gladiators, who were made to fight to the death in honour of Saturn on that date.'

'So, in other words, human sacrifice…'

'Uh-huh… and Saturnalia is specifically a festival of *reversal*, where slaves were treated above their masters and able to insult them without fear of retribution.'

I gave this some thought.

'So, if I understand correctly,' I said, 'what you're saying is that someone is intending on ritually sacrificing someone on the night 17th December, under the light of the full moon, in order to *reverse* the current natural order of things, banishing magic and replacing it with technology?'

Helena looked at me with a serious and slightly scared expression on her face.

'If I'm right, then yes,' she said, 'When future Me told you to "save her," she wasn't just talking about a possible accidental death, but preventing someone being *murdered*...'

'Shit,' I said, looking down at the book, 'this has just got a whole lot more serious.' I glanced at the book, 'You do realise that Master Tweed will be annoyed with you for underlining stuff and making notes in the margins, don't you?'

'That was already there, Alex,' said Helena gravely, 'I think someone else has been researching the same thing...'

Chapter XVI
'You *Shall* Go to the Ball…'

As we'd already worked out the how, why and when, the only bits of information we were missing were the *where* and the *who*.

As we still had two and half months to work out this information, I was fairly confident that we'd be able to figure it out in time.

Helena, now realising the gravity of the situation, had taken to brooding over it and I knew from bitter experience that constantly worrying about things that *might* happen was not good for your mental health.

What she needed was a distraction, something to take her mind off the subject, even if only for a short while. Fortunately, something of this nature occurred at the beginning of the following week.

I headed down to breakfast on the Tuesday morning, having spent a valuable, if long, evening in the company of Mama Lucia. My fabricantation skills were improving and she was of the opinion that I'd soon be ready for a live model.

Once my tray was loaded with a hearty breakfast, I headed over to the table where Helena was sitting with some of the girls from Dee House. I'd put my tray down and was just about to sit down when I noticed that that the conversation they'd been having had ceased and they were all staring at me.

'What?' I asked.

The girls all looked at each other, then Helena spoke.

'Um… Alex,' she said, 'would you mind sitting somewhere else this morning? Only we're having a private discussion and you can't really be part of it.'

'Ahh… This is girl stuff, right?' I asked, 'No problem. I'll just go and sit somewhere else…'

I picked up my tray and looked around. Weirdly, the whole Dining Hall seemed to have divided into tables occupied by either just boys or just girls, with none of the usual mixing you normally saw. Furthermore, they all seemed to be involved in serious whispered conversations, which ceased as they noticed me drawing close.

Now, I don't consider myself a paranoid person, but this sort of behaviour does make you consider the possibility that the reason the conversation stops is because they're talking about *you*. Then you to start question whether you've done something that would cause everyone to talk about you behind your back.

I couldn't think of anything I'd done *recently*, so rather than brood about it – that way leads madness – I just said 'fuck it' and sat down to eat my breakfast. I was sure if it was something important, someone would let me know.

I was halfway through my breakfast, trying to recall the correct incantation for the creation of a lodestone, as that what we would be attempting in Lithometry that morning, when I was interrupted by Sophie.

'Morning Alex,' she purred, 'I was hoping I'd bump into you this morning…' She sat down opposite me, then leaned forward, 'So, have you asked anyone yet?'

I looked at her blankly.

'I've literally just got down here,' I said, 'and, as you can see, I'm not sitting with anyone, so I've not really spoken to anyone or had the chance to ask anyone anything.'

'That's good to hear, Alex,' she said, obviously pleased, 'I just wanted you to know, if you *were* to ask me, I'd probably say "Yes" – so, bear that in mind.'

She then got up, gave my shoulder a squeeze and sauntered off, leaving me mystified in her wake.

I went back to trying to recall the incantation, but Sophie's interruption had caused it to vanish completely from my mind. I groaned and banged my head on the table.

'Sorry about earlier, Alex,' said Helena, sitting down next to me, 'We were discussing… well, it doesn't matter what we were discussing. Was that Sophie I saw you talking to? What did she want?'

'To be honest,' I replied, 'I have no idea. She wanted to know if I'd asked anyone yet and then said if I hadn't and I asked her, she'd probably say "yes" …'

'Oh,' said Helena, then looked down flushing, 'I was hoping you'd ask me…'

I looked at her in puzzlement.

'Ask you?'

'Yeah…' she said shyly, 'Unless you don't want to, that is…'

'Helena, look at me,' I said, waiting until she looked up, 'Will you please explain to me what the *fuck* is going on?'

Helena looked surprised, then a dawning realisation hit her.

'You were in detention, so you weren't there…' she said softly, then went scarlet with embarrassment, 'I'm sorry, Alex, I'd forgotten that you didn't know…um…'

After much cajoling, as Helena was so embarrassed she could hardly look at me, I managed to prise the story out of her.

The previous evening Master Tweed had gathered all the Dee House students together in the common room for an announcement. As was apparently an Oakdene tradition, on the 31st of October, the annual Samhain Ball was due to take place. This was an excuse for both faculty and students to dress up in their finery, enjoy food and drink and dance until the wee hours of the morning. As this happened to fall upon a Friday this year, lessons were suspended from lunchtime on the day of the ball, to give everyone the chance to get ready.

It was *also* traditional that the male students would ask the female students to the ball as their dates, which now explained the why everyone had been indulged in whispered conversations in gender specific groups and what Sophie AND Helena had been banging on about.

'So, Sophie was basically saying that if *I* asked her to the ball, she'd go with me, is that right?' I asked.

'I guess…' said Helena quietly, refusing to look me in the eye, 'I mean, if you'd prefer to go with her…'

I pretended to give it some serious thought, watching as Helena twisted her hair between her fingers.

'Nah…' I said, 'Sophie would eat me alive. To be honest with you, she's actually scares me a little…I can only think of one person that I'd even *consider* asking to be my date to the ball.'

'And who's that?' asked Helena.

'Well, isn't it obvious?' I asked, watching as a shy smile blossomed on her lips, 'Dr Vayne, of course.'

Helena's head shot up with a look of shock and annoyance, then she realised by my expression that I was winding her up.

'I really, really, *really* hate you sometimes...' she said, scowling, but also trying not to laugh.

'Does that mean you *won't* be my date to the Samhain ball, then?'

'Are you *actually,* properly asking me, then?' She said challengingly.

'Yes, I am.'

'Say it properly, then.'

'Helena Morgan,' I said taking her hand in mine and looking her in the eye, 'Would you do me the honour of accompanying me to the Samhain Ball?'

Helena pretended to give it some thought.

'Hmmm... seeing you asked so nicely,' she said, after making me wait a while, 'I will be your date for the ball.'

Unsurprisingly, the upcoming Samhain Ball was all that everyone seemed to be talking about over the next couple of days.

I have to admit that, from my recollections of my school days, I wasn't that popular with the girls, as there was always someone who was that little bit more confident or a bit better looking. I'd go to parties, but I'd be the one who was on the perimeter, joking about with my friends until such time as they sloped off to snog one of the girls.

So, it came as a little bit of a surprise to me that *this* time around, I appeared to be the first choice of date for the upcoming ball.

Since the initial overture from Sophie, several girls had approached me to see if I'd asked anyone, seeming disappointed when they found out I'd already asked Helena. Once this became common knowledge, this petered out, but was replaced with the *boys* now asking for MY advice on the best way to approach the girls.

This was actually quite gratifying, as whilst I don't consider myself a ladies man, the fact that I had decades more experience than my classmates kind of meant that I *was*.

However, I did appear to have taken the big brother approach when it came to certain people...

Due to no longer having to attend lessons for Alchemy or Necromancy, I had the whole of Wednesday afternoons to myself. I usually used this to catch up on any work set in my other classes or to continue my research into the whole saving the world thing.

Regarding the latter, I suspected that the specific instructions that were needed for the ritual were likely to be contained in one of the green-bound "forbidden" books, as Master Tweed had mentioned that these contained 'magic that is no longer practised in our more enlightened age - **blood magic** and the like.'

As whoever had been researching the ritual had resorted to using the commonly accessible books, this would suggest that they currently couldn't access these books.

However, when I'd last asked the Cat, it had confirmed the cataclysmic event *was* still due to occur on 17th December, so at some point whoever it was *would* gain access to the necessary book - unless we could prevent this somehow. I was assuming that there therefore *must* be some way around the blood-lock enchantment, so this was my current focus of study.

I was on my way to the Study Hall for this reason when Mason intercepted me in the corridor.

'Alex,' he said, 'You got a second?'

'Of course, Mason,' I replied, 'What's on your mind?'

Now that he'd got my attention, he seemed to be a little nervous about whatever it was he wanted to talk to me about.

'You've already got a date for the ball haven't you?' he asked.

'Yes, I'm going with Helena.'

'And you're good friends with Yarrow, right?'

'Yes…'

He paused, nervously twisting the strap of his school bag. This was unlike Mason, as he usually came over as a pretty confident guy.

'Do you…do you know if she's got a date yet?' He finally blurted out.

This had been a topic of conversation at lunch, as Yarrow was certain that no-one would ask her, whereas both Helena and I had assured her that they would. Yarrow was not convinced, but it would now appear that she was mistaken.

'Not yet,' I replied, 'Why? Were you considering asking her?'

'Yeah, I was…' he said, 'But… but only if *you're* okay with it?'

I was initially confused as to why he would feel the need to ask my permission, but then realised that it had become common knowledge that I was quite… protective when it came to Yarrow.

Given that Mason had recognised this and wanted to check with me first before asking her, gave me a pretty firm indication of the kind of person he was.

'As long as you treat her with the respect she is due, Mason,' I said, 'I have no problem with you asking her. But…' I paused and gave him one of my best hard stares, 'bear in mind I *will* be keeping an eye on you…'

'I kind of expected that, to be honest,' he said, grinning ruefully, 'I'm sure I won't give you any reason to worry. Thanks, Alex.'

And with that, he headed off to Alchemy and I continued on to the Study Hall.

Given that the majority of the other students were in lessons, the Study Hall was fairly empty, with most of the other occupants being Second Years. As I looked for a free table, I noticed Ashleigh was hard at work, head down, surrounded by what looked like hand - drawn illustrations. As she also had a myriad of coloured pencils scattered across the table, I assumed that she was responsible for them.

As I couldn't think of any subject that required that level of artwork, my curiosity was piqued, and I made my way over.

'Hi Ashleigh,' I said in greeting, 'What are you up to?'

Ashleigh started, spreading her hands protectively over the drawings, until she realised who it was.

'Oh, Hi Alex,' she said, 'Um…I'm just working on…something.'

'I can see that,' I said, 'Mind if I have a look?'

Ashleigh looked at me pensively.

'I…suppose so…' she said slowly, 'but only because it's you and only if you promise not to laugh…'

'Can't think why I would…' I said, sitting down next to her and pulling a selection of the drawings towards me.

They were all illustrations of assorted styles of dress, similar to those that a fashion designer would do, showing a stylised model and two views, front and back. Here was a long, flowing A-Line dress with a square neckline in teal, there a floor length sheath dress with V-neckline and rear cross-strapping in dark navy. Each drawing also had hand-written notes in pencil, with suggestions as to the fabric.

'Wow...' I said, 'These are really *good*.' I looked closer at the notes, 'I think you're right regarding this teal one, it does need to be chiffon... and I'd probably put a split down the front left, from about mid-thigh...'

Ashleigh leaned over and took the drawing, looking at it speculatively, then looked at me in the same way.

'That's actually... a pretty good suggestion, Alex,' she said, 'How did you come up with that?'

'Apparently I have a good eye for this sort of thing, or so I've been told,' I answered, 'What are these for?'

'Well, I *have* got a dress I could wear to the ball, but I don't like it, so I was trying to see if I could come up with something...better.'

If Ashleigh's dress was anything like Helena's, which she'd described to me the other night, I could understand why Ashleigh may not be entirely happy with hers.

During the 1980's, there was a specific style associated with party dresses – whether short or long, the main identifying features appeared to be that they *had* to have an overabundance of ruffles, usually at the shoulders, and they *had* to look like they had been constructed from metallic wrapping paper. So, shiny, fussy, and cheap looking, like the nylon Princess dresses that small girls wear to birthday parties.

'Well,' I said, 'You've certainly succeeded. Any one of these designs would probably be a hundred times better than the dress you've got.'

'Yeah, I know.' Said Ashleigh sighing, 'But it doesn't matter. Whilst I'd love to have any one of these dresses, as I've already got one, I can't see my parents letting me get another one.'

As has been demonstrated before, I am blessed (or possibly cursed) with an inventive mind, the cogs of which can be set to spinning by a chance comment, generating ideas.

True, not *every* idea I come up with is great and sometimes I don't think them through as thoroughly as I should before acting on them, but there are instances where they appear fully formed in my mind and they are fucking *genius*.

This was one of those moments.

I examined the idea from all angles, checking for potential problems and flaws and, not finding any, gave it my official stamp of approval.

'Right, gather all your stuff and come with me,' I said to Ashleigh, 'I think we can solve this little problem. But first, there's someone you *really* need to meet...'

Chapter XVII
A Touch of Class

I was sitting with Helena and Yarrow at lunch on Friday, when Ashleigh came bounding over with a clipboard, a big grin on her face.

'How'd it go?' I asked.

'They all loved them, and everybody wants one!' she gushed.

'That's great,' I said, 'Everything set for tomorrow morning?'

'Yeah, Mama Lucia got quite excited when I told her what we were intending on doing and says she can't wait to get started.'

'Cool. I guess I'll catch up with you in the morning, then?'

'Looking forward to it, Alex.' She said, 'This is going to be so much fun!'

I innocently turned back to my lunch, and then began to mentally count to ten. I'd only reached four when I was interrupted.

'What are you up to, Alex?' asked Helena, frowning.

'Why on Earth would you *possibly* think I was up to anything?' I asked innocently.

'Because I *know* you,' she said, placing her hand at the top of my thigh, 'So unless you want to suffer...' her hand inched closer to a more tender and intimate part of my anatomy, 'I suggest you tell me...'

'Okay, okay,' I said, grabbing her wrist and trying not to laugh, 'I was going to tell you anyway, so there's no need for that. In fact, I was going to tell *both* of you.'

Yarrow looked puzzled, so I gestured for them to draw closer.

'Yarrow, am I right in thinking that you don't have a suitable dress for the ball?' Yarrow nodded, 'And Helena, am I right that you're not overly keen on the dress you *have* got for the ball?'

Helena pulled a face.

'It's...alright, I suppose,' she said, 'but I haven't really got a choice...'

'Well, if you both would care to join myself and Ashleigh in the college theatre tomorrow morning, say...' I did some mental calculations, 'about half ten? Then we will solve both your problems.'

Helena opened her mouth, clearly about to ask another question.

'Nope, not going to tell you anything else,' I said, scooting down the bench out of her reach, 'You're just going to have to wait and see. Trust me, it'll be worth it...'

When Helena and Yarrow arrived the following morning, they were surprised to find the workroom below the theatre was thronged with female student from Dee House, all excitedly chattering and comparing the dresses they were wearing.

Ashleigh and I *had* been rather busy...

As I had anticipated, once Mama Lucia had seen Ashleigh's designs, she immediately started teaching her Fabricantation. Ashleigh proved to be a quicker study than myself and was soon creating fantastic garments based on her own designs. After watching her for a while, I suggested that if she was up for it, we approach all the female Dee House students and ask them if they'd like a more elegant and classy dress for the Samhain ball than the ones they currently had hanging in their wardrobes.

Unsurprisingly, once the girls had seen Ashleigh's designs, they all agreed.

'Ah, there you are,' I said to Helena and Yarrow, 'just in time. Ashleigh, who's next?' I asked, turning to her.

Ashleigh checked her list.

'Sophie.' She answered.

'Sophie, you're up.' I called.

Sophie languidly got up where she had been lounging and sauntered over to the circular platform and stepped on to it. She then slowly untied her robe and let it drop to her feet, looking me directly in the eye as she did so, revealing that she was wearing nothing but black, lacey underwear beneath.

'See anything you like, Alex?' she murmured provocatively, through heavily lidded eyes.

'Answer me this, Sophie,' I said patiently, 'Did you want a nice dress to wear to the Samhain Ball or do you want to wear that ghastly pink thing you showed me earlier that makes you look like you should be on top of a Solstice tree?'

Sophie muttered something.

'I'm sorry, what was that?' I asked.

'I want a nice dress...' she said sheepishly.

'In that case, stop acting like a fucking tart.'

'Sorry Alex.'

I turned back to Helena.

'Do you see what I've got to deal with here?' I said in exasperation, 'Trying to organise this lot is like trying to herd cats...'

'Alex, what on Earth is going on here?' Asked Helena.

'We,' I said, indicating Ashleigh and myself, 'are ensuring that each and every Dee House lady will look elegant, classy and downright stunning on the night of the Samhain Ball, ably assisted by our very own master Fabrician, Mama Lucia.'

'Alessandro, you will make an old lady blush,' said Mama Lucia coming forward, 'Who are these *belle ragazze*?'

'These are my good friend Yarrow,' I said, pointing, 'and Helena...'

'Ah, *Helena*...' said Mama Lucia with emphasis, leaning forward for a closer look, 'You are just as beautiful as Alessandro has said. I thought, perhaps, he was exaggerating, but now I see he tells the truth. He talks about you all the time, but now I can see why.'

'Excuse me,' said Sophie, 'Can we get on with it? I *am* in my underwear here...'

'Sorry, Sophie,' I said, 'You ready Ashleigh?' she nodded. 'Right, tell me what you want...'

Ashleigh looked down at her design.

'Give me a sleeveless floor-length sheath dress to start with...' she said, waiting until I'd projected this onto Sophie. 'I want a square neckline on the bodice, supported by thin double straps criss-crossing over an open back... turn around so, I can see, Sophie... Good. Mermaid skirt skimming the hips, side split in the skirt. Hmm... yes, I think that's it. What do you think, Sophie?'

'I love it,' Sophie said, turning on the spot, 'Does it have to be white, though?'

'That's just the initial pattern, Sophie,' said Ashleigh, 'Alex, what colour d'you think?'

'Green,' I said, 'Dark green satin – it will contrast nicely with Sophie's hair.' I concentrated and the dress changed to the colour I'd suggested.

'Oh yes...' breathed Sophie, 'that's it exactly.'

'Right,' said Ashleigh stepping forward, 'Let's make it real...'

Mama Lucia returned from the storeroom with a bolt of dark green satin, placed the matching thread on the side and stood back. I held the projection in place, and Ashleigh extended her hands, crafting the dress around Sophie. She looked a little nervous, which was an expression I'd not seen on her face before, as the cloth wrapped itself about her, only relaxing once the gown was complete.

She twirled on the platform, examining her reflection in the mirror, then grinned.

'It's perfect,' she said, 'Thank you both *so* much.'

I grinned back and glanced across at Ashleigh, who raised a hand to her face and stumbled slightly.

I rushed to her side and helped her back to her chair. Mama Lucia bustled forward, took Ashleigh's wrist in her hand, the stared into her eyes.

'No more for you today,' she said, 'You have done too much. You must rest.'

Ashleigh looked like she was about to argue, but a look from Mama Lucia stalled her. Then Mama Lucia looked at me, with a questioning look on her face.

'If you think I'm ready...' I said.

'You have been ready for a long time, Alessandro,' she said, 'the only thing holding you back was *you*. You *know* you can do it, so now is time to actually *do*...'

'In that case,' I said, 'I think it's about time Ashleigh got her *own* dress.'

Ashleigh looked surprised.

'But Alex,' she said, 'I've not even *thought* about what I want, let alone done any designs...'

I crouched down if front of her, took her hands in mine and looked her in the eye.

'But I have.' I said, 'Do you trust me?'

Ashleigh searched my face.

'Yes,' she said simply, 'I do.'

'Then get your kit off and up you go.'

Ashleigh slowly got up and approached the platform, disrobing as she went. She stood self-consciously on the platform, wringing her hands nervously.

'Stop that,' I said, 'You *know* you need to stand still... and close your eyes.'

'Why?' she asked.

'Because I want it to be a surprise...'

Ashleigh closed her eyes, put her hands down by her side and visibly relaxed. I nodded to Mama Lucia, who disappeared into the storeroom, returning with a bolt of sky-blue chiffon and some white lace.

I cracked my knuckles, extended my hands and began. I'd been practicing, so no longer needed to project the design, as I could see in my mind's eye exactly what I wanted to create.

The fabric unrolled and swirled around Ashleigh, following the contours of her body and forming the design in my mind. Floor length A-line, with a scoop-necked bodice and cut-in shoulders... double bands angling to the sides of the back, framing a triangular cut-out... skirt flowing out from the waist down to the ground... the lace jumped from the worktop... white lace applique across the front of the bodice... and done.

'Can I open my eyes now?' asked Ashleigh nervously.

'Yeah,' I said, smiling, 'I think you can.'

Ashleigh opened her eyes, looked down at the dress in astonishment, then looked in the mirror, turning this way and that.

'Oh my God...' she murmured, then looked across at me, 'It's *gorgeous*...'

She then squealed, jumped down from the platform and rushed over to me, throwing her arms around me. She was crying.

'Oh Alex,' she said, hugging me tightly, 'It's better than I *ever* imagined it would be. Thank you, thank you so, *so* much.'

'Careful,' I said grinning, 'you'll rumple your dress.'

Ashleigh disengaged, wiped the tears from her eyes and rushed over to the other girls, all of whom had been watching. I could hear murmurs of admiration and excited chatter.

I looked across at Helena and Yarrow, who had looks of shocked amazement on their faces.

'Oh my God,' said Yarrow, 'That was... *amazing*...'

'How... how...' stuttered Helena, then just stopped, at a loss for words.

I ran my hand through my hair and smiled bashfully.

'Yeah, that went better than I thought it would,' I said, 'Ashleigh seems happy, at least.'

'You are too modest, Alessandro,' said Mama Lucia, putting her hands on my shoulders, 'I knew you had the soul of a *benissimo* Fabrician.' She looked across at Helena, 'It's in the eyes – you can always tell.'

'I had a *very* good teacher, Mama Lucia,' I said, 'None of this would have been possible, if it wasn't for you.'

'Pfft, I teach before,' she said, 'My students, they listen, they learn... but unless they have the passion, like you, like Ashleigh, they are *only* good, not great.' She winked at Helena, 'Alessandro, he have *great* passion... and not just for this.'

Helena, once she realised what Mama Lucia was implying, went red.

'So sweet,' said Mama Lucia, chucking her under the chin, 'I leave you now, these girls, they need dresses...'

Helena waited until Mama Lucia was out of earshot, then drew closer, with Yarrow following.

'*You* told me you were sorting clothes, stock-taking and carrying rolls of fabric during detention,' she said accusingly, 'but it turns out you were *actually* learning new magic – stuff that's not taught in normal lessons.'

'Actually, I was doing both,' I said, '*And* didn't I take full responsibility for the other night, risking getting expelled, so that neither of you two would get punished? Is it my fault that I happened to get detention with Mama Lucia AND she decided to teach me fabricantation?'

'I suppose not...' said Helena grumpily, 'But you didn't have to be so *good* at it...'

'Ah, I see what the issue here is...' I said grinning, 'You're jealous, aren't you?'

'No...'

'Yes you are. There was me thinking you'd get all bent out of shape because I'd seen all these girls...' I gestured about the room, 'half-naked, but you're more concerned that I know something that you don't.'

Helena started, as she'd obviously not even considered that in order for Ashleigh and I to have created all these dresses, most, if not all, of the girls would have had to have been in their underwear. She scowled at me and started to raise her fist, but I quickly stepped forward and wrapped my arms around her.

'Don't worry,' I murmured in her ear, 'the only person I actually want to see in their underwear is *you*. In fact, why don't you strip off now...'

'What?!' exclaimed Helena, 'Are you mad?!'

I stepped back and held her at arm's length, grinning.

'I though you wanted a new dress?' I said, 'Why, what did *you* think I was suggesting?'

'You...you...you're *so* annoying,' she said, but even though she was scowling, I could see she was trying not to laugh.

'I know,' I said, 'It's a good thing I'm so goddamn *cute*, otherwise they'd be no hope for me.'

This broke Helena and she snorted with laughter.

'Now,' I said seriously to both Helena and Yarrow, 'I have been giving this a great deal of thought and have a pretty good idea of what would suit you, in both style and colour. My only question is...' I gestured to the platform, 'Who wants to go first?'

Yarrow volunteered to go first and was soon twirling in place on the platform, the dark navy floor-length satin dress I'd created swirling about her.

'Alex, this is the prettiest dress I've ever owned!' she said excitedly, then paused in thought, 'Actually, this is the *only* dress I own... but even if I had a hundred, it would be my favourite. Thank you.'

As Ashleigh and I had already dealt with the rest of the Dee House students, this now only left Helena.

I *had* thought, given that I knew exactly the style and colour of dress that I felt would suit Helena AND that I'd already seen several girls in their underwear that morning, that there would be no issues when it came to Helena.

However, for all my bravado earlier, when it came to Helena I was acutely conscious that it WAS Helena and, as I had feelings for her, the thought of seeing her in her underwear, no matter how innocent the situation, had started my pulse racing. I looked down at my hands and realised that they were shaking.

Helena, it would appear, had come to a similar realisation and, whilst she had stepped red-faced on to the platform, seemed to be having difficulty with the buttons on her blouse and would not look me in the eye.

Mama Lucia looked back and forth between the pair of us, then sighed and stepped forward taking my hands in her own. She looked critically at them, noticed the shaking and tutted.

'Sometimes, the great passion, she overwhelm you,' she said, 'In this state, you will do more damage than good if you try. You will tell Mama what you intended, and I will create the dress. You, Alessandro, you will take a walk and clear your head. Is better for all.'

I thanked Mama Lucia and explained my design, watching as she nodded in understanding. I then made my way upstairs and out into the courtyard.

It was pleasant enough day, if a little cold, so I headed for the Dining Hall, as I knew there was always hot coffee available there and I felt in need of refreshment.

I wandered back over about ten minutes later and made my way back downstairs. Yarrow was waiting at the foot of the staircase, a big grin on her face.

'Helena says you have to wear this,' she said, holding out a strip of cloth, 'she wants to be able to see your reaction when you take off the blindfold.'

I'm not really a fan of not being in control, but as this would only be for a short time, I acquiesced on this occasion and allowed myself to be blindfolded and led into the workroom.

'Are you ready, Helena?' asked Yarrow.

'Yes...' replied Helena nervously. I felt hands on the back of my head and the blindfold was removed.

I blinked once to clear my sight and beheld a vision in burgundy chiffon.

Mama Lucia had followed my instructions to the letter and Helena was wearing an A-line floor-length dress, with a sleeveless bodice in a graceful princess-cut with a scoop neckline. Thin double straps rose from the bodice and continued over the shoulders, before criss-crossing across her back, then lacing up in a corset style. The skirt parted in a side split on the left from mid-thigh, flowing down to the floor.

Helena was watching my face with apprehension.

'What do you think?' she said anxiously.

'Wow...' I said, 'Just...*wow*. You look... *incredible!*' I turned to Mama Lucia, who was standing off to one side, a satisfied expression on her face, 'It's just how I imagined it – thank you.'

'When the vision is clear, is simple enough to do,' she said simply.

I turned back to Helena, who was now smiling shyly.

'But the most important question is...' I said to her, 'do *you* like it? Because if you don't, then it doesn't matter what I think, because I'm not the one wearing it. Is the colour all right? The style? We've got plenty of time before the ball, so if you'd prefer something different, we can...'

Helena gathered her skirt, stepped down from the platform and made her way over to me. She reached out her hand and placed a finger across my lips, ending my rambling.

'Alex,' she said, 'It's perfect. I wouldn't change anything about it.' She then leaned forward and kissed me on the cheek, 'Thank you.'

'It was nothing...' I said, feeling my cheeks flushing and a grin creeping across my face. I then turned and addressed the room.

'Right, Ladies, if you wouldn't mind listening for a moment?' I said, waiting until I had their full attention before continuing, 'Now, you all know what's happening on 31st of October...'

'We're celebrating your birthday?' asked Ashleigh innocently.

'What?! My *birthday*?' I said in surprise, 'How did you know that?'

I looked across at Helena, who was grinning. She tapped the side of her head.

'Oh...right...,' I said, 'Yes, well, whilst it *may* also be my birthday on the 31st, that's not what I was talking about...' I paused to regain my train of thought, 'We have four weeks before the Samhain Ball, so I would suggest that you leave your dresses in the care of Mama Lucia here, as that way they will remain pristine and not get crumpled in your wardrobe. On the day of the ball, you can all assemble in here and get ready together. Now, this is important – do NOT tell *anyone* about your dresses. Yes, you can inform your dates of the *colour* of your dress, so they can coordinate their outfits if they so choose, but that's it.'

There was some rebellious muttering at this.

'I appreciate that you're dying to tell all your friends what an amazing outfit you've got, but consider the impact of your entrance on the night, when everyone else sees your dress for the first time...'

I looked about the room and could see by the expressions on their faces, followed by several grins, that they understood what I was saying.

'And bear in mind if any of the girls from another House hear about your dresses, then they'll want one too...' I let this sink in, 'And surely *you* want to be the centre of attention?'

And with that, I knew I had them. All women, no matter how much they may claim otherwise, when given the opportunity to dress to impress, do actually *want* people to notice that they've made the effort. It's not vanity, it's human nature.

Besides, I could imagine the expressions on everyone else's faces when they swept in the room in their finery and how that would make the girls Ashleigh and I had dressed feel. And birthday or not, that would be *my* gift for the evening.

I made myself scarce whilst the girls were changing out of their dresses, as whilst it had been necessary to see them in their underwear whilst we were creating, hanging around whilst they got undressed again seemed a little... pervy. I decided that the best use of my time would be to ensure that all the unused fabric was returned to its appropriate place in the storeroom, as I would have only had to do it later anyway.

I was man-handling a bolt of crimson chiffon on to one of the upper shelves, which seemed reluctant to be put back where it belonged, when I was interrupted by Helena sticking her head around the door.

'We're all done, Alex,' she said, 'It's safe for you to come out now.'

I pushed the bolt home with a grunt and stepped down from the stepladder.

'Cool,' I said, 'I'm just about done here.'

Helena stepped forward, a look of concern on her face.

'You didn't mind that I told everyone it's your birthday at the end of the month, did you?' she asked, 'It wasn't intentional... it kind of slipped out.'

'Nah, it's fine,' I said, 'With all the other stuff going on, it had kind of slipped my mind. I don't tend to make a big deal about it, but it is kind of cool that the Samhain Ball is on the same day – it's almost like they're throwing a party just for me.'

Helena looked at me with a smile.

'I *think* that some of the girls might be arranging something for you, on the night, as a thank you for all your hard work.'

'Really?' I said, 'That's nice of them... but not really necessary. Ashleigh did most of the work, I just helped.'

'You're too modest, Alex. If you hadn't come up with the idea in the first place, none of this would have happened.'

'Yeah, I suppose it *was* one of my better ideas...' I said ruefully, running my hand through my hair, 'I've not had a good track record so far.'

Helena stepped in closer, her head cocked to one side and a mischievous smile on her face.

'Seeing as you're responsible for the beautiful dress I will be wearing to the ball,' she murmured, '*And* it's your birthday, I feel that I should really give *you* something in return as well.' She moved even closer, put her hand on my chest and looked me in the eye. 'Any ideas?'

I attempted to answer, but all that came out was a strangled 'Yerk.'

Helena grinned and stepped back.

'Guess I'll have to come up with something myself...' she said, turning to leave, 'See you later, Alex.'

I could hear her laughter echoing in workroom outside and grinned ruefully to myself. From the looks of it, my first Samhain Ball would be *quite* the evening.

Chapter XVIII
A Question of Blood

As my assigned detention was now over and I'd already sorted everything I needed to regarding the Samhain Ball, I could shift my focus back to both my curricular and extra-curricular studies.

Having spent several hours reviewing every reference to the blood-lock enchantment in the commonly available books, I was now probably the most knowledgeable person regarding this, second only to Master Tweed himself.

The way the enchantment worked was that it was tied to the blood of the caster, so should anyone else touch what was protected by it, they would trigger the spell and be paralysed. However, I'd discovered from my research that those that shared the same blood, such as siblings or parents, would not trigger the enchantment. What this meant was that both Master Tweed AND his sister could touch the books with impunity. Anyone else touching the books would be caught.

Now, Master Tweed had mentioned that previous students *had* attempted to get around the blood-lock by three different methods; the wearing of gloves, the use of Bibliomantic manipulation and getting a trained monkey to fetch the books for you.

This first would obviously not work, as even if you were wearing gloves, you were still *touching* the books, so would trigger the enchantment.

The same applied to Bibliomantic manipulation, as this relied on the *Vitae* of the Bibliomancer, which was an *extension* of the caster's self and still, therefore, counted as touching the books.

However, the final one was the most interesting, as whilst the person seeking the books would still be subject to the enchantment once they actually touched the books, it had no effect on the monkey itself. As this suggested that the enchantment only applied to *humans*, it was possible that a non-human may be able to touch the books without triggering the enchantment.

Such as a Geist...

However, I dismissed this an option, as whilst there **did** exist the slight possibility that Yarrow *could* touch the books, I wasn't prepared to risk my friend being paralysed, just to test an unproven theory. I didn't need to see the book *that* much...

Having reached a dead end regarding the blood-lock enchantment, I decided to look up *The Ballad of King Athelstan* instead, as the conversation with Mr Ware has piqued my curiosity.

As I had speculated, the text of *The Ballad of King Athelstan* and the poem *Jabberwocky* were identical. And the reason I knew this wasn't because I'd read *Through the Looking-Glass* by Lewis Carroll multiple times, but down to the 1977 film by Terry Gilliam.

As I was only eight at the time *Jabberwocky* was released, I'd not seen it at the cinema, but in the late Eighties it became cult viewing amongst my schoolfriends.

Someone had taped it when it was shown on television, and this tape was then passed around, resulting in people regularly quoting bits of dialogue from the movie. As the poem was featured in the film, I took it upon myself to memorise the entire thing, using a battered copy of *Through the Looking-Glass* – because I thought it would make me look cool.

It didn't, but the end result was that I could quote the entire thing from memory.

Of course, similar to my knowledge of Preseli Spotted Dolerite, this was due to the potential (unless I prevented it) overwriting of the true current history with the false history I remembered, so my knowledge of this poem was probably an echo of me having studied it *now*.

I was beginning to hate this whole time-travel thing, as spending any time thinking about it ended up giving me a headache.

So, in this reality, *The Ballad of King Athelstan* was a fictionalised retelling of King Athelstan's defeat of the last True Dragon on British soil. Sergeant Hades had mentioned Vorpal blades when she'd tested my defensive shield, so I knew that they at least existed, although according to her they were extremely rare, but how much of the rest of it was actually accurate?

As Dr Tweed had mentioned that her brother knew more about this than her, I decided to approach him and ask the question.

'*The Ballad of King Athelstan* was written in 1871 by Charles Lutwidge Dodgson, an Oxford don, scholar and Chimest,' began Master Tweed, 'It consist of seven stanzas, the last being a repetition of the first and is in the style of poetry common to the era from which the legend originates. The first and last framing stanzas can be disregarded, as they have no bearing on the known historical facts, which is evidenced by the reference to 'Toves,' as these did not come into existence until the same year the poem was written. As to the accuracy of the remaining verses, as Dodgson referenced the *Anglo-Saxon Chronicle* for the salient 'facts,' therein lies the problem...'

I must have looked confused, as Master Tweed smiled knowingly, and continued.

'The *Anglo-Saxon Chronicle* originally started off as a *single* manuscript penned in the reign of Alfred the Great, so somewhere between 871 and 899 AD. Multiple copies were then made of that one original and distributed to monasteries across England, where they were independently updated. However, whilst the major historical events were, for the most part, recorded in each copy, due to the individual bias of those updating their particular copy, significant differences *do* exist between the nine surviving copies. This means that the *general* facts of any recorded event are broadly the same, but the minutiae differ. Now, Dodgson, being an Oxfordshire scholar, would probably have referred to what is known as the Peterborough Chronicle, which was and is held in the Bodleian Library in Oxford, but is *actually* a copy of the Canterbury Chronicle, as the original copy from Peterborough was lost in a fire in 1116.'

Master Tweed reached out his hand and two volumes slid off the shelves from the History section and landed neatly on his desk. He reached for the first, and after flicking through the pages, found the entry he was looking for.

'Here we are,' he said, 'Now, we know that Athelstan's defeat of the Jabberwock occurred in 927, as this was the event that consolidated his power and led to him being crowned the first ruler of Anglo-Saxon England as a whole. We also know that this happened on the Berkshire Downs, just south of the village of Woolstone, although the chalk figure commemorating this deed is known as the White *Horse* of Uffington, hence Dodgson's reference to "uffish thought" in the poem. Both the Canterbury AND Peterborough Chronicle notes that Athelstan *slew* the Jabberwock, but the Abingdon Chronicle, having been scribed by someone more local...' Master Tweed reached for the second volume, 'specifically states that "by threat of further harm from the Vorpal Sword, Athelstan gained a binding oath from the Jabberwock to trouble his people no further, and was no longer seen in the land." So, whilst all records agree that Athelstan **did** defeat the Jabberwock, due to the discrepancies of the historical records from that date, it's unclear whether this resulted in the death of the last True British Dragon. As True Dragons can live for centuries, it's *possible*, although highly unlikely, that the Jabberwock may still be alive today.' Master Tweed paused for a moment in thought, 'Although how it would have remained hidden for so long, I have no idea.'

'So, does this mean that the White Horse of Uffington is *actually* a representation of the Jabberwock then?' I asked.

'It is believed so, by serious scholars,' said Master Tweed, 'but over the centuries, as the legend faded, as the chalk figure does resemble a horse, this is what it commonly became known as.'

This would explain why the illustration I'd seen on Mr Ware's wall had struck a chord with me, as once rotated, it did resemble the Tenniel illustration of the Jabberwock, the two 'fangs' sprouting from its head being the barbels evident in that picture.

'What happened to the original Vorpal Sword?' I asked, 'I know from Sergeant Hades that Vorpal blades exist, but I'm guessing these are variants or copies of the original?'

'Not really my area of expertise, I'm afraid, Alexander,' answered Master Tweed, 'You'd be better off speaking to Victoria… sorry, Sergeant Hades, about that. However, as there is no record or mention of the Vorpal Sword being used by Athelstan *after* this event, it's likely that it was deemed too dangerous to fall into his enemies hands, so he may have hidden it for that reason.'

'Mr Ware has an illustration of the White Horse on his wall, which he says is a family heirloom,' I said, 'Is he from that part of the country?'

'Benedict?' said Master Tweed, 'I'm not sure…'

'Mr Ware's first name is Benedict?'

'Yes, it is,' said Master Tweed, 'which rather suits him, as he lives a somewhat monkish existence. However, as with all members of the faculty and staff, you should refer them to by their last name, unless they give you licence to do otherwise.'

Master Tweed glanced at his pocket watch.

'Now, unless you have any further questions, young Alexander, I need to prepare for my next lesson…?'

'No, Sir,' I said, 'thank you for your time, it was very interesting.'

'No need to thank me, Alexander,' he said, 'As teachers, it is our role to impart knowledge. However, it is gratifying when our students actually *want* to learn… so thank *you*.'

Whilst I'd no luck regarding circumventing the blood-lock enchantment, Helena and I had been rather more successful in whittling down the list of potential victims.

As our research had established that a blood sacrifice was necessary for the ritual that would rewrite reality, it stood to reason that the stronger or more magical the blood was, the more likely it would be for the ritual to succeed.

Based on this assumption, which we were fairly certain was correct, this really only left two possible options - Yarrow and Penny.

Yarrow, because she was of a Geist heritage and came from a highly magical race and Penny, or to use her full title, Her Royal Highness the Princess Royal, because she was of an unbroken Royal bloodline dating back to Alfred the Great.

This left me in a bit of quandary.

If it *was* Yarrow and I failed to prevent the ritual, this would mean that I would be responsible for the horrific death of my friend.

However, if it *was* Penny, I'd be placed in the position of trying to save someone that I didn't really like, which might influence my actions when the time came.

So, in order to increase my chances of success, I really needed to resolve my differences with Penny somehow. The fact that Aubrey and Penny had effectively become an item and her opinion of me may have been coloured by *his* opinion of me would make this a little trickier, but I had to at least try.

And as "you can catch more flies with honey than with vinegar," it was time for me to bring the honey...

I'd broadly discussed my plan with Helena, but without going into the actual details, as I wanted her to be aware of the reason I was approaching Penny. I'd also decided that it would be best to do so in a public place, as it was more likely that Penny would hear me out if she knew others were watching.

The opportunity I was looking for came at dinner that evening. Penny was sitting at her normal table, accompanied, as always, by her group of friends and the ever-present Aubrey. Aubrey's presence had been factored into my plan, as if it went the way I intended, he might be forced to reconsider his opinion of me as well.

I checked my pockets to make sure that I had the necessary items my plan hinged on, took a deep breath and walked over to where Penny was sitting.

'Pardon me, your Highness,' I said politely, 'I was wondering if you would be so kind as to spare me a moment of your time?'

'Why would she want to talk to *you*, Crowe?' growled Aubrey, starting to get up.

Penny placed her hand on his arm, stalling him.

'As he has asked politely,' she said, 'I think we can let him speak, Aubrey.'

'Thank you, your Highness,' I acknowledged, 'Having given it much thought, it has occurred to me that I have not really shown you the respect that is due to your standing. I appreciate that our first encounter has coloured your opinion of me and my subsequent actions, and the opinion of those about you, has, perhaps, given you the wrong impression of my character.'

Penny looked at me shrewdly, then nodded for me to continue.

'Whilst a sincere apology for my behaviour would be a good start to making amends, if you were gracious enough to accept this, it would be merely words, so I thought that perhaps a gift, freely offered, may be more amenable to you?'

I'd been watching the faces of those on the table as I made my speech, trying to judge what effect it was having. Aubrey was scowling, which seemed to be his default expression whenever we spoke, but Penny and the others on the table seemed intrigued.

'What exactly did you have in mind?' asked Penny, 'I regularly receive gifts due to my position, so what could you offer me that I haven't already been given?'

'Well, your Highness,' I replied, 'I propose to offer you something both beautiful AND unique, something that I hope you will not have seen before.'

'This is a trick, Penny,' said Aubrey, 'he's up to something...'

'Aubrey, hush,' said Penny, turning to him, 'He's highly unlikely to try anything in front of all these people now, is he?' She turned back to me, 'You were saying?'

'I will need a little assistance with this,' I said, reaching into my pockets and pulling out a black silk handkerchief and a length of bramble stem. I turned to the girl to Penny's right, 'Emma, would you mind holding this for me?' I handed the stem to her, 'Be careful, as I have not removed *all* the thorns.'

Emma cautiously took the length of bramble stem, a puzzled look on her face. I nodded my thanks and placed the folded handkerchief on the table in front of her. I was now ready to begin. I extended my hands towards the handkerchief, watching as it rose spiralling off the tabletop. This garnered a few gasps of surprise from those at the table and I noted that a crowd had started to gather, Helena amongst them. This was good, as the more people who saw this, the better.

'As Autumn fades into Winter, and the winds take the leaves off the trees...' I began, gesturing with my hands and watching as the handkerchief danced this way and that, as though caught in a breeze, 'we look outside and see the bare branches, bereft of blossom and our hearts yearn for Spring, so that we may look again upon the beauty of Nature.'

The handkerchief swirled back across the table, then began to wrap itself around the top of the stem Emma was holding.

'But with the right enchantment,' I said, concentrating on the handkerchief and applying my will to the vision I had in my mind, 'you may be able to mimic the beauty of Nature in a more permanent form, which will last all year round.'

With a final flourish, I completed my creation. Atop what had previously been a bare bramble stem was now a perfectly formed black silk rose. Emma looked at in in wonder, then looked up at me, her mouth open.

I took the completed rose from her unresisting hand, then offered it to Penny.

'A black rose, which will not fade or die,' I said, bowing, 'for the Princess Royal of House Black.'

Penny leaned forward and took the offered rose, a hint of a smile on her lips.

'Well, you promised me something both beautiful and unique, something that I had not seen before...' said Penny, looking me in the eye, 'and you have done just that. Thank you for your gift.'

The watching crowd, which had increased whilst I had been concentrating on my creation, burst into applause now that Penny had accepted my offering.

'It is a small gift, nothing more,' I said modestly, 'and you have Aubrey to thank for this.'

Aubrey looked surprised at this, as I generally did not have a good word to say about him.

'If not for him, I would not have been in a position to learn the necessary enchantment to create this bloom, so equals thanks should go to him.' I nodded at Aubrey and smiled.

He looked confused, as though he'd cornered a wolf, only to discover it was *actually* a sheep.

I bowed to Penny, then turned and walked back to my table, the crowd parting before me. I felt an arm link in with mine and glanced across to see Helena walking next to me, a smile on her lips.

'That was incredibly well done, Alex,' she murmured, squeezing my arm, 'I sometimes forget what a sneaky git you are.'

'Thank you... I think.' I replied, then glanced back at table I'd just left.

It had erupted into animated conversation, but Penny was not paying attention to what was being said - she was watching me walk away, a speculative look on her face, the rose held against her cheek.

102

Chapter XIX
Unexpected Gifts

In the false and overwritten history that I had previously lived through, my birthday always fell in the Autumn half-term week, so I never actually had to go to school on my birthday. My family never really made a big deal of my birthday, so I always considered this the Universe's way of balancing the scales.

But even though this was the first year that I actually *had* to attend lessons on my birthday, as lessons were cancelled after lunch so everyone could get ready for the Samhain Ball AND it was a Friday, which meant all the other Dee House students would be having double Alchemy first thing, I only had an hour and a half of Chimestry lessons mid-morning, which meant I had a relatively relaxing day to look forward to.

'And that's your first gift of the day, Alex' I said to myself, as I stared at the ceiling, contemplating whether I stayed in bed a little longer and had a leisurely morning or headed down to breakfast as normal, in the hope that my friends might have at least got me a card.

My mind was made up for me when Errol swooped in through the window and deposited the half-frozen carcass of a rat on the end of my bed.

Whilst the condition of the corpse meant that there was very little in the way of odour, Errol's table manners were deplorable and watching him messily devour *his* breakfast would definitely put me off *mine*. I scrambled out of bed, grabbed my towel and headed for the bathroom.

As I entered the Dining Hall after my shower, there was a palpable air of excitement in the room, the upcoming Samhain Ball being the only topic of conversation that morning.

Strangely, even though I'd come down a little later than usual, I couldn't see Helena or Yarrow at any of the tables. Come to think of it, there didn't appear to be *any* of the Dee House girls around, which did strike me as a little odd, as usually some of them would have been about.

However, grumbles from my stomach informed me that there were more pressing matters to consider, so I loaded my tray with a full English breakfast - swapping out the bacon for additional sausages, as the bacon looked a little greasier than normal that morning – before heading for the nearest available table.

I was just finishing up my breakfast when I sensed people behind me, and a pair of hands reached around and covered my eyes.

'Happy birthday, Alex,' murmured Helena into my ear, 'stay exactly as you are - we have a surprise for you.'

I could hear my tray being moved and the rustle of paper, as objects were placed on the table in front of me.

'Right, you can look now,' said Helena, taking her hands from my eyes.

There on the table in front of me were a couple of wrapped presents and several envelopes, some of which were bundled together with an elastic band. I looked round in surprise, to see that Helena, Yarrow, Ashleigh, and Sophie were standing behind me, all smiling.

'The bundle was waiting for you in reception this morning,' said Helena, 'I think they might be cards from your family. The rest are from us.'

'Wow,' I said, 'I don't know what to say... I honestly wasn't expecting this... thank you.'

'Well, we could let your birthday go unmarked now, could we?' said Sophie grinning, 'especially after all your hard work getting us ready for the ball. Now, hurry up and open your presents because we've all got lessons to get too...'

As Sophie seemed eager to be off, I opened her gift first, which was a bottle of *Manticore* aftershave, bearing the legend '*Unleash the Beast within*.' It had a pleasant spicy, warming scent, exactly the sort I would have chosen for myself.

Yarrow had gotten me a book, entitled *Leabhar Scáthanna*.

'But not just any book,' she explained, 'this is one you won't find in the Library, or any bookshop for that matter, as it's a collection of legends and folklore of my people and Humans aren't usually allowed access to Geist writings.'

'Oh wow...' I said in amazement, 'That's a really special gift. Are you sure you won't get into trouble for giving this to me?'

'I don't care, Alex,' she said, tears in her eyes, 'You've been the best friend I could have possibly wished for when I came here, so I want you to have it.'

I could feel my own eyes tearing up and stood up, enveloping Yarrow in a hug.

'Thank you so much,' I said, 'I will treasure it.'

'My present's with Mama Lucia,' said Ashleigh, 'So make sure you pop over and see her today, ideally before this evening, as you'll need if before then...'

She refused to elaborate any further, just stating that she really hoped I liked it.

Helena wrapped her arms around me from behind, hugging me tightly and murmured in my ear.

'I have something for you too, but you'll have to wait until later for it...'

She then kissed me on the cheek, grinned at me and headed off to Alchemy with the rest of the Dee House students.

As birthdays go, today was turning out to be one of the better ones.

I headed down the stairs to Mama Lucia's workroom after breakfast, surprised to note that she appeared to be in conversation with a man, judging from the timbre of the voice. Not that there was anything wrong with this, of course, but for all the time I had spent in the workroom, I'd never seen another male down there.

The source of the voice was Mr Beamish, who was sitting drinking coffee with Mama Lucia and looked up with a grin when I walked in.

'And here's the birthday boy himself...' he said, 'A good morning to you, Alex, and a happy birthday.'

'How does *everyone* seem to know it's my birthday today?' I said, sighing, 'It's not like I've been making a big thing of it.'

'You should be happy, Alessandro,' said Mama Lucia smiling, 'your friends, they want you to have a good day, so they tell all those who like you, and these people, they get you gifts to make you happy.'

'That's really kind of them,' I said, 'but it's not really necessary.'

'Does that mean,' said Mr Beamish, tapping his foot against a bag resting at his feet, which clinked, 'that I should take these away?'

'Well, let's not be hasty here...' I said stepping forward, which caused Mr Beamish to burst out laughing.

'Here you go, lad,' he said, handing me the bag, 'You kept your word regarding my little "hobby" and never asked for any more, so I thought, as it's your birthday, you might like to try the latest brew.'

'Thank you very much,' I said, 'if it's anything like the other one I tried, I'm sure it'll be fantastic. And obviously, we never had this conversation...' I said winking.

I then turned to Mama Lucia.

'Ashleigh said that she'd left a present with you for me, but wouldn't tell me anything else,' I said, 'Can I see it?'

Mam Lucia smiled kindly.

'Ashleigh, she speak to me about today,' said Mama Lucia, 'she say that as it your birthday AND you put everyone else before you, that *you* deserve to look as *buono* as everyone else tonight. So, I dig out the *very* special fabric and we make you a new dinner jacket.'

She pointed at a dressmakers dummy, upon which was a beautifully tailored dinner jacket, with black silk lapels. I couldn't immediately see anything special about it, so walked over for a closer look. The jacket seemed to be made of a standard black fabric, but a closer inspection revealed that there appeared to be a pattern of interlocking diamonds woven into the cloth. I looked quizzically at Mama Lucia, as whilst it was very nice, I couldn't really see what made it so special.

'What colour is the jacket?' she asked, her eyes twinkling.

'It's black...' I said.

'Hold the sleeve of your jumper against it.'

I did as I was told, then started in amazement, as where I had held my arm against the jacket, the colour was slowly changing from black to navy blue, rippling out from where my sleeve was touching it.

'Oh my God...' I murmured.

Mama Lucia came over, holding a burgundy handkerchief.

'The jacket, she is made from *mimique*' said Mama Lucia, 'when no other fabric is nearby, is black, but if another fabric is held close to it...' she held the handkerchief against it, and the jacket slowly changed once more, becoming burgundy, 'the fabric, she change to match. Is very rare, but we feel you deserve something a little *speciale*. And this mean, whoever you dance with tonight, your jacket will mirror the colour of their dress.'

'That is probably the coolest thing I've ever seen...' I said, 'Thank you *so* much for this.'

'You thank Ashleigh as well,' said Mama Lucia, 'It was her idea...'

'I certainly will,' I said, watching the jacket slowly change back to the default black, 'Will the pair of you be coming along this evening?'

'As is usual for this event, I will be on duty,' said Mr Beamish smiling, 'someone has to keep an eye on you youngsters to make sure you don't misbehave *too* much...'

'I do not usually go, as usually there is nothing for me to see,' said Mama Lucia, 'but tonight there will many stylish dresses, thanks to you and Ashleigh, I may take a look...'

'Well, if you do decide to come along,' I said, taking Mama Lucia's hand in mine and raising it for a kiss, 'I will be sure to save a dance for you.'

'Well, how can this *Signora* resist such a charming invitation?' said Mama Lucia, obviously pleased, 'Now, off you go, Alessandro – these gifts, they are secret, so take them and put them somewhere safe.'

Whilst I was packing the bag to ensure the half dozen bottles wouldn't clink on the way back to my room, Mama Lucia had hung the jacket and placed it in a suit carrier, to protect it both from damage and prying eyes.

A sudden thought had occurred to me.

'Have you still got some of that *mimique*?' I asked Mama Lucia, 'Because I've just had a *brilliant* idea...'

Mama Lucia nodded, so I explained my idea. She smiled and nodded.

'Yes, we have enough for that...' she said.

Whilst everyone seemed determined to surprise *me* today, I had one final surprise for the girls of Dee House, and it was a *corker*...

Chapter XX
The Samhain Ball

Having spoken to the catering staff earlier that day, I knew that the Study Hall had been dressed and this would be where the evening's buffet and drinks would be served.

The adjacent Picture Gallery had been cleared of furniture and this is where the main reception for the event would take place, followed by dancing later in the evening. I'd also spoken to the band whilst they'd been setting up, and asked a favour, which they had happily agreed to.

I'd arranged to meet all the Dee House girls in the corridor outside the Picture Gallery, waiting patiently until they had all assembled.

As a light drizzle had started earlier that evening, Mama Lucia had provided all the girls with hooded black cloaks to protect their dresses as they made their way across the courtyard, so I was surrounded by darkly cloaked figures. It felt very clandestine, and this seemed to have imparted itself upon the girls, as their excited conversations were being conducted in whispers, rather than the expected volume.

'Ladies, it is time,' I announced, 'remove your capes.'

There was the rustling of fabric and where once there had been an unrelenting wall of black, there was now a veritable riot of colour. I collected the capes and stood back, looking critically at the assembled girls.

'Hmm...' I said thoughtfully, 'whilst you all look fantastic, there IS something missing...'

I pretended to give it some serious thought, then clicked my fingers and put the pile of capes on a side table, picking up the shallow white box I had placed there earlier.

'If you could all come forward,' I said, 'I have something for you...'

I removed the lid from the box and there, nestled in tissue paper, were enough corsages for each girl present. Gabrielle stepped forward and took one.

'It is black,' she said in puzzlement, 'this does not go with my dress...'

'Are you sure about that, Gabrielle?' I asked, grinning, 'look again...'

Gabrielle looked at the corsage she was holding close to her chest, then gasped in amazement as the colour changed to match the red of her dress. The other girls craned round to get a better look, eyes wide with wonder.

'I have one for each of you,' I said, 'each one will mirror the colour of your dress. And as they are not *real* flowers, you don't need to worry about them wilting before the end of the evening.'

Ashleigh came and stood next to me, a smile on her face.

'Looks like you've been busy *again*, Alex,' she said, 'I take it you liked my present?'

'I love it,' I said, 'and as you can see, it gave me a another one of my brilliant ideas.'

Ashleigh took one of the corsages and attached it to her wrist, watching as it changed from black to sky blue.

'They're beautiful,' she said, 'You're really quite inventive, aren't you?'

'I have my moments,' I said, grinning.

'And do you have one for your *actual* date?' said a voice behind me.

Recognising Helena's voice, I turned, and felt my jaw drop open.

Whilst I'd seen Helena in her dress before, this was when she was trying it on, so her bra-straps were on show, and she'd not done her make-up or hair.

Now, however, it was obvious she had spent a great deal of time getting ready. Her make-up, whilst understated, was perfection and where her hair was usually worn loose, cascading in soft curls below her collarbone, she had put this up in a curly messy bun with an accent braid, her face framed with wisps of hair. As the dress had built-in support, no bra was necessary, so no straps were on show and the burgundy chiffon hugged the curves of her body, a glimpse of thigh evident from the side split as she moved.

'*Fuck me...*' I breathed, staring.

'I didn't *quite* catch what you said there, Alex,' said Helena, the quirk of her mouth indicating that she *had* actually heard, 'but I take it from your expression that you approve?'

'Oh my God...' I said, voice thick with emotion, 'You look absolutely *gorgeous*!' I could feel myself welling up, 'I honestly think I may cry...'

Sophie mimed throwing up and Helena flashed her a look of annoyance, then stepped forward and took me in her arms.

'You're just jealous, Sophie,' she said, 'because I've got such a sweet and considerate man as my date.'

'True,' sighed Sophie, 'Lucky bitch...'

'Sorry to interrupt,' said Ashleigh, 'but shouldn't we be going in? Some of the girls are getting a bit antsy...'

'Right...yes...sorry,' I said, reluctantly disengaging from Helena's embrace, 'Now ladies, I want you to line up in front of the two doors to the Picture Gallery. I'll go in first, and when the doors open, I want you to make your entrance.'

'I'm assuming you've *already* planned all this?' asked Helena.

'You know me all too well...' I replied, winking, then opened the door and went through.

The Picture Gallery was thronged with people, both students and staff, all in what they considered to be their finest party wear. The female staff looked elegant, as being of a different generation, were not swayed by the mores of the fashion of the time. As for both the male staff and students, there was a definite trend to the dinner suit, predominantly black, but with a few variations here and there.

Unsurprisingly, most of the male students either had clip-on or pre-tied bow ties, as self-tying a bow tie took a bit of practice and usually several attempts to get right, but it was obvious that the male staff (and myself) had the necessary skill and patience to do it *properly*.

The female students, barring Penny, who was wearing a long, elegant gown in ivory silk, were dressed as expected, shiny satin in various hues and more ruffles than you could shake a stick at.

Mason noticed me standing by the stage and came over, a concerned look on his face.

'You haven't seen Yarrow, have you?' he asked, 'We agreed to meet in here, but I haven't seen her yet...'

'Patience, Mason,' I answered grinning, 'She's on her way and, trust me, the wait will be worth it.'

I then ascended the stage, nodding to the band leader, who stepped back from the edge to give me space. Two of the other band members put down their instruments and took their assigned positions by each of the two doors.

'Ladies and Gentlemen!' I called out, waiting until the hubbub of conversation had ceased and all attention was on me, 'I appreciate that some of your gentlemen have been patiently waiting for your dates to arrive and now that moment is at hand...' I nodded to the drummer, who began a drum roll, 'I would now like to present to you...the ladies of Dee House!'

As I announced this, the two band members threw open the doors and the girls swept in from left and right, crossing in front of me and then lining up in front of the stage.

Ashleigh and I had ensured that every dress was specifically tailored to suit both the body shape and colouring of the wearer and that every dress was of a different hue. The result was a panoply of colour and style that eclipsed nearly every other dress in the room. They looked *stunning*.

There were a few startled gasps of amazement, a pregnant pause, then the room erupted into frenzied and excitable conversation. Those who had been waiting for their dates were cautiously coming forward, quite a few of them with looks of stunned amazement on their faces.

As I stepped down off the stage, Mason had just come forward and was holding onto both of Yarrow's hands, whilst looking her up and down.

'Wow...just wow...' he said, 'Yarrow, you look *amazing...*'

'Thank you,' said Yarrow, colouring slightly. She saw me walking past and mouthed a 'thank you' at me, then smiled back at Mason..

I felt an arm link in with mine and turned to see Helena at my side.

'Looks like all your hard work and planning has paid off,' she said, 'you seemed to have created quite a stir.'

Her proximity had activated my jacket and it slowly changed from the default black to match the burgundy of her dress. Helena glanced across at me, then started in surprise.

'Did your jacket just *change* colour?!' she said.

'It did indeed,' I said, 'It's made from the same material as your corsage, so will always match whoever I'm with, as long as they're close enough. It was a present from Ashleigh. It's pretty damn cool, isn't it?'

'Whoever you're with?' queried Helena, turning to face me a wry smile on her face, 'Are you planning on being with someone *else* this evening?'

'Not planning...' I said, 'but I have a feeling that some of the girls may want at least one dance with me this evening, and who am I to turn them down?'

'As long as dancing is ALL they've got in mind for you, then I suppose I could let you go for a bit...' said Helena, grabbing my arm possessively.

I smiled to myself. Tonight was going to be *fun*.

As anticipated, nearly every girl that Ashleigh and I had provided dresses for had collared me for a dance, with Sophie asking me more than once, much to the annoyance of her date, a tall, athletic looking Second Year from Scot House, whose name I failed to catch.

Having turned her down for the third time, I headed for the Study Hall, as I was in need of a drink and couldn't see Helena in the Picture Gallery. Helena was there, but as she was deep in conversation with Lizzie and Jack, I decided not to interrupt and headed for the bar, which they'd set up in front of the sliding doors to the Library.

These were two immense wooden panelled doors on rollers, which ran from floor to ceiling, which were closed and secured after 10pm, preventing access to the Library after this time.

As I was patiently waiting for the barman to finish serving another student, I heard someone approach from behind.

'Good evening, Mr Crowe,' said a voice I recognised, 'I was wondering if you could spare me a few moments of your time?'

I turned to find Dr Vayne standing behind me. I'd seen her in discussion with Ashleigh earlier in the evening, marvelling slightly that the severe no-nonsense outfits she usually wore had been replaced with an elegant black gown with a halter neck and full skirt, festooned with sequins.

'Of course, Headmistress,' I said, as the barman acknowledged my presence, 'can I order you a drink whilst we're here?'

'Certainly,' she said, placing the empty champagne flute she was holding on the bar top, 'a glass of the Moët, please, James. What are you drinking, Alexander?'

'I'll just have a Coke, Miss,' I said.

'Given that the restrictions on the consumption of alcohol by students have been suspended for this evening,' said Dr Vayne, 'I would have expected you to be indulging, especially since Miss Bond tells me it IS your birthday today...'

'To be honest with you, Miss,' I said, 'I'm not a big fan of champagne. Besides, as this is Yarrow's first social event as a girl, I thought I'd best keep a clear head, just so I can keep a friendly eye on her. We wouldn't want anyone to take advantage of her... lack of experience.'

Dr Vayne gave me a thoughtful look, then took a sip of champagne.

'The reason I called you aside, Alexander, is that I've been speaking to Miss Bond,' began Dr Vayne, 'and she told me that *you* were responsible for the sartorial finery displayed by your fellow House members.'

'Well, I *may* have had the initial idea,' I said, 'but Ashleigh did the majority of the work – I just helped where I could. And it wouldn't have been possible if I hadn't been assigned detention by you with Mama Lucia...er…. Signora Milano in the first place. Actually, I have a question regarding that...'

'Go on.'

'Is there any reason why Fabricantation isn't taught as part of the curriculum?' I asked, 'Ashleigh shows a real talent for it and I'm sure there are other students who, given the opportunity, would also excel at this. As you already have a superb teacher as part of the staff, in the shape of Signora Milano, it seems a bit daft that this isn't offered as an option.' Dr Vayne was watching me shrewdly, 'if you don't mind me saying, that is...' I finished a little self-consciously.

'Hmm,' said Dr Vayne, 'To be honest with you, Alexander, it's not something I'd even considered. I think we just took it for granted that the costumes came from *somewhere*, without actually considering that someone had to create them in the first place. Given that the end result of both your and Miss Bond's efforts have produced some absolutely beautiful garments, I may bring this up at our next review with the board of Governors, as Oakdene does try to provide our students with every educational opportunity, and we appear to have overlooked this.'

'That would be cool,' I said smiling, 'Signora Milano was happy to teach us, so I can't imagine that she wouldn't want to teach other students.'

'One final question for you, Alexander, before I let you get back to enjoying yourself,' said Dr Vayne, who had finished her champagne and indicated to the barman that she required a refill, 'I'm curious as to *why* you took it upon yourself to provide your fellow students with such beautiful dresses in the first place?'

'That's an easy question to answer – if you wouldn't mind following me?' I said, and walked back into the Picture Gallery, Dr Vayne following me with a puzzled expression on her face.

'Now,' I said, 'look at all the girls who Ashleigh and I provided dresses for. Look at their faces. Look at how the dresses make them *feel* and how happy they are…' I smiled in satisfaction, 'I look at them, look at their smiling faces and think of how my humble efforts have spread so much joy… and it makes me happy. It may be my birthday, but I need no greater gift than that.'

I turned to Dr Vayne, who was looking at me with speculative expression on her face.

'You are a very unusual young man, Alexander,' she said, 'Whilst there may have been a few… bumps in the road during your time here at Oakdene, if you continue in this vein, I think we can expect great things of you. I hope you enjoy the rest of your evening.'

Dr Vayne then returned to the Study Hall, leaving me considering what she'd said.

Well, Dr Vayne, I thought to myself soberly, *I've only got to save your entire world from being erased from existence in a month and half's time. I think that **probably** counts… as long as I **actually** manage to do it, that is…*

That sobering thought had a put a little bit of a dampener on my evening, and this was further compounded when Mason rushed over.

'Alex,' he said breathlessly, a look of concern on his face, 'I think you'd better come – there's something wrong with Yarrow…'

I looked over to the other side of the room, where Yarrow was bent double white-faced, a concerned Ashleigh hovering nearby, wringing her hands. I quickly made my way over and reached for her arm.

'Alex…' said Yarrow, tears in her eyes, 'I don't feel very well…'

'Is your friend alright?' asked a voice and I turned to see Mark hovering nearby, a wary expression on his face. At this, Yarrow convulsed, then vomited.

'I would guess not,' I said, taking Yarrow by the arm, 'Let's get you outside. Mason, could you send Helena after us and get some water from the bar?'

Mason nodded and rushed off. I guided Yarrow through the doors, then down the corridor and out on to the rear terrace.

'I'm sorry, Alex,' sobbed Yarrow, 'I didn't mean to spoil your evening…'

'You don't need to apologise,' I said gently, 'I'm more concerned about you. Are you feeling any better?'

'A little,' she said, as I sat her down on one of the benches, shivering, 'I don't know what happened. I was fine and then suddenly, there was this horrible smell, like the stench of rotting meat and I felt my stomach go.'

I took off my jacket and draped it around her shoulders, as it wasn't exactly warm outside that evening. Thankfully, the rain had stopped.

'Thank you,' she said, pulling it around her, 'Aren't you worried I might be sick on your jacket?'

'That's not important,' I said, 'Had you eaten anything that might have disagreed with you? Or drunk anything, possibly?'

Yarrow gave this some thought. Helena burst through the doors, holding her skirt, then rushed over, Mason following in her wake with a large glass of water.

'What happened? Are you alright?' asked Helena breathlessly, crouching down in front of Yarrow and taking her hands.

Mason was looking very worried and wordlessly handed me the glass, which I passed to Yarrow. She took a mouthful, swished it around her mouth, then spat to one side.

'Sorry Helena,' she said meekly, 'I might have got some on your dress...'

'Don't worry about it,' said Helena, 'How are you feeling?'

'A lot better now,' she said, 'but I don't really feel well enough to go back to the party...'

'That's okay, if you're not feeling well, perhaps it's better if you call it a night.' I said, 'Helena, would you mind taking Yarrow back to her room? I'll follow on shortly.'

'Of course, Alex,' she said, a questioning look on her face, 'Anything I need to know about?'

'I'm not sure...' I said, 'I just want to ask Mason a few questions and I'll follow you up.'

Helena helped Yarrow to her feet. She was still shivering and slightly unsteady on her feet, so Helena took her arm, and they made their way back inside.

'You don't think I had anything to do with that, do you Alex?' asked Mason, defensively.

'No, I don't,' I said, 'I just wanted to know what lead up to Yarrow's turn, that's all. You've been with her all evening, haven't you?'

'Yeah,' he said, 'other than when she was dancing with you, that is...'

'And had she had anything to eat or drink?'

'Yeah, she had some of the buffet, but she had the same stuff that I ate. She also had some champagne, but complained it was not as nice or as strong as the mead her parents brewed.'

So, it wasn't a reaction to anything she'd eaten or drunk, then. Something she'd said earlier about 'the stench of rotting meat' rang a bell with me, as I was certain I'd read that exact phrase somewhere recently but couldn't for the life of me remember where. I'm sure it would come to me.

'And you didn't see anybody slip anything into her drink or anything like that?' I asked.

'No, I would have noticed, I'm sure...' said Mason, 'She'll be okay, won't she?'

'Yes, mate, I'm sure she'll be fine,' I said distractedly, the cogs in my mind spinning, 'I'll go check on her now. I very much doubt she'll be back down tonight though, so I suggest you head back inside and try and enjoy the rest of the evening. I'll make sure she knows you've been asking after her.'

'Okay...' said Mason, 'Not sure that I feel like partying now - I think I'll be too worried about Yarrow.'

'Don't worry, she's in good hands,' I said, 'I'll let you know in the morning how she is.'

'Thanks Alex.'

We headed back inside, Mason peeling off into the Picture Gallery, whilst I headed for the main staircase.

'The stench of rotting meat,' I murmured frowning, as I made my way upstairs. Something told me that it was essential that I remember where I'd read that, as it might explain what had happened to Yarrow.

112

Chapter XXI
A Night of Revelations

As I headed down the corridor towards Yarrow's room, I could see Helena stepping out into the corridor, with my jacket draped over her arm. She looked up when she heard my footsteps and smiled in greeting.

'Here's your jacket,' she said, handing it to me, 'She told me to thank you and apologised again for ruining your evening.'

'She has nothing to apologise for,' I said, 'How is she?'

'Now that she's back up here, she seems fine. She just seems to have had a funny turn. Did you find out anything else?'

'Not really. Mason said she did eat from the buffet but had the same as him and she only had one glass of champagne. I also checked to see if anyone had possibly spiked her drink, but Mason assures me he would have noticed.'

'What do you think it was then?'

'I'm not sure, but something she said to me before you came out rang a bell, as though I'd read it somewhere recently and I *think* I've remembered where,' I said, 'but I'll need to go back to my room to check, so if you wanted to head back down to the party, I don't mind.'

Helena linked her arm in mine.

'You're my date for this evening, so where you go, I go,' she said, 'besides, I want to know what happened to Yarrow too.'

I glanced up and down the corridor, checking if anyone was about.

'I *may* have a couple of bottles of beer in my room,' I whispered, 'so at least we can have a drink whilst we're looking.'

Helena grinned at me.

'Even better,' she said, 'let's go.'

I unlocked the door, activated the sprite globe, and slung my jacket over the back of the chair, which changed from black to green, matching the upholstery. Helena closed and locked the door, then looked around the room.

'Where's this beer, then?' she asked.

'In a bag under the bed,' I said, walking to my bookshelf. Now, which one was it?

Helena crouched down, the movement exposing her leg, which I have to admit distracted me a little. She pulled the bag out with a satisfied cry, then turned and saw me staring.

'What?' she asked, then noted the direction of my gaze, 'Are you staring at my legs?'

'Of course not,' I said, a little flustered, turning back to the bookshelf, 'just checking that you'd found them okay...'

'Of course you were,' said Helena with a smirk, 'I mean, why on Earth would you want to stare at my soft, smooth, *naked* leg...'

'I am trying to concentrate here,' I said, 'and that's not helping...'

Helena giggled, then pouted.

'These are warm,' she said, 'Guess I'll have to wait for a *proper* drink...'

'Ah, now that's where you're wrong,' I said, turning with a grin, 'I am about to show you something that is, literally, very cool.'

113

I went to the open window, whistled, and then waited for a moment. Hearing wings outside, I stepped back, and Errol swooped in through the window, flapped a couple of times to right himself, then landed with a thump on the back of the desk chair. I took two bottles out of Helena's unresisting hands and placed them on the desk in front or Errol, who looked at me inquisitively.

'Errol,' I commanded, pointing at the bottles, 'Elsa.'

On this command, Errol turned, opened his mouth, and exhaled over the bottles, the particles of his icy breath covering them in a layer of frost.

'And there we go,' I said, handing one of the bottles to Helena, 'two chilled bottles of beer, courtesy of my little scaly friend.'

She took it with a grin.

'You were right,' she said, 'That was literally "cool." Why "Elsa" as a command word, though?'

'I needed a word that I wouldn't use in normal conversation,' I said, 'and it made me laugh.'

'Why? Who's Elsa?'

As this reality had neither television nor cinema, I spent the next ten minutes explaining the plot to *Frozen*, then a further ten minutes attempting to explain what a Disney film actually *was*.

'So, it's like a theatrical performance, told via Illusioneering *only*, but at a distance?' said Helena, 'Sounds very complicated and not particularly immersive. We'll have to take you to a *proper* performance, so you can see why our way is *better*.'

Let's hope we get the chance, I thought to myself, *if I fail to prevent the upcoming rewriting of reality, then Disney films is the least of your problems...*

This diversionary conversation had made me forget which book I'd read that phrase in, although I was pretty certain it was one in my room. Now, I *could* go through each individual book, but what was the point of learning Bibliomancy if you didn't use it? I held out my hand and intoned, 'the stench of rotting meat...'

The books on the shelf jostled each other, then one leapt forward into my waiting hand. It was the book Yarrow had given me for my birthday, *Leabhar Scáthanna,* which Yarrow had told me roughly translated as "The Book of Shadows." I held my hands flat, the book resting on them and stated the phrase I was looking for again. The book fanned open, the pages riffling, then ceased. And there was the phrase, in the section regarding *mícheart*.

'I *knew* I'd read it somewhere,' I said triumphantly, 'Helena, listen to this... "as guardians of the natural order, the ability to detect *mícheart* is an intrinsic part of our heritage. The foulness and corruption of *mícheart* manifests in many forms, but a primary indicator is by scent, which some have likened to **the stench of rotting meat**..."

Helena looked startled.

'So, does that mean...' she began.

'That someone who was at the ball has been corrupted by dark magic,' I finished, 'I would guess so. And I have a feeling that whoever it was is probably the same person who will be attempting to complete the ritual on the eve of Saturnalia.'

'But there were loads of people in the room,' said Helena in frustration, 'it could be *anyone*...'

'I think we can narrow it down,' I said, closing the book and sending it back to the shelf, 'It has to be someone that Yarrow doesn't have regular contact with, so we can rule out all the teachers she takes lessons with and everyone from Dee House, otherwise, she'd have detected it sooner.'

'Sounds logical,' said Helena, taking a seat on my bed, 'so, someone from either Scot or Watkins House then?'

'Yeah, I think it's safe to assume that. However, if they know enough about Geist and their ability to detect *mícheart,* Yarrow's public display just now might have alerted them to the fact that she may be able to work out who they are, which could put her in danger.'

We both contemplated this in silence.

'I think we need to tell Yarrow what's going on,' I said, 'Not *everything*, of course, but she needs to know about the ritual, not only because she *may* be the target, but also because her ability might be able to help us prevent it.'

'Sounds like a good idea,' said Helena slowly, 'but we don't have to do it tonight, do we?'

'Why?' I asked, 'Was there something else you were planning on doing?'

'Maybe...' said Helena smiling, then patted the bed next to her, 'Come sit with me.'

'How much have you had to drink?' I asked.

'That's not important, Alex. Now, come here – it's not polite to keep a lady waiting.'

I approached slowly and gingerly sat down on the bed next to her, but not *too* close.

'And what exactly did you have in mind?' I asked nervously.

What was *wrong* with me? I'd been in a similar situation many times before, so had a pretty good idea where this was going, but for some reason I felt quite anxious, as though all my previous experience had been wiped away, leaving a blank slate.

'Well,' murmured Helena sliding closer, and putting her hand on my thigh, 'I did say I had something for you at breakfast... and I think that it's time I gave it to you...'

'Helena, wait...' I said, taking her hand in mine and looking her in the eye, 'Do you really think this is a good idea? I mean, you *know* what I am... doesn't it bother you?'

'Alex, listen to me,' she said seriously, 'This isn't some reckless decision, made on the spur of the moment – I *have* given it a lot of thought. I like you... a lot. So what if your mind or soul or whatever is from the future – it's part of who you are *now,* and that's the Alex I'm attracted to.' She reached up, pulled my bow tie undone, took the ends in her hands and pulled me close, 'So... are you going to kiss me or not?'

As I've said before, you only get a handful of these type of moments in your life, where no matter what has gone before, everything falls in to place – just so.

But this time, I wasn't going to fuck it up.

However, the Universe obviously had decided that it was not meant to be, as just before our lips met, we were interrupted by someone pounding on my door.

'Ignore it,' breathed Helena, close enough so that I could almost taste her, 'If we don't answer, they'll go away...'

'We know you're in there, Alex!' Shouted a voice I recognised, 'So you might as well open up!'

'Bloody Sophie...' muttered Helena.

'He might be in bed,' said a second voice, that I recognised as Ashleigh's, 'So maybe we should wait until the morning?'

'If he is, he's not alone,' replied Sophie, 'I heard someone else's voice. Come on, Alex, open up!' She resumed banging on the door, 'We've got something for you!'

'I don't think she's going to give up,' I sighed, 'it IS Sophie, after all...'

'That girl is the bane of my existence,' said Helena darkly, 'Why can't she just leave you alone?'

'Probably because she fancies me,' I said, getting up, 'She couldn't have been *more* obvious when we were dancing earlier unless she'd written "Please fuck me" on her forehead in lipstick.'

Helena snorted with laughter.

'Would that have worked?' she then asked, smiling slyly.

'Depends whose forehead it was written on,' I answered, then paused in thought, 'Got any lipstick on you?'

Helena's laughter followed me as I approached and then opened the door.

'Can I help you?' I asked coolly, barring entry with my arm.

'So macho...' said Sophie, grinning, then ducked under my arm and entered the room.

'Sorry Alex,' said Ashleigh apologetically, 'Sophie insisted... and you know what she's like.'

Ashleigh was carrying a square white box, so I stepped aside and let her in.

'Looks like you're having a little party of your own,' said Sophie, looking around.

'We *were*...' said Helena sourly, 'but then *someone* decided to interrupt us.'

'No need to be like that,' said Sophie, 'We come bearing gifts... well, cake actually.'

Ashleigh carried the box over to my desk and opened the lid. Inside was a large chocolate cake, candles already in place. She glanced at the bottles of beer sitting on the side and frowned.

'Ah yes...' I said quickly, 'as Dr Vayne *herself* said to me this evening, "all restrictions on the consumption of alcohol by students have been suspended," so *technically* there is no problem with me, or anyone else who happens to be in my room *at this precise moment*, from drinking that beer.'

I grabbed the other cold bottle from the side, cracked the lid and handed it to Ashleigh.

'Here you go,' I said, 'Remember, you're off duty tonight...'

Ashleigh took the offered bottle and smiled.

'I saw nothing...' she said, winking.

'The rest of these bottles are *warm*...' whined Sophie. I rolled my eyes, then whistled for Errol, who'd been perched on top of the wardrobe, watching us all. He hopped down on the chair back and I commanded him to chill the other bottles, handing a frosted bottle to Sophie once he was done and taking one for myself.

'Now that's a useful talent,' said Sophie, then took a swig, 'and this is *excellent* beer. I don't mind champagne, but it does make me belch, which seems to put the boys off for some reason.'

'I can't *imagine* why...' said Helena sarcastically.

'So, we didn't interrupt anything, did we?' grinned Sophie, nudging me in the ribs with her elbow.

The problem with being English is that you feel obligated to be polite all the time, even if by doing so, you miss out on things you *really* want to do. However, sometimes you have to make a stand, Like Gandalf on the bridge of Moria, and state "You Shall Not Pass!"

This was one of those times.

'Actually, you did, Sophie,' I said seriously, 'Now, I can't deny that you're an attractive young woman, but I'm not interested in you in that way, I'm afraid. So nothing is ever going to happen between us.' I glanced across at Helena, who was staring at her feet, her face flushed, 'Helena, however, I fancy the arse off...'

'Oh…right…um…' said Sophie, seemingly at a loss for words, which was quite unusual for her.

'I like you, Sophie, but sometimes you're a bit…full-on,' I said, 'if you want a meaningful relationship with someone who actually respects *you* as a person, rather than being purely interested in your body, you might want to consider toning it down a bit.'

Sophie looked at me thoughtfully, then turned to Ashleigh.

'You were right,' she said, 'He IS different. I can see *exactly* why you like him so much.'

'I don't know what you mean…' muttered Ashleigh, flushing.

'And as for you,' said Sophie, turning to Helena, 'I just wish I'd got to him first…'

I walked over to the door and opened it.

'You are welcome to take your beers with you,' I said, 'and thank you for the cake, but would you mind…?'

'Come on, Ash,' sighed Sophie, 'Let's leave these two lovebirds to it.'

Ashleigh quickly made her way to the door, muttering apologies and avoiding my gaze.

I stopped her at the door, took her hand and kissed it.

'I am extremely flattered and there is nothing to be embarrassed about,' I said, looking her in the eye, 'Still friends, yes?'

'Yes, Alex,' she said, smiling shyly, 'still friends.'

Sophie also headed for the door.

'Alex, I…' she said, then faltered 'actually, I'm not sure what I want to say…'

'A first for you,' I said wryly, 'As long as you're happy being just friends, there's no need to say anything.' I then leaned in and kissed her on the cheek. She looked startled, raising her hand to her cheek, and going red.

'I think… I'd like that,' she said, smiling, 'Good night, Alex.'

I shut the door behind them and made sure it was locked, then turned back to Helena, who was watching me with a smile on her face.

'So,' she said, getting to her feet and approaching me, head cocked to one side, 'You "fancy the arse off me," do you?'

She put her arms around my neck and stepped in closer.

'Had you not realised?' I murmured, nuzzling her neck.

'I wasn't *entirely* sure…' she breathed, pressing herself against me.

'Then, perhaps I should prove it to you…' I said.

So I did.

Chapter XXII
Dark Magic

There was no need for either of us to get up early the following morning, due to it being a Saturday, but Helena had decided she ought to go back to her room before anyone else stirred, so as not to draw attention to the fact that she had spent the night elsewhere.

'I'm sure I'm not the only one who didn't sleep in their own bed last night,' she said, climbing back into her dress, 'but I think we should try and keep a low profile – it will help with our investigations.'

She turned to me.

'Now, are you going to just lie there ogling me,' she asked over her shoulder, 'or are you going to help me with this dress?'

'Sorry,' I said, getting out of bed and walking over, 'I was just admiring the view.'

'Oh, shut up you,' she said, but I could tell by the tone of her voice she was pleased by the compliment.

Whilst I had designed the dress Helena was wearing, I'd not really given much thought to the logistics of putting it on, concentrating more on the look of the thing, than the practical aspects. I fed the rear straps through the loops either side, criss-crossing them across her back, then tied them off in a bow at the base of her spine. I then leant forward, and gently started kissing my way along her collarbone, which caused an involuntary intake of breath from Helena.

'Are you *sure* you have to go right now?' I asked, 'Can't you stay for a bit longer?'

Helena stepped forward with a giggle, turned to face me, put her arms around me and drew me close.

'I would love to,' she said, nuzzling my neck, 'but I'm just being sensible here, Alex.'

'Well, if you *have* to go, then I'd best give you something to remember me by...'

And I kissed her deeply, feeling her initially tense, before relaxing into it with a sigh.

'Still sure you have to go?' I asked teasingly.

'It is tempting...' she said, smiling, 'but, yes, I do have to go. I'll see you downstairs in about an hour, yes?'

I reluctantly let her go, agreeing to meet her in the Dining Hall later for breakfast.

After she'd gone, I reflected on the previous day's events. As birthdays go, that was probably the best one I'd ever had.

I decided to take the *Leabhar Scáthanna* down to breakfast with me, in the hopes that Yarrow would be there, as it would help explain what she had experienced the previous evening – and hopefully give Helena and I the opening we needed to discuss the plot to rewrite reality.

Obviously, we couldn't tell her *everything*, as the whole thing was pretty unbelievable, but we could give her the broad strokes, in the hope that she would not only believe us but would also agree to help.

Given that it was a Saturday, was just after 8.00am and everyone was still probably recovering from last night's festivities, the Dining Hall was relatively empty, with only a few students scattered about. The advantage of this was that all the food was freshly cooked and there was plenty of it, so I loaded my plate high and headed for an empty table, as neither Helena nor Yarrow had made an appearance yet.

I was just about to tuck in when I was interrupted, and not by who I expected.

'Good morning, Alexander,' said a female voice, 'Do you mind if I join you?'

I looked up and was surprised to see Penny standing across from me, with a laden tray.

'Of course not, your Highness,' I said, 'Please, take a seat.'

Penny sat down, placing her tray in front of her and leaned forward.

'You don't really need to call me "your Highness," you know,' she said, 'Penny's fine.'

'Well, if you're okay with me calling you Penny, then you can call me Alex – most of my friends do.'

'Fair enough.'

'No Aubrey this morning?' I asked, 'I though you two came as a pair. He was your date last night, wasn't he?'

Penny pulled a face.

'He was *supposed* to my date for the whole evening,' she said sourly, 'but got involved in some kind of drinking game with some of the Second Years, so after that he wasn't really in any fit state to do anything. It was quite disappointing.'

'I regularly find myself disappointed with Aubrey's behaviour,' I said dryly.

Penny looked up at me with a start, then started giggling. This actually transformed her face, as her usual expression was that there was a bad smell under her nose that she couldn't get away from.

'Anyway,' said Penny, once she'd stopped laughing, 'I was hoping to get a chance to speak to you alone. I overheard Dr Vayne and Ashleigh talking last night… it is true that you were responsible for all of the Dee House girls dresses last night?'

'Um…sort of,' I said slowly, 'I came up with the initial idea, but Ashleigh designed and created most of the dresses herself, with Signora Milano's help. I was only directly responsible for three of them.'

'I see,' said Penny, then paused, 'Hang on, did you say YOU designed three of the dresses yourself?'

'Yeah, I did.'

'What, really?' seeming surprised when I nodded in reply, 'Which ones?'

'Ashleigh's, Yarrow's and Helena's…' I said, counting them off on my fingers, 'although Signora Milano actually created Helena's, I just designed it.'

'Gosh…' said Penny, 'I didn't realise you were *that* talented. I mean, that rose you made for me was pretty cool, but I didn't realise that you'd designed AND made dresses too. Especially those ones…' She looked around the room and leaned in conspiratorially, 'Don't tell anyone this, but I was kind of jealous of Ashleigh's dress – I wish mine had looked as nice.'

'Tell you what,' I said, 'next time there's a special event, *I'll* design you a dress myself, if you want…'

'You'd do that for me?' said Penny in surprise, 'but I've not been particularly nice to you since we've been here…'

'Yeah, we didn't get off to the best of starts, did we?' I said, 'What was it you said to me when we first met? "Boy, fetch my trunk," wasn't it?'

Penny flushed.

'Yeah, my dad gave me a right telling off for that,' she said, 'I'm sorry I was so rude to you. I think I may have misjudged you.'

'Don't worry about it. It happens all the time. I am quite a nice guy when you get to know me.'

'Well, you certainly do have a lot of friends, Alex,' she said, 'In fact, I think there's a couple of them now.'

I turned to see that Helena and Yarrow had just walked in. Yarrow gave me a little wave, before going to the counter to get some breakfast. Helena looked surprised to see me sitting chatting with Penny and gave me a questioning look.

'Always room for one more,' I said turning back to Penny. She gave me a thoughtful look, then extended her hand.

'Truce?' she asked, a little shyly. I took her hand.

'Truce,' I agreed, shaking it.

'I'll leave you to it, Alex,' she said, getting up, 'I need to give my dad a call, as he'll want to know how my first Samhain Ball went.'

'And what was all that about?' asked Helena, sitting down, 'You chatting up princesses now? Can't I leave you alone for five minutes without finding you with some other girl?'

I snaked my arm around her waist and pulled her close.

'You *know* there's only one woman for me,' I murmured, 'Do I need to prove it to you *again?*'

'Alex...' said Helena, embarrassed, 'There's people *watching*...'

'Don't care,' I said, 'In fact, I think I'll stand on the table and announce to everyone that you're my girlfriend right now.' I started to get up. Helena grabbed my arm and pulled me back down into my seat.

'Alright, you've made your point,' she whispered, a smile on her lips, 'But I thought we were trying to maintain a low profile?'

'Good point,' I said grinning, 'and I *think* that Penny and I might be friends now, so hopefully that will help with...the other thing.'

'Morning Alex!' said Yarrow breezily, joining us at the table, 'I just wanted to apologise again for last night. I really don't know what came over me...'

Helena and I looked at each other and I placed the *Leabhar Scáthanna* on the table between myself and Yarrow.

'But we think we do,' I said, opening the book to the relevant page and pushing it towards her, 'read the section on *mícheart*...'

Helen and I sat quietly, letting Yarrow read. When she had finished, she looked up with a slightly dazed expression on her face.

'But that means...' she started.

'Not here,' I interrupted, 'We don't know who might be listening. Once we've finished our breakfast, we'll head back to my room, as there's something we *really* need to talk to you about...'

'So, what's going on?' asked Yarrow, once we were secure in my room, 'You're both being very mysterious and it's worrying me...'

Conversation during breakfast had been a little stilted, as both Helena and I refused to be drawn on what we wanted to discuss with her and I was trying to work out the best way to explain, without freaking Yarrow out.

'I think it's best if Alex explains,' said Helena, 'as he knows more than I do.'

'Alex?' queried Yarrow.

'Okay,' I said, marshalling my thoughts, 'We have reason to believe that someone is going to attempt a major sorcerous ritual on 17th December, due to it being the eve of Saturnalia

AND a full moon. We don't know the full details of the *actual* ritual itself, but we're pretty certain that it will involve a blood sacrifice – so we're talking seriously dark magic. Now, we know that the intended victim is female, and, through deductive reasoning, we've whittled down the list of possible victims to two people – Penny...and you.'

'What?!' exclaimed Yarrow, 'Why me?'

'We think that the more magically powerful the blood is, the more chance the ritual will have to succeed,' said Helena, 'Which is why we think it's either you or Penny.'

'How do you know all this?' asked Yarrow.

'Alex was sent here specifically to stop it from happening,' said Helena, 'He's... more than he appears to be.'

Nicely done, Helena, I thought to myself.

'But why haven't you gone to the Headmistress with this?' asked Yarrow, 'If someone's going to potentially hurt one of the students, shouldn't you have reported it as soon as you found out?'

'Well, there's a bit of a problem with that...' I said, 'We don't know who we can trust. Thanks to your ability to detect *mícheart,* we know that someone who attended the ball last night has been corrupted by dark magic and it's likely that it's the same person who is planning on completing the ritual next month – but it could be anyone, even one of the teachers...'

'But surely part of their job is to protect the students?' said Yarrow, 'They wouldn't deliberately harm them, would they?'

'There IS precedent for that sort of thing, unfortunately,' I said darkly, 'So, the only people I *definitely* know I can trust are currently in this room.'

'How long have you known about this?' asked Yarrow.

'Alex only confided in me at the end of September,' said Helena, 'once he knew he could trust me.'

'So, why are you only telling me all this *now*?' asked Yarrow.

'Because there's a strong possibility,' I said, 'that whoever is planning this dark magic knows enough about Geist that they will realise that you can identify them, which puts you in danger.'

'I know it's hard to believe, Yarrow,' said Helena, 'it took me a while to get my head round it, but I do believe AND trust Alex completely. The question is, do you?'

Yarrow looked back and for the between Helena and I, noting how serious we both looked.

'Is this the *only* reason you made friends with me, because of this plot?' she asked plaintively.

'No, of course not!' I said, 'We hadn't worked out until very recently that you *might* be the possible target. We're your friends because we like you and we definitely don't want anything bad to happen to you.'

I could see Yarrow was overwhelmed with what we had told her and close to tears, so I walked over and took her in my arms.

'I know it's a lot to take in,' I said gently, 'I wish I hadn't been given this task, but I was chosen for a reason, and I will do everything within my power to prevent any harm coming to *anyone*. Helena has agreed to help me, even though it could be dangerous for her too. You're already a possible target and I know it's asking a lot, but are you prepared to help too?'

Yarrow pulled back and looked me in the eyes.

'You were the first person who treated me like an actual *person* when I came here,' she said, 'and you've shown me nothing but friendship and kindness since I've known you, Alex. I may not completely understand what's going on and all this talk of dark rituals scares me, but I do know that you're a good person and wouldn't lie to me. If you think I can help, I'll… I'll try my best.'

'That's all that I ask,' I said, 'Thank you. And remember, we're not sure who we can trust, so you need to keep this to yourself.'

I looked across at Helena, who was looking pensive but resolute. Yarrow had rallied and I could see her strength beneath her tears. Unlike the person who was planning on rewriting reality who, by necessity, was working alone, I had trusted allies.

And a bundle of sticks is not easily broken.

Chapter XXIII
The Missing Book

As we were anticipating that whoever was planning on completing the ritual may target Yarrow, due to the fact that she could potentially identify them, it was decided that either myself or Helena would accompany Yarrow whenever she was out of her room. As we were in the same lessons for the most part and it was known that we were close friends, we hoped it wouldn't be too obvious to anyone watching that we were keeping an eye on her.

It would also mean that if Yarrow DID detect *mícheart,* one of us would be present to see who was about and hopefully identify the corrupted individual.

Of course, we had failed to take into account that the person planning all this was not about to be caught *that* easily and had put their *own* plan in place to take Yarrow out of commission…

The first we knew about this was when Master Tweed summoned everyone from Dee House to the common room on Sunday afternoon.

'I apologise for summoning you all here on your day of rest,' he began, a grave expression on his face, 'but a serious matter has arisen that needs addressing.'

Helena, Yarrow, and I looked at each other with puzzled expressions on our faces. What now?

'It would appear that at some point between the Library being secured on Friday night and this morning when it was reopened, someone had managed to enter the Library and remove one of the restricted books,' said Master Tweed, 'As you are all aware, there are enchantments in place that *should* have prevented this from occurring, but the fact remains that this book is missing. As this means that the perpetrator has somehow been able to overcome or disable the blood-lock enchantment placed upon it and, as I have not been able to locate it using my own formidable Bibliomantic talent, also managed to conceal it from me, this would suggest that they are a powerful and skilled sorcerer. Given the particular subject matter of the book in question, this is extremely concerning, as in the wrong hands, this book could do a great deal of damage.'

Helena shot me a worried look, as we'd both realised that whoever was planning on rewriting reality next month now had access to the full details of the ritual they needed.

'Given the seriousness of this theft, the college had no choice but to alert the relevant authorities and they are on their way. Should anyone know anything about this, I would suggest that they come forward as soon as possible, as this will save any possible unpleasantness later. Thank you for your time.'

As Master Tweed left, the room erupted into animated conversation, with everyone speculating on what this could possibly mean. I caught Helena and Yarrow's eye and nodded towards the door, then headed out of the room.

'Alex…' Helena started, before I interrupted her.

'Not here,' I said, 'Too many ears. Let's take a walk outside…'

We headed onto the rear terrace, and I made for the steps leading down to the Dog Walk, with the girls following after me. After checking that no-one had followed us, I turned to them both.

'Right, I think we can be pretty certain that whoever is planning the ritual now has the full instructions on how to complete it,' I said, 'Based on my research on the blood-lock enchantment, unless they have been able to circumvent it, the obvious suspects for this would be either Master Tweed himself...'

'Which we know it's not, otherwise Yarrow would have reacted to his presence,' said Helena.

'Or Doctor Tweed, as she shares the same blood.' I finished.

'Doctor Tweed?' queried Yarrow, 'But she's really nice... it can't be her!'

'We could check,' said Helena, 'Think of some excuse to talk to her with Yarrow present, and see if Yarrow reacts to her?'

'I honestly don't think it's her,' I said, 'but I suppose it is worth checking, just to rule her out.'

Yarrow and Helena started to discuss possible reasons to speak to her, but stopped when they noticed I hadn't joined in.

'What's wrong, Alex?' asked Helena, 'What haven't you told us?'

'You know I did some extensive research into the blood-lock enchantment, to see if I could work out how to get around it?' I said. Helena nodded, but Yarrow just looked surprised, as we hadn't told her this. 'Well, it is *possible* that the enchantment only affects *humans*...'

I waited for this to sink in, watching as they both realised what this meant.

'You're not seriously suggesting...' said Helena, turning to look at Yarrow.

'It wasn't me!' cried Yarrow, eyes tearing up, 'You don't honestly believe I would do something like that!'

'Of course not,' I said, 'All I said was that it was a *possibility*... I don't know if it would affect you or not. But if it doesn't, then we have a problem...'

'I'm not sure I'm following you, Alex...' said Helena, a puzzled expression on her face.

'The book with the ritual in has *publicly* gone missing,' I said, 'So, why *now*? If I'd worked out how to defeat the blood-lock enchantment and was planning on using one of the rituals from the book, I wouldn't advertise the fact. I'd sneak it off the shelf, copy what I needed and put it back, with no-one being the wiser. The only reason I can think of for not doing it that way was if I *wanted* people to discover the book was missing.'

'What's this got to do with me?' Asked Yarrow.

'We've recently discovered that your ability to detect *mícheart* has developed, meaning that you can identify whoever it is that has been corrupted by dark magic, right?' Yarrow nodded, 'Helena, am I right in thinking that Scrying doesn't work on Geist?'

'Yes,' she said, 'it's something to do with how their minds differ from ours...'

'Okay,' I said, 'So, imagine *you're* the bad guy – you've just found out that Yarrow can detect your corruption and need to remain unidentified until it's time to compete the ritual. Plus you've worked out how to get around the blood-lock enchantment, that it's possible that Yarrow CAN touch the restricted books AND that because Scrying doesn't work on Geist, if Yarrow *was* found with the book, even if she denies it, there's no immediate way of knowing if she's telling the truth. What would you do?'

'I'd plant the book in her... Fuck!' Said Helena, 'Yarrow, we need to get back to your room immediately. If Alex is right, someone's trying to set you up...'

We rushed back inside and up to Yarrow's room, but it was already too late. Her door was open, and we could hear adult voices inside. As we approached the open door, Dr

Vayne stepped out into the corridor, followed by Master Tweed. He was holding a green-bound book in his hand, which we assumed was the missing book.

'Ah, Miss Yarrow,' said Dr Vayne, 'I believe you have some explaining to do...'

'Wait a moment, Headmistress,' said Master Tweed walking towards us, 'I just want to check something first.'

He placed the book on the floor in front of us.

'Miss Yarrow, would you mind picking up this book, please?' he said, 'Don't worry, should you be affected by the enchantment, I will immediately lift it.'

Yarrow looked fearfully back at Helena and I.

'I don't really want to, sir...' she said tearfully.

'Miss Yarrow, we are merely trying to establish whether you *could* have taken the book,' said Master Tweed kindly, 'If you are affected by the blood-lock enchantment, then it will be obvious that you could not have taken the book and someone else has placed it in your room. However, if not...' he left the sentence hanging.

Helena reached for Yarrow's hand and gave it a squeeze.

'We're both here, Yarrow,' she said, 'It'll be okay.'

Yarrow smiled gratefully, then crouched down and tentatively touched the book's cover. We all held our breaths.

When nothing happened, she cautiously picked up the book, tears in her eyes and handed the book to Master Tweed, who had a grave expression on his face.

'It wasn't me, sir,' she said, 'You have to believe me!'

'The evidence seems to suggest otherwise I'm afraid, Miss Yarrow,' he said.

'Hang on,' I said, 'all that proves is that Yarrow can touch the book. What if the enchantment on that particular book didn't take completely? What if *anyone* can touch that particular book?'

'Hmm, you have a point, Alexander,' said Master Tweed, 'I suppose it is possible... are you prepared to volunteer to test this theory?'

'If it proves that the blood-lock enchantment isn't present on the book,' I said, 'then, yes, Sir, I am.'

Master Tweed held the book out and I reached out and grasped the cover. I immediately began to feel a tingling in my fingers, similar to the sensation of pins and needles, but rather than the numbness receding, it spread from my hand up my arm, then continued over the rest of my body. I tried to pull my hand away, but couldn't move my arm, or the rest of my body, for that matter. I began to panic slightly but couldn't even make a sound.

'I think that proves that the blood-lock enchantment is in place,' said Master Tweed, making a complicated gesture with his free hand. I was immediately freed from the paralysis and stumbled backwards.

'Are you alright, Alex?' said Helena, stepping forward and taking my arm.

'That...' I slurred, 'was not pleasant.'

'Hmm,' said Dr Vayne, 'This situation presents us with a problem. Miss Yarrow here denies that she took the book and due to her Geist heritage, there is no way of discerning if she is telling the truth, so there is little point in her being questioned by *our* authorities. However, we do need to get to the bottom of this, so we will need to contact the Geist High Council and request an... *iarrthóir fírinne*, I think the term is?' Yarrow nodded.

'Unfortunately, this will take some time to organise, bureaucracy being what it is. Whilst I am fairly certain that you were not responsible for the theft of this book, due to the serious nature of this breach, until we can be certain, I'm afraid you will need to be confined to your room until further notice.'

'You're locking her up?!' exclaimed Helena, 'But she hasn't done anything wrong!'

'That remains to be seen, Miss Morgan,' said Dr Vayne, 'I appreciate that emotions are running high, but do please try to remember who you're speaking to...'

'Sorry, Headmistress.'

Dr Vayne turned to Master Tweed.

'Humphrey, can I leave you secure Miss Yarrow?' she asked.

'Of course, Headmistress,' replied Master Tweed, 'I shall do so immediately. Miss Yarrow, if you could enter your room, please?'

I could see Yarrow was close to tears.

'It'll be okay, Yarrow,' said Helena supportively, 'We *know* you didn't do it, and once the other Geist arrives, they'll prove it too.' She then tuned to Master Tweed, 'Are we allowed to visit her?'

'You'll be able to talk to her through her door, but won't be able to see her, as the door will be secured against all physical or sorcerous forces,' said Master Tweed, 'Once the enchantment is cast, nothing can get in or out, until the spell is lifted. She will be allowed use of the bathroom, naturally, but will be accompanied by a member of the faculty at these times.'

Master Tweed indicated that it was time for Yarrow to be confined to her room and she slowly and tearfully walked to her door and went in. Master Tweed shut and locked the door, then spread his hands towards the door. The perimeter of the door glowed briefly with amber light.

'All done, Headmistress,' said Master Tweed, then turned to Helena and I, 'Whilst I appreciate that you wish to support your friend, which is admirable, there is little you can do for her at present, so I suggest that your return to whatever you were doing prior to this.'

Master Tweed tucked the book under his arm and walked off down the corridor, in conversation with Dr Vayne. Dr Vayne paused at the top of the corridor and looked back at the pair of us, a thoughtful expression on her face.

We watched them turn the corner, then Helena turned to me.

'So, what on Earth do we do now?!' she asked in exasperation.

'Come on,' I said, starting off down the corridor towards my room, 'we need to think this through...'

Chapter XXIV
A Wolf in the Fold

There are many things in life that irritate me – people who play music just loud enough so that you can hear it, but not quite loud enough to be able to identify the particular track; drivers who seem to think that dipping your headlights to prevent blinding other road users applies to everyone else except *them*; and those wankers who start sentences with 'You know what your problem is…' and then proceed to advise you what you're doing wrong and how, by following their *expert* advice, you can improve your standing with the world as a whole.

I know some may think it irrational to get wound up over what they may consider "petty annoyances," but as far as I'm concerned, this kind of behaviour just underlines the fact that these people have no consideration for the others, so it's entirely justified that they be consigned to the Pit, to roast screaming in Hellfire for all eternity.

That'll learn 'em.

However, the things that *really* annoys me, is when someone proves to be cleverer than I thought they were, as it this makes me look like an idiot.

Which I'm not.

Well, most of the time – we all have our off days…

Anyway, this latest stratagem by our shadowy nemesis proved that they were a little more cunning than I had supposed, as by implicating Yarrow in the theft of the book, they had effectively removed her from the playing field, leaving us with no conclusive way of identifying them prior to the ritual taking place.

They were probably hugging themselves in glee, congratulating themselves on how *very* clever they were.

But they had failed to take into account who they were dealing with. As future Helena had stated, I'm a stubborn and suspicious bastard and, like an angry badger, backing me into a corner just makes me more determined to fight.

When we got back to my room, I started to pace back and forth, as this helps me to think. Helena, recognising the expression on my face, left me to it, knowing that once I had worked out what I needed to, I would then start talking.

'Right,' I said, coming to a halt, 'I'm going to talk this through, just to see whether it makes sense. I'm relying on you to be the voice of reason here, so if you think I'm jumping to conclusions or talking out my arse, you need to say, okay?'

'Of course, Alex,' agreed Helena.

'So, we believe our opponent – let's call him Mister X for the time being – planted the book in Yarrow's room, knowing that it would be found, correct?' Helena nodded.

'Okay, so they must have known that once it was found, due to her Geist heritage, Yarrow would not be able to categorically confirm that she had nothing to do with it. This suggests that they know enough about Geist to know that Scrying doesn't work on them. Now, is this something that is common knowledge?'

'Anyone who has studied Scrying would know that, so it IS pretty much generally known,' said Helena.

'Now, this is where it gets interesting,' I said, 'Mister X took Yarrow out of commission, as they were aware that due *their* corruption by dark magic, she could identify them. However, by doing so, they have started a process whereby another Geist, specifically one who investigates "crimes" committed by Geist, will be coming to Oakdene. What's to prevent *that* Geist from identifying Mister X?'

'Depends on how long it takes for them to arrive, I suppose,' said Helena, 'Dr Vayne did say it might take some time…'

'Okay, let's assume that Mister X *knew* that their actions would result in Yarrow being confined AND that a Geist… er… what was that term?'

'*Iarrthóir fírinne*… I think,' said Helena.

'Right, the *iarrthóir fírinne* would be called AND that when they arrived, they would be able to identify Mister X immediately. Now, if they DID know this, they must have been confident that the other Geist would either not arrive *before* the ritual was due to take place, due to bureaucratic red tape, or that if they did arrive before the ritual, Yarrow would be removed from the college for questioning, meaning that Mister X would just need to make themselves scarce on the day the Geist collected her.'

'Let's assume that's all correct,' said Helena, 'What are you getting at?'

'How would they know *enough* about Geist society, specifically how the Geist High Council would deal with something like this, which is NOT common knowledge, unless…'

'…they were a Geist themselves,' finished Helena, looking startled.

'That would also explain *how* they were able to touch the book, as we know the blood-lock enchantment doesn't affect Geist. It all fits.'

'But hang on a second,' said Helena, 'If there was another Geist attending the college, especially if it was one of the other First Years from Watkins or Scot House as we suspect, surely the college would know?'

'That depends,' I said, 'The college was expecting thirty students to arrive on the 1st of September and that's what they got. They would have received the files from their previous school, but if our hypothetical Geist had *replaced* the student who was due to arrive and claimed to be them, who would know?'

'But given the age of the students, surely they wouldn't have transitioned yet?' said Helena, 'Wouldn't it have been obvious that they were a Geist?'

'Only if they were *actually* the age they appeared to be,' I said.

'Are you saying that they may have somehow managed to *alter* their appearance?'

'Possibly. I have a theory, but it's based on folklore from MY world, so it might not apply here… but there is a way to check.'

I reached out my hand towards the bookshelf and said 'Changeling.' Almost immediately, the *Leabhar Scáthanna* jumped from the shelf into my waiting hand, then fanned open.

'Well, I think that proves my theory,' I said, 'let's have a look at what it says… "when encountering *mícheart*, there is the danger that if one is not mentally fortified and protected by the necessary talismans, the corruption can spread, infecting the individual. We refer to these aberrations as **Changelings**. Changelings are especially dangerous, *as they can assume the appearance of others*, masking their true form and masquerading as friends or relatives. However, in order to replace their intended target, they must…." Oh dear God, that's *horrible*…'

'What's wrong, Alex?' asked Helena, leaning forward, 'what does it say?'

'I'm not really sure I want to read it out to you...' I said, holding the book to my chest, a look of disgust on my face.

'Surely it's better if we both know?' said Helena, standing up and walking over, 'Let me see...'

'No, I'll carry on, but it IS particularly gruesome,' I said, 'so brace yourself. Where was I? "...in order to replace their intended target, they must feast upon their flesh, devouring them in their entirety, until not a scrap is left."'

The colour drained from Helena's face and her hand involuntarily covered her mouth.

'Oh my God,' she said, 'that's horrendous!'

'I did warn you it was nasty,' I said, swallowing, 'I honestly think I may actually throw up...'

'So, if your theory is correct...' started Helena.

'A corrupted adult Geist, a Changeling, has replaced one of the students that was due to start on 1st September and in order to do so, they've killed and eaten them.' I finished. 'We knew that whoever was planning on completing the ritual had no qualms in committing murder, but this takes them to a whole new level of malevolence.'

Helena looked shocked, but then a thought must have occurred to her.

'Give me that,' she said, taking the book form me, 'if the book describes what a Changeling *is*, there's a chance that it *also* details their weaknesses...'

She scanned down the page.

'Aha, here we go!' she exclaimed, 'blah, blah, blah... "once *mícheart* has taken full sway, the Changeling is altered both physically and spiritually, resulting in particular substances becoming an anathema to them. The blossoms, fruit and sap of the Rowan tree cause revulsion and the touch of *skiron* is fatal..."'

'Well, I've at least heard of Rowan,' I said, 'but what the Hell's *skiron*?'

Helena looked through the book, scanning the pages.

'It doesn't appear to be in here,' she said in disappointment, 'I guess whoever wrote this assumed that everyone would know what it was...'

I gave this some thought.

'Right, as it's Autumn,' I said, 'there's no chance of getting any Rowan *blossoms*, but we might be able to harvest some berries. What's your tree knowledge like? Would you be able to identify one if you saw it?'

'Not really...' said Helena, 'I *think* it's got red berries, but I'm not sure...'

'I guess we'll have to hit the Library then,' I said, sighing, 'and whilst we're there, it might be worth asking Master Tweed if he knows what *skiron* is...'

Right, Mister Changeling, you may think that you've scuppered our plans, but we're on to you and we have *new* plan.

I'll have you yet, my pretty, and your little dog too...

'*Skiron*?' asked Master Tweed, 'I'm not surprised you couldn't find it in any of the books in the Library.'

After checking to make sure we were the only ones in either the Study Hall or the Library, I'd approached Master Tweed at his desk, whilst Helena searched for a book on trees. As we currently had no way of knowing which of the other students *was* the Changeling, it wouldn't do to advertise what we were looking up, as it may tip them off that we were on to them.

'Why's that, Sir?' I asked, a look of polite interest on my face.

'Well, it's a particularly archaic term and is, in fact, a contraction, which was quite unusual for the time in which it was used,' he explained, 'skiron is a contraction of "sky iron," which actually refers to meteoric iron, which is one of the only naturally occurring forms of iron in *metallic* form, rather than as ore. Prior to the advent of iron smelting, which naturally gave the Iron Age its name, it was the only form of iron available to the Ancients and, due to the fact that it was usually hammered into shape, rather than forged, is also sometimes referred to "cold iron," as no heat was used.' He looked at me in interest, 'Is this something to do with your project on King Athelstan?'

'Not that I'm aware of...' I said, playing along, 'How is *skiron* connected to King Athelstan?'

'Ah, it looks like I can impart some information that is NOT common knowledge,' said Master Tweed, rubbing his hands together with glee, 'such is the life of a teacher, that we derive pleasure from filling the minds of our students with interesting facts... anyway, the connection is the original Vorpal Sword, which, as we've previously discussed, apparently went missing at the same time as the Jabberwock, was made predominantly from *meteoric* iron. It is believed that this contributed to its special properties.'

'Ah, I see... I'll be sure to add that information to my project,' I said. 'So, is meteoric iron quite rare then?'

Well, I've not ever come across any...' said Master Tweed, then paused, 'actually, that's not entirely true. I think that Mr Ware has a bracelet made from it, as I remember noting its unusual design and asking him about it. Apparently, it was bequeathed to him a long time ago. Is there anything else I can help you with?'

I noticed that Helena was waiting for me and tapped her bag meaningfully when she'd got my attention.

'Uh...no...nothing else at the moment, Sir,' I said, 'thank you again for your time.'

'Not a problem, Alexander, always happy to help,' said Master Tweed, 'And I am sorry about this unfortunate business with Miss Yarrow. I know that both you and Helena here are quite close with her and I'm sure once the representative from the Geist High Council arrives, this will all be cleared up.'

'Do we know when they're going to arrive, Sir?' asked Helena, coming forward.

'Not at present, I'm afraid,' replied Master Tweed, 'My understanding is that a formal request has to be submitted, which we have done, then this has to be examined and approved by the Geist High Council, then a relevant *iarrthóir fírinne* assigned to the case, if one is available, who will then join us at the college. It could be anything from a matter of weeks to a couple of months.'

Looking at our crestfallen faces, Master Tweed smiled kindly.

'I'll speak to Dr Vayne and see if she'll allow you two to visit Miss Yarrow in her room,' he said, 'as the Head of Dee House, the welfare of *all* three of you is my responsibility and I think that regular contact with you, her friends, would do her the world of good.'

'Thank you, Sir,' I said, 'that's very kind of you.'

'So, did you get it?' I asked, Helena as we made our way back to my room.

'Yep,' said Helena, tapping her bag, 'a reference book WITH illustrations, so we should be able to locate and identify a Rowan tree.'

She glanced out the window, then frowned.

'Guess we'll have to wait until tomorrow though,' she said sourly, 'it's getting dark, and you know what happened the *last* time we went wandering in the woods after nightfall...'

'Yeah,' I said, 'Not an experience I'm keen on repeating... you haven't got any free periods tomorrow, have you?'

'No, full day, I'm afraid.'

'In that case, we'll have to go after lessons have finished,' I said, 'that should give us about an hour before the sun goes down. Hopefully, that'll give us enough time to find what we need.'

Chapter XXV
A Fruitful Evening

'This one?' I asked, pointing, 'It's got red berries...'

'No,' said Helena, looking at the book on her lap, 'the leaves are the wrong shape... I *think* that might be a Hawthorn.'

After we'd finished our lessons the following day, we had quickly changed into more appropriate clothing and footwear, then headed off into the Arboretum.

Helena was sitting on a tree stump referring to the book we'd "borrowed" from the Library, whilst I ranged about, examining trees.

As neither of us was well-versed in botany, we hadn't realised that there were so many different trees and shrubs that produced red fruit, so whilst we had found several potential candidates, none of them proved to be the Rowan tree we were looking for.

It was becoming a little frustrating, and, due to the fact that in order to examine some of the trees more closely, I'd had to plunge into dripping undergrowth, resulting in the lower part of my jeans now being soaked through, my mood had taken a definite turn for the worse.

'I thought you were country girl?' I complained, 'Surely knowing which trees are which is something you ought to know?'

'Just because I live on a farm, doesn't mean I know anything about trees,' said Helena waspishly, 'It's a sheep farm, you know, rolling green fields and all that. It's not like we have a great deal of trees about.' She looked around the clearing, 'What about that one over there?'

I rolled my eyes, sighed, and made my way over to the one she'd indicated.

'Nope, definitely not,' I called back.

'Are you sure?' asked Helena.

'Of course I'm sure!' I snapped, 'Even *I* can tell what a bloody Holly bush is...'

Somehow, upon turning suddenly to vent my frustration on Helena, I'd managed to get my feet tangled in the undergrowth and teetered for a moment, before falling backwards into the Holly bush.

Helena jumped up and made her way cautiously over.

'Are you alright, Alex?' she said in concern.

'I'm *fucking* fantastic,' I replied, 'Not only am I now *completely* soaked through...' I struggled for a moment in the embrace of the Holly bush, 'I also appear to be stuck.'

'Stop thrashing about and give me your hand,' said Helena, 'I'll see if I can pull you out.'

She put the book down and grabbed my free hand with hers, then leant back, tugging on my arm. I shifted a little, but I appeared to be well and truly lodged in place.

'Wonderful,' I said dryly, 'Not only have we failed miserably to find a Rowan tree, but now I'm jammed in a fucking Holly bush. The Bandersnatch will be *so* pleased to see me again...they're probably tucking little napkins into their collars and licking their lips as we speak.'

Helena covered her mouth with her hand, trying not to laugh.

'You'd best not be laughing at me...' I growled, struggling to get free.

'I can't help it,' said Helena, giggling, 'You look so funny...'

'I thought I heard voices,' said a familiar male voice, 'What brings you two back into the Arboretum, especially as it's nearly dark?'

Mr Ware had appeared from amongst the trees, a questioning look on his face.

'Hello, Mr Ware,' said Helena, 'We were trying to find a Rowan tree and weren't intending on staying out past sunset, but Alex has managed to get himself stuck...'

'So I see,' said Mr Ware, walking forward and looking me over, 'I think we're going to have to cut your free, lad.'

'That would be appreciated,' I said, 'I am quite uncomfortable...'

Mr Ware produced a knife, seemingly out of nowhere, and began to cut away the branches ensnaring me in their prickly embrace. Due to being held pretty much immobile, I couldn't really see what he was doing, but the blade appeared to be quite sharp, as I was soon free.

'You're drenched, lad,' he said, pulling me upright, 'I think you'd best come back to mine to dry out, before heading back up to the college.'

'That sounds like a good idea, Mr Ware,' I said, shivering, 'I am quite sodden. Don't forget the book, Helena – we don't want to give Master Tweed any more reason to tell us off.'

'Oh right...' she said, picking it up, 'Actually, we might need to dry this out a bit too.'

'Luckily for you, I've already got the fire going,' said Mr Ware, 'Follow me.'

Once we'd got back to the Keeper's Cottage, I stripped off my wet coat and jeans and Mr Ware gave me a blanket to wrap myself in, then sat me in a chair by the fire and made the pair of us steaming mugs of cocoa.

'Now,' said Mr Ware, draping my wet clothes over a wooden clothes horse near the fire, 'why were you two out looking for a Rowan tree?'

Helena and I glanced at one another.

'It's for Alchemy class,' said Helena quickly, 'We need some Rowan berries for one of the potions and they'd run out, so we decided to see if we could find some ourselves.'

'Dr Stone has run out already?' asked Mr Ware in surprise, 'I suppose it's lucky for you that I harvested more than she asked for. Wait here, and I'll get some from my stores.'

I waited until Mr Ware had left the room, then looked at Helena in exasperation.

'Are you telling me that you didn't think to check the Alchemy stores *before* we came out here today?' I said, 'if you'd done that, we could have saved a lot of time and effort AND I wouldn't have got soaked to the skin.'

'Sorry, Alex,' said Helena, flushing in embarrassment, 'I didn't realise that they *were* used for potions – I was just making something up to explain what we were doing and that's the first thing that sprung to mind.'

'Well, I *suppose* I can let you off...' I muttered grumpily, 'But you're going to have to make it up to me.'

'And what exactly did you have in mind?' asked Helena, smiling.

'I'm sure I'll think of something... appropriate.' I said grinning.

'Here you go, Miss Morgan,' said Mr Ware, walking back into the room carrying an earthenware jar, 'This should be enough for whatever it is you're brewing.'

As he handed it to Helena, his sleeve pulled back and I noted a heavy bracelet on his right wrist, a dark metallic grey in colour.

Mr Ware noticed my attention.

'Something caught your eye, lad?' he asked.

'Is that the bracelet made from skiron?' I asked.

'How do you know about that?' he said sharply.

'I was speaking to Master Tweed about King Athelstan, and he mentioned that the Vorpal Sword was made from skiron,' I said, 'He also said that skiron was quite rare and he'd only ever seen some when he'd asked you about your bracelet.'

Mr Ware looked at the bracelet thoughtfully.

'I remember Master Tweed being quite interested in this,' he said, smiling, 'he's almost as inquisitive as you.'

'As skiron is really rare, is it some kind of family heirloom, handed down?'

'No,' answered Mr Ware, 'It was given into my safekeeping a very long time ago, by a very great man. I was tasked with looking after it until it was claimed by its rightful owner. So far, they've not come forward, so it remains with me.'

'Master Tweed said that objects made from skiron have special properties,' I said, 'but wasn't able to elaborate. I know skiron's fatal to Changelings, but other than that I don't know much about it...'

'Then you know more than most,' said Mr Ware softly, looking up, 'but sometimes it's better not to know, as it can be a burden.'

'What do you mean? Is the bracelet cursed or something?'

'I think your clothes are now dry enough for you to put them back on,' said Mr Ware, refusing to be drawn further, 'I suggest you get dressed and head back up to the college. I think you've had enough excitement for one day.'

Once I'd got dressed, Helena and I headed back up to the main building, carrying both the book and the jar of Rowan berries.

'That was a bit weird, don't you think?' I said to Helena, 'Mr Ware seemed a bit cagey about that bracelet.'

'Maybe he just didn't want to talk about it,' said Helena, 'You *were* being a bit nosey.'

'I think he's hiding something,' I said.

'You suspect *everyone's* hiding something, Alex. Sometimes people just don't want to talk about personal stuff.'

'I *suppose* you have a point,' I conceded, 'Now, what are we going to do with these Rowan berries? We can't just wave them in people's faces and see if they recoil. We need something a bit more subtle...'

'I've been thinking about that,' said Helena, 'If we create a tincture with them, we can put that into a perfume bottle or something similar, then we could spray it on ourselves and see who reacts to it.'

'A tincture? What's that?'

'Were you not listening in Alchemy class?'

'The last Alchemy class I was in resulted in the Purple Fog of Doom.'

'Ah yes, I'd forgotten about that,' said Helena, 'Do you know that Dr Stone still doesn't know how you managed that? She spent a week trying to replicate your "accident" and finally decided that it was "bloody impossible." Her words, not mine.'

'Impossible stuff seems to follow me around like a bad smell...' I groused, 'Anyway... tincture?'

'In Alchemy, a tincture is usually an extract of plant material dissolved in ethyl alcohol, although you could use grain alcohol, like vodka.'

'And is that something that you have access to in Alchemy? The ethyl alcohol, not the vodka...'

'Um, not exactly...' said Helena, 'The Alchemy store cupboard can only be accessed by First Years under the direct supervision of Dr Stone. I'd need to be a Second Year Alchemy student to have unsupervised access.'

'Well, that doesn't help us then, does it?' I said, then noted that Helena was looking smug, 'Okay, I'm assuming by your expression that you have a way around that?'

'Yes, I do,' she said, 'as we both happen to know someone who IS a Second Year Alchemy student and I think would be willing to help us.'

'Who?'

'Sophie.'

'Sophie?! Really?'

'Yeah, she's really good at Alchemy and is thinking about doing a degree in it.'

'How come I don't know about this?'

'Because, Alex,' said Helena seriously, 'I do actually have conversations with people other than you.'

'That was a dig, wasn't it?' I said. Helena nodded, 'Fair point. But you think she'll help us?'

'If YOU ask her nicely, I'm sure she will,' said Helena smirking, 'she does like you quite a lot, after all.'

'I do have that effect on women,' I said drily, 'I'm surprised you could keep your hands off me once I'd taken my jeans off.'

'You wish,' said Helena, laughing.

'I don't need to wish,' I said grinning, 'You owe me, remember? And I think I know exactly how you can make it up to me...'

After dinner, we made our way up to the second floor and knocked on Sophie's door.

'Hang on!' called a voice, 'I just need to throw something on...'

'No need, I've seen you in your underwear already!' I called back, which earned me a thump on the arm from Helena.

'What?' I said, rubbing my arm, 'It's true...'

'That's not the point,' said Helena, scowling.

The door was flung open, with Sophie shrugging herself into a robe.

'Hi Alex,' she purred, then noticed Helena, 'Oops, didn't see you there, Helena... what can I do for you?'

'Can we come in?' I asked, 'We need a favour...'

Sophie looked puzzled, but stepped back and ushered us in, closing the door behind her.

'Sorry, it's a bit untidy,' she said, picking up various items of clothing and stuffing them into drawers, 'I wasn't expecting company...'

Sophie's room was almost double the size of my room and overlooked the front courtyard, but unlike my room, was quite messy. Clothing was scattered across the floor and draped over the backs of chairs, and books were piled haphazardly on nearly every surface, with a piece of what looked like toast being used as a bookmark in one of them.

However, whilst the rest of the room was pretty untidy, there was one area that was ordered and neat, that being Sophie's desk. Various Alchemical equipment was arrayed across its surface, with flasks and beakers neatly arranged by size. An open case stood to the rear, with several shelves of small, stoppered vials, each labelled in neat, curling script. In the centre of the desk stood a small cauldron, bubbling merrily away, under which was a circular glass tank, containing a salamander.

Sophie noticed my gaze and stepped forward, leaning over the cauldron. She sniffed once, frowned in thought, then took a pinch of brown powder and tossed it into the cauldron, then gave it a quick stir. She then nodded in satisfaction and turned to us.

'I'd just like to point out that I don't *usually* do Alchemical research in my underwear,' she said, 'Prior to your arrival, that...' she said pointing to the cauldron, 'got a little bit vigorous. I'd just finished cleaning up the spillage and was getting changed out of my wet clothes when you knocked.'

'Wet clothes seems to be a theme for today,' I said drily, 'I had a similar issue earlier, although *that* WAS Helena's fault...'

'For which I've already apologised,' said Helena sourly, 'so stop going on about it.'

'Once you've made it up to me, I will,' I said, 'up until that point...'

'Was there actually something you wanted?' interrupted Sophie, 'or did you just come to see me so you could squabble in my room? I get enough of that at home...'

'Sorry, Sophie,' said Helena, 'Alex and I have a favour to ask...'

'Go on,' said Sophie.

'We need a tincture of Rowanberry,' said Helena, 'We've got the berries, but need some ethyl alcohol and, as it's not part of the curriculum, I don't think Dr Stone will let me have some from the Alchemy stores...'

'And I'm banned from the Alchemy lab,' I said, 'So I can't get it either.'

'A tincture of Rowanberry?' asked Sophie, 'That's not something I've come across in my studies. Any particular reason why you need it?'

Helena and I looked at one another.

'We can't tell you,' I said, 'I wish we could, but the less people that know about this, the better. All I can say is that it is important that we get some and once this is all over, Helena will explain everything.'

Helena looked at me with a start.

'Why me?' she asked, 'Why can't you do it?'

'I'll explain later,' I replied, then turned back to Sophie, 'My understanding is that a tincture of Rowanberry is not actually dangerous, but we can't make it ourselves, as we don't have access to one of the necessary ingredients. You do. We're not *technically* breaking any rules here, we're just asking for your help. And we'll understand if you don't feel comfortable doing this and say no.'

Sophie looked back and forth between Helena and I, obviously judging whether we were being serious.

'And if I do this for you,' she said, 'what's in it for me?'

'What do you want?' asked Helena.

'Give me half an hour alone with Alex...'

'What?!' exclaimed Helena.

Sophie started laughing.

'*That* was worth it just for the expression on your face,' she laughed, 'I was winding you up. You've obviously got your reasons for not being able to tell me and, as Alex stated, it's not a dangerous elixir, so of course I'll help. Probably best if you give me the berries and I'll do it here in my room – that way no-one will be the wiser. You can help, Helena, if you'd like. However, given your previous history with Alchemy, Alex, it might be best if you stay out of it – but we may need to borrow Errol.'

'Why?' I asked.

'We'll need to freeze the berries before we add the ethyl alcohol,' said Helena, 'it'll reduce the acidity and make it easier for the essence of the Rowanberries to be absorbed.'

'And my lack of knowledge is one of the many reasons I'm banned from the Alchemy lab,' I said, 'that and the glass-eating toxic purple smoke...'

We agreed that once Sophie had secured the ethyl alcohol, she'd let us know and I'd send the pre-frozen (courtesy of Errol) jar of Rowan berries along with Helena. Sophie warned us that it could take up to six weeks for it to be ready, which was cutting it a bit fine, as we only had about five and half before the ritual was due to take place. But we didn't really have a choice.

Helena was quiet on the way back to my room and immediately turned to me once we'd arrived.

'Why did you say that *I* would explain everything to Sophie, once this was all over?' she asked, 'Surely it would be better coming from you, as you know more?'

'Well, I might not be in a position to explain,' I replied.

'I'm not sure I understand...' said Helena.

'I'll try to explain,' I said, 'but bear in mind this is currently just theoretical, as I don't know for certain. We know that currently there is a plot to perform a sacrificial blood ritual on 17th December which, if successful, will result in this reality being over-written, producing the future that I remember and from which my mind was sent back, correct?' Helena nodded. 'The future version of *you* from this over-written reality will *then* send my mind back in time from this future, May 2020 to be precise, and everything that has happened up to this point will then occur. Now, this is where it gets tricky...'

I paused to marshal my thoughts.

'If I fail to prevent the ritual from taking place, then reality will get over-written, and the whole process will start again. However, If I succeed, there are three possible options. First, everyone survives, and reality continues as it is now, with no changes, other than a hopefully dead Changeling. Second, whilst preventing the ritual from happening, I suffer a fatal injury, which results in my death...' Helena's face had gone white at this, and I could see tears forming in her eyes. I turned away, as I knew that if I looked at her there was chance I'd start crying too.

'Third, I prevent the ritual from happening, but because of this, the future that my mind came from will no longer exist as a possibility. As there would be no future for my mind to come *from*, it is possible that my mind would therefore revert to the Alex that existed *before* I was sent back. In essence, the Alex that you have come to know and care about would be wiped from existence, leaving behind a very confused 17-year-old Alex with a three-month gap in his memories.'

'Are you saying that there's a chance that if you succeed,' asked Helena, 'that you won't be *you*?'

'Yeah, I guess so...' I said, my voice thick with emotion.

'And the Alex who'll be left behind won't know what he's done and... and...' Helena was now actually crying, 'won't even *know* who I am?'

'It's a possibility...'

'Oh Alex,' sobbed Helena, 'Why didn't you tell me all this before?'

'I didn't want to burden you even more,' I said, turning back to her, 'I've already messed with your head enough. I'm trying to save your world, trying to save the friends I've gained since I've been here, trying to save *you*. I couldn't save the woman I loved before, so I'm not about to let the same thing happen again.'

Helena looked up at me through tear-filled eyes, realising what I'd meant by what I'd said and launched herself at me, enveloping me in her arms and hugging me tightly.

Nothing more was said or needed to be.

Chapter XXVI
The Grandfather Paradox

It took a couple of days for Helena to get over the bombshell I'd dropped on her about my possible erasure from existence. However, once she had, she did make some valuable suggestions.

'Firstly, as we know that Yarrow is confined to her room for the foreseeable future,' she said, 'and can only be released by one of the faculty, I think it's pretty certain that Penny is the target of the Changeling, so *you* need to keep a close eye on her, as we might be able to work out which of the other students IS the Changeling based on how friendly they are with her.'

'Sounds like a reasonable plan,' I said, 'especially as you'll be busy with Sophie.'

'Secondly, keep practicing your defensive shield. I know it's pretty good, but extra practice will hopefully make it stronger and there will be less chance of you getting hurt.'

'Okay.'

'Thirdly, you need to talk to the Cat about the mind-wipe thingy. I know you said it's only a possibility, but it may be able to confirm if it *will* definitely happen and therefore *might* know a way around it.'

'I hadn't thought of that,' I said, 'That's a brilliant idea.'

Helena flushed at the compliment.

'I don't want to lose the Alex I know,' she said, 'I like him...quite a lot.'

'I know you do,' I said, 'I quite like him too.'

As Penny and I had resolved our difference, the first part was relatively easy, so I took every opportunity I could to talk to her, making a note of who was in her circle of acquaintances. Unsurprisingly, it was mostly students from Watkins House, other than the ever-present Aubrey, although following on from the events of the Samhain Ball, Aubrey didn't seem to be as much in favour as he had been.

Which he naturally blamed me for, as he seemed incapable of recognising his own part in his fall from grace.

Strangely, rather than confront me about this and threaten me, which I would have expected, he began to furtively follow me about. At least, I assumed that was his intention, as he wasn't very good at it, guiltily starting when I noticed him watching me.

Initially, his inept attempts at spy-craft amused me, but it became burdensome, as his constant presence prevented me from discussing my plans with Helena unless behind closed doors – and even then, I'd have to check the corridor to ensure he wasn't skulking about.

'I really don't know what's got into him,' I said to Helena one evening, as we were talking in my room, 'everywhere I go, there he is. For some reason, he's decided to spy on me. Seems like he's been questioning some of our friends too, asking if they thought I knew anything about Yarrow stealing the book and whether *I'd* convinced her to do it on my behalf.'

'That IS really odd,' said Helena, 'I know he doesn't like you much, but it's almost like he's trying to find some evidence that you were involved.'

'Well, he's wasting his time then, because we both know I wasn't. However, it IS quite annoying having him follow me around all the time.'

'Have you spoken to the Cat yet?' asked Helena.

'No, I was going to do that now,' I replied, 'I was waiting until you were present, as that way you could ask questions that I might not have thought of. It's a shame you can't see and hear it too, as that would save me relaying stuff back and forth.'

I walked over to the mirror and looked into it.

'Cat, are you there?' I called. There was movement in the mirror and the Cat jumped up onto the bed and stared at me.

'If you're going to ask me whether the event is still due to take place,' said the Cat in a bored voice, 'the answer is still "Yes." You do realise that I have other things to do rather than act like some kind of "magic mirror" for you, don't you? And before you ask, I have no idea who the "fairest of them all" is...' The Cat peered around me, 'But your friend there IS quite attractive...'

'Regarding my friend,' I said, 'Is there any way that she would be able to see you?'

The Cat appeared to give this some thought.

'The reason *you* can see me is because of the tachyon particulate clinging to you due to your passage back through time,' it replied, 'Think of it like travelling along a dusty road, with the "dust" surrounding you in a cloud at the end of your journey....'

'So, a bit like the character Pig-Pen from the *Peanuts* comic?'

'Hmm, good analogy...' said the Cat, 'Anyway, anyone in close proximity to you, ideally touching you, *should* potentially be able to see and hear me.'

I turned to Helena.

'The Cat thinks that if you're touching me, you may be able to see it,' I said.

'Are you sure this is not just an excuse to cuddle me?' smiled Helena getting up, 'I've only got your word that this cat *actually* exists...'

'If I wanted to hug you, I wouldn't need an excuse,' I said, 'I'd just do it. Now get your arse over here.'

Helena grinned at me and came and stood in front of me, letting me wrap my arms around her from behind.

'Now what?' she asked.

'Testing, testing, 1,2, 3,' said the Cat, 'Are you reading me? Over...'

'Oh my God...' breathed Helena, 'I can see it...'

'And a good evening to you, Miss Morgan,' said the Cat, 'Nice to finally make your acquaintance.'

'Hello,' said Helena shyly, 'Do you have a name?'

'I like her, Alexander,' said the Cat, 'At least she could be bothered to ask me...unlike you.'

'Um...' I said, 'You have a point. I never thought to ask.'

'It's actually irrelevant, as I don't actually have what you would consider to be a name,' said the Cat, 'and even if I did, I don't think you'd be able to pronounce it. But it was nice to be asked. Anyway, what can I do for you?'

'We have a question for you,' said Helena, 'Alex's mind is from the future, but what will happen to it if he prevents reality from being overwritten? Alex thinks that because there won't be a future from his mind to come back *from*, there's a chance that his current mind will be wiped and revert back to what it was before he was sent back. Is that right?'

'Interesting question,' said the Cat, 'and relates to what is known as The Grandfather Paradox...'

'What's that?' asked Helena, confused.

'Crap, I'd forgotten about that,' I said, 'That complicates things.'

'I don't understand…,' said Helena.

'Basically,' said the Cat, 'The Grandfather Paradox suggests that if a time-traveller went back in time and killed his own grandfather, this would prevent either his mother or father from being born, and thus his own birth, so if he were never born, how was he able to go back in time and kill his grandfather in the first place? It's a paradox, i.e., logically self-contradictory. The same thing *kind of* applies here. Alexander *has* travelled back in time, but if he is successful in preventing the rewriting of reality, then the future his mind was sent back from will no longer exist, so how could it have been sent back?'

'So, *logically* AND *scientifically*,' I said slowly, 'the only way this whole situation will work is if I fail, as that way it will create my future mind to be sent back, but this will result in a recursive time loop, with the events just repeating themselves ad infinitum?'

'Logically and scientifically, yes,' said the Cat, 'However, this is all pure theory, as YOU are the *only* being from the physical timeline that I've ever encountered that has successfully travelled through time, if only mentally. We also have to take into account that as the event you are trying to stop will *rewrite* reality, effectively changing the fundamental laws of the universe, nothing is certain.'

'So, in other words,' said Helena, 'We won't know what will happen, until after it's happened?'

'I'm afraid so,' said the Cat.

'Okay,' said Helena, 'Say Alex's theory IS correct and that his prevention of the rewriting of reality *does* result in a reversion to the original version of Alex from *this* pre-cataclysm timeline… is there any possible way to prevent that?'

'An intriguing question…' said the Cat, 'I suppose that if Alexander stepped *through* the glass into MY realm at the exact moment that reality was due to be overwritten, his mind would remain intact as it is now, as he would be outside of reality and not subject to any of its laws.'

'Then let's do that,' said Helena in relief.

'*However*,' interrupted the Cat, 'Alexander can only enter AND exit my realm due to the tachyon particulate clinging to him. This will be burnt off the longer he remains on this side of the glass and when it is all gone, he would be trapped here, able to see the world he came from, but unable to return to it.'

'That doesn't sound pleasant,' I said, 'What's it like your side of the glass?'

'It's a reflection of your world but would appear slightly skewed from your point of view, as certain things are reversed,' said the Cat, 'If a door is open your side, if would be closed this side, for example. And entities from your world show their true faces on this side of the glass. You, Alexander, appear this side of the glass as an adult, surrounded by a haze of sparkling motes, representing the tachyon particulate clinging to you.'

'If I *were* to become trapped your side of the glass, what would happen to me?' I asked.

'You'd probably lose your mind,' said the Cat simply.

'Then you'd best make sure that you don't stay in there too long, Alex,' said Helena, 'I need you to come back to me – preferably the same Alex that went in.'

'This is all theoretical at present,' I said, 'We're currently planning for a *possible* eventuality, so there's nothing to say that my mind *will* actually be affected by the rewriting of reality. And then we have to consider the logistics of "stepping through" – there will need to be a mirror big enough for me to get through available at the exact moment reality is due to change. As we don't currently know *where* this event is due to take place, how can we ensure *that*? It's not like we can plant mirrors everywhere...'

'Ah, but we don't need to,' said Helena, 'We know that due to the date, the ritual is a sacrifice to Saturn, so it will have to take place somewhere that has *already* been dedicated to him. And as we know it's got to be on the grounds of the college, that only really leaves one place.'

'Which is?'

'The chapel across from the theatre,' said Helena, 'It's multi-denominational, so it's dedicated to lots of gods, as people have different religious leanings, so they have to cater for everyone.'

'Back in my world, they only worship the one god,' I said, 'Well, there are different religions, but they tend to have separate places of worship, so I just assumed that it was a normal church.'

'Just the one god?' queried Helena, 'How weird. What's the name of this god?'

'Um... just God.' I said, 'Well, different religions call him by different names, but the main religion of MY England just refers to him as God.'

'That is so odd...' said Helena, 'Anyway, as far as I am aware, the chapel is the only place that's dedicated to Saturn, so it should be relatively easy to get a reasonably sized mirror in there.' She addressed the Cat, 'Cat, how big does this mirror need to be?'

'Big enough for Alexander to get through, so I'd estimate about four feet square at minimum,' said the Cat, 'and the glass will need to be intact. Any cracks will prevent it being used as a portal.'

'You've said that *I* can cross back and forth due to the tachyon particulate that I've gathered from my journey through time,' I said, 'and you can travel back and forth along the timeline yourself, due to your nature, correct?' The Cat nodded. 'Okay, so how come you can't cross into our world?'

'Well, *technically,* I could,' said the Cat, 'However, a barrier exists between your world and mine that I cannot cross. If this barrier were breached, I could *temporarily* manifest in your world, but these breaches tend to repair themselves fairly quickly. As soon as this occurred, I would automatically be drawn back into my realm. As my true form is not as...palatable to the eye as the one you perceive, it's probably for the best that I stay this side of the glass.'

'So, if I'm *your* side of the glass, I'd see you in your true form?' I asked.

'You would, Alexander,' answered the Cat, 'but I wouldn't recommend it, if you value your sanity.'

'Good tip. If and when the time comes – don't look directly at you,' I said, 'Right, we need to find a mirror of the relevant size and conceal it somewhere in the chapel, prior to the 17th of December. Let's hope that we can identify and disable the Changeling before we need it.'

As the chapel was never locked, due to different religions observing different times of worship, getting into the chapel would not prove a problem. However, we had decided to scout the chapel first, as there was no point finding a mirror of the necessary size and hiding it in there if there was already one place.

This was the first time I had set foot in a place of worship for a number of years, the last being when I'd attended the wedding of some friends in 2015 - my past from a mental point of view, but my future from a temporal point of view.

As with most churches, the interior rose two storeys, with the arched roof being supported by exposed wooden beams. Eight stained glass windows, high above our heads, ran along each of the chapel's long walls, below which were alcoves containing a shrine to whichever God was depicted in the window above. A double row of wooden pews ran down the centre, back-to-back, facing the shrines.

'Right,' I said to Helena, 'where's the shrine to Saturn?'

'Last one on the left,' she said, pointing.

I walked down the nave, glancing at the shrines as I went. Each alcove contained a small altar, with a statue of the relevant deity at the rear and various offerings left in front of them.

I reached the shrine to Saturn and looked it over. The statue depicted a muscular bearded man, in sandals and a toga, cradling a cornucopia in his left arm, overflowing with flowers, fruit and corn, indicating his role as a harvest deity. Various offerings had been left on the altar, including a loaf baked in the shape of a wheatsheaf, a bowl of fruit and a tin of peach halves.

Having satisfied myself, I began to look around the rest of the chapel, looking to see if there was a mirror already present.

'I found one!' called Helena, from back towards the door, 'but I don't think it'll be much use...'

She was brandishing a hand mirror, about six inches in diameter.

'I may be slim, but I don't think I'll fit through there...' I said wryly, 'What's it doing here?'

'Offering to Venus,' said Helena, 'as she is the goddess of beauty, amongst other things.'

Having had a good look around, I returned to Helena's side.

'I think we're going to have to plant a mirror in here,' I said, 'If we lean it face inwards against the wall in the West transept, I reckon it'll just be ignored.'

'The West what?' asked Helena.

'Transept,' I said, 'it's the bit that runs across the nave.' Helena was looking at me blankly.

'The nave is main body of the chapel, running from the doors down there up to the other end,' I said pointing, 'the transept is the bit that runs perpendicular to this, the rectangular area just in front of the curved bit at the top. And the *West* transept is the bit on the left.'

'How do you know all that?' asked Helena, looking puzzled.

'It's something I studied in school,' I said, 'we had to draw the floor plan of a church and label the various bits. Obviously, that bit stuck. I could probably tell you what all the other bits are called too, but it's not *really* that interesting... or useful.'

'I'll pass,' said Helena drily, 'So, where are we going to get a mirror from?'

'Probably the best option is to borrow one from Mama Lucia,' I said, 'She's got plenty and the theatre's just across from here. Although, I think I'll leave that until Friday morning.'

'Any particular reason why?'

'Because I've got the first two periods free, whilst Aubrey will be in Alchemy class along with you, so I won't have to worry about him following me and wondering what I'm doing.'

'Good point,' said Helena, 'There's no point giving him more fuel for his conspiracy theories.'

So that's what I did.

Chapter XXVII
On the Scent

The next couple of weeks were somewhat frustrating, as the date of the planned ritual was creeping ever nearer, and we were no closer to identifying the Changeling.

We knew it wasn't anyone from Dee House, but that still left nineteen possible suspects, nine from Watkins House and ten from Scot House.

As the tincture of rowanberry would not be ready for at least another couple of weeks, we had kind of reached a dead end regarding exposing the wolf in the fold.

However, we had been allowed to visit Yarrow in her room, so were hoping that she might be able to offer a fresh perspective.

'A *Changeling*?!' exclaimed Yarrow, 'are you sure?'

'Alex thinks so,' said Helena, 'and it would explain how the book ended up in your room.'

'It's the best theory we have at the moment,' I said, 'The problem we have is that with you confined to your room, we currently have no way of identifying them. We *are* working on something we hope will help, but it's going to take a couple of weeks, so it might not be ready in time.'

'And you think this Changeling is the one who's planning on completing this ritual?' asked Yarrow.

'Seems likely,' I replied, 'The semi-good news is that because they *planned* for you to be confined to your room, we're pretty certain that you're not the target, as they'll have no way of getting to you. This does mean that Penny's the one in danger.'

'And have you warned her yet?' asked Yarrow, 'You warned me.'

'It's not quite as simple as that,' I said, 'Due to Penny being the Princess Royal, the likely outcome of being informed of a possible threat to her life would be that the college would be swarmed with security personnel, to ensure that she was protected.'

'But surely that's a good thing?' asked Helena, 'If Penny has people watching her to ensure that she's safe, then there won't be any need for you to be involved?'

'Okay, let's assume I leave here and go and tell Penny that I believe there's a possible threat to her life,' I said, 'Even if she doesn't believe me, she WILL report it. Likely outcome is that a security detail will be sent to protect her, along with people whose job it is to investigate and neutralise said threat. The reporting of the threat will be traced back to me, I will be questioned and as there is no *actual* evidence to support this, it would probably result in them declaring it a false alarm and removing the security detail, so we'd be back to where we were before... except for one thing.'

'Which is?' asked Helena.

'I would have been removed from Oakdene and likely "detained," as any attempt to scry me would reveal my... unique condition.'

'Ah, yes...' said Helena, 'I'd forgotten about that. So, if we tell her, there's the possibility that not only will it not do any good, it could result in you not being around when the ritual is due to take place, so you'd not be able to stop it?'

'Possibly...'

Yarrow was looking extremely puzzled.

'Will you two stop talking in riddles,' she said in exasperation, 'What exactly is this "unique condition" you keep talking about? I remember Helena saying you were more than you appeared to be, but what does that *actually* mean?'

Helena and I looked at one another.

'I think we're going to have to tell her,' said Helena, 'It will explain why you can't afford to be scryed by the authorities...'

'Yeah, I guess so...' I said, then turned to Yarrow, 'You're going to have to take our word for all this, because unlike Helena, you won't be able to perform a *visum memoria* on me.'

'Hang on,' said Yarrow, 'Are you telling me that you let Helena view your *entire* memory?'

'Yeah, I did,' I said ruefully, 'Not one of my best ideas, to be honest, as it did cause a few issues...' I reached out and took Helena's hand in mine, then gave it a squeeze, 'but we've got past that now.'

'Is that why you two were not talking for a while?' asked Yarrow.

'Yes, that was the reason,' said Helena, 'it did take me a while to get my head around it. But now that I fully understand the situation, I trust Alex completely... and I hope you will too.'

'Well, you've not lied to me *so* far,' said Yarrow, 'not that I know of, anyway...'

'Okay,' I said, 'I'll try to keep this as simple as possible, as it is a bit complicated. Physically, I am what I appear to be, a 17-year-old boy named Alexander Crowe. However, my mind is from approximately 34 years in the future and has been sent back in time to occupy my teenaged body. Now, this is where it gets a bit complicated... the future my mind has been sent back from currently only exists as a *potential* future, and I have been sent back to prevent that future from ever occurring.'

'O-kay....' Said Yarrow doubtfully, 'Say I believe you... *why* have you been sent back to prevent this future from happening? What's so wrong with it?'

'There's no magic in the future Alex's mind is from,' said Helena distastefully, 'I've seen it. It's... wrong.'

'The ritual sacrifice of the Princess Royal, if it goes ahead,' I said, 'will *rewrite* reality. Everything magical will no longer exist, replaced by cold, sterile technology. There will be no dragons, no sorcery and definitely no Geist.'

'So, are you saying that if you don't stop this ritual,' asked Yarrow incredulously, 'I'll... what, disappear?'

'You, your family, your entire race will cease to exist,' I said softly, 'and no-one will *even* know that you existed in the first place.'

'Oh my God...' said Yarrow, horrified.

'So, you can see why it's *so* important that Alex prevents it from happening,' said Helena. Yarrow turned to me.

'So, why were *you* chosen?' she asked, 'What makes you the best person to do this?'

'I'm not,' I said, 'in fact, I wasn't even the first OR second choice. Unfortunately, the people responsible for this plot, from the future that my mind comes from, eliminated everyone they felt could *possibly* pose a threat to their plans. I'm the only one that was left. I am the basket that all metaphorical eggs have been put.'

'And we know when and where the ritual is due to take place,' said Helena, 'and we've worked out who the target is. The only thing we don't yet know is who the Changeling is. If we can discover their identity prior to the ritual taking place, we can stop them.'

'With you confined, we can't use your ability to sense *mícheart* to identify them,' I said, 'but we do have a backup plan. However, if you could remember *who* was around you when you started feeling ill on the night of the Samhain Ball, it could help.'

'I'll try to see if I can remember,' said Yarrow, 'but there were quite a few people about, so I don't know if I'll be much help.'

'Anything you can remember would help,' I said, 'but don't worry about it too much. As I said, we have a backup plan.'

As we were walking back to my room, Helena stopped me.

'Why didn't you tell her about *your* possible erasure from existence?' she asked.

'I think she's got enough to worry about already,' I said, 'If we don't stop this from happening, her *entire race* will never have existed.'

It took an additional couple of weeks for the tincture of Rowanberry to finally be ready, by which time both Helena and Sophie were fed up with me badgering them every day, asking when it would be done.

'If you'd paid more attention in Alchemy class,' explained Helena, 'you'd know that these things take time… and you probably wouldn't have been chucked out.'

'Fair point,' I conceded, 'so, what do we need to do with it?'

Sophie had supplied us with a couple of atomiser spray bottles, which had previously contained perfume and had been thoroughly cleaned.

'So, we'll decant the tincture into these atomisers,' explained Helena, holding one up, 'They're small enough to be carried in a pocket, so it won't be obvious what we're up to.'

'And then?'

'I *guess* we spray anyone we think may be the Changeling, and see if they react,' said Helena. She looked up and noted my somewhat dubious expression and sighed.

'I *know* it's not the greatest plan in the world, but at the moment, it's the only one we have.'

'I think the *first* thing we need to actually do is smell the tincture ourselves,' I said, 'If it smells disgusting, then everyone will react badly to it, and we'll be no closer in identifying the Changeling.'

'Good point,' said Helena, and held the bottle up to her nose and sniffed.

'Well?' I asked.

'It smells fruity,' she said, 'Here, you try…'

I took the bottle and cautiously sniffed. The scent was familiar…

'It smells like cranberry juice,' I said, handing the bottle back, 'I think we can safely assume that if anyone does have an adverse reaction to it, they ARE the Changeling.'

As we were decanting the tincture into the atomisers, a thought occurred to me.

'I *think* I may have detected a few flaws in our plan…' I said slowly.

'Which are?' asked Helena.

'Well, firstly, I can't imagine that people will take too kindly to being spritzed, as even if we do it surreptitiously, someone is bound to notice,' I started, 'secondly, say we do manage to sneakily spray a couple of people, what happens if they wander off? We won't be able to keep an eye on everyone we've sprayed, so if someone *does* react badly to the scent, we might not be around to see it.'

'Okay, smartarse,' said Helena in exasperation, 'have you got a *better* idea?'

'I *think* so. If we pretend that *this*...' I brandished the atomiser, 'is a new perfume you've developed as an alchemy project, and you need some feedback from other students as to whether or not they like the scent. We can then approach our suspects, get them to sniff it and gauge their reaction. I'll write a list of all the students from our year and pretend to write notes on their reactions. Obviously, we'll try and target our suspects first, but if we include everyone, including our House, it won't look like we're singling people out.'

'That's... actually pretty clever, Alex,' said Helena, 'as well as being a bit sneaky.'

'However, the important thing to remember is that if we DO identify the Changeling, we can't react, otherwise they'll know we're on to them...'

Helena looked slightly alarmed at this.

'They wouldn't try anything, though, would they?' she asked nervously.

'As the ritual is due to take place in nine days' time, they *can't* afford to be exposed before then,' I said, 'However, due to *that* fact, they can't act *directly* against us, as this will not only expose their hand, but also draw unwanted attention. It's likely that if they DO suspect that we know, they'll pull some kind of stunt to take us out of the picture, similar to what they did to Yarrow.'

'So, we're not going to get murdered or anything, then?' asked Helena.

'I would say that's highly unlikely,' I said, with a confidence I didn't really feel. I just hoped that I was right in my assessment of our shadowy foe.

Having prepared a list of the students in our year, we headed down to the Dining Hall, as the majority of the students would be present for the evening meal, giving us our best shot at eliminating a good handful from our list of suspects.

We had decided that we'd approach Penny's table first, as it was likely that the Changeling would be part of her normal entourage or sitting close by, as in order to get Penny to the designated spot on the night of the ritual, we reasoned they would have befriended her and therefore gained her trust.

Sitting with Penny that evening were James Darling, Annabelle Ende, Nicola Quince and Emma Fry from Watkins House and Emma James from Scot House - as the two Emmas had gravitated towards one another during the first week of term and were now pretty much inseparable. As they looked very similar, it was sometimes difficult to remember which one was which.

Aubrey was sitting on a separate table with his two cronies, Ian and Roger, whilst the Mark Levin perched on the end of the same table, nose in a book as usual.

As this fake "project" was supposedly Helena's work, I let her do the talking.

'Hi everyone,' said Helena brightly, 'I was wondering if you wouldn't mind giving me a little bit of help with a class project? It won't take up too much of your time – I just need some honest feedback on a new scent I've been working on...'

'What, like a perfume?' asked James, 'Not sure I'd be much help with that...'

'Don't be so sure,' said Helena, 'I think having a *man's* opinion would be good.'

James visibly perked up at being referred to as a man and he leaned forward.

'Well, in that case,' he said, 'Let's have a whiff.'

Helena sprayed some of the tincture on her wrist and held it forward for James to sniff.

'Hmmm...' he said, 'That's quite nice. Not too strong... smells a bit fruity, like blackcurrant cordial...'

I pretended to make a note of his comments, whilst actually just crossing out his name. One down.

Once the ball had been set rolling, it didn't take too long for the rest of the table to get involved, with the majority of them commenting favourably on the scent, although Annabelle stated that she wouldn't wear it, as she preferred perfumes that were stronger and more floral.

James pulled a face behind her back, holding his nose and pointing at her, which made me chuckle, but earned a thump from Annabelle once she realised what he was doing.

Penny was quite interested in the "perfume," asking what its ingredients were and before I could stop her, Helena has stated that the main ingredient was rowanberries.

She hadn't said it particularly loudly, but a lull in the conversation meant that her voice had carried. Cursing her, I surreptitiously glanced about, to see if anyone had perked up at the mention of rowanberries, but no-one seemed to be paying us more attention than usual... other than Aubrey, who was scowling at me from his table.

'So, that went quite well,' said Helena, after she'd finished speaking to Penny, then noticed the concerned look on my face, 'What's the matter?'

I drew her to one side.

'I know it wasn't intentional,' I said quietly, 'but you *did* just announce the main ingredient of the tincture to all and sundry... which *might* include the Changeling.'

I let this sink in, watching as the realisation dawned on her face as to what she had inadvertently done.

'Oh God, Alex, I'm so sorry!' Exclaimed Helena, 'it just sort of came out...'

'There's nothing we can do about it now,' I continued, 'so we're just going to have to hope that if the Changeling IS here this evening, they weren't paying attention. At least we've managed to whittle down our list of suspects a bit.'

Helena leaned forward to look at the list.

'How many are left?' she asked.

'Fourteen,' I said, looking around, 'As it looks like everyone's heading off for the evening, we'll have to start again tomorrow. We've still got just over a week before the ritual is due to take place, so we've got plenty of time.'

I should have realised that things wouldn't go quite as smoothly as I anticipated, but I wouldn't find out the latest impediment to our plans until the following morning...

As Helena had not shown up for breakfast the following morning, which was unlike her, I'd gone straight to her room afterwards to check on her, but there was no answer, and the door was locked.

I was starting to get a little concerned, so was very relieved when she stormed into Dr Noyce's classroom for double Lithometry, her face like thunder. She threw her bag down on the desk and then slumped in her chair, scowling.

'Right, it's obvious that something's wrong,' I said quietly, 'so you might as well tell me.'

Helena looked across at me, biting her lip. I could tell she was close to tears, so I reached out below the desk and took her hand, giving it a supportive squeeze.

'Tell me...' I said softly.

'*Someone*...' she began, voice thick with emotion, 'reported me to Dr Stone. I had to go and see her this morning and got a right bollocking. Apparently, the "unauthorised" use of alchemy supplies for private projects is not allowed. Not only have I got detention for the next week, she's also confiscated ALL of the tincture we made.'

'Oh shit...' I said.

'Yeah,' she said, 'so, we've now got NO way of telling who the Changeling is before the ritual.'

I gave this some thought.

'Whilst it's not ideal, 'I said, 'it could've been worse. We at least know where and when it's due to take place and who the likely victim is. Whilst the Changeling might suspect that we're on to them, they don't know that we know what they're up to. It still gives us the advantage…'

Or so I hoped. Our elusive quarry was proving to be as cunning and slippery as a greased weasel.

Chapter XXVIII
In the Serpent's Coils

The morning of the 17^{th of} December dawned cold and crisp, something that was all too apparent due to the open window in my room. As Errol was curled up asleep at the foot of my bed, I quickly jumped up and closed it, before retreating back to the warmth of my bed.

I could have attributed my shivering to the cold that ran icy fingers over those parts of my body not covered by my pyjamas, but to be completely honest, I *was* feeling rather apprehensive.

Today WAS the day on which the ritual sacrifice of the Princess Royal was potentially due to take place, which, if I failed to prevent it, would result in the current reality being overwritten and ALL magic being erased from existence.

However, should I succeed in foiling the Changeling's plans, there existed the possibility that whilst I would have effectively saved everyone *else*, there would no longer be a future for my mind to be sent back *from*, so my current consciousness, everything that made me ME, would fade away as reality repaired itself, like grains of sand blown in the wind.

Understandably, I had every right to be a little anxious.

And whilst we had a rough outline of a plan to prevent both the ritual AND my possible erasure from existence from happening, we *were* pretty certain that the Changeling suspected that Helena and I were aware of their presence, even if we hadn't been able to identify *them* yet.

Our shadowy nemesis had chosen not to take any action against us over the preceding week, so they were either confident that we were unaware of what they were *actually* planning, or they were merely biding their time, waiting to an opportune moment to strike.

Either way, we had done all we could possibly do to prepare, so it was just a case of staying alert and being ready to act when the time came.

Of course, unless you're omniscient, have neurotactical wetware or a brain the size of a planet, you cannot "expect the unexpected," no matter how many motivational posters try to convince you otherwise...

The day had progressed without incident, and I was doing some last-minute research in my room, having arranged to meet Helena there around 9.00pm to prepare for the evening's events.

The first sign I had of anything being amiss was the clatter of the key to my room dropping to the floor. I rose from my chair, putting aside the *Leabhar Scáthanna* in which I'd been reading up on Changelings, and approached my door. The key was lying on the floor in front of the door, which was slightly odd, so I picked it up and reinserted it in the keyhole.

Or would have done, had there actually *been* a keyhole to put it back into. I tentatively reached out and ran my finger across the surface, but the backplate was completely blank, with no indication that there had ever been a keyhole in the first place. Reaching up, I tried the handle and was unsurprised to find that it wouldn't budge.

As I was considering this strange turn of events, the open window behind me slammed shut, making me jump. I quickly went to both windows and tried them, but both refused to open or even move. Furthermore, although the moon was full, no light penetrated the room from outside and I could hear a faint rasping noise, although something vast and reptilian was pressed against the glass, its scales rubbing against the outer wall.

It would appear that the Changeling had made their move, trapping me in my room.

I was contemplating this latest development when I heard a muffled voice outside my door.

'Alex? Are you in there?'

I recognised the voice as belonging to Helena.

'Yes, and it doesn't look like I'll be going anywhere soon,' I groused, 'I think *someone* has cast a spell of confinement on my room, as all the windows and door are sealed, and I can't get out.'

'That would explain the glowing sigil on your door,' said Helena, 'I didn't think it wise to try touching it or your door, just in case.'

'Probably for the best,' I said, then paused in thought, 'what does the symbol look like?'

'It's a circle broken at the bottom left, the right-hand end of the break having what looks like the letter V attached and a dot in the centre,' answered Helena.

This sounded familiar, as though I'd seen this somewhere recently...

'Does it sort of look like a snake swallowing its tail?' I asked.

'I suppose...' said Helena dubiously.

'I think I know what it is,' I said, 'but I'll need to look it up. Whilst I do that, check that Yarrow's still safe and see if you can find Penny, but be careful, as I think this definitely confirms that the Changeling knows we're on to them.'

'But what about you?' asked Helena plaintively, 'With both you and Yarrow stuck in your rooms, that only leaves me to try and stop them. I'm not sure I can do it on my own...'

'Let's deal with one thing at a time,' I said, 'go and check on the others and then come back. Hopefully by then, I'll have a plan.'

After Helena had left, I held out my hand and said 'Ouroboros.' The books on my shelf jostled against one another, then one slid free, slowly opening to the relevant page as it floated down into my waiting hands. In the centre of the page was an illustration which matched the glyph Helena had described, so I quickly scanned the contents.

According to Hersent's *Glyphs and Sigils*, I was currently confined by an enchantment which had gone by many names over the centuries but was commonly known as an "infinity trap."

The caster inscribed the ouroboros symbol, usually depicted as a serpent or dragon eating its own tail, on the door to the chamber to be secured. This confined whoever was inside until such time as the caster removed the enchantment, the time limit on the spell expired, or the prisoner somehow managed to escape. It was particular difficult to cast AND also almost impossible to break, as any magic cast nearby was sucked in by the spell, furthering the term of imprisonment - hence the 'infinity' part.

So, not only had the Changeling been hiding in plain sight for the last three months, they'd also been a regular user of the Library, to research both the ritual AND useful spells to ensure they would succeed, as well as stealing one of the restricted books to plant in Yarrow's room.

Suddenly, as though a switch had been flipped in my mind, a series of images flashed past my mind's eye…

…another student already hard at work, surrounded by books and making copious notes. As I walked in, he scowled at me and covered his notes with his arms, as though I was spying on him…

…from the expression on his face and the way he kept shooting glances at the restricted bookcase, it was clear he had been standing there for a while…

…hard at work, with various volumes piled next to him, furiously making notes with a frown on his face. He always seemed to be in here when I came in…

… 'Is your friend alright?' asked a voice…

All the evidence had been right there in front of me, but I'd been so caught up in all the other stuff that I'd failed to piece all the clues together. I now **knew** who the Changeling was…

'Ooohh, you sneaky **bastard**…' I breathed.

And now that I'd solved *that* mystery, which I'd been worrying at like a dog with a bone, my mind was linking together other seemingly insignificant details it had previously registered, coalescing into a fully formed certainty.

Not only did I know what I needed to defeat the Changeling AND where to find it, I also knew how I was going to escape from my room. And all I needed was a little help from my friends…

Whilst I was waiting for Helena to come back, I discussed my plan with the Cat, who confirmed that it *was* possible, although they did state that this could prevent me from avoiding the reality storm should I manage to stop the Changeling.

'I have to admit that I have grown rather attached to you, Alexander,' the Cat said, 'and it would be a shame to lose you. If there is anything I can do to help, you just have to ask.'

'That's appreciated, Cat,' I said, 'At present, I'll just need you to guide me to where I need to be.'

When Helena returned, she sounded out of breath, as though she had been running.

'Yarrow's still in her room and wanted me to tell you to be careful, and wish you luck,' she said, 'but Penny's not in hers. I tried banging on her door, in case she was asleep, but she didn't answer. No-one I asked has seen her since dinner.'

'Bollocks,' I muttered, 'I think the Changeling may have spirited her away somewhere already, but *why* so early? I mean, they need to get Penny to the chapel before midnight, but that's three hours away and the chapel isn't *that* far…'

There was something I was missing, I was certain of it, but the current priority was to extricate myself from the infinity trap, so it would have to be shelved for the time being.

'So, what's the plan? Asked Helena, 'I'm obviously making the assumption that you've thought of *something*…'

'I have,' I replied, 'but I'll need your help.'

'What do you need me to do?'

'Go to the chapel, get the mirror we left in there and take it to Mr Ware's cottage. Make sure you don't drop it on the way, otherwise this won't work. If everything goes according to plan, I'll meet you there shortly.'

'Mr Ware's?' asked Helena, 'Why there?'

'Because Mr Ware hasn't been entirely straight with us,' I said, 'I *told* you he was hiding something, but I've only just worked out exactly *what* it is…'

'And are you going to tell *me*?' asked Helena.

'Not right now, no,' I replied, 'It's probably best you don't know until I'm there too, as I'm not sure how he's going to react.'

'Oh,' there was a pause, whilst Helena digested this, 'Could it be dangerous, then?'

'I honestly don't know,' I said, 'I don't think so, but I'd rather not take the risk. Just take the mirror down to Mr Ware's and tell him that I'm on my way, as there's something I want to ask him. He'll probably want to know what, but as you don't know, you can't tell him. As he knows I'm a nosey bugger, I'm hoping that it'll pique his curiosity and he'll be content to wait.'

'And exactly *how* are you going to get out? You haven't explained that either…'

'I know,' I answered, 'Let's just say that I have an exit that the Changeling had no way of anticipating.'

'Is it dangerous?' Helena asked quietly, 'Could you… get hurt?'

I glanced across at the Cat, who, after some thought, nodded once.

'Possibly,' I said, 'but it's the only way I can think of, and if I don't get out, we can't save Penny.'

'I just want you to know I'm not entirely happy about this, Alex,' said Helena, 'but if you think it's the only choice we have, I guess I'll just have to trust you. However, if you don't turn up in the next twenty minutes at Mr Ware's, I'm going straight to Master Tweed…'

'Fair enough,' I replied.

'Be careful, Alex.'

'I will.'

As Helena went off to fetch the mirror from the chapel, I turned back to the Cat.

'So, how do I do this?' I asked apprehensively.

'Reach out you hand and push *through* the glass,' it said, 'I anticipate there will be some resistance, similar to putting your hand into a bowl of water, but that should be all.'

I swallowed nervously, then reached out my hand towards the mirror. Rather than stopping at the glass, my fingers continued onwards, *beyond* the reflective surface. I could feel a slight tingling in my fingertips, like when you've been out in the cold for too long without gloves and your hands begin to warm up again. It wasn't a pleasant feeling, but I hoped it would only last as I passed through the interface, rather than for the entirety of the time I was on the Cat's side of the glass.

Taking a deep breath, I stepped *through* the mirror…

Chapter XXIX
Through a Glass, Darkly

The first thing I noticed as I stepped into the realm beyond the glass was that the light was... weird.

Everything had a yellowish tinge to it, as though the light had been filtered through an unbleached cotton blind. And the shadows were all wrong - darker than they should have been and shifting subtly, as though whatever casting them was not entirely solid. If you've ever experienced a partial solar eclipse, you'll know what I'm talking about.

The second thing, which was quite jarring, was that the room was reversed. Whilst I had been advised this would be the case, I don't think I'd really mentally prepared myself for this. Navigating this 'mirror realm' would take a degree of concentration, as all directions would be the opposite of what I was expecting, which could lead me to wasting time going the wrong way – time that I couldn't really afford, given that should the tachyon particulate burn off before I managed to exit this realm, I would be trapped here.

I glanced behind me at the mirror I had just stepped through, starting slightly at the image reflected there. There I was, back to my adult form, complete with greying hair and the fine lines around my eyes, yet surrounded by sparkling orange motes, like an updated version of the old Ready Brek adverts from the 70's and 80's.

'Get up and glow indeed...' I muttered to myself.

As I watched, however, one of the motes flickered, then blinked out. This highlighted (pun unintended) that I only had a very limited window in which to get to Mr Ware's, hoping that Helena had done what I asked. Given the reversal of all directions, this *could* present a challenge... unless, of course, you had a local guide.

'Cat? Are you there?' I called.

'I'm waiting for you out in the corridor, Alexander,' came a deeper voice than I was expecting. It was definitely the Cat's voice, but sounded...bigger, somehow. 'I thought it best to wait for you out of your line of sight, as my natural form is not meant to be seen by human eyes and may damage your mind beyond repair.'

'That's very considerate of you, Cat, so thank you for that,' I said, 'Now, I need to get to Mr Ware's cottage as quickly as possible. As directions are reversed, I'm guessing that I'll need to turn left instead of right when I get outside, otherwise I'll end up at the tennis courts... I think. As I will be initially heading for the stairs, which would normally be to the left along the Nursery Corridor, I'll have to turn right, so this is the direction I'll be turning when I step into the corridor.'

'Understood, Alexander,' said the Cat, 'I shall endeavour to stay behind you, providing guidance where necessary. I will also keep an eye on your aura, as you will need to be back your side of the glass before it fades completely.'

'Good point, Cat,' I said, 'Let's get this done.'

Thankfully, my theory that the infinity trap would only confine me in the 'real' world proved to be true, so I just walked out of my room. Progressing through the college was a surreal and disconcerting experience. The layout of the building was reversed, so where my body was screaming at me to turn left, I was turning right and vice versa. It took a great deal of concentration, which wasn't helped by the fact that I could hear the soft padding of paws behind me, which I really shouldn't have been able to hear.

Unless, of course, the Cat was a LOT bigger this side of the glass.

By the time I'd got to the bottom of the main staircase, I had a stiff neck, as when you can hear someone walking behind you, it's your natural inclination to at least glance back.

"Like one, that on a lonesome road,
Doth walk in fear and dread,
And having once turned round walks on,
And turns no more his head;
Because he knows, a frightful fiend
Doth close behind him tread."

Or something like that.

Having navigated the main staircase, which descended counterclockwise in this reversed world, I was disturbed from my reverie by what sounded like muttering coming from up ahead. It appeared to be coming from the entrance hall. As I passed through the main reception, I could see movement up ahead of me – a pair of little legs floating across the doorway towards the entrance to the college.

I slowed and carefully peeked around the door jamb and was confronted by a very strange sight. Bobbing along the ceiling towards the door was a large hairy balloon, beneath which dangled a tiny body, clad in what appeared to be the standard uniform of the college.

Whether it was my sharp intake of breath at this sight, or perhaps some instinctive feeling on the part of the entity, it ceased bobbing and slowly began to rotate towards me.

As it turned, I could see that the large hairy balloon appeared to be a head, but one disproportionate to the tiny body hanging beneath it. There, an ear, and there, spread across the swollen surface of the "balloon," a face. It took me a moment to recognise the face, as I was not used to seeing it spread across such a large surface.

'Aubrey?!' I exclaimed, 'Is that you?'

The balloon-headed entity frowned, looking both puzzled and a little fearful.

'Who are you?' it asked in a high-pitched voice, 'Are you one of the kitchen staff? You're not supposed to be here, no-one's supposed to be here, and I'm not to let anyone out. **HE** told me not to.'

'I'm...' I started to say, then paused.

Based on what the Cat had told me before, this was likely to be Aubrey's reflection this side of the mirror, which suggested that the Changeling had convinced him to wait here (or rather in the entrance hall of college in the real world) to prevent me from leaving, should I manage to escape from the infinity trap. However, as this side of the glass I was in my adult from, Aubrey had failed to recognise me, which I was hoping I could use to my advantage.

'You're right,' I said, 'I'm one of the kitchen porters. I've just been to see Dr Vayne and now I'm on my way home.'

'Well, you can't come out this way,' said Mirror Aubrey, self-importantly, 'I'm guarding the door and I'm not to let anyone out, especially that nasty Crowe boy...'

'Ah, I see...' I said, 'That sounds like a particularly important job. Um... this Crowe fellow you mention – is he a skinny lad with floppy hair?'

'Might be...' said Mirror Aubrey, frowning, 'Why?'

'Well, if it is, I think I saw him the Dee House common room, trying to open the windows. Looks like he might be trying to get out that way...'

Mirror Aubrey bobbed backwards in surprise.

'No!' he said, 'He's not allowed out! **HE** told me so! He must be stopped!'

'Seems to me that if you're going to stop him climbing out the window, you'll have to leave the entrance hall unguarded,' I said, 'Unless...'

'Unless what?' asked Mirror Aubrey quickly.

'Well, it's obvious to me that it's important to that this Crowe fellow doesn't get out, but you can't be in two places at once. I was on my way home, but I *suppose* I could guard the entrance hall for you. That way, you can go and stop him, and if he manages to get past you, I'll be here to stop him. I mean, he's scrawny, so it's doubtful he'd be able get past me, isn't it?'

I could see Mirror Aubrey giving this some thought, his vast brow furrowed.

'A good plan,' he said, 'I'm glad I thought of it. Yes, you stay here and guard the door and I'll stop Crowe.'

'My pleasure,' I said, watching as he drifted towards the reception door, 'I'll keep watch here...'

Once he was out of sight, I quickly made my way outside, got my bearings and headed left. The one thing you could guarantee about Aubrey, be it the real thing or his reflection, was that he was very easy to fool.

'Your aura is beginning to fade, Alexander,' said the Cat from behind me, 'unless you want to be trapped here, you had best hurry.'

Taking the Cat's advice, I took to my heels, hoping that Helena had reached the cottage ahead of me.

I made my way along the front of the college, heading along the road that led to the East Gate (although in this mirror world, I was heading West, of course).

Whilst the air was still, suffused with the weird yellow light of the mirror realm, every tree I passed shivered as though caught in a breeze. I could also hear what sounded like whispering, which appeared to be coming from the trees themselves. I was tempted to stop and try to discern what was being said, as I could *almost* make out the words, but the Cat's warning that the tachyon particulate was slowly blinking out of existence hurried my feet onwards.

I finally reached the spot upon which the Keeper's Cottage stood in the real world, to find that on this side of the mirror the structure had been replaced by what looked like a long barrow, its gaping stone entrance facing towards me. As I drew closer, I could voices echoing from within and could see shadows flickering, as though cast by flames.

Glancing down at my hands, I could see that the remaining glowing motes of tachyon particulate were widely spaced and, as I watched, another blinked out. I didn't have much time left.

I quickly entered the barrow, passing through a long corridor faced with stone slabs, dodging pale roots which dangled from the low ceiling. As I approached the fire-lit chamber at the end of the corridor, the voices I had heard before grew louder and I recognised them as belonging to Helena and Mr Ware.

Or rather, their mirror versions.

The chamber at the end of the corridor was a lot larger than it should have been, given the exterior dimensions of the barrow. A firepit stood in the centre of the room, flames licking from roughly cut branches, casting a warm orange light on the two occupants of the room. One was Helena, who did not look very much different this side of the glass. In her hands she held a glowing rectangle of glass, the mirror I had asked her to bring.

Mr Ware, however, towered above her in all his reptilian glory, a long tail lashing and bat-like wings flexing behind him. He looked almost identical to the Tenniel illustration, even down to the shabby tweed waistcoat that covered his torso.

As I had deduced from the clues my subconscious mind had accumulated, then joined together, Mr Ware was not what he appeared to be. Rather than merely a gamekeeper in the employ of the college, he was THE Jabberwock, the last True Dragon on British soil, revealed in his *true* form on this side of the mirror.

And there, encircling his right wrist, was a brightly shining bracelet, which pulsed and flexed, extruding sharp points which were then reabsorbed. This confirmed my *other* hypothesis.

'Alexander,' came the rumbling voice of the Cat behind me, 'You must hurry – you are almost out of time.'

I made my way swiftly across the chamber, the Jabberwock's flaming eyes narrowing as I approached.

'Don't mind me, just passing through...' I muttered, then quickly dived head-first through the glowing portal held in Helena's outstretched hands.

I tumbled out of the mirror onto the cool flagstone floor of Mr Ware's cottage, landing in a heap at Helena's feet.

'Alex!' Exclaimed Helena, carefully putting the mirror to one side and rushing forward, 'Are you alright?'

'Yeah,' I said, as she helped me to my feet, 'Probably one of the weirdest experiences I've had, but yes, I'm fine.'

Helena looked at the mirror, then back at me.

'You went into the Cat's realm, didn't you?' she asked, 'I thought you were only going to do that when...' she stopped, realising who was listening, 'when the *thing* was supposed to happen...' she finished a little lamely.

'That was the initial plan,' I said, 'but the Changeling didn't give me a lot of choice, and this was the only way I could think of to get free.'

Helena stepped closer and lowered her voice.

'But do you have enough... er... *stuff* left, if you need to go back in?'

I looked over her shoulder, where I could see the Cat gazing out of the mirror at me. It shook its head.

'Yes,' I lied, 'there's enough residue left for when the time comes.'

The Cat rolled its eyes.

Mr Ware, who had been listening to this exchange with a puzzled expression on his face, cleared his throat.

'Now, I don't know exactly what's going on here,' he said, 'but I do know that the pair of you shouldn't really be traipsing around the grounds after nightfall, so I think it best that I escort you back to the college.'

'I'm afraid that's not going to happen, Mr Ware. We've got less than three hours to prevent the death of one of my friends and in order to do so, I'll need that.' I said, pointing at the skiron bracelet that was just visible past his shirt cuff.

'This bracelet? Why?' he said, covering it with his left hand.

Helena looked confused.

'Alex, I know it's made of skiron, which is fatal to Changelings,' she said, 'but I can't see how having that bracelet would be that helpful.'

'Ah, if it was *only* a bracelet, then you'd be right,' I said, 'but it's so much more than that, isn't it Mr Ware? Just as YOU are more than you appear as well...'

'I don't know what you mean...' mumbled Mr Ware, looking uncomfortable.

'I think you'd better explain, Alex,' said Helena.

'You told me that that bracelet was given to you by a very great man, to look after until it was claimed by its rightful owner. You also told me that was a very long time ago.' Mr Ware nodded guardedly. 'However, what you failed to mention was that this "great man" was King Athelstan, and this was just after he'd defeated you, *over* a thousand years ago.'

'What?!' exclaimed Helena, 'What on Earth are you talking about Alex?'

'It took me a while to work it out, as I was concentrating on trying to work out who the Changeling was,' I said, 'But combining what Master Tweed told me about the Athelstan's defeat of the last True British Dragon AND Mr Ware's comments regarding both how he came by that bracelet and my queries regarding *that* picture of the White Horse of Uffington,' I pointed at the illustration on the wall, 'lead me to the conclusion that Mr Ware was not what he appeared to be. If you then add in the first line of the second stanza of *The Ballad of King Athelstan*, then everything becomes clear.'

'I'm not as familiar with that as you, Alex...' said Helena, frowning.

'The first line reads "Beware the Jabberwock, my son!" If you disregard the final two words, break the first word in half and move the comma, it reads as "Be Ware, the Jabberwock" or B. Ware, the Jabberwock. B. Ware, as in Benedict Ware. Mr Ware IS the Jabberwock and *that* skiron bracelet,' I said, pointing at it, 'is the original Vorpal Sword, which King Athelstan bequeathed to you for safekeeping, with the intention that you pass it on to one of his descendants.'

'But...but...' stammered Helena, looking between myself and Mr Ware, 'that can't be right! Are you telling me that Mr Ware is *actually* a dragon?!'

'*Was* a dragon,' said Mr Ware quietly, 'I've been in human form for centuries now – I doubt I have enough magic left in me to assume my true form.'

'That's beside the point,' I said, 'King Athelstan's direct descendant is here, at the college. However, she's been kidnapped by a Changeling, who intends to sacrifice her at the stroke of midnight tonight. We need the sword.'

Mr Ware flexed his right hand and the bracelet flashed once, then flowed down from his wrist into his open palm, extending and expanding from there until it formed into a dull iron sword, about four feet long.

'I was supposed to pass this to its rightful owner,' he said, turning the blade in his hand, 'but it would appear that your need is greater than hers...'

He looked up at me thoughtfully, then obviously came to a decision.

'However, you need to understand what it is you are taking on. The sword can *only* be passed on willingly by its current bearer, it cannot be taken by force. Once accepted, it reacts to the thoughts of its wielder and can form any bladed weapon, which can cut through *anything*, be it matter or enchantment, so you must be careful when you wield it. When not in use, it retracts back into the form of the bracelet you initially saw it as.' He looked me in the eye, 'Are you prepared to accept this burden, as those who are aware of its existence will want to take it from you?'

'I'll only need it to deal with this current situation,' I said, holding out my hand, 'once that's done, I'll pass it on to its rightful owner.'

'In that case,' said Mr Ware, as the sword retracted back into bracelet form, 'I bequeath the Vorpal Sword to your care.'

He reached out and clasped my right hand in his and, as I watched, the bracelet returned to its fluid form, running down his wrist, across the back of his hand and encircling my wrist, where it resumed its solid form.

'Thank you, Mr Ware.' I said seriously, 'And be assured, your secret is safe with us. Isn't that right, Helena?'

'Of course,' said Helena, still somewhat shocked at the revelations she had just witnessed, 'I mean, who on Earth would believe us anyway?'

'Yeah, you've got that right,' I agreed, making for the door, 'Now, we'd best hurry – we have a princess to save.'

Realising what I'd just said, I stopped so suddenly that Helena walked into the back of me.

'Now what?' she complained.

'Do you know what?' I said, a wry grin on my face, 'That's a phrase I genuinely *never* thought I'd ever have reason to say.'

Chapter XXX
Something Borrowed...

'So, what's the plan, Alex?' asked Helena, as we made our way back towards the college, 'We know that Changeling has already kidnapped Penny, but we don't know *where* they've taken her. If we can find them before midnight, we can stop...well, everything.'

'That's the idea,' I said, 'the thing that's been bothering me is *why* he took her so early. We *think* that the likely place for the ritual to take place is the chapel, but what if we're wrong? It's a shame that Yarrow's still confined, because if she wasn't, she *might* be able to track him.'

Helena stopped suddenly.

'Alex...' she said slowly, 'What if we *could* get her out?'

'Master Tweed confined her to her room,' I said, 'in order to get her out, we'd have to break the binding enchantment on her door, and we have no way...' I stopped, then raised my wrist, the moonlight glinting off the skiron bracelet.

'I'm an idiot, aren't I?' I said, turning to Helena, who was grinning, 'Right, let's go get Yarrow.'

As I had encountered the reflected version of Aubrey in the entrance hall and it was likely that he had returned there after my distraction, we decided to sneak back into the college via the Kitchen door.

We made our way upstairs without incident and were soon outside Yarrow's door. I reached out and touched her door with the tip of my finger. As I did so, the confinement charm glowed into life, orange light surrounding the outline of the door.

'Yarrow!' I called out, 'It's Alex. I need you to step away from your door, as we're going to try and get you out.'

'I don't think that's going to be possible, Alex,' came the muffled voice of Yarrow from inside her room, 'Master Tweed was pretty sure that no-one could get in, unless he lifted the enchantment.'

'There's always a way,' I replied, 'you just need the right tools.'

I turned to Helena.

'I think it's best if you stay back whilst I do this,' I said to her, 'as I'm not sure what'll happen when I break the enchantment.'

'Probably best if you raise a shield whilst you're doing it then?' suggested Helena.

'Good idea.'

Concentrating, I summoned a silvery defensive shield, reducing its size to about three feet in diameter and centring it on my left wrist. Once this was in place, I shifted my attention to the bracelet, forming a picture in my mind of the item I wanted it to create. The bracelet flashed and pulsed once, then began to flow from my wrist into my palm, forming a handle, then a shaft and finally, the head of an axe.

'Here's Alex...' I sang, grinning, then drew my arm back and swung the axe towards the door.

As it struck, there was a blinding flash of light and I felt a wave of force buffeting my shield, which flickered, but remained intact. It did cause me to take a step back, however.

'Are you alright, Alex?' asked Helena, cautiously creeping closer.

'I think so...' I said, 'Let's see if it worked.'

I dismissed my defensive shield, then tentatively and slowly reached out with my left hand, pausing just before I placed it on the door handle. When there was no reaction, I grasped the handle, turned it, and gently pushed the door open.

Yarrow was standing wide-eyed on the far side of the room, a look of amazement on her face. Her eyes drifted down to the axe I was holding in my right hand and her brow furrowed.

'How on Earth did you do *that*?!' she exclaimed, 'And where did you get *that*?'

'This,' I said brandishing the axe, 'is the *original* Vorpal Sword, although it *does* look like an axe at the moment, which I managed to convince Mr Ware to lend to me.' I concentrated and the axe returned to liquid form, melting back down until it encircled my wrist, a bracelet once more.

Helena barged past me and rushed into the room, throwing her arms around Yarrow.

'It's so good to see you,' she said, 'we've missed having you around.'

'They'll be time for a proper catch-up later,' I said, looking at my watch, 'we don't have much time and we need your help.'

Yarrow's expression grew serious.

'What do you need me to do?' she asked.

'The Changeling has Penny,' said Helena, 'It looks like he took her about 9 o'clock and Alex thinks this might be because he's taking her somewhere *other* than the chapel.'

'That's my theory, I said, nodding, 'but we have no idea where *else* he might be taking her, so we were hoping that you might be able to track him using *mícheart*…'

'As far as I know,' said Yarrow, 'it only works if I'm in close proximity to someone corrupted by dark magic, so I'm not sure I *can* track him…' She paused, then a thought occurred to her, 'Hang on, how do you know it's a *he*?'

'Alex says he's worked out who it is, although he's not told me yet,' said Helena sourly.

'There wasn't time,' I said, 'I thought it was more important to escape the infinity trap and get the Vorpal Sword.'

'So, who *IS* it then?' asked Helena.

'It's Mark, Mark Levin,' I said, ushering the girls towards the door, 'He was always in the library doing research and he was right next to you at the Samhain Ball when you had your turn – I distinctly remembering him asking whether you were alright, just before you threw up.'

'Now that you mention it, I do recall him being there…,' said Yarrow.

'It's kind of academic *who* it is,' I said, 'unless we can find out *where* he's taken Penny.'

'Are you sure it's not the chapel?' asked Helena, 'We know the ritual must take place somewhere dedicated to Saturn and as far as I am aware it's the only place on the grounds that *is*. I mean, it's not like there's another temple elsewhere…'

'It just seems strange that he abducted her so early,' I said, as we made our way towards the stairs, 'The only reason I can think of for doing that would be that it was going to take him some time to get to where he needed to be….'

I trailed off, as my mind processed what Helena had just said.

'*Another* temple…' I breathed, 'Oh, you sneaky little **wanker**…'

'You know where he's gone, don't you Alex?' asked Helena.

'Yeah, I do,' I replied, 'we need to get down to the lake.'

We were rapidly running out of time, so we hurried down the stairs and headed for the Garden Exit. However, as we made our way towards to the door, a figure stepped into the corridor in front of us from the Picture Gallery, halting our progress.

It was Aubrey.

'I don't know how you manged to get your freaky little friend out,' he growled, 'but I know what's going on. Mark told me everything. I know you're trying to get to Penny and I'm here to stop you.'

'For Fuck's sake, Aubrey!' I exclaimed, '*Mark's* the one who's trying to hurt Penny, we're trying to stop him!'

'I don't believe you,' he said, clenching his fists, 'And this is as far as you go.'

'I really don't have time for your shit, Aubrey,' I said in exasperation, 'Penny's in danger and if we don't get to her in time, she could end up dead.' I flexed my wrist, watching Aubrey's eyes widen as the bracelet formed into a shining broadsword. I pointed it towards him.

'I don't want to hurt you, Aubrey,' I said, stalking forward, 'But you're in my way.'

Aubrey braced himself and began to summon a hex bolt, but as we watched, one of the curtains hanging by the Garden Exit behind him tore itself free, scattering curtain rings onto the ground and launching itself down the corridor towards him.

Hearing the noise behind him, Aubrey had begun to turn, and we briefly saw the shocked expression on his face before the curtain swooped down upon him, binding itself around him and trussing him up like a turkey. He dropped to his knees and toppled to the ground, thrashing as he tried to free himself.

I raised my eyebrows and looked back at Helena and Yarrow, who both looked as mystified as I was.

'Wasn't me...' I said.

'No, it was me,' said a voice I recognised, and Ashleigh stepped into view, 'If what you say is true, Alex, and you've never given me a reason to doubt you, then you don't need Aubrey delaying you. He may be a bit of an idiot, but he IS my brother, so I'd rather you didn't hurt him.'

'Fair enough, Ashleigh,' I said, 'And thank you. I promise we'll explain everything later.'

With our obstruction removed, we ran down the corridor and burst out of the Garden Exit, heading for Oakdene Lake.

We arrived panting at the lake's shore, our exertions temporarily protecting us from the chill December air.

'So,' said Helena, once she had recovered enough to speak, 'why are we here?'

I was still catching my breath, so merely pointed out across the lake, towards the largest island we could see from our vantage point. There, just visible above the trees, was the domed roof of the structure from which the island had got its name, reflecting in the moonlight.

'*Temple* Island...' breathed Yarrow.

'Yes,' I said, 'When I was exploring on our first day here, I remember seeing the island and noting its name, but I never gave it another thought after that, as *why* would I? I'm guessing that it's called "Temple Island" because the building we can just about see IS a temple and I'm pretty certain that we'll find it IS dedicated to Saturn. *That's* where the Changeling has taken Penny.'

I turned to Yarrow.

'I know it might not work at this distance but see if you can sense whether or not the Changeling is there,' I then turned to Helena, 'If the Changeling managed to get Penny to the island, he *must* have used a boat. I seem to recall that student's handbook said something about students being able to use rowing boats on the lake in the summer, so I'm assuming there must be some knocking about somewhere. We need to find one, and quickly.'

Casting about along the shore, Helena spotted a small wooden jetty off to our right, with several shadowed forms nestled against its edge in the water. As she headed in that direction, I heard the familiar leathery flapping of wings and braced myself as Errol descended from the skies and landed with a thump on my shoulder.

'Alright Mate,' I said, tickling him under the chin, 'Just in time. I've got a feeling I might need you tonight.'

'Alex!' called Yarrow, walking towards me, an expression of disgust upon her face, 'I think we can be pretty certain that the Changeling is on the island - there's a horrible smell coming from that direction, which I'm guessing you can't sense?'

'No,' I answered, 'I can't. If you can sense him from this distance, I'm guessing he must have become even more corrupted. That's not a good sign.'

'Alex, we have a serious problem,' called Helena from down by the jetty, 'All of the boats have got holes in them, and it looks pretty recent. Looks like *someone's* deliberately sabotaged them. With no boat, we have no way of getting across the lake. What on Earth are we going to do now?'

'What's he doing?' asked Yarrow, watching as I began to pace back and forth along the edge of the lake, muttering to myself.

'It's what he does when he's trying to work something out,' answered Helena, 'I've found it best to just leave him to it... he usually comes up with something.'

Right, I thought to myself, *we NEED to get to the island. Can't use a boat, as the Changeling has knackered them all, so that's out. No brooms or flying motorcycles, and I doubt Errol could carry me, so flying's out...* I looked at Errol, with a frown on my face, *Errol CAN freeze things, but there's no way he could freeze the surface of the lake to create a bridge...*

a bridge...

abridged*...*

I turned suddenly, looking back towards the college, eyes narrowing.

'That *couldn't* possibly work,' I muttered, 'could it?'

'I recognise that look,' said Helena, looking intently at my face, 'You've had an idea, haven't you Alex?'

'I have,' I said, 'and it's a terrible idea, but I don't see any alternative.' I rolled my shoulders to get the kinks out, then thrust out my arms towards the main college building and began to summon, 'I am going to get in SO much trouble for this...'

There was a brief moment of silence, then the sound of breaking glass echoed across the South Lawn, as several blocky shapes burst from the ground floor windows and started to stream towards us.

Both Helena and Yarrow took an involuntary step back, looks of astonishment on their faces.

'What have you done, Alex?!' asked Helena. Yarrow, who could see better in the dark, suddenly realised what she was seeing.

'Are those *books*?!' she exclaimed.

'This isn't as easy as it looks,' I said through gritted teeth, 'so I'd appreciate a little quiet.'

Helena and Yarrow, mouths agape, watched as hundreds upon hundreds of books – *almost* the entire contents of the Library's shelves (as I'd avoided summoning the restricted volumes – I'm not that daft), streamed over their heads and began to form floating path just above the surface of the lake, leading from the shore to the distant shape of Temple Island.

I could feel sweat breaking out on my brow, as whilst I'd summoned and controlled several books at once, I'd never attempted anything on this scale before. As I strained to keep the books airborne, one slipped from my mental grasp and dropped into the lake, vanishing beneath the surface with a loud splash.

'I won't... be able... to keep... them up... for long,' I gasped, 'So, I'll have to go... on my own...'

I steeled myself, then launched myself forward, leaping on the first book, then the next, speeding up until I was running along the floating pathway I had created. As my foot left each book, I let it fall, concentrating on just keeping just those in front of me aloft.

It was hard work, as although there were less books to control as I ran towards the island, the combination of mental and physical exertion was rapidly tiring me out. The books in front of me were slowly sinking towards the surface of the lake and I increased my pace, hoping that I would reach the island before they dropped.

I almost made it.

I was about ten feet from the shore when I felt the volume I had just leapt onto drop suddenly, so shifted my weight forwards, turning my leap into a dive. The water was just as cold as I had expected it to be, but that didn't prevent my breath from being expelled forcefully from my lungs. I experienced momentary panic as water filled my mouth, until my feet gained purchase on the lakebed and I thrust upwards, spluttering as my head broke the surface. Blinking water from my eyes, I could just make out the dim form of what looked like a rowing boat, tethered to the trunk of a tree, so made my way towards it.

Reaching the boat, I grasped its side and manoeuvred my way along it, teeth chattering, as I knew there was no way I'd be able to drag myself into it. The lakebed rose here, so I staggered from the water, using the rope to drag myself ashore. Once on dry land, I collapsed onto my hands and knees, coughing up the cold lake water.

'That...' I croaked, 'was not fun.'

I heard wooden thump behind me, followed by a chirruping sound. Turning my head, I spied Errol perched unsteadily on the edge of the rowing boat, wings extended to maintain his balance. He had obviously decided to follow me, which made me feel a bit better, as at least I wouldn't be facing the Changeling alone.

Glancing back the way I came, I could see various dark shapes floating on the surface of the water, the remains of Oakdene's library now reduced to water-logged pulp. Looking towards the college, I could see that the Library's windows were now alight, as were other windows of the college and two stick figures, which I assumed were Helena and Yarrow, waving their arms on the shore. I clambered to my feet and waved my arms, hoping that Yarrow's night vision would allow her to see that I was alright.

I checked my wrist, relieved that I hadn't lost the Vorpal Sword after my unscheduled dip in Oakdene Lake, even though it did appear that one of my shoes had been consigned to its watery depths. I pulled the other one off, as limping about in a single shoe probably wouldn't increase my chances of sneaking in on the Changeling, then looked about.

Temple Island had clearly not been visited in some time, as the majority of the ground beneath the low hanging trees was overgrown. However, leading from where the boat had been tied up, a path had been formed, the vegetation along its perimeter curled up and blackened, as though rotted.

I gingerly stepped forward into the gloomy tunnel, cursing quietly as something sharp pierced the sole of my right foot, going straight through my water-logged sock. I lifted my foot up, probing in the semi-darkness to see what it was I had trodden upon. There, attached to the underside of my foot by its thorny stem, was a black silk rose...

Chapter XXXI
Ill Met By Moonlight

Now that I definitely knew that Penny was here on the island, I hastened along the path, trying not to make too much noise as I approached what we assumed was the "temple." As the vegetation had not been cleared back very far, there was limited headroom, so Errol stalked along the ground behind me.

I could just about make out the walls of the temple ahead of me, shrouded in ivy, but there appeared to be some kind of obstruction in front of the entrance. As I drew closer, I discovered that it was a large mirror, angled backwards away from the doorway.

Looking above the mirror, I could see that the foliage above it had also been cleared to the treetops, allowing light from the moon above to be reflected into the temple. I could see the distinctive flickering of sprite lanterns from within, so wasn't entirely sure why this had been done, but realised that I would have to be careful manoeuvring myself past the mirror, as disturbing either the mirror or interrupting the reflected light could alert the Changeling to my presence.

Motioning Errol to stay outside, I carefully stepped through the angled gap, hugging the wall as to reduce my profile, and hoping that the flickering from the sprite lanterns would mask any changes to the reflected moonlight.

The interior of the temple was round, with a low wall circling the perimeter, forming a balcony looking down into the main room of the building, which appeared to be below ground level. Two sets of stone steps led down to the tiled floor below, one immediately in front of the entrance and the other opposite, on the far side. I quickly ducked down behind this wall, then waited listening, to see if my presence had been detected. I could hear a low muttering coming from the floor below me, as well as what sounded like whimpering, so cautiously raised my head above the top of the wall, to get a better view.

In the centre of the floor was a stone altar, upon which Penny had been securely tied, a gag across her mouth, her eyes wide with fear. Suspended above her was *another* large mirror, also angled at 45 degrees, which reflected the moonlight from outside down upon her, bathing her in silvery light. Five sprite lanterns had been placed equidistant around the altar and a shadowy form, clutching a sheaf of papers was pouring some kind of powder along the floor. I looked closer and realised that the powdered lines were forming a pentagram, with sprite lanterns positioned at the points of the star.

I ducked back down, then concentrated on the skiron bracelet, watching as it formed into a short sword in my hand. As I did this, the low muttering ceased.

'So, it would appear that we're no longer alone, Princess,' came a rasping voice from below, 'and from the stench, they have armed themselves appropriately...'

'Bollocks,' I muttered, 'so much for the element of surprise...'

'I'm assuming that you've come here to try and stop me,' continued the voice, 'and you can hardly do that if you're skulking in the shadows now, can you? So, you might as well come out...'

The Changeling had a valid point and *seemed* unconcerned that there was someone there, but as they were attempting to draw me out, that suggested that the confidence I could heard in his voice was false. From my understanding, the ritual *needed* to be completed by the stroke of midnight, which was now only half an hour away. In order to do so uninterrupted, the Changeling would need to deal with my unforeseen presence before then. I could almost guarantee that if I stepped into view, I would get a hex bolt between the eyes, which would seriously hamper my attempt to prevent reality from being overwritten.

I knew that confronting the Changing directly, even though I was armed with the Vorpal Sword AND my defensive shield was almost impenetrable, was *not* the sensible option.

Fools rush in, and all that.

So, what I needed was an *indirect* plan of action. How could I disrupt the ritual, but without exposing myself or Penny to harm?

Then I remembered what Helena had said back in the Study Hall, when we were trying to work out why the 17th of December was significant.

'The *light* of the full moon is supposed to enhance any sorcery performed...' I breathed, looking back towards the entrance. *That's* why he'd set up the mirrors, as he needed Penny to be bathed in the light of the full moon in order for the ritual to succeed.

I scrambled towards the entrance, mentally commanding the Vorpal Sword to alter its form, as I needed something more suitable for wholesale destruction.

'Leaving so soon?' echoed the grating voice from behind me, amusement evident in its tone, 'I assume you've realised that your actions would have been futile?'

'Not at all, Mark, or whatever your name really is,' I called back, 'I've just had a *smashing* idea...'

I gripped the haft of the axe with both hands, raised it above my head and swung it down, hard. The blade of the axe impacted on the angled surface and there was a bright flash of light, a loud cracking noise and the mirror split down the centre, then collapsed into two pieces, shattered glass tumbling from the ruptured frame.

'*That's* the way to do it,' I said, grinning.

'You little shit!' shouted the voice from behind me and I felt something snaking around me, entwining my body and limbs, lifting me off the ground. I was able to briefly glance down before my head was restrained, realising that I had been engulfed by the woody vines of the ivy that covered the temple. The vines above me twisted and I was rotated, the frowning visage of the creature that was wearing Marks' face coming into view.

'Well, well, well,' he said, 'Alexander Crowe. I thought I recognised the voice. I'll have to admit that I'm impressed that you managed to escape the infinity trap I set for you, even if I'm not exactly certain *how* you managed it.' The Changeling looked down at the axe still grasped in my hand, 'and you seem to have acquired a genuine vorpal blade forged from skiron from somewhere...' He twitched his hand and one of the vines encircled my wrist, tightening until I had no choice but to drop the axe, 'which I think we'll leave here.'

As the axe tumbled from my numb fingers, it pulsed, returning to bracelet form as it dropped to the ground.

He looked me directly in the face, and I could see madness lurking behind his eyes.

'I don't know how you worked out what I was up to,' he said, an amused grin on his face, 'and frankly, I don't care. And whilst you may *think* the destruction of this mirror has stopped me, it is merely a minor delay, as I anticipated that one or more mirrors may get damaged in transit and therefore brought some spares.' He paused, cocking his head on one side.

'It would be far too easy to kill you now, and who would be there to witness my triumph? So, I've decided to give you a break... '

He grinned savagely, then twisted his right hand, 'the leg, I think.'

167

I felt the vines move around my body, then with a sudden wrench, the vines pulled in opposite directions, breaking my left leg. White hot pain filled my head and I let out an involuntary scream, tears filling my eyes.

I must have blacked out for a moment, as when I next opened my eyes, I was no longer outside, but suspended against the interior wall of the temple to left of the door, bound in ivy.

A dull throbbing was coming from my leg, sending out pulses of pain and I felt rather sick. Having suffered a broken a bone only once before, when I'd misjudged the weight of a cabinet that someone had left in my way and managed to drop it on my foot, I recognised the symptoms. Thankfully, as I was not putting any weight on the leg I was assuming was broken, I had only briefly passed out and the pain was... manageable.

I couldn't see the Changeling but could hear muttering and the sound of something heavy being moved outside, then moonlight streamed in through the door, striking the suspended mirror and illuminating Penny once more. The light shifted as the Changeling made his way back inside, rubbing his hands together.

He turned to look up at me and I started, as the face looking up at me was no longer Mark's, but gaunt and pale, the dark, hollow eyes feverish with excitement and the mouth stretched in a rictus grin. Looking closer, I could see that he was now also taller, but painfully thin.

'As I no longer needed to maintain my ruse,' said the Changeling, 'I took the opportunity to resume my real form. It certainly made positioning the mirror easier, as Mark's body was quite weak, although...' He licked his lips, 'he *was* quite tasty.'

He turned away from me and started to make his way down the steps.

'Now that the interruption has been dealt with and everything is in place,' he said, running his finger along the recumbent form of Penny, who flinched from his touch, 'we merely need to wait until the appointed hour...'

He bent down behind the altar, then stood, holding a pocket watch in one hand and a sharp knife in the other.

'As no doubt your little friends have alerted the staff of the college as to what they *think* is going on, you are probably thinking that reinforcements will arrive *just* in the nick of time to save you both.' The Changeling looked up at me, his dark eyes boring into mine, 'You are mistaken. Time is on MY side.'

It would have been easy to give into despair at this point, as the Changeling appeared to have the upper hand. However, whilst he may have managed to restrain me *physically*, he couldn't stop my mind from working and I believed I *may* have detected a fundamental flaw in his plan.

In order to complete the ritual, the Changeling needed to meet specific criteria – he must sacrifice someone of a highly magical bloodline, under the light of the full moon, *exactly* at the stroke of midnight. The moonlight merely increased the chances of the ritual succeeding, the condition that the whole plan hinged upon was the *time*. All I needed to do was prevent the Changeling from killing Penny at the specified time.

That would be simply a matter of casting a defensive shield over Penny, but I couldn't do that unless I was free from the vines restraining me. If I still had the Vorpal Sword, I could have easily cut myself free, but that was lying on the ground outside.

I was interrupted from my thoughts by a chirruping noise from below me. Looking down, I could see that Errol had crept inside and was squatting just below me, looking up at me, a quizzical expression on his face. Lying at his feet was the skiron bracelet, which I had no way of reaching from where I was.

But the Vorpal Sword was *not* the only way I could get free…

I twisted my hand, until I had managed to point my finger at the vines surrounding me. 'Errol, *Elsa*…' I hissed.

Errol leapt into the air, hovering in front of me, then opened his mouth. I closed my eyes, hearing the distinctive hissing sound as Errol breathed all over me, coating me with his freezing breath. I could feel my waterlogged clothing becoming brittle, something I'd not considered when I came up with this idea but hoped that the vines restraining me would be affected in the same way.

I flexed my arms and heard a cracking noise, as the vines wrapped about my arms dropped away in pieces. I reached down and wrenched those encircling my torso away, feeling my body drop slightly as the support was removed.

'Oh crap…' I said as I began to fall. I twisted as best as I could, as if I landed on my broken leg, the pain would disable me for some time, time I couldn't afford to lose.

I landed with a thump on my side, my hands gripped about my left leg, trying to stop it from impacting on the ground. I grit my teeth as a wave of pain shot up my leg but seemed to have prevented any further damage and at least I was still conscious. I scrabbled out with my hand, searching for the skiron bracelet, a feeling of relief washing over me as my fingers gained purchase on the heavy links.

'You are beginning to get on my nerves, Alexander,' growled the Changeling, 'I probably should have killed you when I had the chance.'

I poked my head over the top of the wall and could see the Changeling had positioned the knife across Penny's throat, waiting for the exact moment to end her life. He was too close for me to effectively block his strike with a shield, so I needed a distraction.

I looked behind me.

'Errol, get him!' I called, watching as the tiny blue dragon took to the air and swooped over the wall, diving towards the Changeling.

The Changeling took an involuntary step back as Errol swooped towards his face, giving me the opportunity I needed. I concentrated, covering both Penny and the altar she was laid upon with a shimmering dome of silver light.

Let's see you get through *that*, I thought.

The Changeling slashed at Errol with the knife he held, nicking one of his wings and causing him to spiral from the air, landing with a thump on the tiled floor below.

'That's taken care of *that* distraction,' the Changeling spat, then looked at the watch he held, 'And I still have time to dispose of you AND complete the ritual…'

I looked down at the skiron bracelet I held in my hand, remembering what Mr Ware had told me about the properties of the Vorpal Sword, then looked at the mirror suspended above the altar.

'It will cut through *anything*…' I breathed, then quickly commanded the bracelet to form the shape in my mind. The bracelet pulsed, then swiftly became what I'd imagined, five curved arms radiating from a central hub. I flicked my wrist and five curved blades popped from the ends of each arm.

I was now holding probably the coolest weapon ever to grace the silver screen in the 1980's – the Glaive, from *Krull*.

I raised my arm, took aim, and launched the Glaive. The Changeling's eyes had widened as I'd formed the weapon, and he threw himself down behind the altar as soon as it left my hand. The Glaive spun through the air with a whirring sound, spiralling around the perimeter of the temple, before angling upwards and striking the centre of the suspended mirror, where it lodged, cracks radiating out from the point of impact.

There was a moment of silence, then I could hear rasping laughter coming from the floor below.

'Not only did you miss,' said the Changeling, climbing back to his feet 'but you've also thrown away your only weapon. Such a pitiful attempt...'

'I never miss what I'm aiming for,' I said coolly, 'Cat, take him...'

The glass from the suspended mirror exploded outwards, as *something* burst through from the other side with a bestial roar.

The Vorpal Sword could cut through anything, *including* the barrier between our world and that of the Cat. True, the Cat could not remain in our world before the barrier repaired itself and drew it back to where it belonged, but I was counting on it being here just long enough.

Remembering what the Cat had said about its true form, I shielded my eyes, but not before I caught a glimpse of something large and raw looking, speckled with mirrored shards, leaping across the room towards the Changeling.

I limped along towards the steps using the wall to hold me up, being careful to maintain the shield around Penny. The mingled sound of screams and snarling met my ears, but with a tearing sound, the screaming suddenly faded, replaced by gurgling and the slithery sound of something wet being dumped upon the floor.

I *really* did not want to see what.

Of course, averting my eyes from whatever was happening on the far side of the room was not the most sensible option when attempting to negotiate steps with a broken leg, causing me to try and place my foot on a step that wasn't actually there. This resulted in me tumbling down the steps and ending up in a screaming heap, black spots appearing before my eyes. Panting, I grit my teeth, rolled on to my stomach and dragged myself towards the altar, pain pulsing up my leg.

The defensive shield had popped out of existence after my fall, and I could hear Penny sobbing above me. I looked up and could see the Glaive still embedded in the wooden back of the mirror's frame, so reached out my hand and summoned it. It twitched, then worked its way free, spinning down in a slow circle until I snatched it from the air. I used my left arm to lever myself up to surface of the altar, panting with exertion, sweat beading on my brow. Darkness was encroaching on the edges of my vision, and I could feel my consciousness ebbing.

I shook my head to clear my vision, then concentrated on the Glaive, which pulsed, then reformed as a dagger, which I used to cut through the ropes binding Penny to the altar. She sat up, tear tracks streaking the grime on her face and pulled the gag from her mouth.

She then launched herself forward, wrapping her arms around me, sobbing.

'It's alright,' I croaked, stroking her hair, 'You're safe now.'

'Alexander,' came the rumbling voice of the Cat, 'I can feel the barrier reforming, so will soon be drawn back into my realm. I have dispatched your foe, so you are no longer in any danger. As the tachyon particulate has completely burnt off, you will no longer be able to perceive me, so this is sadly farewell. I hope that you remain as you are, but nothing is ever certain, in either this world or mine.'

Penny had begun to turn when she heard the voice of the Cat, but I held her head.

'Best if you don't look,' I said, 'it's not something you want to see.'

There was movement behind us, and then the looming presence of the Cat was gone.

I could feel my mind drifting, images forming in my mind of everything I had experienced since being thrust back in time, then dissolving, like film left exposed on a projector for too long.

I had successfully foiled the plot to sacrifice Penny, which meant that reality would now not be overwritten, Yarrow and her Geist brethren would not be wiped from existence and magic would continue to exist in this world.

However, that did mean that the future that my mind had been sent back from no longer existed as a possibility, so it was probable that all my memories, everything that made me ME would fade away, as the Alex of this world returned to what he was before I occupied his body.

And I'd not even had a chance to say goodbye to my friends.

My consciousness was fading. Whether this was due to the pain from my broken leg or reality restoring the status quo, I couldn't be certain, but there was something I needed to do before that happened.

'Penny, listen to me,' I said urgently, 'This is important. You must tell them what happened, tell them everything and... and...' I gulped, blinking back tears, voice thick with emotion, 'and tell Helena that I'm sorry.'

'What?! No!' she wailed, 'You can tell them, Alex! Alex, wake up! Alex...'

I could feel her shaking me, but this, along with her voice, faded as darkness enveloped me, carrying me away in its embrace.

And once again, I was falling backwards, away from the light...

Chapter XXXII
Second Chances

After floating for an indeterminate time in warm, featureless darkness, I could feel a slight tugging, as though my body was reeling my mind back in from wherever it currently was.

I initially resisted, as I was genuinely scared as to what would confront me when I finally opened my eyes. I appeared to have all of my memories intact, but that might just mean that everything I had experienced had merely been a construct of my subconscious mind and I would wake up back in my adult body, in the future I believed I had left behind.

Which was a depressing thought, because it would mean that everything that I had experienced and done whilst *there* was completely worthless.

As I surfaced from unconsciousness, I began to sense my body, which felt heavy and numb. However, I couldn't feel any pain from my leg, which I fervently hoped was because I was dosed up with painkillers, rather than returning to a body whose leg had never been broken in the first place.

I knew that at some point I *would* have to open my eyes, but for the time being I was content to keep them closed, existing like Schrödinger's Cat in neither one state nor another.

However, a couple of things prevented me from remaining like this.

Firstly, my bladder was indicating that as some point in the very near future, it would need to be emptied, unless I wanted to lie in a pool of my own urine. Secondly, my ears had detected a noise close by, which sounded like the pages of a book being turned.

Whilst I vaguely recalled that St. Peter was supposed to look up your name in a book before allowing you admission to Heaven, I seem to remember that having left your mortal form behind you were no longer subject to bodily functions, so unless there was a public toilet just outside the Pearly Gates, I was fairly certain that I wasn't dead.

'I appreciate that you have only just regained consciousness, Mr Crowe,' said a male voice that seemed somewhat familiar, 'but there are important matters we need to discuss before I allow those waiting outside to enter.'

As whoever this man was knew I was awake, I really had no choice but to open my eyes and discover what my current situation *was*. With a feeling of trepidation, I forced open my gummy eyes and looked around.

I appeared to be lying in a bed in a high-ceilinged room that I did not recognise. Light streamed in from several tall, arched windows positioned at the foot of the bed. Given the quality of the light, I estimated that it was mid-morning, but I had no way of knowing for sure.

I raised my arms from where they had been lying on the bedspread, noting that they were the slim arms of my teenaged self, and there, encircling my right wrist, were the dull, grey links of the bracelet that was the Vorpal Sword in its passive form.

I felt a wave of relief wash over me.

It would appear that my mind had **not** been wiped from existence, as I had theorised *might* happen, and I remained as I had been prior to the point in which reality was due to be overwritten.

I looked over to my right, where the voice had come from and was surprised to see that the owner of the voice was the King, who was perched on a wooden chair, a familiar book spread across his lap – my copy of the *Leabhar Scáthanna*.

He noticed my gaze and gave me a wry smile.

'As you have been asleep for some time, I needed something to occupy myself until you regained consciousness,' he said, looking down at the book, 'And whilst I have *heard* of the *Leabhar Scáthanna*, this is the first time I have actually seen a copy, so I couldn't resist taking a look.'

He carefully placed the book on the floor beside the chair, then leaned forward, a frown upon his face.

'How are you feeling?' he asked.

'Um...' I gave this some thought before answering, 'Not too bad, I think. I don't seem to be experiencing any pain from my leg, which I'm assuming is because I've been given something for it.' Then I remembered to whom I was speaking, 'Er... your Majesty.'

'I believe that Dr Stone has reset your leg and dosed you with the appropriate medication,' said the King, eyes twinkling, 'although you do not appear to be one of her favourite students, for some reason...'

As I had been recovered from Temple Island, returned to the college, and received medical treatment AND it appeared to be mid-morning, at *least* nine hours must have passed since the events of the (possibly) previous evening.

As you've probably gathered by now, I don't like not knowing what's going on, and wanted to question the King extensively, so I could fill in the gaps. However, as I wasn't sure how much the King knew and what my current status *was*, i.e. how much trouble I was in, I chose to ask a question that I knew he would definitely answer.

'Where's Penny? Is she alright?' I asked.

'Given the extensive property damage you caused last night and the numerous college rules that you have broken, I find it interesting that your first question relates to the condition of my daughter,' said the King, 'However, I am unsurprised, as having spoken to both your teachers and your friends, it does appear that you have a tendency to put others before yourself. To answer your question, Penny is currently in her room and whilst a little battered and bruised, physically, she appears to be fine. What lasting effects the trauma she suffered last night will have on her remains to be seen, but she has been asking after you, as she was concerned when you lapsed into unconsciousness, which would suggest that she is better than could be expected.'

He paused, marshalling his thoughts.

'Had you not intervened, I could have lost her,' he said, his voice thick with emotion, 'Penny's mother, my wife, passed away a number of years ago and had I lost Penny too, I'm not sure what I would have done. But you would know all about that, having lost your *own* wife...'

My wife? How did he *know* that?

'Yes, Mr Crowe, I am aware of your... *unique* situation,' continued the King, 'When I questioned Miss Morgan, the tale she told was, in parts, frankly quite unbelievable. However, it was clear that she believed it was true and, given the nature of the situation, I took it upon myself to verify this information using *Visum memoria*. Whilst generally this kind of intrusion is considered... *impolite*, I felt that the situation warranted it.'

'Ah, I see...' I said, 'So, what happens now? Is it off to the Tower for me, to be questioned by serious-looking men in suits? Or to a research facility, to be prodded and probed?'

The King looked startled by this question.

'Why would you think that?' he asked.

'Well, in my current state, I shouldn't exist,' I said, 'I'm an anomaly, a time-displaced consciousness, from a reality that is no longer going to *be*. My head is filled with knowledge of that reality – doesn't that mean I'm a security risk? Wouldn't the Order of Vulcan want to get their hands on me and extract this information for their use?'

The King considered this, then smiled.

'I understand your concerns, Mr Crowe, but I really don't think that is the case,' he said, 'From viewing your memories, I believe that in the reality you come from, you have a device called a "fridge," which provides the same functions as the iceboxes we have here, correct?'

I nodded.

'So, were you provided with the necessary components and tools, could you construct one of these "fridges"?' he asked.

'Er… no,' I said, 'That would be beyond my capabilities.'

'Exactly,' said the King, 'The knowledge you have of this… *alternate* reality is from living within in. But it is not *practical* knowledge. You would know how to operate the technology from your reality, but you could not provide detailed instructions on how to replicate it.'

'So, I'm useless to the Order of Vulcan due to being… useless?' I asked.

'Well, I wouldn't have put it in quite those terms,' said the King, chuckling, 'but essentially that is the case. Whilst the Order of Vulcan may be interested in getting hold of you, they would first have to have knowledge of your existence. At present, only a select few are aware of your unique condition, myself included. And I have no intention of revealing this and I am certain that your friends will not either. These fanatics have, up to this point, been a minor irritation, but now that they have made this… *personal*, I will ensure that my considerable resources are focused on stamping them out.'

I have to admit to being somewhat relieved by this, as I had been imagining a future in which I was consigned to a small cell, buried deep under the Tower of London, scratching the days on the wall with a blunt spoon.

'Whilst I am having difficulty in appreciating the enormity of what your failure would have resulted in,' continued the King, 'I do know that *I* owe you a debt of gratitude which cannot be adequately repaid. If not for your actions, I would have not only lost my daughter, but also my existence, and that of my country. Furthermore, you did this with the full knowledge that you were potentially risking both *your* life AND *your* continued existence should you succeed. I therefore feel that you should be rewarded in some fashion, but am unsure as to what form this reward should take…'

'A reward? For me?' I exclaimed, 'That's not really necessary. I mean, the fact that I'm still here and still *me* is enough. I don't need anything else. Besides, I should be giving YOU something…'

I held up my wrist, from which hung the dull skiron bracelet.

'I believe *this* is rightfully yours,' I said.

The King leaned forward.

'And this would be the *original* Vorpal Sword, I take it?' asked the King, then held up his own wrist, where an almost identical bracelet hung, 'As you can see, I have one of my own. It may merely be a copy of the original, but it is a superior copy. Being King does have some perks, after all. For the time being, I believe that you should retain ownership of the original. You have earned the right to carry it, as you used it in defence of your future Queen. But this still begs the question of a suitable reward…'

'As I said before, I don't need a reward.' Then a thought occurred to me, 'however, I *may* have inadvertently destroyed the college library...'

'Say no more,' said the King, smiling kindly, 'I shall speak to Master Tweed and see what we can do about replacing the books that you... borrowed.'

The King rose to his feet.

'You have my sincerest thanks for what you have done, Mr Crowe,' he said, 'I still feel that I owe you more than you have asked, so you may very well hear from me again. Be advised that you are now a Person of Interest to the Crown, so we will be keeping a close eye on you, mainly for your own protection. Now, I have kept your friends waiting impatiently for far too long and I also need to speak to Dr Vayne, as she no doubt will want some kind of explanation.'

He paused, his hands resting lightly on the back of the chair.

'Knowing you as I do now,' he said, 'counselling you to try and avoid trouble would be like telling the sun not to shine, so I will merely say this – should you require any future help from the Crown, all you have to do is ask. However, I sincerely doubt you will, as you seem to be somewhat... reluctant about requesting help from authority figures. For the time being, I will leave you to convalesce.'

The King turned and strode from the room. I could hear him conversing with someone beyond the door, although I couldn't make out what was being said, then it was flung open and Helena ran in, followed by Yarrow at a slower pace.

Helena faltered as she drew closer to the bed, her face a mixture of concern and anxiety.

'Alex..?' she asked, falteringly.

It was obvious that she wasn't entirely sure *which* Alex she was addressing, and I did momentarily consider pretending that I didn't know who she was, but that would have been a bit mean.

'Yes, I am Alex,' I said, 'and yes, I AM *still* the same Alex who you last saw falling into the lake.'

Helena's lips quivered, tears filling her eyes and she flung herself forward, enveloping me in her arms.

'Gods, I was so worried about you,' she said, 'We didn't know what was happening, if you'd got there in time, and if...if...you'd come back the *same*...'

'Well, other than some bruises and a broken leg...' I said, which caused Helena to leap backwards, muttering apologies, 'I'm pretty much okay. What happened to Errol? Is he alright?'

Yarrow carefully perched on the end of the bed.

'Dr Tweed took charge of him when she saw he'd been injured, and she's looking after him at the moment.' She leaned forward, 'Now, tell us *everything*, as none of the teachers will say anything...'

'I will,' I said, 'but first, I need the loo.'

Once I'd hobbled back from the toilet, which was a challenge in itself, I explained what had happened after I'd got to the island and how I'd managed to stop the Changeling.

'So the Changeling is dead, then?' asked Helena.

Images of what I'd glimpsed from the corner of my eye as I'd struggled to free Penny flashed across my mind's eye – raw meat, steaming in the cold air, the sound of something heavy and wet slithering to the ground and blood... lots and lots of blood. I shuddered.

'Yes,' I said, licking my lips, 'I think we can definitely state that the Changeling is dead.'

'So, what happens now?' asked Helena, 'Are you in trouble?'

'Um, I don't appear to be...' I said, 'Well, at least not with the King. However, the fact that I've broken *several* college rules AND destroyed the library means that Dr Vayne isn't going to be my biggest fan. There IS a possibility I might be expelled...'

'But you saved Penny!' exclaimed Yarrow, 'Surely that's got to count for something?'

'I guess we'll find out...' I said gloomily.

It wasn't until the following evening that Dr Vayne paid me a visit. After asking how I was feeling, she took a seat and marshalled her thoughts.

'I have been headmistress of Oakdene for many years now,' she started, 'and in that time, I have been presented with a number of challenges. I inherited some staff from the previous head who were unsuitable for the positions they held, including the previous Unnaturalism master, whose disregard for safety protocols resulted in the gym being burnt down when a mature salamander got loose. After I had instigated a full review of all staff and regulations, the college flourished and other than a few unruly students over the years, we have had no further problems. And then you came along...'

I swallowed nervously, as I felt that this was the part where I got a serious telling off and then informed that my time at Oakdene was at an end.

'This year we had decided to open our doors to a wider selection of students,' Dr Vayne continued, 'We had been approached by the Geist High Council about the possibility of including our first Geist student, the King had expressed an interest in allowing his daughter to attend Oakdene and, after much careful consideration, we decided to allow in our first scholarship student – you, Mr Crowe.'

Dr Vayne paused.

Here it comes, I thought.

'As the college had been running smoothly, I guess that I had become complacent and assumed that everything would run as it normally had. Whilst consideration had been given to the safety of the Princess Royal, we could not anticipate that a plot would be hatched that could have resulted in her death, if not for your actions. I am not entirely certain how you became aware of this plot, nor exactly how you managed to prevent it, but the King has assured me that whilst the Changeling masquerading as one of our students met a violent end, this was not perpetrated by you and that you do not represent a present or future threat to anyone here at Oakdene.'

She sighed.

'The reason I have not visited you before now,' she continued, 'was that you present me with a quandary, Mr Crowe. On the one hand, you have flouted several college rules on numerous occasions, encouraged others to also break certain rules and have destroyed the school library. On the other hand, you excel at your studies, your teachers all speak highly of you, and you are a considerate and loyal friend. If we add to that the fact that your recent actions prevented the death of one of the students under my care, with no apparent thought for your own safety, the scales do seem to weigh in your favour. I hope that the remainder of your time here at Oakdene proves to be less... eventful.'

It took me a moment or two to digest what Dr Vayne was saying.

'I'm sorry, Miss,' I said, 'but are you saying I can stay?'

'Yes, Mr Crowe. After careful consideration, as well as several impassioned... discussions with your teachers, I have decided to allow you continue your education here at Oakdene,' she said, smiling, 'With one condition...'

'Which is?' I asked.

'Should anything else of such a serious nature comes to your attention, come and see me *first*.'

'Um, yes Miss,' I stuttered, 'Of course, Miss...'

'Now, I believe that your little dragon is becoming a little fractious, so I have agreed with Dr Tweed that he can be brought here whilst you complete your recovery.' She turned to leave, 'I will be watching you, Mr Crowe, so please do not make me regret my decision.'

It's human nature to look back on the decisions you've made in your life and speculate on how your life would have turned out differently, had you chosen an alternate path. It's usually a pointless exercise, as no matter what decisions you think you may have changed with the benefit of hindsight, the past is immutable and cannot be changed.

Unless someone decides to cast your consciousness back in time to occupy your teenaged body, for the sole purpose of foiling a murderous plot to rewrite reality. In which case, should you survive with body, mind, and sanity intact, you *may* find yourself in the unique position of being able to rewrite your own history.

Of course, it's *highly* unlikely that would happen to you and, having experienced it myself, I wouldn't really recommend it.

However, having been given a second chance at a life I thought had, for the most part, already run its course, I felt an excitement building that I had not experienced for many years.

I had no idea what the future would bring, what further challenges I may face, but I was certain of one thing - I was *definitely* looking forward to finding out.

Printed in Great Britain
by Amazon

50797967R00101